MICHELLE MORAN was born and grew up in California. ᴗ ᴡ ᴏᴉᴋed as a teacher for six years, travelling around the world during school holidays, including to an archaeological dig in Israel, which inspired her to write. Her novel, *Nefertiti*, was published around the world in 2007. She now writes full time and lives in California with her husband. *Cleopatra's Daughter* is her third novel.

ALSO BY MICHELLE MORAN

Nefertiti
The Heretic Queen

CLEOPATRA'S DAUGHTER

Michelle Moran

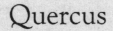
Quercus

First published in Great Britain in 2009 by Quercus
This paperback edition published in 2010 by

Quercus
21 Bloomsbury Square
London
WC1A 2NS

Grateful acknowledgement is made to Jon Corelis for permission to use
his translation from Ovid's Amores from Roman Erotic Elegy by Jon Corelis,
copyright © Jon Corelis (University of Salzbury, 1995).

A CIP catalogue reference for this book is available
from the British Library.

ISBN 978 1 84916 079 7

10 9 8 7 6 5

Printed and bound in Great Britain by Clays Ltd, St Ives plc

For Matthew,
amor meus, amicus meus

TIME LINE

323 BC   After the death of Alexander the Great in Babylon, the empire he had so rapidly built begins to disintegrate. Ptolemy, one of Alexander's Macedonian generals, seizes control of Egypt. Thus begins the Ptolemaic dynasty that will end with Kleopatra Selene.

47 BC   Julius Caesar's forces defeat Ptolemy XIII in the Battle of the Nile, and Kleopatra VII is installed on the throne of Egypt. Later that same year, she announces that she has borne Caesar a son, Caesarion ('little Caesar'). The relationship between Julius Caesar and Kleopatra will continue until his assassination.

46 BC   Juba I, King of Numidia, allies himself with the republicans' losing cause in their war against Caesar. After the calamitous Battle of Thapsus, his kingdom of Numidia is annexed as a Roman province, and a servant is instructed to take Juba's life. His infant son, Juba II, is taken to Rome and paraded through the streets during Caesar's Triumph. Juba II is raised by Caesar and his sister, forming close ties with Caesar's young adopted heir, Octavian.

44 BC   The assassination of Julius Caesar. In the aftermath, an uneasy alliance is formed: the Second Triumvirate, composed of his supporters Octavian, Marc Antony, and Lepidus. The three unite to defeat the forces of Caesar's killers, led by Brutus and Cassius, who have amassed an army in Greece.

42 BC   After victory over the forces of Brutus and Cassius at the Battle of Philippi, the three members of the Second Triumvirate go their separate ways. Marc Antony begins his tour of the eastern provinces by summoning the Queen of Egypt to meet him.

41 BC   Meeting of Marc Antony and Kleopatra VII. Antony is so charmed that he returns to spend the winter with her in Alexandria, during which time their twins are conceived.

40 BC   Birth of Kleopatra Selene and Alexander Helios. The following eight years see escalating mistrust and eventual hostilities between Octavian and Marc Antony.

36 BC   Triumvirate breaks up when Lepidus is removed from power by Octavian. Rome is now governed by Octavian and Marc Antony.

    Birth of Ptolemy, Queen Kleopatra and Marc Antony's third and last child together.

31 BC   Marc Antony and Kleopatra's forces are defeated at the sea battle of Actium by the young Octavian and his indispensable military aide, Marcus Agrippa.

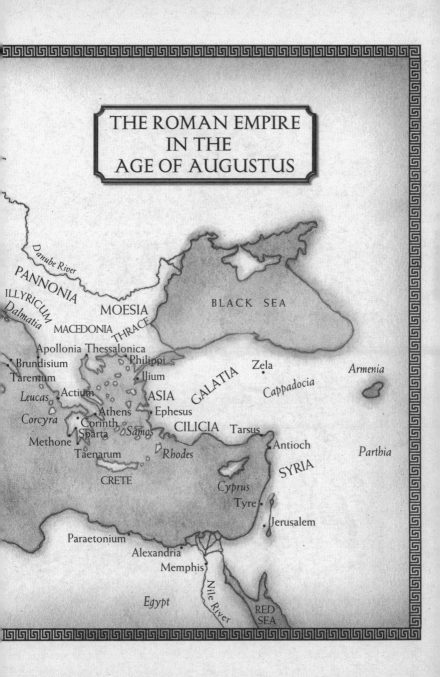

THE ROMAN EMPIRE IN THE AGE OF AUGUSTUS

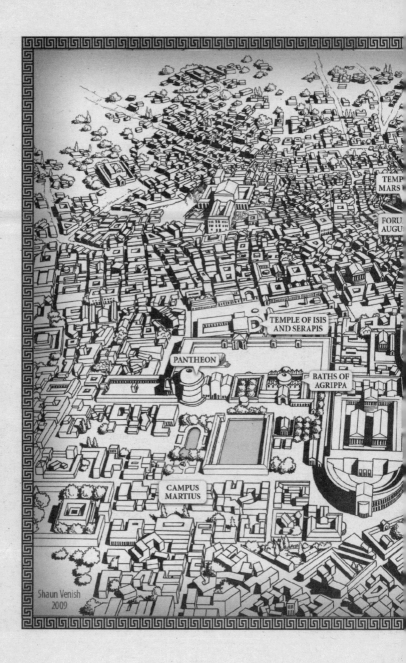

TEMP
MARS

FORU
AUGU

TEMPLE OF ISIS
AND SERAPIS

PANTHEON

BATHS OF
AGRIPPA

CAMPUS
MARTIUS

Shaun Venish
2009

Rome in the Age of Augustus

TEMPLE OF VENUS GENETRIX

PALATINE HILL

HOUSE OF AUGUSTUS

CIRCUS MAXIMUS

BASILICA AEMILIA

ROMAN FORUM

TEMPLE OF SATURN

TEMPLE OF JUPITER

TEMPLE OF APOLLO

THEATRE OF MARCELLUS

TIBER RIVER

PORTICO OF OCTAVIA

TIBER ISLAND

CHARACTERS

Agrippa. Octavian's trusted general; father of Vipsania.

Alexander. Son of Queen Kleopatra and Marc Antony; Selene's twin brother.

Antonia. Daughter of Octavia and her second husband, Marc Antony.

Antyllus. Son of Marc Antony and his third wife, Fulvia.

Claudia. Daughter of Octavia and her first husband, Gaius Claudius Marcellus.

Drusus. Second son of Livia and her first husband, Tiberius Claudius Nero.

Gallia. Daughter of Vercingetorix, king of the defeated Gauls.

Juba II. Prince of Numidia, son of the defeated King of Numidia, Juba I.

Julia. Daughter of Octavian and his first wife, Scribonia.

Kleopatra VII. Queen of Egypt, mother to Julius Caesar's son Caesarion and to Marc Antony's children Alexander, Selene, and Ptolemy.

Livia. Wife of Octavian; Empress of Rome.

Maecenas. Poet; friend of Octavian.

Marcella. Second daughter of Octavia and her first husband, Gaius Claudius Marcellus.

Marcellus. Son of Octavia and her first husband, Gaius Claudius Marcellus.

Marc Antony. Roman consul and general.

Octavian. Emperor of Rome; known as Augustus from January BC onwards.

Octavia. Sister to Octavian; former wife to Marc Antony.

Ovid. Poet.

Ptolemy. Younger son of Queen Kleopatra and Marc Antony.

Scribonia. First wife of Octavian; mother of Julia.

Selene. Daughter of Queen Kleopatra and Marc Antony.

Seneca the Elder. Orator and writer.

Tiberius. Son of Livia and her first husband, Tiberius Claudius Nero.

Tonia. Second daughter of Octavia and Marc Antony.

Verrius. A freedman and a schoolteacher of great renown.

Vipsania. Daughter of Agrippa and his first wife, Caecilia Attica.

Vitruvius. Engineer and architect; author of *De architectura*.

CLEOPATRA'S DAUGHTER

CHAPTER ONE

ALEXANDRIA

August 12, 30 BC

WHILE WE waited for the news to arrive, we played dice. I felt the small ivory cubes stick in my palms as I rolled a pair of ones. 'Snake eyes,' I said, fanning myself with my hand. Even the stir of a sea breeze through the marble halls of our palace did little to relieve the searing heat that had settled across the city.

'It's your turn,' Alexander said. When our mother didn't respond, he repeated, 'Mother, it's your turn.'

But she wasn't listening. Her face was turned in the direction of the sea, where the lighthouse of our ancestors had been built on the island of Pharos to the east. We were the greatest family in the world, and could trace our lineage all the way back to Alexander of Macedon. If our father's battle against Octavian went well, the Ptolemies might rule for another three hundred years. But if his losses continued . . .

'Selene,' my brother complained to me, as if I could get our mother to pay attention.

'Ptolemy, take the dice,' I said sharply.

Ptolemy, who was only six, grinned. 'It's my turn?'

'Yes,' I lied, and when he laughed, his voice echoed in the silent halls. I glanced at Alexander, and perhaps because we were twins, I knew what he was thinking. 'I'm sure they haven't abandoned us,' I whispered.

'What would you do if you were a servant and knew that Octavian's army was coming?'

'We don't know that it is,' I snapped, but when the sound of sandals slapped through the halls, my mother finally looked in our direction.

'Selene, Alexander, Ptolemy, get back!'

We abandoned our game and huddled on the bed, but it was only her servants, Iras and Charmion.

'What? What is it?' my mother demanded.

'A group of soldiers!'

'Whose men?'

'Your husband's,' Charmion cried. She had been with our family for twenty years, and I had never seen her weep. But as she shut the door, I saw that her cheeks were wet. 'They are coming with news, Your Highness, and I'm afraid—'

'*Don't* say it!' My mother closed her eyes briefly. 'Just tell me. Has the mausoleum been prepared?'

Iras blinked away her tears and nodded. 'The last of the palace's treasures are being moved inside. And . . . and the pyre has been built exactly as you wanted.'

I reached for Alexander's hand. 'There's no reason our father won't beat them back. He has everything to fight for.'

Alexander studied the dice in his palms. 'So does Octavian.'

We both looked to our mother, Queen Kleopatra VII of Egypt. Throughout her kingdom she was worshipped as the goddess Isis, and when the mood took her, she dressed as Aphrodite. But unlike a real goddess, she was mortal, and I could read in the muscles of her body that she was afraid. When someone knocked on the door, she tensed. Although this was what we had been waiting for, my mother hesitated before answering, instead looking at each of her children in turn. We belonged to Marc Antony, but only Ptolemy had inherited our father's golden hair. Alexander and I had our mother's coloring, dark chestnut curls and amber eyes. 'Whatever the news, be silent,' she warned us, and when she called, in a steady voice, 'Come in,' I held my breath.

One of my father's soldiers appeared. He met her gaze reluctantly.

'What is it?' she demanded. 'Is it Antony? Tell me he hasn't been hurt.'

'No, Your Highness.'

My mother clutched the pearls at her neck in relief.

'But your navy has refused to engage in battle, and Octavian's men will be here by nightfall.'

Alexander inhaled sharply, and I covered my mouth with my hand.

'Our *entire* navy has turned?' Her voice rose. 'My men have refused to fight for their queen?'

The young soldier shifted on his feet. 'There are still four legions of infantry—'

'And will four legions keep Octavian's whole army at bay?' she cried.

'No, Your Highness. Which is why you must flee—'

'And where do you think we would go?' she demanded. 'India? China?' The soldier's eyes were wide, and, next to me, Ptolemy began to whimper. 'Order your remaining soldiers to keep filling the mausoleum,' she instructed. 'Everything within the palace of any value.'

'And the general, Your Highness?'

Alexander and I both looked to our mother. Would she call our father back? Would we stand against Octavian's army together?

Her lower lip trembled. 'Send word to Antony that we are dead.'

I gasped, and Alexander cried out desperately, 'Mother, no!' But our mother's glare cut across the chamber. 'What will Father think?' he cried.

'He will think there is nothing to return for.' My mother's voice grew hard. 'He will flee from Egypt and save himself.'

The soldier hesitated. 'And what does Your Highness plan to do?'

I could feel the tears burning in my eyes, but pride forbade me from weeping. Only children wept, and I was already ten.

'We will go to the mausoleum. Octavian thinks he can march into Egypt and pluck the treasure of the Ptolemies from my palace like grapes. But I'll burn everything to the ground before I let him touch it! Prepare two chariots!'

The soldier rushed to do as he was told, but in the halls of the palace, servants were already beginning to flee. Through the open door Alexander shouted after them, 'Cowards! *Cowards!*' But none of them cared. The women were leaving with only the clothes on their backs, knowing that once Octavian's army arrived there would be no mercy. Soldiers carried precious items from every chamber, but there was no guarantee that those items would end up in the mausoleum.

My mother turned to Charmion. 'You do not have to stay. None of us knows what will happen tonight.'

But Charmion shook her head bravely. 'Then let us face that uncertainty together.'

My mother looked to Iras. The girl was only thirteen, but her gaze was firm. 'I will stay as well,' Iras whispered.

'Then we must pack. Alexander, Selene, take only one bag!'

We ran through the halls, but outside my chamber, Alexander stopped.

'Are you frightened?'

I nodded fearfully. 'Are you?'

'I don't think Octavian will leave anyone alive. We have defied him for a year, and remember what happened to the city of Metulus?'

'Everything was burned. Even the cattle and fields of grain. But he didn't set fire to Segestica. When Octavian conquered it, he allowed those people to survive.'

'And their rulers?' he challenged. 'He killed them all.'

'But why would the Roman army want to hurt children?'

'Because our father is Marc Antony!'

I panicked. 'Then what about Caesarion?'

'He's the son of Julius Caesar. No one's in more danger than he. Why do you think our mother sent him away?'

I imagined our brother fleeing toward India. How would he ever find us again? 'And Antyllus?' I asked quietly. Though our father had children with his first four wives, and with perhaps a dozen mistresses, Antyllus was the only halfbrother we'd ever known.

'If Octavian's as merciless as they say, he'll try to kill Antyllus as well. But perhaps he'll spare your life. You're a girl. And maybe when he realizes how clever you are—'

'But what good is being clever if it can't stop them from coming?' Tears spilled from my eyes, and I no longer cared that it was childish to cry.

Alexander wrapped his arm around my shoulders, and when Iras saw the two of us standing in the hall, she shouted, 'We don't have the time. Go and pack!'

I stepped into my chamber and began searching at once for my book of sketches. Then I filled my bag with bottles of ink and loose sheets of papyrus. When I glanced at the door, Alexander was standing with our mother. She had exchanged her Greek chiton for the traditional clothes of an Egyptian queen. A diaphanous gown of blue silk fell to the floor, and strings of pink sea pearls gleamed at her neck. On her brow she wore the golden vulture crown of Isis. She was a rippling vision in blue and gold, but though she should have had the confidence of a queen, her gaze shifted nervously to every servant running through the hall.

'It's time,' she said quickly.

A dozen soldiers trailed behind us, and I wondered what would happen to them once we left. If they were wise, they would lay down their weapons, but even then there was no guarantee that their lives would be spared. My father had said that Octavian slaughtered anyone who stood against him – that he would kill his own mother if she slandered his name.

In the courtyard, two chariots were waiting.

'Ride with me,' Alexander said. The two of us shared a chariot with Iras, and as the horses started moving, my brother took my hand. We sped through the gates, and from the Royal Harbor I could hear the gulls calling to one another, swooping and diving along the breakers. I inhaled the salty air, then exhaled sharply as my eyes focused in the dazzling sun. Thousands of Alexandrians had taken to the streets. My brother tightened his grip. There was no telling what the people might do. But they stood as still as reeds, lining the road that ran from the palace to the mausoleum. They watched as our chariots passed, then one by one they dropped to their knees.

Alexander turned to me. 'They should be fleeing! They should be getting as far away from here as they can!'

'Perhaps they don't believe Octavian's army is coming.'

'They must know. The entire palace knows.'

'Then they're staying for us. They think the gods will hear our prayers.'

My brother shook his head. 'Then they're fools,' he said bitterly.

The dome of our family's mausoleum rose above the horizon,

perched at the rim of the sea on the Lochias Promontory. In happier times, we had come here to watch the builders at work, and I now tried to imagine what it would be like without the noise of the hammers and the humming of the men. *Lonely,* I thought, *and frightening.* Inside the mausoleum, a pillared hall led to a chamber where our mother and father's sarcophagi lay waiting. A flight of stairs rose from this room to the upper chambers, where the sun shone through the open windows, but no light ever penetrated the rooms below, and at the thought of entering them, I shivered. The horses came to a sudden halt before the wooden doors, and soldiers parted to make way for us.

'Your Majesty.' They knelt before their queen. 'What do we do?'

My mother looked into the face of the oldest man. 'Is there any chance of defeating them?' she asked desperately.

The soldier looked down. 'I'm sorry, Your Highness.'

'Then leave!'

The men rose in shock. 'And . . . and the war?'

'*What war?*' my mother asked bitterly. 'Octavian has won, and while my people scrape and bow at his feet, I'll be waiting here to negotiate the terms of my surrender.' Across the courtyard, priestesses began to scream about Octavian's approaching soldiers, and my mother turned to us. 'Inside!' she shouted. 'Everyone inside!'

I gave a final glance back at the soldiers' fear-stricken faces, then we plunged in. Within the mausoleum, the summer's heat vanished, and my eyes slowly adjusted to the darkness. Light from the open door illuminated the treasures that had been taken from the palace. Gold and silver coins gleamed from ivory chests, and rare pearls were strewn across the heavy cedar bed that had been placed between the sarcophagi. Iras trembled in her long linen cloak, and as Charmion studied the piles of wood stacked in a circle around the hall, her eyes began to well with tears.

'Shut the doors!' my mother commanded. 'Lock them as firmly as you can!'

'What about Antyllus?' Alexander asked worriedly. 'He was fighting—'

'He's fled with your father!'

When the doors thundered shut, Iras drew the metal bolt into place. Then, suddenly, there was silence. Only the crackling of the torches filled the chamber. Ptolemy began to cry.

'Be quiet!' my Mother snapped.

I approached the bed and took Ptolemy in my arms. 'There's nothing to be afraid of,' I promised. 'Look,' I added gently, 'we're all here.'

'Where's Father?' he cried.

I stroked his arm. 'He's coming.'

But he knew I was lying, and his cries grew into high-pitched wails of terror. 'Father,' he wailed. 'Father!'

My mother crossed the chamber to the bed and slapped his little face, startling him into silence. Her hand left an imprint on his tender cheek, and Ptolemy's lip began to tremble. Before he could begin to cry again, Charmion took him from my arms.

'I'm sorry,' I said quickly. 'I tried to keep him quiet.'

My mother climbed the marble staircase to the second story, and I joined Alexander on the bottom step. He shook his head at me. 'You see what happens from being kind?' he said. 'You should have slapped him.'

'He's a *child*.'

'And our mother is fighting for her crown. How do you think she feels, hearing him crying for Father?'

I wrapped my arms around my knees and looked at the piles of timber. 'She won't really set fire to the mausoleum. She just wants to frighten Octavian. They say his men haven't been paid in a year. He needs her. He needs all of this.'

But my brother didn't say anything. He held the pair of dice in his hands, shaking them again and again.

'Stop it,' I said irritably.

'You should go to her.'

I looked up the stairs to the second story, where my mother was sitting on a carved wooden couch. Her silk dress fluttered in the warm breeze, and she was staring out at the sea. 'She'll be angry.'

'She's never angry at you. You're her *little moon*.'

While Alexander Helios had been named for the sun, I had been named for the moon. Although she always said her *little moon* could never do anything wrong, I hesitated.

'You can't let her sit there alone, Selene. She's afraid.'

I mounted the steps, but my mother didn't turn. Clusters of pearls gleamed in her braids, while above them, the vulture crown pointed its beak to the sea as if it wished it could leap away and take flight. I joined her on the couch and saw what she was watching. The wide expanse of blue was dotted with hundreds of billowing sails. All of them were pointed toward the Harbor of Happy Returns. There was no battle. No resistance. A year ago our navy had suffered a terrible defeat at Actium, and now they had surrendered.

'He's a *boy*,' she said without looking at me. 'If he thinks he can keep Antony's half of Rome, then he's a fool. There was no greater man than Julius, and the Romans left him dead on the Senate floor.'

'I thought *Father* was Rome's greatest man.'

My mother turned. Her eyes were such a light brown as to be almost gold. 'Julius loved power more than anything else. Your father loves only chariot races and wine.'

'And you.'

The edges of her lips turned down. 'Yes.' She gazed back at the water. The fortunes of the Ptolemies had first been shaped by the sea when Alexander the Great had died. As the empire split, his cousin Ptolemy had sailed to Egypt and later made himself king. Now, this same sea was changing our fortunes again. 'I have let Octavian know I am willing to negotiate. I even sent him my scepter, but he's given me nothing in return. There will be no rebuilding Thebes.' Sixteen years before her birth, Thebes had been destroyed by Ptolemy IX when the city had rebelled. It had been her dream to restore it. 'This will be my last day on Egypt's throne.'

The finality in her voice was frightening. 'Then what do we have left to hope for?' I asked.

'They say Octavian was raised by Julius's sister. Perhaps he'll want to see Julius's son on the throne.'

'But where do you think Caesarion is now?'

I knew she was picturing Caesarion, with his broad shoulders and striking smile. 'In Berenice with his tutor, waiting for a ship to take him to India,' she said hopefully. After the Battle of Actium, my eldest brother had escaped, and the princess Iotapa, who had been promised in marriage to Alexander, had fled back to Media. We were like leaves being blown about by the wind. My mother saw the look on my face, and took off her necklace of pink sea pearls. 'This has always brought me protection, Selene. Now I want it to protect you.' She placed it over my head, and its golden pendant with small onyx gems felt cold against my chest. Then her back stiffened against the wooden couch. 'What is that?'

I held my breath, and above the crashing waves I could hear men pounding on the door below us.

'Is it he?' my mother cried, and I followed the silk hem of

her gown to the bottom of the stairs. Alexander was in front of the door, and his face was gray.

'No, it's Father,' Alexander said. But he held out his hands before she could come closer. 'He tried to kill himself, Mother. He's dying!'

'Antony!' my mother screamed, and she pressed her face against the metal grille in the door. 'Antony, what have you done?' Alexander and I couldn't hear what our father was saying. Our mother was shaking her head. 'No,' she said, 'I can't . . . If I open this door, any one of your soldiers could seize us for ransom.'

'*Please!*' Alexander cried. 'He's dying!'

'But if she opens the door—' Charmion began.

'Then use the window!' I exclaimed.

My mother had already thought of it. She was rushing up the stairs, and the five of us followed swiftly at her heels. The mausoleum wasn't complete – no one could have predicted it would be needed so soon. Workmen's equipment had been left behind, and my mother shouted, 'Alexander, the rope!'

She flung open the lattice shutters of the window overlooking the Temple of Isis. Below, waves crashed against the eastern casements. I can't say how long it took for my mother to do the unthinkable. Of course, she had Alexander and Iras to help. But as soon as our father's bloodied litter on the ground below was fastened to the rope, she lifted him two stories and moved him onto the floor of the mausoleum.

I stood with my back pressed against the marble wall. The happy sound of the gulls outside had faded, and there were no more waves, or soldiers, or servants. Nothing existed but my father, and the place where he had pushed his own sword between his ribs. I could hear Alexander's ragged breathing, but I couldn't see him. I only saw my mother's hands, which came away bloodied from my father's tunic.

'Antony,' she was crying. '*Antony!*' She pressed her cheek to my father's chest. 'Do you know what Octavian promised after the Battle of Actium? That if I had you killed, he would let me keep my throne. But I wouldn't do it. I wouldn't do it!' She was becoming hysterical. 'And now . . . what have you done?'

His eyelids fluttered. I had never seen my father in pain. He was Dionysus, larger than life, bigger than any man who stood next to him, faster, stronger, with a louder laugh and a wider smile. But his tanned good looks had gone pale, and his hair was wet with perspiration. He looked unfamiliar without his Greek robes and crown of ivy, like a mortal Roman soldier struggling to speak. 'They said you were dead.'

'Because I told them to. So you would *flee*, not kill yourself. Antony, it's not over.' But the light in his eyes was growing dim.

'Where are my sun and moon?' he whispered.

Alexander led me forward. I don't think I could have crossed the chamber without his help.

My father's eyes fell on me. 'Selene . . .' He took several deep breaths. 'Selene, will you bring your father some wine?'

'Father, there's no wine in the mausoleum.' But he didn't seem to understand what I was saying.

'Some good Chian wine,' he went on, and my mother sobbed. 'Don't cry.' He touched her braids tenderly. 'I am finally becoming Dionysus.' My mother wept loudly, and he had enough strength to grasp her hand in his.

'I need you to stay alive,' she begged, but our Father had closed his eyes. '*Antony!*' she screamed. '*Antony!*'

Outside the doors of our tomb, I could hear the Roman soldiers approaching. Their chanting carried over the water, and my mother clung to my father's body, grasping him to her chest and pleading with Isis to bring him back.

'What is that?' Alexander asked fearfully.

'The *evocatio*,' Charmion whispered. 'Octavian's soldiers are calling on our gods to switch sides and accept them as the rightful rulers.'

'The gods will *never* abandon us!' my mother shouted, frightening Ptolemy with her rage. He buried his head in Charmion's lap as Mother stood. My father's blood stained the blue silk of her gown; it soaked her chest, her arms, even her braids. 'Downstairs!' she commanded. 'If they try to break down the door, we will set fire to every piece of wood in that chamber!'

We left my father's body on his litter, but I turned to be sure he wasn't moving.

'He's gone, Selene.' My brother was weeping.

'But what if—'

'He's *gone*. And the gods only know what's happening to Antyllus.'

I felt a tightening in my throat, as if the air I was breathing suddenly wasn't enough. At the top of the stairs, my mother handed daggers to Charmion and Iras. 'Stay here and watch the windows,' she commanded. 'If they force their way in, you know what to do!'

My brothers and I followed my mother's bloodied steps to the first floor. Outside, soldiers were beating on the door and pressing their faces, one by one, to the grille.

'Stand behind me,' my mother instructed.

We did as we were told, and I dug my nails into Alexander's arm while our mother approached the door. There was the muffled sound of voices as she appeared before the grille, and then a man on the other side of the door told her to surrender. She raised her chin so that the vulture's carnelian eyes would look directly at this Roman soldier. 'I will surrender,' she told him through the iron bars, 'when Octavian gives me word that Caesarion will rule over the kingdom of Egypt.'

We moved closer to the door to hear the soldier's reply.

'I cannot give that assurance, Your Majesty. But you may trust that Octavian will treat you with both respect and clemency.'

'I don't care about clemency!' she shouted. 'Caesarion is the son of Julius Caesar and the rightful heir to this throne. The Ptolemies have ruled over Egypt for nearly three hundred years. What do you propose? To have Roman rule? To burn down the Library of Alexandria and do murder in the streets of the greatest city in the world? Do you think the people will stand for it?'

'Your people are already falling over themselves to show deference to Caesar Octavian.'

My mother reeled back as though the man had slapped her from the other side of the door. 'He has taken Julius's name?'

'He is the adopted son and heir of Gaius Julius Caesar.'

'And Caesarion is Caesar's son by blood! Which makes them brothers.'

I had never thought of it this way, and as I moved forward to glimpse the soldier's face in the window, a man's arm caught me around the waist, I felt the cold tip of metal at my neck.

'Mother!' I screamed, and before Alexander could leap forward to defend me, a line of soldiers descended the stairs from the second story. They had come through the open window. Two held Iras and Charmion, and a third held Ptolemy by the arm.

My mother unsheathed the dagger at her waist, but a broad-shouldered Roman caught her wrist in his hand while another man unlocked the door.

'Let go of me!' My mother's voice was a sharp warning, and although she had no power to command Roman soldiers, once the man had disarmed her, he freed her wrist. He was built like my father, with well-muscled legs and a powerful chest. He could have snapped her arm if he had wanted to. I wondered if this was Octavian.

'Take them to the palace.' His words were clipped. 'Caesar will wish to see her before he speaks with the people of Alexandria.'

My mother raised her chin. 'Who are you?' she demanded.

'Marcus Agrippa. Former consul of Rome and commander in chief of Caesar's fleet.'

Alexander looked across the chamber at me. Agrippa was the general who had defeated our father at Actium. He was the secret behind every one of Octavian's military successes, and the man our father had feared above any other. His face was round, and although I knew from our father's descriptions that he was already thirty-one or thirty-two, he looked much younger.

'Agrippa.' My mother caressed his name like silk. She spoke Latin to him, and though she knew eight languages flawlessly, her words were accented. 'Do you see this treasure?' She indicated the leopard skins on the floor, and the heavy chests wrought from silver and gold that nearly obscured the rugs from view. 'It can be yours. All of Egypt can be yours if you wish. Why give it to Octavian when you are the one who conquered Antony?'

But Agrippa narrowed his eyes. 'Are you proposing that I betray Caesar with you?'

'I am saying that, with me, you would be accepted as Pharaoh, by the people. There would be no war. No bloodshed. We could reign as Hercules and Isis.'

The man holding my arm chuckled softly, and my mother's eyes flicked to him.

'You are asking Agrippa to betray Octavian,' he said. 'You might as well ask the sea to stop meeting the shore.'

Agrippa clenched the hilt of his sword. 'She is desperate, and doesn't know what she's saying. Stay here with the treasure, Juba—'

'Juba.' My mother said his name with as much loathing as one word could carry. 'I know you.' She stepped forward, and Juba unhanded me. But there was nowhere for me to run. The mausoleum was surrounded by Octavian's soldiers. I stood next to Alexander as our mother advanced on the man who wore his black hair longer than any Roman. 'Your mother was a Greek, and your father lost his kingdom to Julius Caesar. And now look.' Her gaze shifted from his leather cuirass to his double-edged sword. 'You've become a Roman. How proud that would have made them.'

Juba clenched his jaw. 'If I were you, I'd save my speeches for Octavian.'

'So why isn't he here?' she demanded. 'Where is this mighty conqueror of queens?'

'Perhaps he's looking over his new palace,' Juba said, and the suggestion robbed my mother of her confidence. She turned to Agrippa.

'Don't take me to him.'

'There is no other choice.'

'What about my husband?' She drew his gaze toward the top of the stairs, where my father's body lay illuminated by the afternoon sun.

Agrippa frowned, perhaps since the Romans did not recognize our parents' marriage. 'He will be given a burial that befits a consul.'

'Here? In my mausoleum?'

Agrippa nodded. 'If that's what you wish.'

'And my children?'

'They will be coming with you.'

'But what . . . what about Caesarion?'

I saw the look that Agrippa passed to Juba, and I felt a tightening in my chest.

'You may ask Caesar yourself what will become of him.'

CHAPTER TWO

MY MOTHER paced her room. She had changed from her blood-stained gown into one of purple and gold, colors that would remind Octavian that she was still Queen of Egypt. But even the new pearl necklace at her throat didn't disguise the fact that she was a prisoner. The red plumes on the helmets of the Roman soldiers waved in the breeze outside every window, and when my mother had tried to open the door to her chamber, soldiers were posted there, as well.

We were hostages in our own palace. The halls that had rung with my father's songs now echoed with the gruff commands of hurried men. And the courtyards, where evening was beginning to fall, were no longer filled with servants' chatter. There would be no more dinners on candlelit barges, and never again would I sit on my father's lap while he recounted the story of his triumphant march through Ephesus. I pressed closer to Alexander and Ptolemy on my mother's bed.

'Why is he waiting?' My mother paced the room, back and forth, until it made me sick to watch her. 'I want to know what's happening outside!'

Charmion and Iras implored her to sit down. In their plain white tunics, huddled on my mother's long blue couch, they reminded me of geese. *Geese who don't know that they've been penned for slaughter.* Why else would Octavian be keeping us under guard? 'He's going to kill us,' I whispered. 'I don't think he's ever going to set us free.'

There was a knock, and my mother froze. She crossed the room and opened the door. 'What?' She looked at the faces of the three men. 'Where is he?'

But Alexander scrambled from the bed. 'It's him!' He pointed at the man who was standing between Juba and Agrippa.

My mother stepped back. The blond man with gray eyes wore only a simple *toga virilis.* Although extra leather had been added to his sandals in order to increase his height, he was nothing like the man my father had been. He was thin, fragile, as unmemorable as one of the thousands of white shells that washed up daily along the shore. But what other man would be wearing the signet ring of Julius Caesar? 'Then you are Octavian?' She spoke to him in Greek. It was the language she'd been born to, the language of official correspondence in Egypt.

'Don't you know any Latin?' Juba demanded.

'Of course.' My mother smiled. 'If that's what he prefers.' But I knew what she was thinking. Alexandria possessed the largest library in the world, a library even larger than Pergamon's, and now it would all belong to a man who didn't even speak Greek.

'So you are Octavian?' she repeated in Latin.

The smallest of the three stepped forward. 'Yes. And I presume you are Queen Kleopatra.'

'That all depends,' she said as she sat down. 'Am I still the queen?'

Although Juba smiled, Octavian's lips only thinned. 'For now. Shall I sit?'

My mother held out her hand toward the blue silk couch with Iras and Charmion. Immediately they stood and joined my brothers and me on the bed. But not once did Octavian's gaze flicker in our direction. He had eyes only for my mother, as if he suspected she might grow wings like those on her headdress and take flight. He seated himself while the other men remained standing. 'I hear you have tried to seduce my general.'

My mother threw Agrippa a venomous look, but didn't deny it.

'I'm not surprised. It worked on my uncle. Then on Marc Antony. But Agrippa is a different kind of man.'

Everyone in the room looked to the general, and although the power of kings rested on his shoulders, he glanced away.

'There is no one more modest or loyal than Agrippa. He would never betray me,' Octavian said. 'Neither would Prince Juba. I suppose you know that his father was King of Numidia once. But when he lost the battle against Julius Caesar, he gave his youngest son to Rome and then took his own life.'

My mother's back straightened. 'Is that your way of telling me I shall lose my throne?'

Octavian was silent.

'What about Caesarion?'

'I am afraid your son will not be able to take the throne either,' he said simply.

Some of the color drained from her face. 'Why?'

'Because Caesarion is dead. And so is Antyllus.'

My mother gripped the arms of her chair, and I covered my mouth with my hands.

'However,' Octavian added, 'I will allow them a burial with Marc Antony in the mausoleum that you have prepared.'

'Caesarion!' my mother cried, while Octavian turned his eyes away. 'Not Caesarion!' Her favorite. Her beloved. There was heartbreak, and betrayal, and a mother's deep anguish in her voice, and that was when I knew the *evocatio* had worked. The gods had really abandoned Egypt for Rome. I wept into my hands, and my mother tore madly at her clothes.

'Stop her!' Octavian rose angrily.

Agrippa held her arms, but my mother shook her head wildly. 'He was your *brother*!' she shouted. 'The child of Julius Caesar. Do you understand what you've done? You've murdered your own brother!'

'And you murdered your own sister,' Octavian replied, coolly.

My mother lashed out with her feet, but Octavian easily avoided her wrath.

'In three days, I will sail with you and your children to Rome, where you will take part in my Triumph.'

'I will never be paraded through the streets of Rome!'

Octavian gave Juba a sideways glance, then rose to depart. When he reached the door, my mother cried out. 'Where are you going?'

'To the Tomb of Alexander, the greatest conqueror in the world. Then on to the Gymnasium, where I will address my people.' He turned, and his gray eyes settled on me. 'Shall your children come?'

I ran from the bed and fell to my knees at my mother's feet. I wrapped my arms around her legs. 'Don't send us with him. Please, Mother, please!'

She was shaking uncontrollably. But instead of looking down at me, she was watching Octavian. Something seemed to pass between them, and my mother nodded. 'Yes. Take my children with you.'

'No!' I cried. 'I won't go.'

'Come,' Juba said, but I wrenched my arm from his grasp.

'Don't make us go!' I screamed. 'Please!'

Ptolemy was crying, and Alexander was pleading with her.

At last she threw up her hands and shouted, '*Go!* Iras, Charmion, get them out of here!'

I didn't understand what was happening. Charmion pushed us toward the door, where my mother embraced Alexander. Then she came to me, touching my necklace and running her hands over my hair, my arms, my cheeks.

'Mother,' I wept.

'Shh.' She put a finger on my lips, then took Ptolemy onto her lap, burying her head in his soft curls. I was surprised that Octavian waited so patiently. 'You listen to whatever Caesar says,' she told Ptolemy. 'And you do as you're told, Selene.' She turned to my twin brother. 'Alexander, be careful. Watch over them.'

My mother stood, and before her face could betray her entirely, Charmion shut the door, and we children were alone with our enemies.

'Walk next to me and keep silent,' Agrippa said. 'We go first to the Tomb of Alexander, then on to the Gymnasium.'

I held one of Ptolemy's hands in mine, and Alexander held the other, but it was as if we were walking through a foreign palace. Romans occupied every room, sniffing out our riches to fill Octavian's treasury. The carved cedar chairs which had graced our largest chambers had disappeared, but everything left was being taken. Silk couches, cushions, ebony vases on towering silver tripods.

I whispered to Alexander in Greek, 'How does he know these men aren't stealing things for themselves?'

'Because none of them would be so foolish,' Juba responded. His Greek was flawless. Alexander's eyes were full of warning.

For the first time, Octavian looked at us. 'The twins are handsome children, aren't they? More of their mother than their father, I think. So you are Alexander Helios?'

My brother nodded. 'Yes. But I go by Alexander, Your Highness.'

'He is not a king,' Juba remarked. 'We call him Caesar.'

Alexander's cheeks reddened, and I sickened at the thought

that he was speaking to the man who had killed our brothers. 'Yes, Caesar.'

'And your sister?'

'She is Kleopatra Selene. But she calls herself Selene.'

'The sun and moon,' Juba said wryly. 'How clever.'

'And the boy?' Agrippa asked.

'Ptolemy,' Alexander replied.

The muscles clenched in Octavian's jaw. 'That one's more of his father.'

I tightened my grip protectively on Ptolemy's hand, and as we reached the courtyard in front of the palace, Agrippa turned to us.

'There will be no speaking unless spoken to, understand?' The three of us nodded. 'Then prepare yourselves,' he warned as the palace doors were thrown open.

Evening had settled over the city, and thousands of torches burned in the distance. It seemed as though every last citizen of Alexandria had taken to the streets, and all of them were making their way to the Gymnasium. Soldiers saluted Octavian as we approached the gates, with right arms held forward and palms down.

'You can forget a horse and chariot,' Juba said, surveying the crowds.

Octavian stared down the Canopic Way. 'Then we will go by foot.'

I could see Juba tense, and he checked the sword at his side and the dagger on his thigh. He was younger than I had first assumed him to be, not even twenty, but he was the one Octavian trusted with his life. Perhaps he would make a mistake. Perhaps one of my father's loyal men would kill Octavian before we sailed for Rome.

We waited while a small retinue was gathered, some Egyptians and Greeks, but mostly soldiers who spoke Latin with accents that made them hard to understand. Then we began the walk from the palace to the tomb. Every dignitary who came to Alexandria wished to see it, and now Octavian wanted to pay obeisance to our ancestor as well.

I wished I could speak with Alexander, but I kept my silence as I had been instructed, and instead of weeping over my father, or Antyllus or Caesarion, I studied the land. *Perhaps this will be the last night I will ever see the streets of Alexandria*, I thought, and I swallowed against the increasing pain in my throat. On the left was the Great Theater. I tried to remember the first time my father had taken us there, climbing with us to the royal box that was erected so high it was possible to see the island of Antirhodos. Beyond that was the Museion, where my mother had sent my father to become cultured, and professors had taught him Greek. Alexander and I had begun our studies there when we were seven, walking the marbled halls with men whose beards fell into their flowing himations. North of the Museion were the towering columns of the Library. Half a million scrolls nestled on its cedar shelves, and scholars from every kingdom in the world came to learn from the knowledge stored inside. But tonight, its pillared halls were dark, and the cheerful lamps that had always lit the porticos from within had been extinguished. The men who studied there were making their way to the Gymnasium to hear what would become of Egypt now.

I blinked back tears, and as we reached a heavy gate, a Greek scholar whom I had often seen in the palace produced a key from his robes. We were about to enter the Soma, the mausoleum of Alexander the Great, and as the gate was drawn open Agrippa whispered, '*Mea Fortuna!*'

I noted with pride that even Octavian stepped back. I had

sketched the building a dozen times, and each time Alexander had wanted to know why. He wasn't moved as I was by the luminous marble dome, or the beautiful lines of heavy columns that stretched like white soldiers into the night.

'When was this built?' Octavian asked. Instead of turning to either Alexander or me, he looked at Juba.

'Three hundred years ago,' Juba replied. 'They say that his sarcophagus is made of crystal, and that he's still wearing his golden cuirass.'

Now Octavian turned to my brother and me. 'Is it true?'

When I refused to answer him, Alexander nodded. 'Yes.'

'And the body?' Agrippa asked Juba. 'How did it come here?'

'Stolen, by his cousin Ptolemy.'

We passed through the heavy bronze doors, and the scent of burning lavender from a tripod filled the empty antechamber. Torches blazed from iron brackets on the wall, sputtering in the rush of night air we'd let in. The priests here had not abandoned their duties, and an old man in golden robes appeared.

'This way,' he said, and it was clear we were expected.

We followed the old man's footsteps through a maze of halls, and the soldiers who had chattered all the way there like monkeys, without ever once pausing for breath, were silent. In the dull glow of the priest's lamp, the men regarded the painted exploits of Alexander. I had sketched these images so many times that I knew them by heart. There was the young king with his wives Roxana and Stateira. In another scene Alexander was lying with Hephaestion, the soldier he loved above all others. And in a last mosaic he was conquering Anatolia, Phoenicia, Egypt, and the sprawling kingdom of Mesopotamia. Octavian reached out and touched the painted locks of Alexander's hair.

'Was he really blond?'

The priest frowned, and I was certain he had never heard such a question before. 'He is depicted on these walls as he was in life, Caesar.'

Octavian gave a small, self-satisfied smile, and I realized why he had wanted to come. Facially, there did not appear much difference between the painting of Alexander and Octavian. Both men were fair, with small mouths, straight noses, and light eyes. Now Octavian imagined himself as Alexander's heir, the next conqueror not just of Egypt, but of the world. Hadn't his great-uncle, Julius Caesar, already begun the conquest for him?

We reached a flight of stairs descending into greater darkness, and I heard Ptolemy whimper. 'It's only a few steps down,' I whispered, and when I saw that he was going to protest, I put my finger to my lips.

The priest led the way, and the only noise was the whisper of our footsteps and the crackling of torches. Juba was the last to descend. When the door swung shut behind us, my brother let out a frightened cry. Immediately, Alexander put his hand to Ptolemy's mouth.

'Not here,' he whispered angrily. 'There's nothing to be afraid of.'

But no one was paying attention to Ptolemy. In the dimly lit chamber, the men's gazes were fixed on the crystal coffin of the world's greatest king. The air smelled heavily of embalming spices: cinnamon, myrrh, and cassia.

Octavian approached the coffin with hesitant steps, and the priest pulled back the lid so that everyone could observe Alexander as he had been. There was a gasp of admiration throughout the chamber, and even Ptolemy wanted to draw closer.

'Only thirty-two,' Octavian said. The king's face was beautiful in its three-hundred-year repose; his arms against the muscled cuirass were still pink with flesh and strikingly large. Octavian called Agrippa and Juba to his side, and although Octavian's hair was a similar gold, it was Juba, with his broad shoulders and impressive height, who most resembled Alexander. In the poor light of the tomb, I studied the Numidian prince. From his hobnailed sandals to his scarlet cloak, he was every bit a Roman soldier, and only his long dark hair betrayed his ancestry.

'Agrippa, the crown,' Octavian said, and from the folds of his cloak Agrippa produced a thin golden diadem of twisted leaves. Octavian placed it carefully on Alexander's head, and as he straightened, he caught sight of the Conqueror's ring. He bent closer to inspect it, and when he saw that it had been engraved with Alexander's profile, he announced, 'This shall be the ring of Imperial Rome.'

'But, Caesar, that belongs—'

Agrippa turned, and the priest's protest died on his lips.

Octavian held the stiff hand of Alexander, but as he tugged on the ring his elbow swept back and there was a sickening crunch.

'His nose!' the priest cried. Octavian had broken off Alexander's nose.

There was a moment of terrified silence. Then Octavian exclaimed, 'What does it mean?' He spun around. 'Shall I send for the augurs?'

'No,' Juba said.

'But then what does it portend?'

'That you will break the Conqueror's hold on the world and reconquer it yourself,' Juba replied. His dark eyes gleamed, and though I thought he was being sarcastic, Agrippa nodded.

'Yes, I agree.'

But Octavian didn't move, and his hand with the golden signet ring was frozen over the king's body.

'It can only be a good sign,' Agrippa repeated.

Octavian nodded. 'Yes ... Yes, a sign from the gods,' he suddenly declared, 'that I am the successor of Alexander the Great.'

The priest asked meekly if Octavian wished to visit the rest of our ancestors. But Octavian was too full of his prophecy.

'I came to see a king, not a row of corpses.'

I looked back at the shattered face of the great man who was responsible for the long reign of the Ptolemies, and wondered if Egypt would have a similar fate.

Although Juba and Agrippa had proclaimed the breaking of Alexander's nose a good portent, Octavian's retinue fell into an uneasy silence as we made our way up the stairs through the Soma. But the throngs of people in the streets – soldiers, Alexandrians, foreign merchants, even slaves – were loud enough to wake the gods. The soldiers were rounding up every Alexandrian they could find.

'What's happening?' Ptolemy worried.

'We're going to the Gymnasium,' Alexander said.

'Where Father gave me a crown?'

Juba raised his brows. Although Ptolemy had only been two and could not have had many memories from that time, he clearly recalled the Donations of Alexandria, when our father had seated himself with our mother on a golden throne and proclaimed our brother Caesarion not just his heir, but the heir to Julius Caesar as well. That evening, he'd announced his marriage to our mother, even though Rome had refused to recognize it. Then he'd given Alexander the territories of Armenia, Media, and the unconquered empire of Parthia. I'd received Cyrenaica and the island of Crete, while Ptolemy became king of all the Syrian lands. Although the Ptolemies wore simple cloth diadems bedecked with tiny pearls, our father had presented us with gold-and-ruby crowns, and this was what had stayed in Ptolemy's memory. Only now, those crowns were being melted to pay Octavian's men, and we were the inheritors of dust.

Alexander's lips turned down at the corners, and I knew he was fighting back tears as well. 'Yes, that is where Father made you a king.'

We approached the Gymnasium, longer than two stadia, and a murmur of surprise passed among the soldiers. Surrounded by shaded groves, the porticoes had been carefully plastered with gypsum so that even in the moonlight they glittered. But Octavian didn't stop to appreciate the beauty. He twisted the ends of his belt in his hands.

'Repeat to me what I wrote,' he instructed.

Agrippa quickly unfurled a scroll he had been keeping in his cloak. 'First is the matter of the city itself,' he said.

Octavian nodded. 'And then?'

'The matter of how many citizens will become slaves in Rome.'

Octavian shook his head curtly. 'None.'

Agrippa frowned. 'Your uncle took a hundred and fifty thousand men from Gaul. When Marius . . .'

'And what did he get for it?'

'Spartacus,' Juba broke in contemptuously. 'An uprising of slaves who didn't appreciate what Rome had given them.'

'That's right. There is enough gold in the queen's mausoleum to pay every man who's ever fought for me. This time, we don't pay them in slaves.'

'And the men who wish to take women?' Agrippa asked.

'Let them pay for whores.'

We reached the steps of the Gymnasium, and a phalanx of soldiers with heavy shields formed a wall between us and the people. Suddenly, I couldn't go on.

'What are you doing?' Alexander hissed.

But I was too afraid to move. Armed men surrounded the Gymnasium, and I wondered what would happen if Octavian decided to set fire to the building. There would be chaos, women and children crushed as men scrambled over their bodies to escape. But their paths would be blocked by Roman soldiers. The doors would be barred, as they were at my mother's mausoleum. I stood at the base of a long flight of steps, and Agrippa came to my side.

'There's nothing to be afraid of,' he said. 'Caesar wouldn't have kept you alive this long if he intended to kill you tonight.'

Of course not, I realized. *He wants us alive for his Triumph.*

I followed Agrippa's red cloak up the stairs. Inside the Gymnasium, thousands of people fell to their knees in silent obeisance.

Octavian quipped, 'I see why Antony liked Egypt so much.'

'You are Pharoah,' one of the soldiers remarked. 'They'll dance naked in the streets if that's what you wish.'

Juba smirked. 'I thought the Egyptians did that anyway.'

For the first time, I saw Octavian smile, and as we mounted the dais I wondered if Alexander felt as sick as I did. Our father had told us how Octavian had ordered the massacre of every last captive at the Battle of Philippi. When a father and son had begged for mercy, Octavian determined that only one should live and ordered the father to play *morra* with his child. But the old man refused, asking for his life to be taken instead, and nineteen-year-old Octavian himself had wielded the blade that executed him. And when the son wished to commit suicide, Octavian had mockingly offered him his own sword. Even my father, no stranger to battle, had seen only cruelty and single-mindedness in this pretender to Caesar's throne.

When we reached the top of the dais, Octavian held out his

arms. He wore only a simple tunic of chain mail beneath his toga, and I wondered again whether there was a brave Alexandrian who might give his life to rid Egypt of its conqueror. 'You may rise,' he said into the silence.

The sound of thousands of unbending bodies echoed in the torch-lit Gymnasium. All along the perimeter, next to every window and heavy cedar door, armed soldiers stood seven deep in case of revolt. But the people stood silent, and when Octavian began his speech I saw men holding their breaths in anticipation of what was to come. When he explained that there would be no taking of slaves, that the city could not be blamed for the errors of its rulers, and that every soldier who had fought against him would be pardoned, the silence remained. 'For Egypt does not belong to Rome,' he announced. 'It belongs to me, the chosen heir of the Ptolemies. And I always protect what is mine.' Women shifted their children on their hips, looking to their husbands in confusion. Octavian's cruelty was known throughout Egypt.

It was the High Priest of Isis and Serapis who broke the silence. 'He has even saved our queen's youngest children. Hail, Octavian the Merciful, King of Kings!'

'Octavian the Merciful!' the people shouted. Then one of the men took up the cry of 'Caesar,' and the Gymnasium reverberated with it.

'What are they doing?' I shouted to my brother in Parthian, certain that was one language Juba didn't know. 'Why are they chanting his name? He's a conqueror!'

'And now he's their savior,' Alexander said bitterly.

'But our father.' My eyes burned. 'Antyllus and Caesarion. Don't they know?'

'Perhaps. But they're thinking of themselves.'

Octavian held up his arms, and the cries immediately died

away. Then Agrippa stepped forward and explained how the wealthy villas around the Soma now belonged to Rome.

'The statues of Kleopatra and Marc Antony have been spared by a generous donation of two thousand talents. Those who would like to spare their own works of art, perhaps even their own villas, may have their chests of gold talents ready when soldiers come.'

'Greed!' I whispered angrily. 'Octavian will make them pay for the very bricks they're walking on.'

'But Alexandria is saved. The Museion, the Library—'

'For *whom*? For *what*? These Romans don't even know how to speak Greek!'

The people beneath us were cheering, even the men who would pay two-thirds the value of their villas to Caesar in order to keep what was rightfully theirs. Octavian, flanked by Juba and another soldier, descended the steps of the dais. Immediately a path through the Gymnasium was cleared as the citizens of Alexandria stepped back.

'Follow me,' Agrippa said gruffly, and I wondered if this was the moment when someone would attempt to kill Octavian. My father would have risked everything to do it, but as we made our way through the frightened silence, nobody moved. A child cried in his mother's arms, and somewhere in the mass of people a man shouted, 'Hail, Caesar.' But when we stepped outside the Gymnasium, Octavian's cloak snapped in the breeze; he was still alive. No one had risked his life for my mother. I could feel the bile rising in my throat, and I didn't even have the strength to hold Ptolemy's hand as we made our way back to the palace. Soon, we would surely sail for Rome.

'Is there anything I forgot?' Octavian demanded. Though he was small, he walked with confidence through the streets, unafraid of the dark corners along the Canopic Way. Forty soldiers surrounded him, their enameled cuirasses reflecting the light of the moon.

'Nothing,' Agrippa promised. 'It was the right decision to let the temples stand. The priests will never incite rebellion.'

'And the people?'

'They called you king,' Juba said. 'They will find the gold talents to ransom their villas, I have no doubt.'

Octavian smiled, but as we reached the palace, his steps grew uncertain. In the courtyard, a woman was screaming. She ran toward Octavian, and in a single, flawless motion his forty soldiers joined shields.

'Caesar!' she cried. 'Caesar, there is news!'

'Put down your shields,' Octavian ordered.

I glimpsed her face between the armor of two soldiers and cried, 'Euphemia!'

'Princess, your mother! You must come. She is dying!'

Agrippa looked to Octavian, and neither of them stopped us when the soldiers parted and I ran with Alexander and Ptolemy through the palace. I don't remember if anyone followed. Perhaps there were a hundred men, or perhaps we were alone when we reached the open door of my mother's chamber.

'Move away!' Alexander shouted at the servants. 'Move!'

Inside, there was a sickening silence. My mother, in her purple gown, lay peacefully on a couch in the center of the room, her smooth skin gilded by the candlelight. On the floor, Iras and Charmion rested their heads on two silk pillows, looking as though they might be sleeping.

'Mother?' I crept forward, while behind us Octavian crowded the doorway with Agrippa and Juba. When she didn't move, I screamed, 'Mother!' My brother and I ran to her. 'Mother,' I pleaded. I shook her by the shoulders, and the crown she had carefully placed on her head struck the floor with a hollow clank. Below her, Charmion didn't stir. I took Charmion's hands in mine, but the aged fingers that had taught me to sketch were cold. I grasped her arm and reeled back at the sight of two puncture wounds. 'Alexander, she used a snake!' I turned and saw Octavian and Agrippa standing in the doorway, surrounded by soldiers.

Juba rushed to my side and felt for my mother's heartbeat, then bent down and felt the necks of Iras and Charmion. 'How do you know it's a snake?' he asked quickly.

'Look at her arm!'

Juba rose swiftly to his feet. 'There are asps in this chamber.' He turned to Octavian. 'Seal off the room!' he ordered. 'Selene, Alexander, Ptolemy—'

'No!' I moved closer to my mother. 'A snake-doctor could drain the wound!'

But Juba shook his head. 'She's already gone.'

'You don't know that!' I cried.

He looked to Octavian for an answer.

'Find a snake-doctor!' Octavian ordered sharply.

The white-haired soldier next to him didn't move. 'But Caesar,' he whispered, 'you have what you want. She's dead. And in ten months you can march into Rome—'

'*Silence!* Find a snake-doctor and bring him here at once!'

Juba took my brother's arm, knowing he would have less of a fight with him. 'Stand at the door,' he instructed sternly. 'There is at least one cobra in this room. Do *not* step inside.'

We waited at the entrance to the chamber, and Alexander looked like one of my mother's statues, thin and pale and immovable.

'It was a lie,' I whispered in Parthian. 'He was never going back to Rome in three days. He wanted her to die. He wanted her to commit suicide.'

A snake-doctor arrived, and his black skin shone in the lamplight as he worked. My brother remained silent, and I could hear the rush of my heart beating as I watched him. He located the wounds on Mother's arm and made a thin cut above the bites. Then he pressed his lips against her skin and attempted to suck the venom from her body. We watched for what felt like an eternity. Then, at last, he stood up. His lips were red with my mother's blood, and I knew from his face that we were orphans.

Alexander asked quietly, 'Will our mother be buried in her mausoleum?'

Octavian raised his chin. 'Of course. She was the Queen of Egypt.' But there was no remorse on his face, not even surprise.

'Will you really keep the children alive?' Agrippa asked.

Octavian's eyes swept over me the way they had swept over my mother's treasure. 'The girl is pretty. In a few years, some senator will need to be silenced. She'll be of marriageable age and make him happy. And neither of the boys has reached fifteen years. Keeping them alive will seem merciful.'

'And Rome?' Juba wanted to know.

'In a few months, when affairs are settled here, we'll sail.'

CHAPTER THREE

ALEXANDRIA

July 1, 29 BC

THE VESSEL that was to bear us toward Rome was my mother's *thalamegos*, a ship so large that its pillared courtyards had once hosted my father's mock battles on horseback. From the docks, I could hear the Roman soldiers exclaiming in delight over every small detail on board: the fountains and potted palms in the grottos, the ivory-paneled bedrooms with their gilded images of Isis, the cedar chairs and embroidered couches. But even though all of our trunks were packed, Octavian wouldn't leave before the taking of the auspices.

Alexander and I stood together on the dock while Octavian held up a frightened quail. Juba passed Agrippa a newly whetted knife, and with a deft flick of the wrist, Agrippa slit the neck of the terrified bird. The quail's blood dripped between Octavian's fingers, staining them red before trickling onto the planks. The five of us looked to the augur, whose head was covered by a heavy linen cloth.

'What does it mean?' Octavian demanded.

The augur held up his hand and shook his head. 'It must make a pattern first.'

Next to me, Juba smiled. 'He thinks that by reading the splattering of some blood he'll be able to tell us whether the gods plan to send this ship to the bottom of the sea,' he said in

Parthian. 'Of course, if the augur's wrong, there'll be no one alive to challenge him.'

'How do you know Parthian?' my brother whispered.

'I'm Caesar's spy among the people. I wouldn't be very successful if I didn't know a few languages, would I?'

I suspected he was being sarcastic when he said 'a few,' and suddenly I felt sick. 'So you've been telling Caesar what we've been saying?'

'Why would I do that when nothing you've said has been of any interest? But the walls in Rome have ears, Princess.'

'*Your* ears.'

'And many others.'

Octavian was watching our exchange with interest.

'So you send men to their deaths,' I said to Juba. 'To prison.'

'Only if they're assassins. Why, you're not planning to assassinate Caesar, are you?' His voice was mocking, but his dark eyes were serious.

'What's happening?' Agrippa asked.

Juba's eyes lingered on mine for a moment, then he turned and said pointedly, 'I am simply warning the queen's children that in Rome, many things will be different. I think they understand.' He smiled, but his words were directed at me.

The augur raised his hands to the sky.

'Well? What is it?' Octavian snapped.

'The signs are favorable,' the priest announced, and Octavian exhaled audibly. 'Neptune blesses this voyage.'

Agrippa passed the augur a bag of coins. Then the three men escorted Octavian down the dock before I dared to whisper, 'He's heard *everything*.'

'There's nothing we've said that's been suspicious. Just questions.'

But Juba had looked into my eyes and known what I wanted

to do. Octavian had murdered Antyllus and Caesarion. He had given my mother and father no choice but to take their own lives. Even Charmion and Iras were dead. After eleven months, it still hurt to swallow when I thought of them all resting in their marble sarcophagi inside my mother's mausoleum. Seven days after Octavian's speech in the Gymnasium, their funeral processions had wound through the streets of Alexandria, collecting so many mourners that the Roman army had needed every last soldier to keep order in the city. Now everyone was gone. Everything but a few chests of silks had been taken from us. And when my brothers each turned fifteen, what would happen to them? Death was inevitable, perhaps preferable to what we would suffer in Rome. And if death was inevitable . . .

We watched the soldiers as they tried to force a horse from the sand onto the wooden dock. The horse wouldn't move. The men tried whistling to it. Octavian slapped its rear, and when one of the soldier's raised a whip to beat it, Ptolemy covered his eyes.

'Stop!' Alexander shouted. He crossed the pier and approached the men. 'He's just afraid of the water,' Alexander told them.

Some of the soldiers laughed. A fat soldier shouted to the one with the whip, 'So beat the horse until it moves.'

'No!' Alexander said angrily. 'He still won't move.'

The man with the whip crossed his arms over his chest. 'Why not?'

The fat one sneered. 'Are you going to listen to an eleven-year-old boy?'

'He should,' I said quickly. 'He knows horses better than anyone else.'

'So why won't the horse move?' Octavian demanded.

Alexander's hair was wet with sea spray, and in the bright summer sun his skin had turned to bronze. He was handsome, and some of the soldiers were leering. 'Because he isn't the lead horse. My father trained the lead. If you bring *him*, he'll board your ship, and if the others are watching, they will, too.'

Agrippa turned to look at the herd of horses shifting nervously on the shore. 'Which one is the leader?'

My brother pointed to a large bay mount. 'Heraclius.'

Octavian glanced at my brother. 'Fine. Then bring him up.'

Alexander walked confidently toward the pack, and the soldiers' murmuring died down. Upon seeing him, the horse immediately lowered his head, sniffing my brother's outstretched hand for the treats he normally brought. My brother whispered something into Heraclius's ear, stroking his wide flank with one hand as he took the horse's reins in the other. Slowly, whispering all the time, he walked onto the dock, and Heraclius followed obediently.

'You can bring the others now,' Alexander said, and when none of the horses put up a struggle, Octavian studied my brother.

'I remember your father was a great man for horses,' he remarked.

Alexander looked away. 'Yes.'

Octavian nodded. 'Has everything been loaded from the mausoleum?' he asked Juba, and my father's memory returned to dust.

'Every last talent.'

But the soldier with the paunch squinted in the sun. 'Not the girl's necklace. And what about the children's crowns?'

'They're simple bands of pearls,' Juba said testily. 'Perhaps you'd like to take their clothes as well?'

'The children may keep whatever they're wearing. I want to leave,' Octavian announced.

Alexander reached out to take my arm, but I stepped away.

'This might be the last time we ever see the Museion,' I said.

Or the palace, or the Temple of Isis and Serapis. 'I've never sketched Alexandria from the harbor,' it occurred to me.

'We'll be back,' my brother said sadly. He looked beyond the water to the city of marble that had been built over hundreds of years by the Ptolemies. In the brilliant sunshine, the city rose like a blinding white beacon, home to the greatest minds in the world.

'I want to stay.'

'Octavian is already on board,' my brother warned.

'And who cares what Octavian is doing?'

'You should.' Alexander, always the practical one, added bitterly, 'You've seen how it's been these past months. Nothing happens for us now without his say.' He took little Ptolemy's hand in his. But I remained on the pier, and only turned away when Agrippa said that it was time. He led the three of us to our cabin, the same one Alexander and I had shared when our mother took us to Thebes every winter.

'This door is always to remain open,' Agrippa instructed. 'Do not close it. Do not lock it.'

'Even when we sleep?' Alexander asked.

'Even then. If you would like food, you may ask me. If you are sick, go to the railing, but never disturb Caesar for anything.'

Our room faced onto an open courtyard where Octavian was already reclining on a couch, scribbling across a scroll with his reed pen.

'Caesar spends most of his day writing,' Agrippa explained. 'There is never a time when he isn't busy. If he wants to hear noise, he will ask for the harp.'

Alexander and I both looked to Ptolemy. How would a seven-year-old child keep silent on a two-month voyage? And we weren't even allowed to shut the door.

I sat on one of the cedar beds and pulled Ptolemy onto my

lap. 'You are going to have to be very quiet on this ship. Do you understand?'

He nodded, and his curls bounced up and down. 'Will Mother be coming?'

I looked at Alexander.

'No, Mother won't be coming,' he said softly. 'Don't you remember?'

Two small lines creased Ptolemy's brow. 'She's with Father, in Elysium?'

'That's right.' Alexander seated himself on the second bed, and we avoided each other's gaze. Outside, Juba and Agrippa joined Octavian in the courtyard as the ship wrenched away from the port. With the door open, we could hear their conversation.

'It's finally over,' Juba said, reclining on a separate couch.

'It's never over.' Octavian looked up from his scroll. 'Only the dead have seen the end of war.'

'Then perhaps Plato was wrong, and you'll forge something different. Who in Rome is going to challenge you now?'

Octavian smiled. 'Antony did me a favor by getting rid of Cicero. He taught the Senate a powerful lesson. Seneca and the rest of the old beards will keep their silence.'

'For now,' Agrippa warned.

'Yes,' Octavian said, after a pause. 'The danger is no longer with the old men. I must restore the prestige of the Senate. I must make equestrians' sons want to be senators again.'

'That would mean convincing them to come out of the whorehouses first,' Agrippa said dryly.

'Then I will close the whorehouses!' Octavian flushed. 'They are breeding grounds for rebellion.'

'And you will have a different kind of rebellion on your hands,' Juba said. 'The boys visit them because they have nothing better to do. But if you increase the Senate's pay and power, they will think you are bringing back the Republic and they'll leave the whorehouses on their own. That was what Caesar forgot, and what Antony never knew.'

The three of them looked into our cabin, and Octavian beckoned to Alexander with his finger.

'Me?' my brother asked.

Octavian nodded, and my brother stood.

'What are you doing?' I demanded.

'He wants me to go.'

While Alexander crossed the short distance between our room and where Octavian sat, Ptolemy cried sharply, 'You're hurting me.' I was holding him so tightly I was crushing his chest.

'Tell me about your father,' Octavian said.

Alexander looked back at me, wondering what kind of game Octavian was playing.

'He loved my mother,' Alexander replied.

'And horses.'

Alexander raised his chin, and the long white chiton he was wearing flapped in the warm sea breeze. 'Yes. He taught me to ride as soon as I could walk.'

'They say your father held races every day of the week. Is that true?'

Alexander grinned. 'Yes. There was nothing he loved more than the races.'

'Even his kingdom,' Octavian remarked, and I saw Alexander flinch. 'Tell me about your sister. Did he teach her to ride as well?'

My brother's voice was not so bright when he replied. 'No. She sketches.'

Octavian frowned.

'Drawings of buildings and temples,' he explained.

'Bring one to me.'

Alexander returned to our cabin, and I shook my head angrily.

'*Never!*' I hissed. 'Didn't you hear him? He thinks our father squandered away his kingdom.'

'And what *did* our father like more than races and wine?'

I thought of my father's last request, and sat back among the cushions.

'He asked, Selene. What if this is a test? *Please*. Give him the one overlooking Alexandria. The one you drew at the Temple of Serapis.'

Ptolemy looked up at me with his wide blue eyes, waiting for me to tell him to get my book.

'Selene,' Alexander whispered nervously, 'they're waiting.'

It was true. Beneath the potted palms of the courtyard, the three men were watching us, though so long as we kept our voices low they couldn't hear what we were saying. 'Pass me my leather bag.'

Ptolemy scurried across the bed for my bag. He handed it to me as if it were a rare and precious stone, and I took out the leather-bound book of sketches, with its title neatly penned by Charmion in gold ink. Her father had been a great architect in Egypt. When she was young he had taught her the beauty of building and the precise penmanship required of architects, and then she had passed these abilities on to me.

'Hurry,' Alexander implored.

I flipped through the pages and unfolded a loose sheaf. It was an image of Alexandria: her roads, her temples, the palaces that spread like the feathery wings of a heron across the Lochias Promontory. Charmion had taught me to pay attention to even the smallest details, and I had captured the sea foam as it broke against the Lighthouse, and the still faces of the marble caryatids that lined the Canopic Way.

Alexander snatched the parchment from my hand and

returned with it to the sunny courtyard. Agrippa saw it first, then Juba, and by the time it made its way to Octavian, all three men had fallen silent. Octavian pushed back his wide straw hat to see it better.

'Your sister drew this?'

'When she was nine, from the Temple of Serapis.'

Octavian ran his finger over the drawing, and I didn't need to lean over his shoulder to know what he was seeing. His eyes would be drawn first to the Lighthouse, whose four corners were crowned by bronze images of the sea god Poseidon. Then he would see the great statue of Helios, copied from the colossal masterpiece in Rhodes and straddling the Heptastadion. From there he would see the Museion, the towering obelisks taken from Aswan, the theater, the public gardens, and the dozens of temples dedicated to our gods.

'Your sister has great talent. May I keep this?'

From the cabin, I gave a little gasp. 'No!'

The men turned, and Alexander said quickly, 'She's talking to Ptolemy. Of course you may keep this.'

I pressed my nails into my palms, a nervous habit I had picked up from Charmion, and Ptolemy asked, 'What's the matter?'

'Our brother is giving away my things.'

His little features were bunched up in confusion. 'But we already gave away all of our things from the palace.'

'No,' I replied, barely containing my rage. 'They were *taken*. And now Octavian wants this as well.'

When Alexander returned, I couldn't bear to look at him.

'What's the matter with you?' my brother whispered harshly, pushing back the hair that escaped from his diadem. 'We're not in Alexandria anymore.'

'No, because the man you are giving gifts to murdered our family!'

'Do you think if our father had won he would have kept anyone alive? Even Octavian's heirs?'

'He has no heirs! Just a girl.'

'Then if he did?'

'So we're alive! For now. And only because Octavian doesn't want to parade three stinking corpses through the streets of Rome. Wait until the Triumph is over,' I warned. 'Antyllus was murdered at the feet of Caesar's statue, and Caesarion was beheaded. What do you think will happen to us?'

'Exactly what he said. We will be given away in marriage.'

'And how is that better than death? To marry a Roman?'

'Our father was Roman.'

'Perhaps by blood, but in every way that counted he was Greek. The way he dressed, the gods he worshipped, the way he spoke—'

'Not on the battlefield.'

I looked up, and Alexander's light brown eyes were blazing.

'You didn't see him in the stadiums,' he said, 'preparing for battle or racing chariots. All he ever spoke was Latin.'

'I don't believe you.'

'Why would I lie? Our father was a Roman, even if he never put on a toga.' When I didn't say anything, Alexander shook his head. 'You are very stubborn.'

'And you are very trusting,' I said accusingly.

'Why shouldn't I trust? We have no other choice!'

'Stop it! Stop it!' Ptolemy cried. He put his hands on his ears and screeched, 'Stop fighting!'

Octavian had gone back to his work, but Juba looked up from his couch.

'You see what you've done?' Alexander said to me, casting a look over his shoulder. 'Agrippa warned us to be silent.'

'Ptolemy, we aren't fighting,' I said comfortingly. But he had put his head down on my pillow, and I could see that his pale skin was flushed. I placed the back of my hand on his cheek. 'Alexander, he's hot.'

My brother crossed the cabin to feel Ptolemy's brow. 'He probably needs sleep.'

But even though Ptolemy slept for much of the next few days, his cheeks remained flushed. Alexander and I devised quiet games to play with him, even while he lay on the pillows of his bed, but by the third day, he was too tired to even play.

'There's something the matter with him,' I said. 'It isn't normal.'

'It's just a fever,' Alexander replied. 'We had it in Thebes. It'll break with enough water and rest.'

So we brought Ptolemy fresh juices and fruit. And while he lay, I sketched my mother's *thalamegos*. Alexander read from my mother's library, scrolls she had chosen for the ship herself. But it hurt me too much to read them, and whenever he brought them back to our cabin I turned away so I wouldn't have to smell the faint scent of her jasmine on the papyrus.

On our fifth morning at sea, Alexander lowered a scroll onto his lap. 'Who do you miss the most?' he asked quietly.

I glanced at Ptolemy, to make sure he was still sleeping. 'Charmion,' I admitted. 'And Mother.'

My brother nodded.

'And you?'

'Petubastes,' he replied, and I could see that he was struggling to hold back his tears as he recalled the young priest of Ptah who had been our Egyptian tutor in the Museion. 'And Father, of course. Have you seen all the statues they took from Alexandria? Octavian has them in the library, and there's one of Petubastes. Juba is labeling each one for sale.'

'And what does Juba know about Egyptian history?' I demanded.

'He's a writer.' I didn't know where Alexander came by this information, but he seemed certain of it. 'He's already written three books on history.'

'At eighteen?' I challenged.

'Nineteen.'

'So he's a writer as well as a spy.' I despised the Prince of Numidia, who had turned his back on his ancestry to become close to Octavian. But that afternoon, when I had run out of subjects to draw, my curiosity overcame my dislike. I had intended to keep away from my mother's library, but I wanted to see what had been taken from Egypt.

When I arrived, the doors of the library were already thrown open, and light streamed from the windows onto the rich panels. Hundreds of statues and stolen shrines were pressed against the walls. But aside from marble faces, the room was empty. I stepped inside, then heard the swift footsteps of someone rushing to hide.

'Who's there?' I demanded, and a man appeared at my mother's wooden desk. I could see from his unmarked tunic that he was a sailor, and he was holding a statuette of Isis in his hands.

'Well, good morning.' He took several steps toward me and smiled. 'The men were right. You are a pretty girl.'

Immediately, I turned to run. Then a streak of metal flashed in the doorway and someone's arm lashed out. A heavy blade struck deep into the panels where the sailor was standing, and at once the man dropped the statuette. I didn't move. I didn't even breathe.

'I hope you are going to return that,' Juba said.

The man bent to collect the statuette, but as he replaced it on the table, his trembling hands knocked it over and broke a tiny arm. When he rushed to leave, Juba caught him by the neck.

'You will never touch anything that belongs to Caesar.' The man did his best to choke out a response, but Juba tightened his grip. 'The next time, I will aim for your throat,' he promised. He shoved the man away, then turned his black gaze on me. 'What are you doing here?'

'A scroll,' I lied swiftly. 'I – I just wanted something to read.'

'So find it,' he said angrily, and made his way to the desk. He picked up the broken arm of the goddess and held it up to the light before discarding it into an empty amphora.

'No! Don't throw it away.'

He looked up, and I could see that he did not wish to be disturbed.

'That's a very old statue,' I told him.

'Well, thank you, Princess. Unfortunately, not many Romans are interested in purchasing broken statues of Egyptian goddesses. But since you're so interested in art, why don't you tell me which pieces you believe to be the most important?'

I had seen Juba in his fury, and did not wish to make him any angrier, so I pointed to a statue, and he raised his brows.

'Tuthmoses I?' Juba asked.

I was impressed that he could identify a Pharoah whose reign had been more than a thousand years earlier. 'How did you know?'

'I can read hieroglyphics,' he said curtly. 'What else?'

I pointed to the bronze bust of Dionysus, and suddenly tears were welling in my eyes. I tried to blink them away before Juba could see.

'You can weep, but it won't bring them back,' he said cruelly. 'Kingdoms rise and fall on whims of the gods.'

'Isis has never turned her back on Egypt! She will bring me home.'

Juba's voice grew threatening. 'I would be very careful where I said that, Princess.'

But I raised my chin, determined not to be afraid. 'I know about you. Julius Caesar killed your own mother and brother. But I'll never bow to Rome.'

'How very brave.' Juba's lips twisted into a sardonic smile. 'Perhaps you'll feel differently after the Triumph.'

I spun around and crossed the library. But before I left, I glimpsed the basalt statue my brother had seen of Petubastes. The priest's face was beautiful even in stone, and a hastily chiseled inscription indicated the day of his death at sixteen years old. When I reached out to touch it, I glanced back and saw Juba watching me, then thought better of it and walked away.

Inside our cabin, Alexander was pacing.

'Where have you been?' he cried.

'In the library.'

'Well, I've been looking for you.' I followed his gaze to the bed. Ptolemy was a sickly color. He lay between the cushions, hardly moving. 'He's burning even hotter than before.'

'Then we must find the ship's physician!'

'He already came.'

When my brother didn't add anything more, I felt my chest constrict. 'And?'

Alexander remained silent.

'And what did he say?' When Alexander only shook his head, I rushed to Ptolemy's side. 'Ptolemy,' I whispered, pushing his hair away from his brow. He was as hot as Alexander had said. Slowly he opened one of his pale blue eyes.

'Selene.' He reached out and placed his small hand in mine; the tears ran hot down my cheeks onto his palm.

For the next three days Alexander and I kept a constant vigil at Ptolemy's bed. When Octavian took his meals in the courtyard, we didn't join him. When the sailors spotted dolphins alongside the ship and pronounced it a good omen, we didn't go to see. The three of us were the last of the Ptolemies. We had nothing more in the world than each other.

Several times a day, Agrippa brought trays of fruit, and once, when the physician said there was no hope, Agrippa found a slave in the galleys who had studied medicine in his native Macedonia.

'Caesar wants all three children alive for his Triumph,' Agrippa explained. 'I will give you a hundred talents to cure him.' But even for the price that would buy his own freedom, there was nothing the Macedonian could do. Frustrated, Agrippa shoved a bag of gold at the man. 'Take it!' he said angrily.

'But I can't heal him, domine.' He used the Latin word for 'master,' and I could see he was afraid. 'He's too sick.'

'Then just take it and go!'

The man left the cabin before Agrippa could change his mind, and I buried my face in my hands.

'You will keep the door closed,' Agrippa said. 'Caesar sickens easily. We must move the two of you to a different cabin.' But even though Alexander and I protested at this, Agrippa was firm. 'Caesar wants you alive.'

In the end, it didn't matter. Before a new cabin could be found near the royal courtyard, Ptolemy began to moan. I pressed his little hand in mine, and whenever the pain was too great, he bunched his fingers into a fist, squeezing his eyes shut as if he could squeeze out the world. He couldn't eat, he couldn't even drink, and by morning his small body lay rigid on the silk sheets of the bed.

'Ptolemy,' I whispered when he didn't move. 'Ptolemy!' I cried.

Alexander shook him. 'Wake up! Ptolemy, we're almost there. Wake up!' But even such a lie wouldn't open his eyes. Although Alexander began to weep, I was too numb to cry. Perhaps the

Ptolemies had angered the gods. Perhaps Juba was correct, and we would all die by Fortune's whims.

I smoothed my little brother's hair from his brow, then opened his fingers so they could finally relax. 'My little prince,' I whispered.

But my brother stood up from Ptolemy's bed in a rage. 'What have we done? Why are the gods punishing our family like this?'

'Shh!' I said sharply. 'Give him some peace! He heard enough anger in life.'

Alexander sank to the bed and put his face in his hands. 'Why?'

I didn't have an answer.

When the news was sent to Octavian, the Macedonian slave returned to collect Ptolemy's body for a burial at sea. But Alexander stood guard in front of the bed.

'Only murderers are buried at sea!' he cried.

'I'm sorry, domine, but these are orders from Caesar himself.'

'Then tell him no!' my brother shouted.

Agrippa appeared, and the Macedonian shook his head. 'They want to keep the body.'

Agrippa stared at my brother. 'We have many days left at sea, and no embalming materials to keep his body fresh. Let your brother rest with Neptune, Alexander.'

While the Macedonian wrapped Ptolemy in the sheets of his bed, I strained to see his golden head one last time, and the little lips that had so often trembled in fear. He'd been a timid child and my mother's favorite after Caesarion. *I should have looked after him better,* I thought. *He was too young to survive so much upheaval.*

We followed the slave into the crisp morning air, then through the royal courtyard to the side of the ship. All the important members of Caesar's retinue were gathered. A priest of Apollo said several words in prayer, and each face was solemn, even

Octavian's. I held on to Alexander's arm to keep myself from collapsing on the deck. And when the Macedonian dropped the tiny body into the sea, my brother dashed to the railing. 'Ptolemy!' he cried desperately. '*Ptolemy!*' Agrippa held him back.

'Take him to the courtyard,' he instructed. 'Find him some food and good Chian wine.' Several men escorted my brother away, but I remained on the deck, letting my hair whip in the wind, too tired to push it away.

He hadn't even been given a decent burial. The blood of Alexander the Great and Marc Antony had run through his veins, and he'd been tossed into the sea like a criminal. But what better fate lay ahead for Alexander and me? Octavian had said he would keep us alive, but if he'd lied to the Queen of Egypt about leaving for Rome in three days instead of eleven months, what would stop him from lying to us? He was never going to parade my mother through Rome. I knew now that Caesar had tried it with Arsinoë, and instead of cheering, the people had revolted. They were shocked by such treatment of a woman, and the sister of the Queen of Egypt, no less. My mother had never faced any future but imminent death, and if Octavian hadn't fooled her into taking her own life, he would have found someone to kill her. And once his Triumph in Rome was finished, why should our future be any different?

I thought of the many terrible ways there were to die, and wondered if Ptolemy had escaped worse pain. I put my hand on the polished rail. With one jump, there would be no more tears, no more loneliness.

'I wouldn't think it, Princess.'

My back tensed. I had thought everyone had left, but I spun around to face Juba. In his vermilion toga, he looked more regal than Octavian in his homemade tunics and broad-brimmed hats.

'Have you ever seen the body of a drowned man?' he asked. 'It swells five, even six times its size, then turns black until the skin peels away.'

My knuckles grew white as I gripped the rail.

'Do you want to end up as a bloated corpse abandoned at sea?'

'Better than a corpse abandoned in Caesar's prison!' But I turned from the railing and Juba got what he wished for. Alexander and I would be alive for Octavian's Triumph.

CHAPTER FOUR

ROME

AS THE ship approached a harbor for the first time in weeks, Alexander and I rushed to the prow.

'Is this Rome?' I asked. There was no Museion gleaming in the afternoon light, and the villas that hugged the vast stretches of shore were plain, without columns or ornamentation. There was nothing to distinguish one squat white building from the next except the colors of their wind-beaten shutters.

My brother shook his head. 'Brundisium. I heard it's another ten days by litter to Rome.'

Hundreds of soldiers waited on shore, their red standards emblazoned with a tall, golden eagle and the letters *SPQR*, for *Senatus Populusque Romanus.* Brundisium's port was large enough to berth fifty ships, but there was nothing like my mother's *thalamegos.* I could see the soldiers' reactions as the ship came near, her banks of ebony oars catching the sun as her purple sails snapped in the wind. The men shielded their eyes with their hands, and they shook their heads in wonder.

Agrippa appeared with Octavian on the prow. Both men were dressed as if for war. *To remind Rome that they've returned as conquering heroes*, I thought bitterly.

'Caesar's carriages are waiting on the shore,' Agrippa told

Alexander. 'The pair of you will travel with his nephew, Marcellus.'

I tried to pick out Octavian's nephew, but Agrippa remarked, 'Don't bother.' There were too many horses and soldiers.

'Do you have your sketches?' Alexander asked.

'Yes. And do you . . . ?'

Alexander nodded. He had hidden books from our mother's library in his bag – a last reminder of her before we left her *thalamegos* to the Romans at Brundisium. I looked one last time at the polished decks as the tinny sound of trumpets pierced the air. Three of her children had boarded her ship, but only two had reached her enemy's shore.

Octavian was the first to disembark, followed by Agrippa and Juba. When it was our turn to walk the wooden steps, Alexander held out his hand. I shook my head. 'I'm fine.' But we hadn't felt land in more than three weeks, and suddenly my legs gave way beneath me.

'Alexander!'

But it wasn't Alexander who caught me. Instead, it was a young image of Hercules.

'Be careful.' He laughed. He was tall and broad-shouldered, with hair the color of summer's wheat. His eyes were lighter than Ptolemy's had been, a turquoise made even brighter by the darkness of his skin. I felt my cheeks growing warm at the sight of him, and he smiled. 'Now, don't faint on me,' he warned. 'I'm the one who's supposed to take care of you.'

'You're Marcellus?' Alexander asked.

'Yes. And there she is.' He indicated a horse-drawn carriage.

'But that's a king's carriage,' I replied.

Marcellus laughed. 'I wouldn't say that too loudly. My uncle likes to think of himself as consul. If the people should get the idea he wants to be king, there'll be another mess on the Senate floor.'

'Romans don't want kings?' my brother asked.

Marcellus led us from the docks, and his toga flapped at his heels. 'There was a time. But it has passed, and all they can think of now is a republic. Of course, there's been a hundred years of civil wars with their republic, and the first end in sight was Julius Caesar. They all want a vote, but they vote for their own clans, and nothing but bloodshed ever gets accomplished.' We had reached one of the carriages beyond the shoreline, and as Marcellus held open the door for us, he said warmly, 'Prince Alexander, Princess Selene.'

Inside, I looked meaningfully at my brother. Why were we being treated so kindly? What had Octavian written to his family from Alexandria? We listened while Marcellus chatted genially with Juba and Agrippa outside, and his voice carried far beyond our carriage.

'And the Egyptian women?' he was asking.

I could hear Juba's wry laughter. 'They would have swooned at your presence,' he promised. 'Falling into your arms like the princess Selene.'

When my brother looked over at me, I blushed.

'And the fighting?' Marcellus pressed.

'The gods were with us,' Agrippa replied.

'With us, or with *you*? They say the Egyptian fleet—' Marcellus cut himself off, and his voice grew serious. 'I am glad to see you've returned safe, Uncle.'

'Marcellus,' I heard Octavian reply, 'I hope you've been applying as much passion to your studies as you do to your gossiping.'

'Yes, Caesar,' he said quietly.

'Good. Then you may tell me what kind of ship this is.'

There was an uneasy silence, and I could imagine Marcellus's extreme discomfort as he stood in front of Octavian. I pressed my mouth close to the window and whispered, '*Thalamegos.*'

'Selene!' Alexander mouthed, but Marcellus had heard and repeated the word.

'It's the queen's *thalamegos,* I believe.'

I could hear Octavian step back on the gravel. 'He's going to be your equal someday, Agrippa. A titan in the Senate and on the battlefield as well.'

I couldn't see Agrippa's face to know his reaction. But when Marcellus joined us in the carriage, he looked immensely relieved.

'I don't know how I can thank you, Selene.' He took a seat across from me, next to Alexander. 'I would have had to study ships all the way to Rome if you hadn't come up with it.'

'Is he really so strict?'

'All he does is write letters and prepare speeches for the Senate. He wouldn't leave Syracuse if not for his wife.'

Alexander frowned. 'The city?'

'No. His study. He named it for Archimedes, the Greek mathematician who lived there.'

'But he doesn't speak Greek,' I protested.

Although my brother glared at me, Marcellus only laughed. 'It's true. But everything is theater with my uncle. You'll see.'

In front of our carriage, there was a confusion of voices. Then someone shouted and the crack of a whip set the long procession rolling. I looked at Marcellus and decided he wasn't more than two or three years older than Alexander and me. He was dressed in an undistinguished white toga, but the fabric was superior to anything I'd seen Octavian wear. When he caught me looking at him, he smiled.

'So you are Marc Antony's daughter, Selene,' he remarked.

'Strange. There's almost no resemblance between you and Tonia or Antonia.'

'Are those my father's children with Caesar's sister Octavia?' Marcellus nodded. 'Yes, with my mother.'

Alexander sat forward. 'So you are our brother?'

'No. I'm Octavia's son with Marcellus the Elder. It's very confusing, I know. Prepare to be confused much of the time you are in my mother's house.'

'We're going to Octavia's house?' I asked.

'Of course. You're to live with us.' Marcellus saw the look I gave to Alexander, and shook his head. 'I know what you're thinking. Your father left my mother for yours. But don't be nervous. My mother loves children. Of course, Livia won't like you at all.'

'That's Caesar's wife?' Alexander asked.

'Yes. She doesn't like anyone but her own sons, Tiberius and Drusus.'

I was confused. 'I thought Caesar only had a daughter.'

'Yes. Julia, from his first wife. Then he divorced that wife and married Livia when she was pregnant with her second son.' When I inhaled sharply, Marcellus laughed. 'It was a scandal. But now my uncle has two adopted sons.'

'Then they are his heirs?' Alexander asked, wondering whom we should be careful to impress.

Marcellus shifted uncomfortably in his seat. 'Actually, I think he may be more partial to me. He hopes to make me a senator in ten years or so.'

'So is a senator a prince?'

'No!' Marcellus thought my question was wildly funny. 'Didn't your father tell you anything about the Senate?'

'Our mother forbade it. I don't think she cared much for Roman politics,' Alexander remarked.

Marcellus sat back against the padded seat. 'Well, the Senate is just a group of men from the most powerful clans in the Roman empire.' When I frowned, Marcellus said, 'You know. Like the Julii and the Claudii. Or your father's clan, the Antonii. They have to be at least ranked as equestrians first, and then there's different types of senators. Quaestors, aediles, praetors, consuls. Of course, the consuls are the most powerful.'

I nodded, pretending to understand. 'So what do they all do?'

'Meet in the Senate house. Argue about politics. Make decisions about taxes or free grain. My uncle pretends to be one of them, and they always vote for him as consul, or tribune, or censor. It doesn't matter which. So long as the show continues and he's still writing the script.' He began chatting merrily about what we would see in Rome, from the Temple of Venus Genetrix to Julius Caesar's Forum, and for seven days, while the carriages rattled over the roads, he entertained us with stories. At night, when we stopped to sleep in the sprawling villas belonging to Octavian's friends, I dreamt of Rome. I imagined how much larger it would be than Alexandria, and when the cry came up that we were in sight of the city walls, I threw back the curtains and held my breath. Alexander pressed his face next to mine in the window, then we both drew back.

'This is Rome?' Alexander asked uncertainly.

'The greatest city on earth!' Marcellus said proudly.

For as far as either of us could see, faded brick houses crowded together like cattle in their market-day pens. Posts, which Marcellus called 'milestones,' indicated at every mile that Rome was just ahead, but there was no Museion rearing its marble head in the distance, no towering theater crowning any of the hills. A few marble tombs had been constructed on either side of the Appian Way, which seemed to be a favorite burial place for the Romans, but most of the markers were made from roughly hewn stone.

Marcellus saw my disappointment and explained, 'Romans have been fighting one another for centuries. It wasn't until Caesar that there were finally enough slaves and gold to rebuild. But there's the tomb of Caecilia Metella.'

The tall, round building was perched on a hill, and though beautiful crenellations decorated its top, it, too, had been made of plain stone. There was a sharp twisting in my stomach, and I could see from Alexander's face that he felt the same. This was the city whose army had conquered Alexandria. This was where Octavian had studied his Latin, and failed to learn Greek, but had amassed enough power to defeat my father and wipe the Ptolemies from Egypt.

'Someday,' Marcellus said, 'everything you see will be marble. And those are Agrippa's aqueducts.'

For the first time, Alexander and I sat forward, impressed. Arching across the horizon, so tall that the gods alone might have reached them, the aqueducts were the largest structures we had seen so far.

'What do they do?' Alexander asked.

'They carry water to the city. Agrippa has also built baths. There are more than two hundred of them now. My uncle thinks the only way he'll remain in power is to give the people a better Rome.'

So while my father had been adorning himself with gold in Alexandria, drinking the best wines from my mother's silver *rhyta*, Octavian had been working to improve his city. Was this why my father's own people had turned against him? I could hear my father's raucous laughter in my mind. His men in Egypt had loved him, adored him, even. There had been nothing he wouldn't do for a soldier who'd fallen on desperate times.

But the Romans he'd left behind hadn't known this. They hadn't known the man who could ride all day and still stay up until the early hours of the morning with me and Alexander on his lap, drinking and telling stories about his battles against the Parthians.

Our procession of carriages came to a sudden stop, and Alexander and I both looked to Marcellus. 'Are we there?' I asked nervously.

Marcellus frowned. 'We haven't even passed the Servian Wall.'

'And then we'll enter Rome?' my brother asked.

Marcellus nodded, then leaned out of the carriage. There was a commotion happening in front of us. I could hear the raised voices of Agrippa and Octavian.

'What's happening?' Marcellus shouted. When no one answered, he opened the carriage door and I caught a glimpse of soldiers. 'I'll be right back,' he promised, shutting the door behind him.

'What do you think it is?' I asked Alexander.

'A broken carriage wheel. Or probably a dead horse.'

'But then why the soldiers?'

Marcellus returned and his look was grave. 'You might as well get out and take in some fresh air. We won't be going anywhere for a while.' He helped Alexander and me from the carriage, then explained, 'Some sort of rebellion is going on inside the walls.'

'And now we can't enter?' my brother exclaimed.

'Well, we *could*.' Marcellus ran a hand through his hair. 'But it would be much more prudent not to. It's a slave rebellion a few thousand strong.'

As word began to spread among the carriages that there would be no progress for several hours, doors swung open and tired-looking men stumbled out onto the cobblestones. We approached a group of soldiers who were explaining to Octavian how it had happened. Agrippa and Juba stood on either side of Octavian, listening intently as the prefect described the scene just inside the walls.

'Many of them are gladiators who escaped from the training arena – the Ludus Magnus. It began this morning, and since then, more slaves have joined the rebellion.'

'And who is leading them?' Octavian demanded.

'No one. They've been stirred up by' – the prefect hesitated – 'by years of listening to the Red Eagle's messages, and now ... Now they've taken to the streets,' he finished quickly. 'It's nothing to worry about, Caesar. The rebellion will be put down before sunset.'

The prefect remained at attention as Octavian turned to face Marcellus. 'Was there any trouble when you left Rome sixteen days ago?'

'None,' Marcellus swore. 'The streets were peaceful.'

'I doubt there would be rebellion if not for this Red Eagle,' Agrippa said. 'When we find him—'

'We will crucify him,' Octavian finished. 'I don't care that he isn't leading these men. His messages will breed the next Spartacus. And remember,' he said darkly, 'a third of Rome's population is enslaved.'

Alexander whispered to Marcellus, 'Who's Spartacus?'

'Another slave,' he answered quietly. 'Almost fifty years ago, he led more than fifty thousand of them in a revolt against Rome. When they were crushed, six thousand were crucified. Crassus refused to have their bodies taken down, so for years their crosses lined this road.'

Octavian looked out from our perch on this same road to the Servian Wall. Along the road, a soldier was fast approaching. His horse's hooves kicked up clouds of dust, and when the horse stopped before Octavian, the soldier slid off and saluted.

I was surprised to see Octavian smile. 'Fidelius,' he said swiftly, 'tell me the news.'

Fidelius was young, perhaps seventeen or eighteen, and he began eagerly, 'A thousand slaves have already been killed. The ones who remain are trying to find more men to join them, but they haven't had much success.'

'Yet,' Octavian warned.

But Fidelius shook his head. 'They are penned in by the walls, Caesar. The gates have held strong and your men are slaughtering them by the hundreds.'

'Good. And the legions understand they are to take no one alive?'

'Of course.'

There was a moment's hesitation before Octavian asked, 'And your mother, Rufilla?'

Fidelius grinned. 'Well. She sends you her love. And this.' He pulled a lightly wrapped package from the leather bag on his horse. It looked thin enough to be a portrait, and when he opened the linen wrapping, I saw that it was.

The color in Octavian's cheeks rose slightly. 'Very nice,' he said softly, studying the woman's face inside the faience frame. She was pretty, with long black hair and a straight Roman nose. Octavian passed the image to Juba. 'Put it away.'

Fidelius frowned. 'My mother has missed you a great deal these months.'

'Has she?' Octavian raised his brows. 'Well, send her my regards and let her know that I will be very busy in the coming days.'

'But you will see her, Caesar?'

'If I have the time,' Octavian snapped. 'There is the matter of a rebellion and a Senate to placate first!'

Fidelius stepped back. 'Yes . . . yes, I understand. The Senate has been tense while you've been gone.'

Octavian's gaze intensified. 'Really?' he said with rising interest. 'And why is that?'

Fidelius hesitated, and I wondered if he had said more than he should have. 'Well, the matter of the war. Not knowing who would win. You or Antony.'

'And?'

Fidelius glanced uneasily at Agrippa. 'And the succession. No one knew what would happen if both you and Antony were killed. A few names were mentioned as possible successors.'

Octavian smiled disarmingly. 'Such as?'

'Just . . . just a few men from patrician families. No one with any real power.' Fidelius laughed nervously.

'Well, if the Senate thought enough of them to mention them, perhaps those men can be useful to me somehow.'

Fidelius was surprised. 'Really?'

'Why not? Which men did they think might be good replacements?'

'Oh, all sorts of people were mentioned. Even my name was brought up.'

The smile vanished from Octavian's face.

'Of course, he's too young,' Marcellus said swiftly. 'And he could never lead an army. Who would follow him?'

Fidelius looked at Marcellus and realized what was happening. 'That's – that's right. They only mentioned my name because of who my father was and how much wealth he left me. Marcellus can tell you. I – I would never want to be Caesar.'

'Of course. Come.' Octavian put his arm around Fidelius's shoulders and passed a look to Agrippa. 'Let's take a walk. There are some things I'd like to speak about in private.'

Fidelius looked back at Marcellus, who tried to intervene, asking, 'But can't he stay here and play dice?'

Octavian's glance rooted Marcellus in his place. 'No.'

Agrippa joined Octavian and Fidelius, and the three wandered off back the way we had come.

My brother and I looked to Marcellus. 'What will happen to him?' Alexander whispered.

Marcellus looked away, and I thought there might be tears in his eyes. 'His mother will be told that her son died fighting the rebels.'

'They're going to kill him?' I cried. 'For what?'

Marcellus put a finger to his lips. 'If the Senate thought Fidelius would make a good Caesar two months ago, then what stops them from thinking the same thing three years from now?'

'But he doesn't want to be Caesar!' I protested.

There was a sharp cry at the rear of the wagons, then silence. Marcellus closed his eyes. 'He was my closest friend as a child,' he whispered. 'I looked up to him like a brother.'

'And your uncle doesn't care about that?' I exclaimed.

'No. He cares more about the stability of Rome than about anyone's life.' He opened his eyes and looked at both of us. 'Be careful with him.'

The revolt was crushed before the sun had risen to its highest point in the sky. We were sitting by the side of the road rolling dice when Agrippa brought the news. 'It's time to leave,' he said shortly. 'The rebellion is finished.'

'And all of them killed?'

Agrippa nodded in answer to Marcellus's question. 'Every last slave.'

'And Fidelius?'

Agrippa hesitated. 'Unfortunately, his life was lost.'

We stepped into our carriage, and as it began to roll, Alexander tried to distract Marcellus from his sadness. 'How old is the Servian Wall?'

Marcellus shrugged as we passed through the gates. There was no sign of any rebellion, and if the bodies of wounded slaves had littered the streets, they had since been taken away for Octavian's arrival. 'Extremely old,' he said.

'And the Seven Hills? What are their names?'

Marcellus pointed to the hill directly in front of us. 'That's the Quirinal.' He sighed. 'Nothing special there. The one next to it's the Viminal. It's the smallest hill. But the Esquiline' – he indicated a hill to the right – 'is where wealthy visitors lodge. The problem is getting to the inns at the top.'

'Why? Is the road steep?' I asked.

Marcellus smiled good-naturedly at my question. 'No. It's just filled with escaped slaves, and thieves. Men you don't want to know,' he assured me. Then he pointed out the Caelian, capped with handsome villas. 'To the right of that is the Aventine. Nothing there but pleb houses and merchants.'

'Pleb houses?' Alexander repeated.

'You know, houses for the plebeians. Men who aren't *equites* and don't own much land.'

'So Caesar is an equestrian?' I asked.

'Oh no.' Marcellus waved his hand. 'Our family's much higher than that. We're patricians. We live on the Palatine, where Octavian is building the largest temple to Apollo.' He indicated a flat-topped hill where buildings of polished marble and porphyry gleamed. It wasn't Alexandria, but there was some beauty in the way the buildings climbed the hillside and shone white against the pale blue sky.

The last of the Seven Hills was the Capitoline. 'My father used to take me up there to see the Tarpeian Rock,' Marcellus recalled with a shiver. 'That's where criminals are thrown from if they're not used in the Amphitheater.'

'And is your father still living?' I asked quietly.

'No. He died ten years ago. A few months later, Octavian arranged for my mother to marry Antony.' Even though our mother had already given birth to me and Alexander. I felt my cheeks warm, knowing that only five years after her marriage, Octavia had been abandoned. I wondered who had been a father to Marcellus.

'So your mother has three children,' I said.

'Five. She had two daughters from my father, but they were sent away when she remarried.'

I didn't understand. 'Why?'

'Because that's what's expected of a newly married woman.'

I stared at him. 'That she give up her previous children?'

'If they are girls. This is why my mother won't marry again.'

I thought of my father welcoming Octavia into his home but refusing the small girls who huddled fearfully behind her. Was that how it had been? Though he had never spent much time with me, my father had always been affectionate. Suddenly, I became afraid of Rome: afraid of her dirty streets, of her terrible punishments, and, most of all, of what it would be like to live with the woman my father had spurned.

We passed a forum where slaves were being sold by the thousands. Most of them were flaxen-haired and blue-eyed.

'Germans and Gallics.' Marcellus saw my look and shook his head. 'It's a sickening display.' As our procession of carriages rattled along, I could see the shame of the naked girls whose breasts were being squeezed by men who would buy them for work as well as pleasure, and my brother covered his mouth at the sight of grown men whose testicles had been removed.

'Eunuchs,' Marcellus said angrily. 'Some men like them, and

they go for a higher price. Don't look,' he suggested, but there was nothing else to see on the streets but starving dogs, jostling merchants, and mosaics whose crude images depicted men in various positions with women. 'This is the unsavory part of the city.' He twitched the curtain closed and sat back against his seat. 'In a moment, we'll be at the Temple of Jupiter. Then it's a short ride to the top of the Palatine and we'll be home.'

You'll be home, I thought. *We'll be prisoners waiting for Caesar's Triumph.* My brother reached out and took my hand. Then there was a sudden clamor of voices outside our carriage, and Marcellus opened the curtain again. The road was filled with petitioners being told to step back, and Marcellus said proudly, 'Almost there.'

My brother pointed to a strange structure peeking out from a grove of oaks. 'What is that?'

'The Temple of Magna Mater.'

'How is that a temple?' I asked rudely. It was a simple altar bearing a heavy rock.

'The goddess came to earth in the shape of a stone, foretelling Rome's victory over Hannibal.'

I wondered what foolish story the Romans would concoct for Octavian's victory over Egypt. Marcellus indicated a crude hut whose muddy walls would never have withstood the first gale in Alexandria. 'And that's where Romulus lived,' he said. 'Do you know that story?'

Alexander and I both shook our heads.

'Your father never taught it to you?' he exclaimed. 'Romulus and Remus were twins. When their mother abandoned them, they were raised by a she-wolf. That doesn't sound familiar?'

We shook our heads again.

'They founded Rome, and this hut was where the she-wolf raised them. It was Romulus who first built walls on the Palatine.

And when Remus mocked his brother's work, Romulus killed him. But there weren't enough women in Romulus's tribe, so he decided to steal them from the neighboring Sabines. He invited their men to a festival, and while the men were drinking and enjoying themselves, Romulus's men carried off their wives.'

I gasped. 'Is that what's meant by the Rape of the Sabine Women?'

'Then you've heard of it?'

'Only the name.' It was an event my mother had always alluded to when talking about the barbarism of Rome.

'Well, the Sabine men wanted revenge. But their king could never defeat Romulus, and since the women didn't want to see their husbands die, they begged for peace. It's a disgusting tale,' Marcellus admitted, 'but the beginning of Rome.' We had arrived at the top of the Palatine, and the carriage rolled to a stop. 'Are you ready?'

He stepped outside, then held out his hand, first for Alexander, then for me. 'Rome,' he announced, and beneath the Palatine spread the most disorganized city I had ever seen. Markets and temples crowded together while brick kilns belched smoke into the blazingly hot sky. People crushed one another on the narrow streets, rushing from one shop to the next. Although the Palatine was far above the stink of the urine used in the laundries, the pungent scent wafted upward on the breeze. Even Thebes, which had suffered destruction at the hands of Ptolemy IX, was far more beautiful than this. There was no organization, no city plan, and though buildings of rare beauty stood out among the brick *tabernae* and bathhouses, they were like gems in a quarry of jagged stone.

'So this is Rome,' I said, but only Alexander understood my meaning.

'And this is my mother's villa.'

I turned, and a sprawling home filled the horizon above us. There were villas up and down the Palatine, but none of them commanded such a beautiful view or boasted such elaborate columns. The shutters were carefully painted the same earthy color as the tiled roof, and a pair of metal-studded wooden doors were thrown open onto a broad portico. A crowd had gathered on the steps, watching as the soldiers unloaded Egyptian statues and rare ebony chests filled with cinnamon and myrrh.

Octavian led the way, and I took Alexander's arm. The group on the portico chattered excitedly, and when Octavian mounted the marble steps with Marcellus, one of the women stepped forward.

'That must be Caesar's sister, Octavia,' I whispered to Alexander in Parthian.

The woman wore a silk stola of Tyrian purple, and though her clothes subtly suggested great wealth, her face conveyed simplicity. She had not painted her eyelids with malachite, or even lined them with antimony, as my mother would have done. Her light hair had been pulled back into a simple chignon, and when she spread her arms to embrace her brother, I saw that her only jewel was a thin golden bracelet.

'*Salve, frater,*' she said warmly, and for the first time since meeting him, I saw Octavian's smile reach his eyes. 'You look well. And only a little red this time. But I suppose that conquering the world is difficult work.'

'Not the world,' he said without a trace of irony. 'Just Egypt.'

'Well, there will be a feast tonight. Your wife has arranged it.'

A woman appeared behind Octavia, and I felt my brother tense at my side. This was the woman Marcellus had warned us against.

'Livia,' Octavian said, and though he'd embraced his sister, he simply squeezed his wife's hand.

'*Mi Caesar.*' There was nothing to distinguish her from any woman on the street, and if Octavia's dress was simple, then Livia's was austere. Her stola was made of simple white cotton, and her dark hair had been braided before being swept back into a tight bun. She was small, and while my mother's build had been slight, at least her voice had been remarkable. There was nothing remarkable about Livia. Yet Octavian had wanted her, wooing her while she was still married to another man and pregnant. She looked up at him with wide-eyed adoration. 'All of Rome is waiting for your Triumph,' she said breathlessly. 'And while you've been gone, I've arranged it all.'

'You have the notes?'

She nodded eagerly. 'You may look them over tonight. Or even sooner, if you wish. They're right here.' She held up a scroll she'd been concealing in her stola.

Octavian unrolled it and skimmed the contents. 'So the celebration will last for three days.'

'Your sister thought it should be longer, but I knew you wouldn't want to appear like Antony, turning your victories into endless Triumphs.'

'I hardly think five days is an *endless Triumph*,' Octavia said sharply.

'Five days or three, it doesn't matter,' Octavian ruled. 'We will only be participating on the first day. The rest is just entertainment for the plebs, and since Livia has planned for three, that's what it will be.'

Livia preened a little, smiling smugly at Octavia, and I thought that if she were my sister-in-law, I would want to slap her.

Octavian handed the scroll to Agrippa. 'Look this over and prepare the soldiers. I'll wish to see the final plans tomorrow.'

'And are these the children?' Octavia asked.

Octavian nodded. 'Alexander and Selene.'

She blinked rapidly. 'They are beautiful.'

Marcellus laughed. 'What did you expect? A pair of Gorgons?'

Octavia walked down several steps so that we were standing on the same level. Instinctively, Alexander and I moved back, but there was no menace in her face. 'I know you must have had a terrible voyage,' she said, 'but welcome to Rome.' She smiled at us, then turned to her brother, whose face did not reflect the same tenderness. 'Shall we?' she asked him, and the group followed Octavia onto the portico. Although Alexander and I were the last in the party, there was no doubting that we were of the most interest. The women craned their necks around Agrippa to see us, and Juba even stepped back so that a young girl could get a better view.

'Caesar's daughter, Julia,' Alexander whispered. Although many of the girls on the portico were attractive, there was no one with the same dark beauty as Julia. Her mass of black hair shone in the sunlight, and her large dark eyes were framed by long lashes. Even her mouth was pretty, not small or thin-lipped like the rest of her family's. Her gaze shifted from me to my brother. Then Marcellus went to her and whispered something in her ear so that she giggled. I felt a strange annoyance, but didn't have time to understand why.

Octavian held up his arm and announced, 'Since you are more interested in seeing the children of Kleopatra than me, I shall present them to you.' There were sharp denials from all around, but Octavian didn't appear angry. 'Prince Alexander Helios and Princess Kleopatra Selene.'

Dozens of faces turned in our direction. Many in the crowd were not much older than us. 'Great Jupiter!' Julia cried. 'What are they wearing?'

'Greek clothes,' Marcellus explained. 'But,' he warned her, 'they speak perfect Latin.' Color flooded her cheeks.

A handsome man in a crimson toga stepped forward. 'Are they—'

'Roman citizens,' Octavian said dryly.

'What a shame.' The man cooled himself with a fan. 'They're quite a pair. Especially the boy.'

'There are plenty of boys in the market, Maecenas.' Octavian looked around. 'Now, who will make the introductions?'

Though Marcellus dutifully stepped forward, Livia pushed another young man toward Octavian. The boy shrugged off her hand, and I wondered if this was one of her sons. 'What are you doing?' he demanded.

Livia's lips grew even thinner. 'Caesar has asked for someone to make the introductions.'

'And because Marcellus wants to do it, I should, too? Perhaps I should be more like Marcellus and gamble away Caesar's allowance, as well.'

Marcellus laughed uneasily. 'There's nothing wrong with gambling.'

But Octavian glowered. 'Not when it's done in *moderation*.'

Everyone heard the implied criticism, and Marcellus colored a little. Then he introduced us to those gathered on the portico, beginning with Livia's son Tiberius, who had shaken off his mother's hand. His nine-year-old brother was Drusus, and each of them was the very image of Livia, with sharp noses and too-thin lips. Though I knew I would never remember so many names, Marcellus went on, pointing out our half sisters Antonia and Tonia, shy girls who clung to Octavia's stola and had none of our father's gregariousness. There was Vipsania, Agrippa's little girl whose mother had perished in childbirth, and a cluster of old men whose names I had heard of in the Museion, Horace and Vergil among them.

When Marcellus was finished, Livia held out her arm for her husband. 'Shall we prepare for your Feast of Welcome?'

'But I haven't asked Marcellus about his journey,' Julia complained.

'Then you may ask him tonight,' Livia said tersely.

Julia looked for reversal from her father, but he gave her none, and they left with Agrippa and Juba, trailing a dozen slaves behind them.

When they were gone, Octavia said softly, 'Marcellus, show Alexander and Selene to their chamber. When their chests have been brought, I will come myself to prepare them for Caesar's feast.' She looked down at the small girls clinging to her legs. 'Shall we pluck some roses for the dinner?' The little girls nodded eagerly, then chased each other to the end of the portico.

We followed Marcellus into a long hallway whose mosaic floor spelled out the word SALVE, welcoming visitors into Octavia's home. 'This is the vestibulum,' he said, leading us through it into another columned room he called the atrium. A beech-beamed opening overhead admitted sunlight, and terra-cotta gutters led into a marble pool. I asked Marcellus, 'How often does it rain?'

'Well, in summer, almost never. But in winter the streets of Rome turn to mud.' He gestured toward several doors leading from the atrium. 'Those are the guest rooms. And that is the tabulinum, where my mother keeps her desk.' He pointed to the far side of the room, and through the slightly open door I could see a long table of polished oak. 'Over there is the lararium.'

'And what is that?'

Marcellus turned in surprise to Alexander. 'Aren't there lararia in Egypt?' he asked. 'That's where we greet the Lares every morning.' Alexander and I looked at the alcove, with its long granite altar and ancestral busts of the Julii. When Marcellus saw our expressions, he explained, 'They're the spirits of our ancestors. We give them a little wine and bread every morning.'

'And do they like it?' I asked curiously.

'Better ask the slaves.' Marcellus laughed. 'They're the ones who end up taking it.'

We crossed the atrium and reached another open-air space, the peristylum, where bronze sculptures peered from the shadows. There was a long garden in the center, and a fountain that channeled water through the mouths of marble lions. Several men reclined on benches, shaded by trellised vines and flowering shrubs. They raised their hands in quiet greeting, and Marcellus mumbled, 'My mother's builders.'

At the end of the portico was the triclinium, where the household ate, and across the hall, next to the baths, were more chambers. 'This is my room,' Marcellus said. 'This is my mother's.' He indicated a wide door painted with a garden scene. 'These are for my sisters. And this is for you.' He opened a wooden door, and I heard my brother Alexander breathe in sharply.

It was a magnificent chamber. Curtained windows opened out onto a balcony, where a variety of palms grew from painted urns. The room itself was unlike anything in Egypt, with three wide couches, instead of beds, and only one painting. But the furniture was unmistakably rich: four chairs inlaid with bone and ivory; a pair of lamps fashioned into triple-headed Cerberus, whose bronze serpent's tail could be lit; a cedar folding stool; three tables; and three heavy chests. Everything had been prepared for three children, only Ptolemy had never made it to Rome. I blinked back my tears and tried not to think about Egypt. The northern wall had been painted with images from Homer's epics, so that whenever we fell asleep our last thoughts would be on the greatest poet Greece had ever produced. I could pick out Agamemnon, Achilles, and even Odysseus among the painted men.

'I thought we were prisoners,' my brother said.

'In my mother's house?' Marcellus sounded offended. 'You are guests.'

'Caesar killed our brothers,' I reminded him sharply. 'And tomorrow, we will be taken through the streets.'

Marcellus's face became grim. 'My uncle rids himself of anyone he thinks might be an enemy now or in the future. And he surrounds himself with useful people. He has a wife who is more like a secretary to him, and my mother advises him on matters of the Senate. He keeps Agrippa for his knowledge of war, and Juba for his knowledge of the people and for protection. Do you think he would have any interest in me if I weren't my mother's eldest son? I serve a practical purpose as well. But so long as you are here,' he said firmly, 'you are guests.'

Several slaves appeared behind us with the ironbound chests we had taken from Egypt. But before we could look through them to see what we had been allowed to keep and what had been taken, Octavia entered the chamber.

'It's time to prepare,' she said quickly. 'Marcellus, take Alexander to your room and give him what's been laid out on your couch. He may keep his diadem, but the chiton and the sandals must go.' As she turned to me, I noticed the strikingly beautiful woman standing behind her at the door. Her long hair was the color of honey, and Marcellus smiled winsomely as he passed.

'*Salve*, Gallia.'

She inclined her head slightly, and I guessed her age to be about twenty. 'I am glad to see your safe return, domine.' She used the word for master, which indicated her position as a slave, yet her tunic was embroidered with gold.

'Selene,' Octavia said, 'this is my *ornatrix*, Gallia. We are going to prepare you for tonight, and give you clothes that will be suitable for Rome.'

'It is a pleasure to meet you, domina.' When Gallia smiled, I noticed that she had the high cheekbones that artists in Alexandria loved to capture. *She's like a sculpture carved from marble*, I thought, and wondered if she was one of the twenty thousand women Julius Caesar had brought back as slaves from his conquest of Gaul. She spoke Latin with an accent and pronounced her words with exaggerated care to make sure she was getting them right. 'Why don't you come with us into the bathing room?' she asked, indicating a room in the corner. Inside was a tub of heavy bronze. She turned a handle and a pipe that led from the ceiling released hot water into the bath. The mosaic floors depicted sea nymphs and mermaids, and a large mirror of polished brass hung on the wall. A small brazier was tucked away in the corner for colder nights when the chamber would need to be heated. Several stools were arranged before a long cedar table.

Octavia led me to one of these seats, then studied me carefully with her pale gray eyes. 'What do you think?' she asked Gallia nervously.

'How old are you?' Gallia asked me.

'I turn twelve in January,' I replied.

Gallia stepped forward. 'Almost twelve. Still, just a little bird.' No one had ever called me a 'little bird,' and when I straightened indignantly, Gallia laughed. 'No, it is good that you are so small.'

'We want you both to appear as young as possible tonight,' Octavia said, busying herself with Gallia's basket. She took out vials of antimony and saffron, piling them on the long table along with hairnets and pins with ruby tips.

Not understanding, I looked at both women. 'Why?'

'So that no one feels threatened by you,' Gallia said simply. She lit a fire in the brazier and plunged a metal rod into the burning charcoal.

'Do you wish to wear your diadem tonight?' she asked.

I touched the thin band of pearls in my hair, remembering the time my mother had given it to me. 'Yes.'

'And your pearl necklace?'

'Of course.'

'Then they will stay. But the rest must go.'

I stood and slowly removed my chiton and loincloth. I was not yet so developed as to need a breastband. Then Gallia pointed me to the steaming bath.

'Inside. Do not wet your hair. It will never dry in time to curl it.'

'But I already have curls.'

'These will be smaller.'

I stepped into the bath as I was told, and let Gallia rub lavender oil into my back.

'Look at this, domina!' Gallia turned to Octavia. 'You can see the bones. What do they feed her in Alexandria?'

'She has been on a ship for weeks,' Octavia reminded her, 'and has lost nearly every member of her family.'

'Domina will feed you well here,' she promised, motioning for me to stand. Then she started drying me with a long white linen cloth.

I didn't reply, knowing that if I did I would only cry. From her basket, Gallia produced a silk tunic of the deepest green. I lifted my arms obediently. She slipped the tunic over my head and fastened it at the shoulders with golden pins. When Octavia passed her a belt of light olive, Gallia held it in front of her and frowned.

'Under the breasts, at the hips, or at the waist?' she considered.

The women studied me, and now I really felt like Gallia's bird, being preened for a life in a cage.

'At the waist,' Gallia decided herself. 'It's simple.' She tied the sash above my hips, then slipped a pair of leather sandals on my feet. On my neck, she fastened a golden necklace with a disc that was hidden by my mother's pearls. She didn't have to tell me that it was a *bulla*. I had seen Roman children in Alexandria wearing the same protective amulet.

'What about her hair?' Octavia worried.

Gallia took the metal rod from the brazier and held it in front of me by its cool end. 'Do you know what this is?'

We had them in Alexandria. 'A hot iron,' I said.

'Yes. A *calamistrum*. If you will remove your diadem . . .'

I followed her instructions and seated myself on one of the chairs. When Gallia was finished, Octavia said eagerly, 'Now her eyes.'

I had powdered the lids carefully with malachite, and lined them with antimony as Charmion had taught me. But Gallia wiped my eye makeup away with a cloth, and when she didn't make any motion to replace it, I protested. 'But I've never gone anywhere without paint.'

Gallia passed a look to Octavia. 'Domina,' she said to me, 'that is not proper in Rome.'

'But I wore it every day on the ship.'

'That was at sea. You must not look like a *lupa* in front of Caesar's guests.'

'A what?'

'You know' – she gestured – 'one of those women.'

'A whore,' Alexander said from behind us, and Octavia gasped. 'Sorry,' he said quickly. But I knew that he wasn't. He was smiling, and Gallia nodded at him.

'You look very handsome, domine.'

I turned. 'Handsome? You look like you're wearing a bedsheet. How will you walk? It's ridiculous.' I spoke in Parthian, but Alexander replied in Latin.

'It's a *toga praetexta*. And,' he added indignantly, 'it's what Marcellus is wearing.' A red stripe ran along its border, but the material wasn't nearly as beautiful as that of my tunic. Just then he noticed my red sandals, and whistled. 'A Roman princess.' I glared at him, but he ignored my anger. 'So nothing for your eyes, then?'

'We want to remind Rome that she is a girl,' Gallia repeated, 'not a woman in some dirty *lupanar*.'

'That will do,' Octavia said sternly, and I imagined that a *lupanar* was a place where women sold their sexual favors.

But Gallia only smiled. 'He asked.'

I went to Alexander and touched the golden disc at his throat. 'So we really are Romans now,' I said darkly. My brother avoided my gaze. Then Marcellus appeared behind him, smiling in a way that made me forget we were prisoners masquerading as citizens. His freshly washed hair curled at the nape of his neck, and the color contrasted with the darkness of his skin.

'You're a goddess in emerald, Selene. This must be the work of Gallia. She could stop Apollo in his chariot, if she wanted.'

'Very pretty, domine.'

Octavia looked from my brother to me. 'Are they ready?'

Gallia nodded. 'They are as Roman now as Romulus himself.'

Alexander risked a glance at me. We followed Gallia through the halls and out to the portico, where Octavia's youngest daughters sat patiently in the shade. I couldn't recall ever sitting patiently anywhere as a child, but these children were all sweetness and gold. *Like their mother,* I thought, and stopped myself from thinking of my own mother lying cold in her sarcophagus next to my father.

As we followed the cobbled road to Caesar's villa, Gallia explained, 'When we reach the triclinium, a slave will ask you to take off your sandals.'

'To wash our feet?' Alexander asked.

'Yes. And then you'll enter the chamber. A *nomenclator* will announce your arrival, and all of us will be taken to our assigned couches.'

'Romans eat on couches?' I asked.

'Don't Egyptians?'

'No. We eat at tables. With chairs and stools.'

'Oh, there will be tables,' Gallia said easily. 'But not stools, and chairs are only for old men.'

'But then how do we eat?' Alexander worried.

'While reclining.' Gallia saw our expressions and explained, 'There will be a dozen tables with couches around them. Caesar's couch is always at the back, and the place of honor is opposite the empty side of his table. Whoever sits there at Caesar's right is his most important guest.'

'Which tonight,' Octavia predicted, 'will be the both of you.'

'But we don't know what to do!' I exclaimed.

'Oh, it's nothing,' Marcellus promised. 'Just recline on your left elbow, then eat with your right hand. And if they serve the Trojan pig,' he warned mischievously, 'don't eat it.'

'Marcellus!' Octavia said sharply.

'It's true! Remember Pollio's dinner party?'

'Pollio is a freedman without the sense to cook a chicken,' Octavia pronounced, and turned to us. 'Here you may eat whatever is served.'

Behind her, Marcellus shook his head in warning, making the gesture of throwing up with his hands. Alexander snickered, and I suppressed a smile. But when we reached the wide bronze doors of Octavian's villa, I pressed my nails into my palms. I could hear my mother's voice in my head, scolding me to relax my hands.

'This is it,' Alexander said nervously. I took his arm, and as we crossed the threshold into the vestibulum, I was shocked by the room's simplicity. There were no cedar tables inlaid with gems, or lavish chambers hung with Indian silks. A faded mosaic depicted a stage with tragedians, and on the wall an old mask from a comedy stared back at us with its sightless eyes and ghastly smile. As we passed though the atrium, there were candlelit busts of the Julii, but no great statues of Octavian or his family. Aside from the blue-veined marble of the floors, there was nothing to indicate that this was the home of a conquering hero.

'This could be a merchant's villa,' I whispered.

'Or a peasant's. Where is the furniture?' Alexander asked.

But as we reached the triclinium and a slave hurried out to wash our feet, I peered inside and realized what Octavian had done. In every room a visitor might frequent, the crudest furniture had been used. But inside the summer dining room, where only his most intimate friends ever gathered, the tables had been set with silver egg cups and matching bowls. Maroon silk covered the dining couches, and lavender water trickled from a marble fountain. Because one side of the room opened onto a garden, long linen curtains blew in the breeze, keeping out the glare of the setting sun.

'He wants the people to think he's humble,' I said critically in Parthian.

'Meanwhile, his friends are dining like kings,' my brother added.

The *nomenclator* announced each person's arrival, and when it was our turn, I noticed that every guest in the triclinium turned.

'Alexander Helios and Kleopatra Selene, Prince and Princess of Egypt.'

There was a murmur of surprise, then the guests turned to one another and began to chatter eagerly.

'Just follow me,' Octavia instructed softly, and Gallia departed to take her meal with the household slaves in the atrium. As we crossed the room, I saw Julia stand up from a table in the corner. She was Octavian's only child, but she looked nothing like him, and I assumed she had inherited her looks from her mother.

'Marcellus!' She smiled. She was wearing a tunic of the palest blue, and her dark gaze, cool and appraising, flicked in my direction. 'Come,' she told him, and led him away, putting her slender arm through his.

When I made to follow, Alexander pulled me back. 'We're not eating with them. We're at the next table.' He indicated the couch where Caesar was scribbling something on a scroll. We would be sitting with Livia, Juba, and Agrippa.

'Your guests of honor,' Octavia said.

Her brother looked up, and a faint smile touched his lips. 'Very nice.' He meant our clothes. He rose to a sitting position and the others around the table immediately did the same. 'Almost Roman.'

'They are Roman,' Agrippa pointed out.

'Only half. The rest of them is Greek.'

'But a stunning combination,' Maecenas said approvingly.

Octavian rose, and the entire triclinium fell silent. 'I present to you the children of Queen Kleopatra and Marc Antony,' he announced. 'Selene and Alexander have journeyed from Egypt to take part in tomorrow's Triple Triumph, a celebration of my success in Illyricum, my victory in the Battle of Actium, and the annexation of Egypt.'

There was tremendous applause, and I refused to let my lower lip tremble.

'And tonight,' Octavian continued, 'there will be an auction for each of these prizes.' He snapped his fingers and a group of male slaves wheeled twenty covered statues into the triclinium. Some were very large, but others were no bigger than my hand. An excited murmur passed through the room. 'Bidding, as always, will be blind.' He smiled briefly. 'Enjoy your meal.'

He returned to the table, and Octavia motioned that it was time for us to recline on the couches. It was impossible to get comfortable, and Juba smiled across the table at me.

'Just like a Roman now,' he said. 'And I must say, a tunic suits you much better than a chiton. You've even donned the *bulla*.'

I narrowed my eyes at him. 'It belongs to Octavia.'

'But you wear it so well.'

Octavia smiled. 'Alexander, Selene, I see you've met Juba. Perhaps you remember Maecenas as well.' Maecenas's dark eyes hadn't left my brother's face since our arrival. 'And this is Maecenas's wife, Terentilla. A good friend of mine and a great patron of the theater.'

When Terentilla smiled at us, a pair of dimples appeared in her cheeks. 'It is a pleasure.'

'And this is the poet Vergil, and the historian Livy.' That completed our table, and while women appeared with food in large silver bowls, Octavia whispered, 'This is the *gustatio*.' I presumed that meant the first course. There was cabbage in vinegar, snails, endives, asparagus, clams, and large red crabs. Each person was expected to take what he or she wanted from the middle of the table, and just as in Egypt there were napkins, and spoons whose opposite end could be used as a knife. I chose several clams, and while I was wondering what to do with the empty shells, I saw Agrippa toss his to the floor. Alexander merrily followed his example, discarding his crab shells onto the tiles.

'Alexander,' I hissed.

'What? Everyone else is doing it,' he said guiltily.

'But who cleans it up?'

Alexander frowned. 'The slaves.'

Even Octavia was dropping her shells onto the floor, wiping them away with a flick of her wrist as she asked Terentilla to help describe the plays Octavian had missed while he was gone. There was talk of a play in which female actors had actually undressed on stage, and one at which the entire audience rose and walked out because the actors had been so terrible.

When the second course came, Alexander said eagerly, 'Look!' Slaves with large platters came to our table first, setting in front of us a variety of meats that would have contented even my father. There was roasted goose in white almond sauce, ostrich with Damascene prunes, and pheasants. There was even a peacock, served on a platter decorated with its own feathers. But when Alexander saw the thrushes in honeyed glaze, his eyes went wide.

'You'd think you'd never eaten before,' I said critically.

'I'm growing.'

'Into what? Remember what happened to our grandfather.' He had grown to the size of a bull by the time he died.

A slave came to fill our cups with wine, and Octavian whispered something into Terentilla's ear. She giggled intimately, and his eyes lingered on hers. *Perhaps this is why Livia has never given him a son*, I thought.

'And would you like to see what I picked up along my travels?' I heard him ask. Her dimples appeared, and when she nodded, Octavian snapped his fingers. 'The chest from Egypt,' he ordered one of his slaves. 'Bring it here.' Though he had eaten only a few olives and some bread, it appeared that he was finished with his meal.

When the chest was placed on a table behind Octavian, Terentilla clapped her hands with joy. 'Your treasures!' she exclaimed, and her long lashes fluttered on her cheeks.

'A few,' Octavian admitted, and I was curious to see what he had stolen from Egypt. The slave who had brought the chest to the table produced one curiosity at a time, and Octavian named each one and then passed it around.

'Shall I write down the names?' Livia asked eagerly. 'In case you forget?'

'Yes,' Octavian said, and Livia produced a scroll and a reed pen from a hidden drawer in the table. 'This is called the Eye of Horus,' he said, and his guests made the appropriate noises of delight. It was a small faience amulet, something that would have impressed a peasant farmer outside of Alexandria but would never have found its way inside the palace. I wondered where he had taken it from. 'And this is a statue of the war goddess Sekhmet.' Terentilla thought it was the most beautiful image she had ever seen. When the statuette came to her, she stroked the goddess's leonine face and drew her finger over the breasts.

'Can you imagine worshipping a goddess with a lion's head?' she asked Juba. 'I've heard they have a goddess with a hippo's head as well!'

'Tawaret,' I said through clenched teeth. 'They are old gods, and today the people worship Isis, who is no different from your Venus.'

'I think what Selene is trying to say,' Juba interpreted, 'is that the Ptolemies do not worship goddesses with animal heads anymore, but women with wings.'

'I believe your Cupid has wings as well,' I said sharply.

Alexander kicked my shin, but the men around the table

laughed. 'It's true!' Vergil said, nodding sagely. Terentilla looked contrite, and I saw that she hadn't meant any offense. But Octavian wasn't interested in our banter. He had produced the sketch he'd taken from me on the ship, and Terentilla was the first to murmur her surprise.

'What is *that*?'

'An image of Alexandria by Kleopatra Selene,' Octavian replied, though when he looked at me there was no warmth in his eyes. 'The princess appears to have great talent in art.'

My drawing was passed around the table, and even Juba seemed impressed, staring at the picture for a second time. Livia made several markings on her scroll, misspelling my name with a *C* in place of a *K*. I didn't believe there was any person left in Rome who couldn't spell my mother's name or mine in Greek, and I knew she did it on purpose.

'The artist and the horseman,' Agrippa remarked. 'A pair of very interesting siblings. I wonder—' His words were cut off by a commotion outside the doors of the triclinium. Guests sat upright on their couches; then the doors flew open and a soldier appeared.

'What is this?' Octavian demanded. When he stood, Juba and Agrippa rose as well.

'Forgive me, Caesar, but there is news I thought you might want to hear.'

'Has our illustrious traitor been caught?' Juba demanded.

'No, but one of the Red Eagle's followers—'

'Are the soldiers now glorifying him as well?' Octavian shouted.

The soldier stepped back. 'No. I – I meant to say *the traitor*. One of the traitor's followers was discovered posting this on the Temple of Jupiter.' The soldier produced a scroll, and Octavian snatched it. 'Another actum,' the soldier said. 'And the symbol of the same red eagle at the bottom.'

'Has the man been tortured?' Octavian asked.

'Yes.'

'And what has he said?'

'That he was paid by a stranger in the Forum to nail it up.'

'And who was this stranger?'

The soldier shook his head. 'He swears it was a farmer.'

Octavian's look was murderous. 'The man who produces this cannot be a farmer. He is literate and has access to the Palatine. He is a soldier, or a guard, or a very foolish senator. The man is lying!'

'Chop off his hand,' Livia said at once, 'and nail it to the Senate door.'

The soldier looked for confirmation from Octavian.

'Yes. And if he still doesn't remember who paid him to post this, then crucify the rest of him. Agrippa will make sure that it's done.' When the soldier hesitated, Octavian said sharply, 'Go!'

An uneasy silence had settled over the triclinium. Octavian looked to the harpist. 'Keep playing!' he commanded. The girl placed her trembling hands on the strings, and when Octavian resumed his seat, the room filled with nervous conversation.

I turned and whispered to Octavia, 'I don't understand. Who is the Red Eagle?'

Octavia glanced uneasily at her brother, but he was giving instructions to Agrippa. 'A man who wants to put an end to slavery.'

'Then he's inspiring slaves to rebel?' I asked.

Octavia shifted uncomfortably. 'No. The attempts to do that have already failed. Slaves have no weapons or organization.'

'So what does he want?' Alexander asked.

'For the *patricians* to rebel. He wants men with money and the power in the Senate to put an end to servitude.'

My brother made a face. 'And he thinks that will happen?'

Octavia smiled sadly. 'No. The most he can hope for is a leniency of the laws.'

'And if he thinks he will achieve even that, then he's a fool,' Juba said darkly. 'Rome will always have its slaves. Gauls, Germans—'

'Egyptians, Mauretanians. If not for an accident of Fortune,' I said hotly, 'you and I might be slaves as well!'

Marcellus looked over from the table next to us, and I realized my voice had been louder than I intended.

CHAPTER FIVE

'THAT WAS very brave, what you told him,' Marcellus said.

'Or very foolish,' my brother put in angrily.

'Why? Isn't it the truth?' I demanded. The three of us sat on separate couches, and Marcellus looked like golden-haired Apollo in the lamplight of our chamber. His strong, tanned arms seemed capable of anything. It was no wonder Octavian preferred him over his bitter stepson Tiberius.

'It doesn't matter if it's the truth,' my brother warned. 'You're lucky Caesar didn't hear you.'

I glanced at the door. Soon Octavia would appear and order us to bed. 'What do you think will happen to that prisoner?'

'Exactly what my uncle said. His hand will be nailed to the Senate door.'

'And Agrippa will do it?' Alexander asked quietly. He had removed his diadem, and his hair tumbled over his brow. He pushed it back with his palm.

'Or someone else. But there is no one more loyal than Agrippa. He would strike down his own daughter if she threatened Rome. And they'll catch this rebel eventually.'

'But why does he use the image of a red eagle?' I asked.

'Because the eagle is the symbol of Rome's legions. He is trying to say that Rome is dripping with the blood of its slaves. The freedmen all think it's very brave. But don't ever use the name in front of my uncle. He thinks it glorifies the rebel's cause.'

'But if the senators haven't rebelled,' I asked, 'how has the Red Eagle gone against the law?'

'By sneaking into the arenas and freeing gladiators. And by helping husbands and wives who've been separated by slavery escape.'

'Escape where?' my brother exclaimed.

'Possibly to their homelands. Gallic slaves were caught on the Flaminian Way a few months ago with enough stolen gold to return to Gaul.'

I glanced at my brother, who must have known what I was thinking, because he shook his head sternly. But what else was there to hope for? If this Red Eagle was willing to help slaves return to Gaul, why wouldn't he help us return to Egypt? Alexander had heard Octavian's warning just as well as I had. *The girl is pretty. In a few years, some senator will need to be silenced. She'll be of marriageable age and make him happy. And neither of the boys has reached fifteen years. Keeping them alive will seem merciful.* And when it wasn't merciful anymore? When Alexander came of age and posed a threat?

Marcellus continued, 'There is some honor in what the rebel does. It's only an accident of Fortune that we were born on the Palatine. We could just as easily be living in the Subura, sleeping with the rats and begging for our food. Or we might have been like Gallia, and sold into slavery.'

Alexander sat forward. 'She wasn't born a slave?'

'No. Her father was King Vercingetorix.'

'She's a Gallic *princess*?' I gasped.

Marcellus nodded. 'When she was a girl, she was brought to Rome in chains, and years later her father was paraded in Caesar's Triumph and then executed.' He saw my look and added quickly,

'That would never have happened to an Egyptian queen. Vercingetorix was the leader of the Gauls. A barbarian. My mother told me that when Gallia came here, she knew neither Latin nor Greek.'

'Then she isn't twenty.'

'No. I should say more like thirty.'

My brother hesitated. 'So then why did your uncle spare us from slavery?'

'Because your father was a Roman citizen, and you carry the blood of Alexander the Great.'

'Juba's father wasn't a Roman,' I pointed out.

'No. His ancestor was the warrior Massinissa. But my uncle must be thankful he didn't make Juba a slave. Juba saved his life at Actium, and there were many days leading up to the battle when my uncle feared he would be defeated.'

Just as there had been many days leading up to the battle when my mother had thought Egypt could still be saved.

An uneasy silence settled over the room. Marcellus cleared his throat. 'So I saw your sketch of Alexandria,' he said. 'You are very talented.'

'You should see her other drawings,' Alexander added. 'Show him your book of sketches, Selene.'

I crossed my arms over my chest.

'She has a leather book,' Alexander explained. 'It's not like anything you've ever seen. Go ahead. Get it,' he coaxed.

When Marcellus looked at me, I went to the chest in the corner of the room and took out my mother's present. His eyes widened in the candlelight, and when he held the book in his hands, he asked in amazement, 'What *is* this?'

'Calfskin,' Alexander said.

'All of it?' Marcellus turned the pages, and I don't know what impressed him more, my sketches or what I had drawn them on. 'I've never seen anything like this,' he admitted. 'Where did it come from?'

'The library on the Acropolis in Pergamon,' my brother said.

'The greatest library in the world!'

'The *second* greatest,' Alexander corrected. 'And when our family stopped exporting papyrus to them, they started using calfskin to make books like these.'

'Books,' Marcellus said wonderingly.

'There were two hundred thousand of them in Pergamon, and our father made a present of them all to our mother. She was reading them, one by one. A different book every night.' He looked at me, and I knew he was remembering our seventh birthday, when we had been allowed to choose anything we wanted from Pergamon's library. My brother had chosen a book on horses, and I had chosen an empty book for sketches.

When I looked away, Marcellus said quietly, 'Queen Kleopatra was a remarkable woman.'

'Yes,' Alexander said quietly.

Footsteps echoed in the hall, and Marcellus stood. 'My mother,' he said, returning my book of sketches to me. The door of our chamber opened, and Octavia's face appeared next to an oil lamp.

'Marcellus,' she said sharply. 'What are you doing?'

'Going to sleep.' He grinned back at us, then kissed his mother on the cheek. 'I'll see you in the morning,' he promised us. When he was gone, Octavia set the oil lamp on a table.

Alexander and I lay back on our couches and waited to see what she was going to do. Despite the heat, I covered myself with a thin linen blanket. She came and sat at the edge of my couch. When I inhaled, I could smell her light scent of lavender. My mother had always worn jasmine.

'How was your day?' she asked kindly.

I shot a questioning look at Alexander. 'Tiring,' I admitted.

'It will be even more tiring tomorrow,' she warned. 'I would like to prepare you for my brother's Triumph, though it will only be for one day.'

'I thought it was three.'

'Yes, but you will only be a part of it tomorrow. In the morning, clothes will be delivered to your chamber. You'll be expected to put them on, then ride behind Caesar on a wooden float. There may be chains as well. But I will not allow them to cuff your necks. That is only for slaves.'

'And then?' Alexander asked steadily.

'You will return for the Feast of Triumph. It will be larger than what you have seen tonight. But you must be prepared to see things tomorrow. Things that will make you very upset.'

'Will they spit at us in the streets?' I whispered.

'I don't know. The plebs are very angry. They believe what they've heard about your mother and father.'

'Such as?' I asked urgently.

Octavia's shoulders tensed. 'Such as your father wore a Greek chiton and put away his toga while in Egypt.'

I raised my chin. 'That's true.'

'What else do they believe?' Alexander asked.

'That Antony instructed that he be worshipped as Dionysus. That he crowned his head in ivy and carried a *thyrsus* instead of a sword.'

I could see my father in his robes of red and gold, holding Dionysus's stalk of fennel just as Octavia had described. 'All of that is true.'

Octavia sat forward. 'And did he really strike a Roman coin with your mother's likeness?'

'Yes. Three years ago,' my brother replied. 'What's so terrible about a coin?'

When she didn't answer, I asked sharply, 'So is that all the Romans believe?'

She hesitated. 'There were rumors of dinners on the Nile . . .'

'Of course,' Alexander said frankly. 'Our mother and father had a club. The Society of Inimitable Livers.'

'And what did this society do?' she asked breathlessly.

'They had banquets on ships and discussed literature with philosophers from around the world.'

'Then they changed it to the Order of the Inseparable in Death,' I added, 'when our father lost the Battle of Actium. Now all of that is gone,' I said. 'Just like our mother and father.'

Octavia sat back and looked from my brother to me. She seemed to have trouble reconciling the Antony she had known as her husband with the Antony who had been our father. 'So did . . . did your father spend a great deal of time with your mother?'

I realized what was happening and felt my cheeks warm. She had loved him.

Alexander answered quietly, 'Yes.'

'Then he didn't spend all of his time with his men?' It was me she was asking.

'No.' I was too ashamed to meet her gaze. 'Are you glad that he's gone now?'

'I would never wish death on anyone,' she said. 'When he left me,' she admitted, 'it was a great embarrassment. All of Rome knew I had been rejected.'

I tried to imagine how she must have felt, abandoned so publicly by my father. Antonia and Tonia, my half sisters, wouldn't even have known him, since he had come to live with us permanently when they were just a few years old.

'My brother wanted him dead,' she confessed. 'But I . . .' She hesitated, saying at last, 'There wasn't a woman in Rome who didn't love your father.'

'They don't love him now,' I remarked.

She stood up from my couch, then touched my cheek with the back of her palm. 'Because they think he abandoned his people to become a Greek. But all of that is past,' she said tenderly. 'What matters is tomorrow. Be brave,' she said, 'and it will all end well.'

When she closed the door, leaving the oil lamp near Alexander's couch, I turned to him and we watched each other in the flickering light.

'Our mother never came to us at night,' he remarked.

'Because our mother was a ruler, not the sister of one.'

'Do you think Father really loved Octavia?'

It seemed cruel to say no, but Octavia was nothing like our mother, and I couldn't imagine my father ever racing chariots with her on the Canopic Way, or spinning her in his arms whenever she won. 'Perhaps he loved her kindness,' I offered, and Alexander nodded.

'Marcellus has the same compassion, doesn't he? And I doubt there's anyone in Rome more beautiful.'

I stared at him. 'You're not a Ganymede, are you?'

'Of course not!' He blushed furiously.

I kept staring at him, but he blew out the light, and in the darkness, I was too tired to argue.

The clothes that were brought to our chamber the next morning were insulting. Alexander held up his linen kilt, and I crumpled the beaded dress in my hands.

'Is this what Romans think Egyptians wear?' I asked angrily. The hills were still pink with the blush of dawn, but I could hear that the villa was already awake.

'Of course,' Gallia said, and I could see that she wasn't mocking me.

'A thousand *years* ago queens wore beaded dresses,' I told her. 'Now they wear silk chitons!'

'That is not what I have seen in the paintings or statues.'

'Because they're stylized,' Alexander explained patiently. 'I have never worn a kilt in my life.'

'I am sorry,' she said, and I could see that she was. As a child, she must have suffered the same humiliation when she was paraded through the streets of Rome. 'But this is what Caesar has instructed.'

I did not fight her when she took me to the bathing room. I could see that Gallia was unhappy, but when she helped me to put on the beaded dress and I looked in the mirror, my cheeks grew hot. The beads covered only the most important places; otherwise I might as well have been naked.

But when Octavia arrived, her hand flew to her mouth. 'What is she wearing?'

'What Caesar ordered,' Gallia said indignantly.

'She will not be paraded through the streets like a whore!' She turned to me. 'Have you brought other clothes?'

'Silk tunics and wigs,' I answered swiftly.

'And that's what you wore in Alexandria?'

'With paints.'

'Then fetch them.' She closed her eyes briefly. 'Better paint than this.'

Octavia watched while Gallia fit the wig over my hair, and she frowned a little when I showed Gallia how to extend the dark lines of antimony outward from the corners of my eyes. Gallia wanted to know about everything I unpacked. The henna for my hands, the moringa oil for my face, the pumice stone for removing extra hair around my brows.

'You are too young for that!' Gallia said sternly. 'You will rub your face raw.'

'That's what this is for.' I showed her the cream Charmion had used on my face every morning. She held it to her nose, then passed it to Octavia.

'And all women wear these things?' Octavia asked quietly. 'Henna and wigs?'

'On special occasions,' I told her.

She glanced at Gallia, who said, 'It's not much different from the malachite that Romans use for eye shadow, domina. The Egyptians just prefer more of it.'

When we left the bathing room and returned to the chamber, I suppressed a laugh. My brother was dressed in a long linen kilt. A golden pectoral shone from his chest, and a pharaoh's blue and gold *nemes* headdress had replaced his diadem. When he turned, he crossed his arms angrily. 'How come you get to wear your tunic, and I have to wear this?'

'Because Caesar wanted me to wear a beaded dress.'

He gasped. 'Like a *dancer*?'

'Or a whore,' I said in Parthian.

Octavia cleared her throat. 'We are going to the atrium now.' She smoothed her stola nervously. 'My brother is coming here to make an offering. Then the procession will begin at the Senate. Nothing will happen to you,' she promised.

'You will be on the float behind Caesar,' Gallia explained. 'And the plebs will never risk hurling stones if they think they might hit him.'

'But they might hurl other things,' my brother ventured.

Gallia looked to Octavia, who shook her head firmly. 'No. You will be close to Octavian. I will see to that.'

I took my brother's arm. In the atrium, Octavian and Livia had already arrived. They were instructing Marcellus and Tiberius on where they would ride during the Triumph, though Marcellus seemed to be more intent on smiling at Julia. As soon as we appeared, the conversation faltered. Agrippa and Juba stopped polishing their swords.

'By the Furies!' Marcellus exclaimed, and moved toward me. 'Look at this wig.' While everyone turned to look, Julia watched me with unveiled disgust. *There will be trouble with her*, I thought.

'Where is the beaded dress?' Livia demanded, and I realized it wasn't Caesar who had ordered the dress for me, but Livia. She wanted to see me humiliated. But when no one answered her, she repeated, 'Where is the dress?' She advanced, but Gallia stepped in front of me.

'There was an unfortunate accident with the dress this morning. It appears that domina's cat mistook it for a plaything.'

'You arrogant little *lupa*. Move!'

Gallia stepped aside, but Octavia took her place. 'The dress is gone, Livia.'

'Liar! I know you took—'

'You are speaking to the sister of Caesar, who does not lie,' Octavian said angrily.

Livia lowered her eyes in shame. 'Forgive me, Octavian.'

'It is my sister you have offended, not me.'

Everyone watched while Livia turned to Octavia. 'I am sorry,' she said, though her words sounded more bitter than contrite.

Octavia merely nodded. She hadn't lied. The dress was gone, given to one of the slaves to sell in the marketplace. It was Gallia who had twisted the truth, and I wished my wig could make me disappear when Livia's eyes settled on me. *She will never forget this humiliation. She will blame me for this. Me and Gallia.*

'Where is my speech?' Octavian demanded.

Livia produced it slowly from her sleeve. He took the scroll from her, and when he unrolled it, he nodded approvingly. 'This is good.' I noticed he was wearing a steel corselet beneath his toga, and he shifted uncomfortably under the weight.

'Agrippa, Juba, you understand not to move during the speech?'

'I will be on your left,' Agrippa promised. 'Juba will be on your right. If a senator moves toward you—'

'Then you have my permission to draw your sword. We are a family,' he said sternly, looking from Octavia to Livia to Marcellus. 'Family members protect one another, and the people of Rome must see this. The plebs look to the Julio-Claudii to understand tradition, unity, morality. And if *we* cannot be happy, what chance is there for a brick-maker to be happy? So there will be smiles, even from Tiberius.'

Tiberius made a purposely ugly grin, and Marcellus snickered. 'How handsome!'

'I'm sorry I can't be as beautiful as you,' Tiberius snapped at Marcellus.

But Octavian was not in the mood for banter. 'Enough! Octavia, the Lares.'

Octavia reached into a small cabinet and took out a vessel of wine. She poured a cup's worth into a shallow bowl beneath the bust of Julius Caesar, and, together, everyone in the room intoned *'Do ut des'*: I give so you will give.

There was a short silence. Then Octavian straightened his shoulders and announced, 'Let the Triumph begin.'

I expected the Senate to be the grandest building in all of Rome, a place so enormous that every senator who had ever served could have sat within its marbled chambers. So when I saw that it had been made of concrete and brick, the lower half faced with marble slabs, the upper half with imitation white blocks, I asked Marcellus, 'Is this it?'

'The Curia Julia,' he said reverently. 'Romans call it the Senate.' Graffiti covered the steps, and some of the images were undoubtedly of Caesar. If my mother had ever found graffiti of herself, the men responsible would have been hunted down and sentenced to death. Yet Octavian hadn't even bothered to order it removed for his Triumph. A single flight of stairs led to a pair of bronze doors, and Marcellus lamented, 'We're not normally allowed inside.'

'Why not?'

'Because we're still too young, and women are never allowed within. But they're making a special exception for you.'

I glanced nervously at my brother.

'And what will we do?' Alexander asked. The morning's light shone so brightly from his golden pectoral that Marcellus had to hold up a hand to see him.

'Sit there while my uncle gives his speech. Then the Triumph will begin. I'll be riding only a few paces ahead of you,' he said reassuringly.

'On a float?'

'A horse. To the right of Caesar.' The position of honor.

'Come.' Agrippa beckoned Alexander, and as we mounted up the steps, I glanced over my shoulder at Marcellus, who gave me an encouraging smile.

'This is the Senate,' Agrippa said as we entered. 'There is no one inside because it's still too early. But in a few moments, all of this will be chaos.' The wooden benches for the senators rose in tiers, and across from the door was a raised platform where Octavian would give his speech.

Alexander craned his neck to see the whole building. 'How many senators are there?' he asked.

'Nearly a thousand,' Agrippa replied.

'And there's room for all of them in here?'

'No. Some of them will have to stand in the back.'

We crossed the Senate floor toward the platform, and Agrippa held back so that Alexander and I could follow Juba up the three small steps. A statue draped in linen stood next to the dais.

Octavian looked at Juba. 'Is this it?'

'The statue of Victory,' Juba said. 'Sculpted two hundred and fifty years ago in Tarentum and completely unharmed. It is authentic.'

Octavian tore away the linen, and Alexander and I both stepped forward.

'Just like Nike,' I whispered in Parthian, 'our goddess of victory. I wonder if these Romans ever come up with anything original.' My brother pinched my arm, but I had the satisfaction of knowing that when the senators filed into the building, they would be looking at a statue sculpted by a Greek.

As the senators arrived, they greeted one another with raised arms, and their voices echoed loudly in the chamber. Men in purple and white togas filled the benches, carrying scrolls under their arms and wearing wreaths on their heads. There were five chairs on the platform, and Agrippa instructed us to sit on his left, freeing his right arm in case he had need of his sword. Alexander seated himself next to Octavian, and on the other side of Caesar was Juba. Both men took their seats, but while Octavian studied his notes, Juba searched the crowd. No one coughed, or stood, or even bent forward to chase an errant scroll without Juba's notice.

When there was no more space in the Senate, Agrippa cleared his throat. 'It is time.'

Octavian smoothed his palms against his toga, and I wondered how he could be nervous. These were his people, his victory, his Senate. He unrolled the scroll that Livia had given him outside of Octavia's villa, and I could see that his hands were shaking. But his eyes were filled with determination. He stood, and the room fell silent. Though it was early in the morning, the chamber was already unbearably hot, and I was thankful for the doors that were propped open so that the senators' sons could watch the proceedings from outside.

'*Patres et conscripti*,' Octavian addressed the men formally. 'If you and your children are in health, then all is well. For I and the legions are in health.' There was a roar of approval, though he hadn't said anything of importance. But then he told them about his conquest over Dalmatia, his victory at Actium, and finally his acquisition of Egypt, which would remain his personal property and not a kingdom to be governed by the Senate. 'For Antony shamed himself in the streets of Egypt. He shamed himself in the palace of Alexandria. And he shamed himself by allowing a foreign queen to give commands to our Roman legions. But that shame is over!' There was thunderous applause. I looked at my brother, whose face was as pale as his linen kilt.

'From this day forward, the name of Marc Antony shall be obliterated from the Fasti. His statues shall be removed from the Forum, and no member of the Antonius clan shall ever be named Marcus so long as there is a Senate in Rome.' The applause rose up again. 'Finally, I propose that the birthday of the traitor become a *dies nefastus,* an unlucky day on which public business shall never be conducted!' There was a roaring cheer, and I assumed that Octavian's proposal had passed. He looked behind him and smiled at Agrippa. The scroll in his hand was no longer shaking.

'In the wake of such victories,' Octavian went on, 'some of you are wondering why there are no slaves. Perhaps you remember when Julius Caesar conquered Gaul and brought back forty thousand blond barbarians. Now, every woman in Rome wants to be blond. But I will not have our women painting themselves like the whores of Egypt! If your women must paint, let them decorate your villas. Let them buy Egyptian statues. But we are Romans, and we shall look like Romans!'

The applause that met this statement was deafening.

'There shall be no temples to Isis within the boundary of

Rome. Let Romans worship Roman gods. As for the Senate, I propose an increase in pay. What job in Rome is more important than leading its people and making the decisions that will affect their lives?' There was a hum of approval throughout the building. 'This is the dawn of a bright new age. For the first time in several hundred years, we have peace, and there will be prosperity. With my own denarii I shall create not only battalions of fire watchmen but crime watchmen, and increase the number of people who are allowed free grain from three hundred thousand a year to four hundred thousand.' His voice boomed over the Senate, and I realized that this was part of his theater – a way of enslaving citizens to him without chains. 'For every victory or personal triumph,' he continued, 'I encourage you to contribute to the building of this new Rome. My commander Titus Statilius Taurus has already begun the first amphitheater constructed of stone. My consul Agrippa has put his own denarii into baths that have welcomed tens of thousands of men. Now, he will erect the Pantheon, the greatest temple ever built for our gods. Lucius Marcius Philippus is rebuilding the Temple of Hercules Musarum. What are you building?' he demanded. 'On which monuments shall your name be written for eternity?'

I could feel the senators' excitement. There was no talk of punishing those who had supported my father, no talk of anything but a new Rome. Octavian made a small, graceful bow. Then suddenly everyone was moving.

'What's happening?' I asked Alexander.

'The Triumph has begun,' Agrippa replied.

Horns blared in unison outside the Senate, and an old man appeared at the bottom of the platform holding a pair of golden chains. 'For the children,' he said.

I looked to Agrippa.

'It is only for the Triumph,' he explained, and when he instructed us to hold out our hands, tears betrayed me. He fitted them first around Alexander's wrists, then turned to me, but didn't meet my gaze. *His daughter Vipsania is four years younger than I am. I wonder if he's imagining her humiliated this way.* He made sure the chains were loose around our wrists, and when a senator smiled at the picture we presented, I forbade myself from crying.

I was too ashamed to look at my brother as we followed Octavian through the double doors into the Forum. When I tripped over my tunic, Juba said harshly, 'Keep walking.'

'I am,' I retorted.

'Then you can quit feeling sorry for yourself. You're still alive.'

Outside, thousands of people were singing and dancing to the music of flutes. Soldiers attempted to keep the plebs away from the senators, who were organizing themselves in lines for the procession, but it was a fool's task. Juba led us through the madness to a wooden float, which had been decorated to look like an Egyptian chamber, and began to mount the steps. In front of me, my brother stopped suddenly, and I followed his gaze. At the top, a wax figure of my mother lay on a couch with a cobra coiled between her breasts.

'Don't look,' he said angrily. 'They want us to weep in front of Rome.'

I bit my lower lip so hard I tasted blood, and Juba pointed to a pair of gilded thrones, where we were supposed to sit beside the likeness of our mother. 'You will not move,' he instructed. 'Or even think of escape.' My eyes flashed, and though I didn't ask *Or what?* he added, 'There are thousands of soldiers here today, and every one of them would love to claim that he killed one of Marc Antony's children.'

I sat obediently and forbade myself from thinking of Charmion. She had hated the noise and closeness of parades, and her heart would have broken to see us sitting there amid the signs of all the cities that Octavian had conquered. Some of the men below were dressed as personifications of rivers the Roman legions had crossed, including the Euphrates and the Rhine. But what would have saddened Charmion the most were the women who had been chained together, naked except for signs on their chests that identified their conquered tribes.

Alexander surveyed the scene below us; then suddenly he turned to me and whispered, 'No one is ever kept alive after a Triumph.'

'Then why give us rooms? Why let us stay with Octavia?'

'To keep us obedient!'

I searched my brother's face. 'Then what do we do?' Alexander lifted his kilt, and when I saw the outline of a knife, I exclaimed, 'How did you—'

'Shh. I took it from Marcellus. I told him I needed to cut the ropes on our traveling chests and he never asked for it back. We may still be executed, but not without a fight.'

When the Triumph began, it became a blur of people and soldiers. I was aware of the chariot in front of us, pulled by a team of four white horses and carrying Octavian with his wife and sister. All three were wearing wreaths of laurel, but only Octavian's face had been stained with vermillion to remind the people of Jupiter, the father of the gods and administrator of justice. I watched Octavian smile through his dark-red mask, and wondered what role he would perform once the procession reached the temple. Would he be the executioner?

We passed the Temple of Divus Julius, where a speaker's platform had been built from the prows of ships Octavian had captured at Actium. And while crowds of people screamed below us, I couldn't hear anything but the sound of blood rushing in my ears. From the tops of porticoes streamed long crimson banners, and in a courtyard where children were playing games, a statue of the Egyptian god of death had been erected, with a collar below its canine head and a sign that read, BARKING ANUBIS HAS BEEN TAMED. There were other signs as well, rewards for slaves who'd gone missing or had been captured. Slave catchers, who called themselves *fugitivarii*, clearly thought that this was the time to advertise their services, and I wondered if slaves used public days like this to escape from their households. I looked down at the chains around my wrists, thinking it might be possible for us to escape. But Juba hovered next to Octavian like a hawk, studying the crowds with his sharp black eyes, watching, waiting.

When we reached the Capitoline Hill, the floats were surrounded by the cheering, drinking mobs, as they groaned their way toward the top. The senators tried to push the men back, and soldiers made threatening gestures with their shields, but no one wanted to shed Roman blood on a day of victory. The crowds chanted, '*Io Triumphe!*' and when I turned my head I could see that, below us, the smaller floats carried treasures from my mother's mausoleum. Gold and silver gleamed from open chests, and the sun was reflected from the beautiful wine bowls and golden *rhyta* my father had used when he was alive. We rolled to a stop before Jupiter's temple, and for the first time I could see Marcellus and Tiberius on their horses. Both of them dismounted, but it was Marcellus who came toward us. I glanced at my brother, whose hand went swiftly to his knife.

'Marcellus would never hurt us,' I said.

'He will do whatever Octavian commands.'

But as Marcellus mounted the steps of our float, he looked from my brother to me and his color rose. 'What is this?' he shouted. 'Somebody take off these chains!' The same old man who had appeared in the Senate approached the base of our float with a key. 'Today!' Marcellus snapped impatiently. As soon as we were free, he led us down the steps and shook his head understandingly. 'It's over now.'

But Alexander hesitated. 'So what will your uncle do with us?'

'When?'

'Today,' my brother replied.

'I doubt you will be the guests of honor, if that's what you mean. He will probably ask Agrippa—'

'But are we to be executed?' I cried.

Marcellus recoiled. 'Of course not.' He looked at both of us, startled by our solemn silence. 'Is that what you were thinking?' When neither of us answered him, he swore, 'My mother would never let that happen. You're like her own children.'

'So was Antyllus,' Alexander reminded him, 'and he was slaughtered at the feet of Caesar's statue in Alexandria.'

Marcellus nodded gravely. He had been raised with our half brother Antyllus during the years that Octavia was married to our father, and had known him far longer than we ever had. 'This is different,' he promised. 'You're too young to threaten him.'

'And when we turn fifteen?' my brother demanded.

'He will marry you off. Until then, you'll just have to suffer through school with the rest of us.' There was a blast of horns and Marcellus motioned quickly. 'Hurry!'

Inside the Temple of Jupiter, men stepped aside when they recognized Marcellus, and as we made our way past the bodies of sweating senators, an old man held out his hand to me. 'For you, Selene.'

I recognized the symbol of Isis on his belt at once. To anyone else, the knot would have been unremarkable, but I knew it was a sacred *tiet*. I looked around, but the temple was too crowded for anyone to see. Quickly, I took the slip of papyrus from his hand.

'A thousand blessings,' he said as I passed.

As we reached the altar I pretended to adjust the brooch at my shoulder. I unpinned it and, slipping the scrap of papyrus beneath, repinned it so that no one could see. Then my heart began to beat faster in my chest. I wondered what the message might be – rebellion, rescue, delivery from Rome – and when I looked up, I saw Juba watching me.

CHAPTER SIX

WE WERE given time to prepare ourselves before the Feast of Triumph, but I didn't show Alexander what I had received. Instead, I slipped the secret message into my book of sketches. Then, while Gallia brushed my wig and laid out a fresh tunic, I took the book with me into the bathing room and read the note.

> There is hope in the Temple of Isis. Egypt is lost only so long as the Sun and Moon are imprisoned. I wish for the Sun to come, and we shall prepare for a time when the Moon may rise again.

It was written in hieroglyphics, and even if the message was short, its meaning was clear. If I could make my way to the Temple of Isis, the High Priest would find a way to return us to Alexandria. I thought of the madness in the Temple of Jupiter, where a thousand senators had crowded together, laughing and drinking and chanting 'Io Triumphe!' Those same senators would be invited to Octavian's villa, and I was certain I could slip away unnoticed. Of course, Alexander couldn't come. If both of us disappeared, the alarm would be raised, and there would be no time to meet with the High Priest. Besides, if I told Alexander what I was doing, he would argue against it. I closed my book of sketches, and when Gallia returned, I asked casually, 'Do you know of a temple to Isis in Rome?'

She gave me a long look before sweeping my hair into a knot and fitting the wig over my head. 'There is a temple to Isis on the Campus Martius. It is outside the boundary of the city,' she said. 'But I would not think of asking to go there,' she warned. 'Domina will not like it.'

'Why?'

Gallia gave an elegant shrug. 'Domina worships Roman gods. She does not believe in the gods of other nations.'

'So when you came to Rome,' I asked quietly, 'did you lose your gods as well?'

She laughed sharply. 'The gods cannot be lost. These Romans can shatter our statues,' she whispered, 'and replace them with images of Jupiter and Apollo, but the gods remain here.' She touched my chest briefly. 'And here.' She indicated the space above us. 'Artio still watches over me.'

Octavia entered the chamber behind us, followed by Alexander and Marcellus, who were dressed in matching kilts and pharaonic crowns. They poked their heads into the bathing room and Marcellus asked, 'So? Could I pass for an Egyptian?'

I rose from my chair. 'Where did you get that?' I exclaimed. A golden collar gleamed from his neck, as bright as newly minted coins.

'My uncle had it made for me and sent from Alexandria.'

I studied the collar closely. The hieroglyphics were etched in silver, and the name of a nineteenth-dynasty Pharaoh was written on the side. 'Are you sure you're not wearing the possessions of the dead?'

Octavia covered her mouth in horror. 'If that is something from one of the tombs—'

'Your brother would never steal anything from a tomb. He's

afraid of lightning,' Marcellus reminded her, 'and his entire chamber is filled with amulets. Do you really think he would go digging in cursed sands?'

'No,' she agreed.

But I wasn't so sure. Perhaps one of Octavian's soldiers had thought it was easier to steal than to create. After all, Octavian himself had stolen the ring from the body of Alexander the Great.

'Besides,' Marcellus added mischievously, 'this is far too nice to have been made a thousand years ago. Ready?' He took my arm, and Alexander fell into step beside us.

'Is this how Romans see Egyptians?' I asked. 'In kilts and pectorals?'

'And crowns and gold cuffs,' Marcellus added.

Alexander held up the linen flap of his blue-and-gold-striped headdress. 'No one has worn this in three hundred years.'

'Well, prepare for a resurgence,' Marcellus warned, and in Octavian's villa hundreds of senators were dressed in similar crowns, with thick bands of gold encircling their wrists. The women wore golden snakes on their arms, and their short black wigs were cut sharply to the chin. Despite the proclamation that Romans must dress like Romans, the senators and their wives were happy enough to try and look like Egyptians so long as it was in mockery and in celebration of Octavian's triumph. 'Julia!' Marcellus called excitedly, and when she crossed the garden where dining tables and couches had been arranged, I heard Marcellus draw in his breath. Julia's long white sheath was completely transparent when her back was to the sun. I wondered pettily if her father had seen her dressed like that. 'You look like an Egyptian princess,' Marcellus swore. 'Doesn't she, Selene?'

Julia fixed me with her dark-eyed glare.

'Yes. Just like an Egyptian,' I lied.

Julia turned to Marcellus. 'Did you hear what my father plans to build?' She snapped her fingers at a passing slave who was balancing a platter on his palm. He held out the tray and Julia handed the largest cup of wine to Marcellus, leaving Alexander and me to take our own. 'He is going to begin his mausoleum,' she said merrily.

'Excuse me,' I said. 'I think I will go and sit with Octavia.'

Alexander grabbed my arm before I could leave. 'Where are you going?' he whispered in Parthian.

'Where I won't have to hear about Octavian's mausoleum!' When he moved to come with me, I shook my head. 'Stay here with Marcellus,' I told him. As I left, I looked behind me to make sure he wasn't following. The sun had disappeared beneath the hills and the gardens were illuminated now by hanging lanterns. As I made my way through the crowded villa, I saw Octavian in his formal *tunica Jovis* standing with Terentilla in a corner of the triclinium. She was tracing the palm leaves on his tunic with her finger, and the two of them were laughing intimately. Neither of them looked in my direction, and it wasn't difficult to make my way to the vestibulum and out the front doors into the dusk.

I was surprised there was no one following me. Perhaps Octavian couldn't imagine a scenario in which Alexander and I might try to escape, or perhaps we had simply finished being useful to him, and if we were foolish enough to run away, then our punishment would be of little consequence. I wondered what that punishment might be, and decided that whatever it was, I was willing to take the risk. *My mother would want this*, I told myself, making my way down the Palatine Hill. *And if anyone sees me, they'll simply think I'm another senator's daughter.*

The sky was the color of blooming hibiscus, a red that turned to purple and gradually black. I didn't know where I might find the Campus Martius, but I was determined to ask the priest in the small temple to Jupiter at the base of the hill. The noise of the festivities drifted down from above, and the sharp laughter of women made my heart race. Would one of them want to speak with me and find that I was gone? I walked as quickly as the steep incline would allow, being careful not to trip over my sandals.

Bands of drunken men lumbered up the road, singing about Bacchus and inviting me to drink with them. 'Come here, my pretty Egyptian queen. There's a thing or two I'd like to teach you about Rome.' But I had seen enough leering drunks with my father to know that I must simply avoid their gaze. I made my way around several groups of men, but when one of them reached out to grab me, I was too slow.

'Get off of me!'

'What's the matter?' His friends began to laugh, and he pushed his lips roughly against mine. 'You're not too young for paint.'

He dragged me toward a copse of trees, and when I screamed, the laughter of his friends grew more distant. *They're leaving me with him to be violated*, I realized. I kicked at his shins, but he wrestled me to the ground. His heavy stomach pushed against the front of my body, and I could feel his desire beneath his kilt. I turned my head to scream, but as his hand reached down to lift my tunic a shadow loomed behind him. There was the flash of a knife and suddenly my attacker grew still. I didn't wait to see who the shadow was. I crawled through the darkness to the cobbled road, then ran the rest of the way down the hill. When I placed my sandal on the first step of the temple, a hand grabbed my arm and I cried out.

'What do you think you're doing?'

Frightened, I turned around, and Juba shook me with both hands.

'What are you doing out here?' he shouted.

'I'm—'

'Think carefully before you lie.' I didn't say anything, so he guessed. 'You were going to the Temple of Isis.'

My eyes must have given me away, because he took my arm and wrenched me up the hill.

'You're hurting me!' I cried.

'You were prepared to risk worse.'

'Where are you taking me?' I was ashamed that my voice trembled. When he didn't answer, I asked quietly, 'Did you kill that man?'

'Would you rather he lived?'

We kept walking, and his grip on my arm was hurting. 'You have no right to touch me.' I tried to pull away. 'I'm a princess of Egypt!'

'And what do you think makes a princess?' he demanded.

I raised my chin. 'Her education.'

He laughed mockingly. 'Her gold! Did you really think the High Priest was going to help you return to Egypt out of kindness? I saw what he gave you in the Temple of Jupiter, and there's only one reason he would contact you. He wanted payment. Of one kind' – his eyes lingered on my diadem – 'or another.' He made a point of studying the rip in my tunic.

'No.' I shook my head. 'Not a high priest of Isis.'

'Oh no. And not a citizen of Rome. Do you understand what that man would have done to you?'

'Of course!'

'Then understand this.' He stopped walking, and his face was so close to mine that I could see the muscles of his jaw working angrily. 'Women who walk the streets by themselves are kidnapped by men and sold as slaves. So far, Fortuna has smiled on you, although I have no idea why she wastes her time on such a pampered little girl. You have your brother in Rome, a tidy sum in the Temple of Saturn for whatever you need—'

'I don't have any *sum*.'

'Of course you do,' he said bitterly. 'I know because I transferred it there myself. So unlike some of us who were captured at war, *Your Highness* will never have to dirty her fingers to make her way in Rome. Octavia may want to see you survive, but I can promise you this. Fortuna's smiles don't last forever. And if I ever hear of escape or rebellion associated with your name, I will not bother to knife the next man in the back.'

He released my arm and I staggered backward. 'You're Octavian's man through and through,' I said, intending to insult him. But he only smiled.

'That's right. Everything belongs to Caesar.'

'Not me!'

'Yes, even you, *Princess*.'

A group of men dressed as Egyptian pharaohs passed us by, but none of them looked in my direction. They all eyed Juba warily and then moved away. He caught my arm and we continued walking up the Palatine.

'Where are you taking me?'

'Back where you belong,' he said.

In the vestibulum of Octavia's villa, I heard footsteps coming toward us and held my breath.

'Selene!' Octavia put her hand on her chest. I could see the shadows of Marcellus and Alexander behind her. 'We couldn't find you anywhere!' she exclaimed. 'We thought you were—' She looked from me to Juba, and her expression grew wary. 'You weren't planning on running away?'

'No,' he said. 'I found her near the Temple of Jupiter. I think she was planning on making an offering.'

Octavia studied me with her soft eyes, refusing to admonish me for what she must have known I'd attempted.

When everyone had left, Alexander kept staring at me. 'You didn't really—'

I turned from him and stalked into our chamber. 'I had a message from Egypt.'

'What do you mean?' He slammed the door.

'In the Temple of Jupiter, the High Priest of Isis and Serapis gave me a message.'

In the lamplight, Alexander watched me, aghast. 'And you thought you would travel across Rome to visit him? Without telling me?'

'You would have said no!'

'Of course I would have! Gods, Selene. How could you be so foolish? Ptolemaic rule of Egypt is finished.'

'It will *never* be finished!' I ripped off my wig, too tired to bother with my paint and tunic. 'As long as we are alive—'

There was a sound outside our door, then a soft knock. Alexander glanced uneasily at me. 'Come in,' he said. We both rushed to our couches and pulled the linens over our chests.

Octavia appeared, and I was certain that she had come to reprimand me. She placed her lamp next to Alexander, then sat on the edge of his couch so that she could look at both of us. I held my breath.

'Tomorrow, school will begin,' she said softly. 'Gallia will take you to the Forum, where you will meet Magister Verrius near the Temple of Venus Genetrix. He will be the one to instruct you over these next few years.' When we didn't say anything, she added, 'Marcellus will be there, as well as Tiberius and Julia.' When there was still nothing either of us felt we could say, she asked awkwardly, 'Did both of you enjoy the feast?'

Alexander nodded against his pillow. 'Caesar's villa is magnificent,' he replied. But I knew he was lying. My mother's guest houses had been larger than Octavian's villa, and all of the lanterns in Rome could not have illuminated the smallest palace garden in Alexandria. But Octavia was pleased. 'My brother is turning Rome from a city of clay into a city of marble. He and Agrippa have great plans.'

She placed her hand tenderly on Alexander's forehead, and I saw him flinch. 'Sleep well.' She stood, then gazed down at me in a way that only Charmion ever had. '*Valete*,' she said softly. When she opened the door, I could see the figure of a thin, balding man waiting near her chamber. He wrapped his arm around her waist, and as the door swung shut, I sat up and looked at Alexander.

'The architect Vitruvius,' he said.

'The one who wrote *De architectura*?' He was the only Roman architect we'd ever studied in the Museion. 'Are they . . . ?'

'Lovers? I guess. He came here to see your sketches, but you had disappeared. You should be thankful she isn't going to tell Octavian. Instead, she came in here and wished us happy dreams. You have no idea how fortunate we are—'

'And how is losing your kingdom fortunate? How is losing our brothers, our mother, our father, even Charmion and Iras, fortunate?'

'Because we could be dead!' Alexander sat up. I heard the sound of a window opening in the chamber next door. I imagined it was Marcellus letting in the fresh air, and suddenly I felt hot. 'We could be prisoners,' he went on, 'or slaves like Gallia. You're just lucky that Juba found you before someone else did!'

My brother blew out the lamps, but in the darkness I could still see Juba's eyes, full of anger and resentment.

Gallia woke us while the sun was still rising. She placed a pitcher of water on our table, and two slaves brought in bowls of olives and cheese. But even the fresh bread, which smelled deliciously of herbs, couldn't tempt me to move.

'Up with the sun!' Gallia said forcefully. 'Domina has clients waiting for her in the atrium, and her morning *salutatio* has already begun. Take off your tunics and put on your togas!'

I opened one eye and saw that Alexander had placed a pillow over his head. 'What is a *salutatio*?' I groaned.

Gallia clapped her hands so loudly that Alexander jumped. 'It is when clients come to the villa to ask for the money they are owed, or, more likely, favors. Every Roman with a few denarii to rub together has a *salutatio* in the morning. How else do the baker and the toga maker get paid?'

Alexander sat up and eyed the food warily. 'Olives and cheese?'

'And bread. Come,' I said wearily, 'I can already hear Marcellus.' He was singing in the hall, possibly something crass about the priestesses of Bacchus.

'What are you doing?' Gallia exclaimed. 'Up! Get up!'

We both rose, and I looked at Alexander. 'Our first day at school,' I said mockingly. 'I wonder who will be more cheerful, Julia or Tiberius?'

'Well, you know why she dislikes you.'

'Who says Julia dislikes me?'

My brother gave me a long look, and I followed him into the bathing room. 'She's already been engaged twice,' he said, washing his face in a bowl of lavender water. 'Once to Antyllus, another time to Cotiso, the king of the Getae. But Octavian can't betroth her to a foreign king, because now he needs an heir. So he's hoping to marry her to Marcellus. She's jealous that you get to live here with him.'

'How do you know this?'

He glared at me. 'She told me last night. While you were at the bottom of the Palatine.'

I looked at Gallia and asked if it was true. 'Is Julia really engaged to Marcellus?'

'Yes,' she said cautiously, and I put my face above the bowl of water so that no one could see my disappointment. 'But engagements among Romans are like the wind,' she added. 'They come and go.' She passed me a square of linen.

'Why?'

'That is simply how it is,' she explained while I dried my face. 'Most women are married four and five times.'

She handed me a small jar of toothpaste and I paused to look at her. 'But how can a woman love so many men?'

'Your mother loved many men,' she pointed out.

'My mother had two men,' I said sternly. 'Julius Caesar and Marc Antony. That was it.'

When Gallia looked disbelieving, my brother added, 'It's true. Whatever the gossip may be here in Rome, she had only two men, and she was loyal to our father until his death.'

'Like a *univira*,' Gallia said reverently.

I frowned.

'A one-husband woman,' she explained. 'Well, you will not find many of those in Rome. A woman may be married for fifteen years, but if her father decides on a better match . . .' She snapped her fingers and I understood that to mean the marriage would be over. 'It is also expected that a woman will remarry if her husband dies, even if she is fifty years old.'

'And who expects this?' I asked with distaste. I began to scrub my teeth.

Gallia held up her palms. 'Romans. Men. It is the fathers and brothers who arrange these things. Domina Octavia is very fortunate not to have to remarry. Caesar has granted her special dispensation, and now she may keep her own house by herself.'

She led us back into our chamber, and while Alexander and I put on freshly washed clothes, I thought of Juba's angry accusation that I would never have to dirty my fingers in Rome. Perhaps not, but I would be expected to marry and then remarry at Caesar's whim. And Alexander . . . *If* Octavian kept Alexander alive once he turned fifteen, who knew what would happen to him? We would be a pair of dice, thrown anywhere across the board so long as it pleased him, then picked up and thrown again and again.

Gallia tied the belt of my tunic, and I asked her quietly, 'Are women of so little value in Rome?'

'When a girl is born,' Gallia replied, 'a period of mourning is begun. She is *invisa*, unwanted, valueless. She has no rights but what her father gives her.'

'Was it that way in Gaul?'

'No. But now we are worse than *invisae*. Worse even than thieves. My father was a king, but Caesar defeated him and brought so many of our people to Rome that slaves are worth only five hundred denarii now. Even a baker can afford to keep a girl to pleasure him.' I winced, and Gallia spoke solemnly. 'Become useful to Caesar. Do not let him hear you wish to run away, because there is nowhere you can go,' she warned. 'Find a skill.' She turned to my brother, whose toga was immaculate. If not for the white diadem in his hair, he might have been a Roman. 'Let him see that you are both worth something to Rome.'

'Why?' I asked bitterly. 'So that I can be married off to a senator, and Alexander can be married to some fifty-year-old matron?'

'No. So that you can return to Egypt,' she said firmly, and her voice became a whisper. 'Why do you think that dominus Juba keeps company with Caesar? He hopes to be made prefect of his father's old kingdom.'

'And Caesar would do that?' Alexander broke in.

'I do not know. Not even dominus Juba knows. There is nothing left of my kingdom.' Her eyes grew distant, and I knew she was seeing some faraway horror. 'But yours remains, and if you are obedient—'

There was a sharp knock on our door, then Marcellus bounded in. 'Are we ready?' He smiled.

Gallia put her hands on her hips. 'What is the purpose of knocking, domine, if you are not going to even wait for an answer?'

Marcellus looked from my brother to me. 'But I heard voices,' he said guiltily. 'And how long could it take to put on a tunic?' His eyes swept over the pretty blue silk one that Octavia must have found for me, and he added, 'A very *pretty* tunic.' My cheeks grew warm, and he offered me his arm. 'To the Forum,' he said. 'Of course, I don't know what Magister Verrius thinks we'll do today. The streets will be filled with so much noise he'll have to shout over it just to be heard. But my mother insists.'

'Doesn't she want you to be a part of the celebrations?' my brother asked.

'And miss school?' Marcellus asked sarcastically. 'No. Besides, my uncle thinks one day of celebration is more than enough. He doesn't want us to get used to so much excitement.'

We followed Gallia through the villa, and as we crossed the atrium, I saw that Octavia's clients filled every available bench.

'Will her *salutatio* last all day?' I asked.

Marcellus shook his head. 'Just another few hours. Then she'll do her charity work in the Subura. She would feed all of Rome if she had enough grain.'

'Will we be doing charity work with her?'

Marcellus laughed at Alexander's question. 'Gods, no. After school, we'll be in the Circus Maximus. I brought a few denarii so we can all place bets.'

Julia and Tiberius appeared on the portico, and at once I withdrew my hand from Marcellus's arm.

Tiberius saw the gesture and laughed. 'Don't bother,' he said. 'Julia has already seen you together and is working herself into a jealous frenzy as we speak.'

Julia smiled sweetly at Marcellus. 'Don't pay any attention to him. Selene and I are going to be great friends.' She made a show of taking my arm.

'Will your father be sending soldiers to escort us?' I asked.

'Who needs soldiers?' she replied. 'Gallia was a warrior in her tribe.'

I looked at Gallia. With her wheat-colored hair and proud Gallic chin, she was the image of a queen, but as the sun filtered through her tunic I saw the outline of a leather sheath on her thigh. It was a companion to the knife she wore openly at her waist, and I blinked in surprise. 'You fought?'

'When the men are all gone, or have been killed, it is up to the women. But I cannot fight off a mob if their intent is evil. That is what *they* are for.' She gestured behind her to a group of men. If not for the short swords at their sides and chain mail beneath their togas, they might have been senators or wealthy patricians.

'Have they been following us all along?' I asked.

Julia sighed loudly. 'Every day. From the moment we leave our villas.'

Gallia led us down the Palatine, and as the silence grew heavier between me and Julia, I said quietly, 'You know, there is nothing to be jealous of. Marcellus has been treating me like a sister.'

She stared ahead at the figure of Marcellus, who was leaning on Alexander's shoulder and laughing. I guessed the pair of them were talking about gambling. Tiberius, meanwhile, lagged several steps behind, his long nose buried in a scroll. 'That may be,' Julia began, 'but you aren't his sister, are you? And it's hard to resist such a pretty smile.'

'I wouldn't know.'

'You don't think about him?' she demanded.

'I think about Egypt, and returning to the land of my birth.'

Her grip on my arm relaxed, and for the first time, her smile was genuine. 'You know, I'm engaged to be married to him.'

'At eleven?'

'I was engaged when I was two,' she said crossly. 'So why not now, when I'm nearly twelve? And when we marry, everyone in Rome will see who my father's heir is intended to be. Then Tiberius can finally disappear into the army, and we can all stop pretending he's of any importance.'

'Is that what he wants to do?'

'Who knows what Tiberius wants to do?' she asked nastily, glancing back at him. 'And I doubt if anyone cares but his mother.' Her voice grew low. 'You know, she has two thousand slaves on the Palatine.' When I gasped, she nodded, and a curl escaped from the golden band nestled in her dark hair. 'They live on the western end of the hill.'

'But I haven't seen them.'

'Of course not. That's because there are underground passages. We don't want them crowding up our roads. But you would think she did all of the work herself, with the way she complains about needing more slaves. And she sells any girl who falls pregnant.'

'Because she can't get pregnant with Octavian's heir?'

Julia raised her brows at my astuteness. 'My father said you were clever.' She studied me with her dark, intense gaze, as if trying to determine whether she liked this or not. 'Yes. She punishes the girls by selling them to farms, where the labor will break them and there's no chance of ever seeing the man who made them pregnant. And if she finds the one who did it . . .' Julia shook her head.

'And your father loves her?' I asked hesitantly.

'Oh, I doubt it. But Romans don't marry for love. Of course,' she added brightly, 'I will. And when Marcellus becomes Caesar, the laws will change.'

'What about Agrippa?'

'He'll watch over the army.'

'And he's content with that?'

'He'll do whatever my father wants. If my father tells him to serve Marcellus, he'll do that as well. They are very old friends, and my father only keeps loyal men around him.'

We had come to the place on the Palatine where Juba had killed the man who was assaulting me. I searched for the body, but someone had taken it. I shivered anyway. 'So is that why he keeps Livia as a wife?'

Julia looked at me, and I could see that this had never occurred to her before. 'Yes. It probably is. It's certainly not for children.'

'But she birthed Tiberius and Drusus.'

'With her first husband,' she said coldly. 'Not with my father. And no one can say it's my father's fault, when he had me with his first wife. Which makes it obvious, doesn't it?'

I frowned.

'Their marriage is cursed! My father left my mother the day I was born to take up with Livia, who was already married and pregnant. When Livia was granted a divorce, her previous husband appeared at the wedding and gave her away. Imagine!' she said, scandalously, and I could almost believe she was talking about someone other than her own father. 'Of course, it's no surprise why he wanted her. Your father used to taunt mine in the Senate, saying he was *ignobilis* and the grandson of a pleb.'

I could imagine my father saying those things, enjoying the anger it would have aroused in Octavian, and secretly I was proud.

'My father had all the power he needed, but he lacked *nobilitas*. And Livia comes from a long line of Claudii. But do you know what happened the year they were married?' I shook my head. The sun bathed the Temple of Jupiter in its rosy glow, which also fell like soft blush across Julia's skin. I didn't think there was a more beautiful girl in Rome. 'The hut of Romulus burned down, and a statue of Virtus fell on its face. Then Livia produced a stillborn, and that's been it. Not another child.'

A stillborn after two healthy sons. It did seem like a curse. 'And Terentilla?'

'He will never marry her,' she said quickly. 'Livia will make sure of it by weaving his togas and brewing his tonics.'

'Doesn't he have slaves for that?'

She smiled. 'Of course. But there's no slave in the world he could trust the way he trusts Livia. And what is Terentilla?' she asked with brutal frankness. 'Just a pretty actress who can talk about the theater.'

We reached a wooden door inside the Forum, and Gallia led the four of us into a small chamber.

'Is this it?' I asked nervously.

Julia sighed. 'The ludus.'

When my eyes adjusted to the dimness, I saw a man in a neatly arranged toga behind a desk. I had imagined he would be much older than Gallia, but he was no more than thirty, with the same light hair as Marcellus, though darker eyes. As soon as he saw Gallia, he rose.

'Magister Verrius.' She smiled, and when he crossed the room and took her hand in his, I noticed that his kiss lingered longer than it needed to.

'Good morning, Gallia. And this must be the Prince and Princess of Egypt,' he said in Greek.

'Yes, dominus Alexander and domina Selene.' I was shocked when Gallia replied in Greek. 'They have been educated in the Museion, and domina Octavia tells me that the princess is gifted in art.'

Magister Verrius looked at me. 'What kind?'

'I'm interested in architecture,' I replied. 'Buildings and cities.'

'And Prince Alexander?'

When I hesitated, Marcellus laughed. 'Alexander races horses,' he offered in Greek. 'He's also exceptional at dice.'

A small frown appeared between the Magister's brows, and Julia giggled.

'Squandering time isn't funny,' Tiberius said sharply.

'And neither is arrogance.' Julia smiled, and a deep flush crept from Tiberius's neck into his pale cheeks.

Magister Verrius ignored them both. 'I assume you studied Vergil in the Museion?' he asked me.

'And Homer, and the Athenian dramatists.'

Magister Verrius looked immensely pleased. 'Then you will be very welcome additions to this ludus.' He glanced briefly at Marcellus and Julia, and I wondered how welcome they would be if not for their positions on the Palatine. He pointed us to separate tables, each with its own wax tablet and stylus, and Gallia left.

'Will all of our schooling be conducted in Greek?' my brother asked.

'As Cicero said, we must apply to our fellow countrymen for virtue, but for our culture we must look to the Greeks.'

I met Alexander's gaze and saw the smile at the corners of

his mouth. There would be almost nothing required of us if all we were expected to do was learn the language of our ancestors.

For the rest of the morning we read Athenian plays. If the lessons weren't difficult, at least they were interesting, and Magister Verrius held a contest to see who could answer his questions first. For every correct answer he gave out a small token, and by the end of the class, it had become a competition between Tiberius and me. Alexander had seven tokens on his desk, Julia three, and Marcellus one. But Tiberius and I had each answered eleven questions correctly. I didn't know what we were competing for, but I was determined to win.

At the front of the room, Magister Verrius smiled broadly. 'The last question.'

I looked at Tiberius, whose thin lips were pursed with determination.

'Aside from Sophocles,' Magister Verrius said, 'which dramatist also wrote a play called *Antigone*?'

'Euripides!' I exclaimed.

Tiberius sat back in defeat. He studied me, and I could see the warring emotions of respect and jealousy on his face. 'Finally,' he said at last, 'another student worthy of Magister Verrius's teaching.'

The Magister came to my table and presented me with a scroll. 'For you. Sophocles' *Antigone*.'

I looked up. 'To *keep*?' It would be my first real possession in Rome.

'Of course. What else?'

When I had thanked him and returned the tokens to his desk, he dismissed us with a wave of his hand. 'To the Campus Martius for your exercise,' he said.

Marcellus turned to me. 'How do you know so much?'

'All she does is read and draw,' Alexander commented, but I could see that he was proud.

'Well, you'll have your own library soon,' Julia predicted. 'It's about time someone put Tiberius in his place.'

I glanced at Tiberius, whose jaw clenched angrily, but he didn't say anything.

Outside, Gallia was waiting for us, shielded from the intense summer's heat by a leather *umbraculum*. 'Well, domina Selene, domine Alexander. How was it?'

I held out my scroll, and she grinned.

'I knew Magister Verrius would be happy to have you! Let me guess – you snatched it from the hands of Tiberius.'

Tiberius shrugged. 'She's a worthy opponent,' he said to Gallia. 'Not a useless stone weighing down another chair. But we'll see how much she knows when it comes to Sallust.'

I looked from Tiberius to Gallia. 'Who's that?'

Tiberius looked pleased with my ignorance. 'Who's Sallust?' he repeated. 'Only the greatest writer of Rome's military history. Haven't you read his *Jugurthine War*? or *The Conspiracy of Catiline*?'

'No one's interested in those boring works but you,' Marcellus said.

Gallia cleared her throat before the argument could continue. 'To the Campus,' she said.

'If we make it there,' Julia grumbled. 'Look at these people. They're *everywhere*.'

It was the second day of Octavian's Triumph, and a parade had just passed by the Forum, where thousands of spectators had come for the entertainment. Children, chased by screeching sisters and brothers, ran between the columns, while mothers scolded and fathers laughed. There was no breeze as there had been in Alexandria, so the scent of incense from the Temple of

Venus Genetrix lingered in the air along with the scent of *ofellae*, round pieces of baked dough topped with melted cheese. Men and women from every corner of the world were crowded together, and I recognized German and Gallic men from their height and flaxen-colored hair. Dark women from the southern parts of Egypt, balancing colorful baskets on their heads, wove lithely between groups of drunken men and Assyrian shopkeepers.

'This way,' Gallia said, pushing back the strands that had escaped from her long braid. The sun was at its highest point, baking the stones beneath our feet so that even through the leather of our sandals we could feel the rising heat.

'So what kind of exercise do we do?' I asked Julia.

She sniffed dismissively. 'It's the men who exercise. And while they get to practice their sword fighting and horse riding, we get to sit with Livia and weave. Gallia will stay with us, and Octavia will be there with her girls, and Vipsania.'

'But I don't know how to weave!'

'At all?'

'Of course not.'

'But what did you do while your brother exercised?'

'I swam with him.'

'In the river?' she exclaimed.

'No. In the pools. Why would anyone want to weave?'

'They wouldn't.' she said grimly. 'But Livia thinks it will keep us modest.'

'Perhaps I can draw,' I said feebly, and indicated the leather bag at my side with my book of sketches and Magister Verrius's scroll.

But Julia warned, 'She will teach you to weave even if your fingers bleed.' She looked up and sighed. 'Here we are.'

As the Campus Martius came into view, Alexander looked at

me in surprise. Hundreds of buildings filled the horizon, jostling for space outside the walls of Rome. Marble baths nestled against the concrete walls of theaters, and giant arches competed for attention next to bustling forums.

'Have you ever seen so many *buildings*?' my brother asked.

'Not all in one place,' I said disapprovingly. We walked past the strangest jumble of shops – built without uniformity or any attention to design. From sweaty bakeries, men tried to tempt us with sows' udders and crab cakes, while on the polished steps of the marble baths, merchants hawked Egyptian linen and scented oils.

'That will be the site for Agrippa's Pantheon,' Marcellus said, indicating a field strewn with broken columns and abandoned carts.

'*That* will be a temple?' I confirmed.

He laughed. 'It doesn't look like much now, but once my mother's architect lays his hands on it . . .'

I searched the streets for the Temple of Isis, but too many buildings were crowded together to tell them apart. 'And what about the Egyptian temple?' I asked.

'It's just a few streets away,' Marcellus said eagerly. 'Would you like to go?'

'Absolutely not!' Gallia said sternly, giving me a dark look. 'Caesar is waiting.'

'But it's on the way,' Marcellus protested.

'So is the *lupanar*,' she said angrily. 'Would you like to go there, too?'

'I've never been inside the Temple of Isis,' Tiberius said suddenly, and everyone looked at him. 'I think we should go.'

'You see?' Marcellus said. 'Even Tiberius thinks it's a good idea. We'll be quick,' he promised. 'Alexander and Selene could show us what all of the strange paintings mean.'

'And those masks,' Julia added. 'Haven't you ever wanted to go inside?'

It was five against one. Gallia glanced at the guards.

'Don't worry about them,' Marcellus swore. 'They won't say anything.'

'Really?' I asked. 'How do you know?'

He turned to me and grinned. 'Trust me.'

Gallia looked at Tiberius. I suspected that if anyone would go running to Octavian, it would be him.

'I'd like to go,' he said simply. 'No one will find out. And if they do, you can just blame it on Selene and say that she took off running. That wouldn't be so unlikely, would it?' he asked pointedly.

Marcellus saw my discomfort and interjected, 'Come on!'

We walked briskly down several crowded streets, and I tried not to show my excitement. Despite Gallia's misgivings and Juba's anger, I would be meeting with the High Priest of Isis and Serapis.

'Do you think this is a wise idea?' my brother asked in Parthian.

'Of course it is.'

'If Octavian finds out, he might banish the Temple of Isis from Rome altogether.'

'We *have* to meet the High Priest, Alexander. If he can't help us return to Egypt, then perhaps he knows someone who can.'

'What?' my brother exclaimed. 'Are you mad?' Marcellus and Julia both looked in our direction. My brother lowered his voice. 'It will never work. Don't even think it. You've caused enough trouble.'

'For you!'

He flinched.

'Don't you want to return?'

'Of course. I'm the rightful King of Egypt.'

'Well, you heard Octavian as well as I did. He plans to marry me off and keep you alive only so long as it seems *merciful*.'

'He . . . he might change his mind.'

'And if he doesn't? Don't you think we should have a plan for that?' I could already smell the strong scent of *kyphi*, just like in Alexandria. 'I would rather risk my life trying to escape,' I said firmly, 'than wait for Octavian to cut you down like Antyllus or Caesarion.'

My brother didn't say anything, but as we approached the temple, he hesitated. On the steps, a group of soldiers had surrounded a young man and woman.

'Domine, this is not a good idea!' Gallia exclaimed.

'Why? What's the harm in a few soldiers?' Marcellus asked. 'They're probably just hassling a beggar.' He pushed his way through the crowd of onlookers, while Tiberius snapped, 'Stand back.'

'Domine, do not interfere!'

'What's happening?' Marcellus demanded.

A gray-haired centurion at the edge of the circle studied Marcellus. 'Who are you?'

'Son of Caesar,' Tiberius announced proudly.

The centurion looked at Octavian's guards, who stood behind us. 'And what are you doing here?'

'That's none of your business,' Tiberius snapped.

'Who is the woman?' Marcellus asked.

The centurion narrowed his eyes. 'A slave. Claims this man is her husband and that the pair of them were freed.' He held up a small leather bag and shook it up and down. Coins clinked against each other. 'Obviously stolen gold, probably from Caesar's caravan.'

'The one that was attacked last week on its way to the Temple of Saturn?' Tiberius demanded.

The centurion grinned. 'Very good.'

'And *she* attacked it?' Marcellus challenged. He looked at the young woman, who made a pitiful sight in her ragged tunic and broken sandals.

The centurion made a noise in his throat. 'If not her, then him. And we have reason to suspect they were working for the rebel the plebs like to call the Red Eagle.'

'May I see the bag?' Marcellus held out his hand.

'What are you doing?' Julia whispered. 'You'll get us all in trouble!'

The centurion hesitated, then passed him the gold.

Marcellus made a show of inspecting the leather. 'She isn't lying,' he said suddenly. 'The gold belongs to her.'

The soldiers raised their voices in protest, but Marcellus was louder. 'This comes from the House of Octavia.'

The centurion's jaw tightened. 'I believe if you take a better look, you will discover that you are wrong.'

'No. I'm not.'

'Are you saying,' the centurion's voice rose angrily, 'that the sister of Caesar gives so freely of her gold?'

'No, I do.'

The soldier looked at Gallia, whose face had gone pale, then at Tiberius, who maintained a careful silence. Suddenly, he waved his hand. 'Fine. Less work for us,' he announced grandly. 'Let them go.'

The man and woman rushed to thank Marcellus, but he shoved the bag at them and said forcefully, 'Get out of here.'

The group of soldiers dispersed, though I noticed that the centurion cast a suspicious look over his shoulder before leaving. The four of us watched Marcellus, and I suspected that behind us even the guards were passing questioning glances among themselves. It was Tiberius who broke the silence.

'Well done. Perhaps if we make a visit to the Carcer you can free the rest of the slaves who are imprisoned.'

'That was incredibly foolish,' Julia said. 'Who cares what happens to a pair of runaway slaves? They were *thieves*.'

'No. They were a husband and wife who wanted to be free,' I replied, and Marcellus's light eyes met mine. 'I think it was kind.'

Julia looked from me to Marcellus and said hotly, 'Are we going to the temple or not?' She marched up the remaining steps and Marcellus smiled at me.

'Thank you,' he mouthed.

'This must be quick,' Gallia cautioned. 'One look inside and that is all. Caesar is waiting on the Campus Martius.'

We hurried up the steps behind Julia, and as we passed beneath the arch, I blinked back tears. It was just like the temple in Alexandria. The cool interior was painted with the familiar images of Isis and Serapis, and bald-headed priests dressed in long linen robes were dispensing incense from gilded balls. A statue of the Mother Goddess, with eyes of sapphire and necklaces of gold, rose at the opposite end of the temple. Marcellus gave a low whistle.

'Welcome home.' A tall man emerged from the shadows, and I saw Gallia tense.

'The High Priest,' my brother said swiftly in Parthian. 'Is that the one . . . ?'

I nodded.

'Prince Alexander and Princess Selene.' The High Priest opened his arms in a gesture of welcome. 'And you've brought your distinguished friends.'

'How does he know you?' Tiberius was immediately suspicious.

'He must have seen us in the Triumph,' my brother said levelly.

'Have you come to see Isis and Serapis?' The High Priest stepped forward.

'Yes,' I replied, and I struggled to ignore the overwhelming feeling of homesickness. The towering granite statues and pink-veined marble had all been shipped from Egypt. Even the statues in the cleansing pool had probably been sculpted by Egyptian hands. 'Shepsit!' The High Priest snapped his fingers and a young woman appeared at his side. 'Show our new friends around the temple.'

The girl inclined her head dutifully. While everyone followed her, I remained with the High Priest.

'Aren't you coming?' Alexander called.

'I want to place an offering. I'll join you in a moment.' I saw the hesitation in his face, then Julia took his arm and he was gone.

The High Priest looked down at me. 'You read my note?'

'Yes. That's why I came.'

'Then you understand what Caesar plans for you,' he said, directing me toward a room behind a beaded curtain. Baskets and chests filled the little chamber, and I tried not to think of how similar baskets had adorned our palace in Alexandria. 'How long do you think it will be until Caesar decides to do away with the last of Kleopatra's children?'

'I – I don't know. That's why I've come to you. For help.'

He smiled. 'You want to return to Egypt?'

'If our lives are in danger.'

'Of course they are!' He moved closer to me. 'What happened to your mother? Your father? Your brothers? What happened to the priests of Isis and Serapis in Alexandria?'

I pressed my back against the marble wall. 'They're gone,' I whispered.

'That's right.' He stopped walking. 'But I can help you escape.'

I glanced at the beaded curtain. 'To Egypt?'

'Or India, or any place you wish.'

'And how long would we be in hiding?'

'Until your brother is old enough to raise an army and challenge Caesar.'

'My father failed and he had half of Rome's legions! What makes you think my brother would succeed?'

The High Priest narrowed his eyes. 'He might not. Perhaps in the very first battle he'll be crushed along with all of his men. But what do you think Caesar will do if he remains here?'

'He's kept my father's sons by Fulvia alive. I have older brothers—'

'Who are not the sons of an Egyptian queen!'

We watched each other in tense silence. Even amid so much incense, I could smell his fetid breath. Men with rotten teeth often smelled this way.

'Do you value your life?'

'Of course.'

'Then escape is your only option.'

I searched his face. 'And who would help us?'

He reached out and trailed a bony finger along my necklace. 'People who would do anything for the right price.'

My necklace could keep a man fed for the rest of his life. It might very well buy a passage to India. But I could never give away my mother's pearls. 'And if I don't want to pay the price?'

The High Priest grabbed my wrist. 'Everyone pays something.'

'Take your hands off of me!'

'Just give me the pearls,' he hissed. 'I'll have you free of Rome for the rest of your life.'

'Step away from her!' Marcellus parted the beaded curtain. Julia stood behind him with four stone-faced guards.

The High Priest dropped my arm and smiled blandly. 'Did you enjoy your tour?'

Marcellus glanced at me. 'Has he hurt you?'

'No.'

He met the High Priest's gaze. 'Isis is not so beloved in Rome that her priests can afford to abuse Caesar's guests.'

'Is that what she is?' His smile widened. 'A guest?'

'Yes,' Marcellus said forcefully. He held out his arm, and I hurried past the High Priest.

'Think about what I said,' the High Priest warned darkly. 'It's a small exchange for the protection of Isis.'

Although the priestesses were shaking their gilded sistra in the courtyard outside, all I could hear was Juba's voice in my head.

'So was that part of the offering?' Julia asked archly when we reached the steps of the temple.

My brother gave me a disapproving look, and I said angrily, 'Don't say it!'

'It might have happened to anyone,' Marcellus said. 'You just happen to have a queen's ransom around your neck. Priests of every goddess are greedy.'

I tried a smile, but it didn't come out right.

'Here,' he said compassionately, and offered me a small square of linen. As I dabbed at my eyes I could smell his scent on the cloth, and wanted nothing more than to weep into his shoulder. But Julia was there. And Tiberius.

'You see what happens, going into strange places?' Gallia demanded.

'I thought it was beautiful,' Julia said to be contrary.

'If you enjoy men dressed as jackals,' Tiberius said.

'You liked the women well enough,' she challenged.

Color tinged Tiberius's cheeks, but no one mentioned the High Priest again, and when we reached the Campus Martius, even my brother forgot his anger at me. 'Look at this!' he exclaimed.

It was hundreds of acres of low-lying plains bordered on the west by the Tiber River, and on the east by the Quirinal hill. There was a space for horses and chariot races, a place where marathon runners practiced, and in a series of grassy fields hundreds of soldiers wrestled, and boxed, and played games with leather balls. I saw men who were oiled and sweaty from their exertions jump into the Tiber, and I thought, *They must be brave not to have any fear of the crocodiles.*

'What are those buildings?' my brother asked. He pointed to a number of domed structures dotting the plains.

'Stables,' Marcellus replied. 'The Campus is where wealthy men keep their horses. There are baths inside them as well, for washing and changing. Those are my uncle's stables.' He pointed to a large building near the river.

As we drew closer, I could see that Octavia and Livia were already seated in the cool shade of the portico, working on their looms. The younger children were there as well; Antonia and Tonia patiently following their mother's instructions while Drusus and Vipsania giggled. Octavian stood between Juba and Agrippa; all three men were dressed in short tunics, with thin linen belts around their waists and sandals whose laces crisscrossed up their muscled calves. But only Octavian wore a broad-brimmed hat in anticipation of an afternoon in the sun.

'Alexander,' Agrippa said in greeting. 'Since you are a horseman, we've decided on riding. Go and change with Marcellus and Tiberius. They'll show you where the tunics are, and they'll find you a sword.'

But Alexander looked back at me. 'What about Selene?'

'Selene will be enjoying her time weaving,' Juba said.

'But she doesn't know how.'

'What girl doesn't know how to weave?' Livia demanded.

'She's a princess of Egypt,' Octavia replied. 'Her mother taught her languages, not how to work the loom.'

'Then perhaps her mother should have taught her some modesty so she doesn't end up clutching a cobra to her neck.'

I saw my brother tense, but Marcellus stepped forward. 'Come on.'

Alexander looked back at me, and I nodded. 'Go. There is riding to be done.' I smiled bravely, then watched the men disappear into the stables. I turned back to Octavia. 'I could study instead of weaving, if that would please you. Or perhaps I could draw—'

But Livia snapped, 'You will weave like the rest of us!'

I seated myself between Julia and Octavia, and Julia whispered, 'Just do as she says.'

'Why should she?' Octavia asked suddenly, and her girls looked up from their looms with wide eyes. Vipsania, Agrippa's seven-year-old daughter, gasped. 'There's no point in teaching Selene how to weave, and even less of a point in teaching her how to spin. When will she ever use those skills?'

'For her husband,' Livia retorted angrily.

'Very few men prefer homespun tunics. And I doubt that her future husband will be one of them. I don't see any reason not to let Selene sketch.'

Livia dropped the wooden shuttle onto her lap. 'What? Silly buildings and painted urns? For what purpose?'

'Well, if everything must have a purpose, then Vitruvius can train her as an architect.'

Livia sat forward. 'You think he would train a *girl*?'

'Why not?'

'Your brother would never allow it!' she swore. But when Octavian appeared with Agrippa and Juba, I noticed that Livia was silent.

Swiftly, I took out my sketches, and Julia regarded me with quiet fascination. I knew she was wondering why Octavia would choose to fight for me this way. But I thought I understood. It was her chance to anger the petty, jealous woman her brother had chosen for a wife.

When my brother emerged with Marcellus and Tiberius, I didn't dare say anything, even when Tiberius boasted that he was going to teach Alexander how to ride. After they'd left, there was an uncomfortable silence until mid-afternoon. No one spoke, and when I looked up to make a comment to Julia, she shook her head sternly.

When Marcellus and Alexander finally came galloping toward us, followed by the others, Julia rose. 'They're back!'

'Sit down,' Livia commanded, and I saw Octavia pass her niece a sympathetic look.

Alexander reined in his horse at the edge of the portico. With Marcellus beside him, he looked triumphant. The pair were the first to dismount.

'Your brother is a fine horseman,' Marcellus announced.

I looked from Alexander to Tiberius. 'Where did you go?'

'To the tracks, where the horses raced around poles. It was better than anything in Alexandria, Selene.'

Juba slid easily off his horse. 'There's something in Rome that's better than Alexandria?'

Octavian smiled at Juba's humor. 'He's an exemplary horseman,' he said matter-of-factly, walking toward us. 'Finer than Marcellus and possibly even as good as Tiberius.'

'Yes, but what does he know about tactics on the battlefield?' Tiberius demanded. 'You said so yourself. Anyone who hasn't read Sallust shouldn't be on a horse.'

'Well, there's always time to remedy that,' Agrippa said.

Tiberius laughed sharply. 'You really think he'll be as good a scholar as I am?'

Agrippa studied my brother. 'You never know.'

Juba placed his hand on Tiberius's shoulder. 'Come into the Tiber and cool off,' he suggested. 'It doesn't matter who did better today.' But when he moved to lead Tiberius away, I stood.

'Don't follow him!'

Juba and Tiberius turned.

'You shouldn't go into the river,' I said. 'You don't know what's in there.'

Juba laughed. 'What, are there sea serpents lurking beneath the waters?'

'Of course not,' I said angrily. 'There are crocodiles.'

Juba grinned. 'I am sorry to be the one who must tell you this, Princess, but there are no crocodiles swimming in the Tiber.'

I looked to Tiberius, who smiled arrogantly. 'I guess you don't know everything.'

Octavian and Agrippa followed them to the river bank, and when I returned to my seat, Julia suggested, 'Just ignore him.'

'But what happened to the crocodiles? Have they all been killed?'

'There have never been crocodiles,' Octavia replied, putting down her spindle. 'There are only fish. And all of them are harmless.'

I wondered what it would be like to swim in a river, and as we watched Marcellus and Alexander strip down to their loincloths, I asked Octavia, 'Will we be swimming, too?'

'What? In a loincloth?' Livia exclaimed.

'And a breastband,' I offered, but Vipsania giggled.

'Perhaps you would like to parade naked as well!' Livia added.

'She almost did,' Octavia remarked pointedly, reminding her of the Triumph and the beaded dress that Livia had chosen for me.

Livia sat forward and fixed me in her gaze. 'My father committed suicide because of your father. And now your father has killed himself because of my husband. It's a strange little world, isn't it, Selene? And I imagine that when your mother came to Rome, she thought it would be only a matter of time before she stood in the Senate and declared herself queen. But Romans don't accept women who paint their faces, or dress themselves in beads, or swim in rivers. And they won't accept a little whore from Alexandria who thinks she can come here and take her mother's place. I know what you want.' She laughed bitterly. 'You think my husband is going to send you back to Egypt, but the Greeks will be settling their debts on the Kalends before that ever happens!' In Rome, the Kalends was the first day of every month, but the Greeks had no such day.

When Livia sat back, Octavia smiled. 'Charming as always, Livia. And every afternoon a sweet reminder of why my brother chose you for his wife.'

I risked a glance at Julia, but her eyes were fixed on the wooden loom in front of her, and for the next hour we worked in silence while the men enjoyed themselves in the river. As the heat rose and it became unbearable even in the shade, no one moved. Octavia wiped the sweat from her brow with a small square of white linen. Julia's hair had gone limp in the heat. I thought of my brother pushing through the cool waters of the Tiber and felt a mounting anger. My mother had always given the two of us the same opportunities. If Alexander was allowed to swim, then so was I. If he had lessons in the Museion, I went with him. Nothing had ever been forbidden to me simply because I was a girl.

When the men returned, my brother had the good sense not to look too pleased. Instead, he saw me suffering in the heat and asked uneasily, 'So how was the drawing?'

'Hot,' I said curtly in Parthian. 'And your swim?'

'It was all right.'

I glowered at him. 'I'll bet it was better than sitting here with the Gorgon.'

'I'm sorry.' He hesitated. 'I won't go next time—'

'That's not what I want,' I said petulantly.

He looked at Livia. 'She really is a monster, isn't she?'

'Can you imagine if we were living with her?'

My brother shivered. 'Come.' He held out his hand. 'Gallia's taking us to the Circus Maximus.'

'And will I have to stand outside and watch through the arches?'

My brother chuckled. 'Marcellus says anyone can go.'

'I guess women's money is just as good as men's.'

Julia watched us, trying to follow our conversation, and when my brother went inside the stables to change, she asked me, 'How many languages can you speak?'

'Four. Plus a little Hebrew.'

'But how did you learn them?'

'I was raised with them. Like you were raised with Latin.'

'And did you study them in school?'

'Six days a week.'

Julia was thoughtful. Then she said quietly, 'Sometimes, I wonder how it would be if your father's ships had won at Actium.'

'He probably would have had you killed,' I said honestly.

'Or perhaps I would have come to Alexandria and studied in the Museion with you.'

When the men returned from the changing rooms, Octavia instructed Gallia to bring us home well before the sun set. 'I want them in the villa in time to have a rest and take a bath. And don't let Marcellus spend every last denarius, even if he's being charitable to his guards.'

'Are you coming?' Marcellus asked Tiberius.

'To the Circus? No, thank you.'

'What?' Marcellus laughed. 'You have something better to do?'

'Drusus and I are studying with Agrippa.'

'More Sallust?' I questioned.

'We finished Sallust two years ago. We're studying Rome's greatest generals now. My brother knows the entire history of Catiline from his career with Pompey to his revolt against the Republic.'

'So why doesn't he study with us in the ludus?' I asked.

'He's only nine. But even he knows that watching horses run around in a circle is a waste of time.'

As we started to walk, Julia demanded, 'Why do you invite him when he's so nasty?'

'I feel sorry for him,' Marcellus admitted.

'Well, you shouldn't,' she said. 'He's just like his mother.'

'Only because she bullies him.'

'So what?' she exclaimed as Gallia led the way. 'He allows it!'

'And what other choice does he have?'

'He can be silent.'

Marcellus made a face. 'Tiberius will never be silent. His dying breath will be a complaint.'

'But why does Livia stand for it?' my brother asked. 'She doesn't stand for anything else.'

Julia and Marcellus exchanged meaningful looks.

'Because he's her greatest hope,' Marcellus said. 'She wants to see Tiberius as ruler of Rome. Even though he'd rather join the army and go off fighting the Gauls.'

'But *you're* Octavian's heir!' Alexander exclaimed. 'Not Tiberius!'

'For now. But what if something should happen to me? What if I'm wounded in battle, or I fall from my horse—'

'*Marcellus!*' Julia cried.

'What?'

'From your lips to Juno's ear,' she reminded him. 'You shouldn't say such things.'

'Why?' He laughed dismissively. 'Do you think the gods really care what we say?'

'My father says so.'

'Because that's what he wants the plebs to think. A religious people is a people with purpose. So if the grain fails, or the aqueducts turn muddy, it can be Jupiter's fault, not his.'

Julia hesitated. 'I could believe it. Everything with my father is a show. And that's why he'll make you his heir, and not Tiberius. You're willing to act.'

'You mean I'm willing to be his puppet.' When he saw that Julia was going to protest, he smiled. 'I don't mind. But it's Alexander and Selene who need to be careful.'

We followed the Tiber past the Forum Boarium, a cattle market whose stench must have reached up to Elysium itself. Julia took a small wooden ball from her bag, pressing it to her nose and inhaling. 'Here,' she said to me.

I inhaled. 'What is this?'

'An amber ball. All the women use them.'

I inhaled deeply, then held my breath so that the earthy scent from inside the ball would stay with me for as long as possible. But eventually, when I had to breathe again, I coughed.

'It's terrible, isn't it?' Marcellus asked. 'If I were Caesar, I'd move the Forum Boarium to the other side of the Tiber.'

'Is it always this crowded?' Alexander complained.

We passed a bull with pads of hay tied on its horns, and Marcellus jumped back to avoid being trampled. 'Always. Even on days when there isn't a Triumph.'

When we reached the Circus Maximus, Marcellus and Gallia paused, allowing us to look up at the concrete megalith adorned with arches and marble statuary. I had seen the Circus from the Palatine, where Octavian had built a long wooden platform on which he could overlook the games from the privacy of his villa, but I hadn't understood just how truly great an accomplishment it was until we stood beneath the steps.

'This is one for your book of sketches,' Alexander said.

I could hear the wild excitement of the crowds inside, cheering as the chariots made their laps. Gallia fought against the heavy tide of people until we stood in front of the western gates. A man in a toga waved us through, shouting a greeting that we couldn't make out, and we climbed a flight of narrow stairs toward Caesar's box.

'Be careful,' Gallia warned us loudly. 'There are men who crack their necks here every day.'

'Usually because they're drunk,' Julia added.

'Or racing into the arms of one of their *lupae*.' Marcellus laughed, but I noticed that this time Gallia didn't smile.

'Was that what those cubicles were for?' my brother asked. 'Beneath the arches?'

Julia giggled. 'The *fornices*. And they're always crowded, night or day.'

When we reached the top of the stairs, the Circus Maximus slumbered beneath us like a giant in the sun. The track extended from the slopes of the Aventine to the Palatine, and all around it the seats rose in three tiers.

As soon as we reached Caesar's box, a portly man appeared below us asking for bets.

'Over here!' Marcellus shouted, waving the bet-maker toward us.

The man puffed his way up the stairs, and I wondered how he could have such a stomach when his job demanded so much rigorous activity.

'I have seventy-five denarii,' Marcellus said.

Gallia sucked in her breath. '*Domine!*'

'What? It's for Alexander and Selene as well. And Julia, if she doesn't have any.'

But Julia tipped a handful of coins from her bag onto her palm. 'I want twenty denarii on the Whites,' she said, handing them over.

'It won't be until the next race,' the bet-maker warned.

She made a small gesture of indifference with her hand. 'Doesn't matter.'

'And for you?' The man looked at Marcellus.

'What will it be?' Marcellus turned to us. 'Each team has three chariots in every race, and there's four different teams. The Reds, the Whites, the Blues, and the Greens.'

'Which are your favorite?' Alexander asked carefully, his eyes on the horses.

'The Whites.'

'Are they better?'

Marcellus frowned. 'Who knows? I always bet on the Whites.'

'But shouldn't you bet on which drivers are most capable? Or which horses have won in previous races?'

'Who thinks of those things?' Marcellus exclaimed.

'You should, if you want to win! Look at the rider in red,' my brother said. 'He's the only one left on his team because he's light. His horses don't have to pull such a heavy burden, so the chariot goes faster.'

Marcellus and Julia both stared at him. 'So you favor the Reds?' Marcellus asked hesitantly.

'I don't know. I'd have to watch the races for several days to see.'

'Well you don't have several days,' the bet-maker said sourly. 'I have other customers, so place your bets.'

'The Reds, then,' Alexander said firmly.

When Marcellus turned to me, I said, 'My brother wouldn't

waste his time drawing a portico, and I won't waste my time pretending I know horses. Whatever he says.'

'Twenty-five on the Whites, and fifty on the Reds.' Marcellus handed a bag full of coins to the man, and I saw Gallia flinch at the sum. It was probably a hefty percentage of what she would need to purchase her freedom, if Octavia allowed it, and half of what Magister Verrius made in a year as a teacher at the *ludus*. But she didn't say anything, and Marcellus went on. 'I come here every day,' he said cheerfully, 'and Gallia is good enough to put up with it.' She gave a weary smile, and even when she looked hot and bored, she was beautiful. 'We will have to ask my mother to go to the Temple of Saturn and withdraw several bags of denarii for you both.'

'Then we will go shopping,' Julia promised me. 'I'll take you to the markets and we'll pick out something we can wear to the theater. When my father's here, we go once a month.' The sound of trumpets echoed in the Circus, and Julia became distracted. 'The Reds are out in front, just as Alexander said!' She stood up, and while she and Marcellus shouted for the Whites to hurry, I took out my book of sketches. She looked back at me. 'You're not going to draw right now?' she exclaimed.

'Why not? There is nothing like this in Alexandria.'

'No stadia?' she shouted over the jubilation of the crowds. The charioteers were on their final lap.

'Certainly, but nothing this large.'

When the Reds won, Marcellus sat down and clapped Alexander on the back. 'You know your horses, don't you? But you think they'll really win a second time?'

'If the Reds have the same kind of riders, I don't see why not.' Below, the track was being cleared, and the body of a charioteer who'd fallen under the hooves of an opponent's horses was being dragged away. A troupe of musicians appeared to entertain the crowds while the track was being smoothed, and slaves clambered toward us to pull an awning over the western section of the Circus, where the wealthy had their seats.

Julia watched as I began my sketch by drawing the long *spina* in the center of the track. Unlike the stadium in Alexandria, where the *spina* had been a plain stone barrier, the Circus had two rectangular basins filled with water. In each basin were seven bronze dolphins spouting water from their mouths, and with every completed lap, an official turned a dolphin in the opposite direction. And for those whose eyes weren't good enough to see whether the dolphins were facing north or south, there were seven bronze eggs and a second official to take one down for every lap.

'Those were built by Agrippa,' Julia explained.

'How much has he constructed?' I asked. 'It seems to be half of Rome.'

She laughed. 'That's because he's my father's greatest builder.'

'So he does it himself?'

'He just comes up with the ideas and the denarii. I suppose the architect Vitruvius does the drawing. Have you seen him?' she asked. 'You know, he's Octavia's lover.'

'I saw him in the villa. How long have they been living together?'

'Since your father announced he was going to divorce her. She'd already been alone for several years.'

'Do you think she loved him?'

Julia looked at me askance. 'Your father? Of course! Why do you think she raised all those legions for his eastern campaigns?'

My response was cut off by the sudden clamor of people below us. Thousands of spectators were on their feet, looking in our direction and pointing above us. 'The Red Eagle!' someone next to us cried, and when I looked up, I saw that the vast gold awning that the slaves had fastened above the western end of the Circus had been painted with a bird. Its wings were spread and from its outstretched talons a pair of children were struggling to be free. I didn't have to see the Egyptian wigs or the white diadems to know who they were supposed to be.

'That's you,' Julia whispered, aghast.

Immediately, Gallia rose to her feet. 'Go!' she shouted, and then we were moving.

'What about our bets?' Marcellus cried.

Gallia spun around. 'Caesar is watching these races right now, and what do you think he's seeing from the Palatine?'

'But how did he do it?' Marcellus marveled. He looked up at the red eagle. It was beautifully painted and had been completely hidden from view until the awning was opened.

Alexander shook his head. 'He must have come during the night.'

Julia held on to my arm as we descended into the chaos. Men and women with the best seats in the Circus were rushing toward the gates before they could be accused of bearing witness to treachery. But slaves were taking up the chant of 'Red Eagle,' which could be heard over the water horns of the musicians, and those who wanted the races to go on began throwing their food at the canopy.

'Hurry!' Gallia exclaimed. 'Before there's a riot and we can't get out!' She pressed forward in the madness, and we shoved our way down the stairs onto the street. As we reached the gates, I felt someone's hand on the bag at my side, and when I turned, the young boy who was going to steal from me held up his hands in innocent protest.

'Do it again and I'll knife you,' I swore. He leered, and I wondered if he knew that I was bluffing.

In the streets, we could finally breathe again, but Gallia didn't stop. Although it would have been undignified to run, that is nearly what we did all the way to the Palatine.

'Look!' Marcellus pointed. A crowd was gathering around the doors to the Temple of Jupiter, and the people stepped back when they recognized Marcellus.

'Another actum from the Red Eagle!' Julia pushed forward, despite Gallia's objections, and read the actum aloud to us. 'He's complaining about the Triumphs,' she said, quickly reading the papyrus. 'And look at this! He's freed a hundred and fifty slaves coming from Greece.' Three sheets with the same content had been posted, and the crowd regarded them silently. 'He's also purchased the freedom of twenty children and returned them to their parents in Gaul.'

She read a short list of names, and I wondered whether it was possible that he might help me and Alexander next. He had risked his life to paint our image above the Circus, and his message had been clear. Our fate was to be the same as that of any slave who could be killed on his master's whim. If he knew that Octavian planned to kill us, surely he would help us escape from Rome. But that would be costly. 'He must be wealthy,' I observed.

'He must be brave.' Julia sighed.

A priest emerged from the temple to see what was happening and shouted angrily, 'Get out of here or Caesar will hear of this!' He tore the three sheets of papyrus from his temple doors and flung them to the ground.

CHAPTER SEVEN

ONLY A small party gathered in Octavian's triclinium for the evening meal. Juba and Agrippa were both in attendance, and Maecenas was there with his attractive wife, Terentilla, but no one was in a particularly merry mood. Although we were at a separate table, Marcellus and Julia spoke softly, afraid their voices might arouse Octavian's wrath.

'I don't know why everyone's whispering,' Tiberius said suddenly. 'It's not like this rebel hasn't pulled pranks like this before. So he painted an awning.'

'On a day of *Triumph*,' Marcellus whispered. 'And with another to go.'

'So what?' Tiberius asked arrogantly. 'Tomorrow, Octavian will toss coins in the Circus, and the people will fight one another for them like animals and it will all be forgotten.'

We looked at Octavian, who was scribbling furiously on a scroll. The boiled capons in front of him had gone neglected, and he seemed to be eating a simple salad of rosemary flowers.

'What do you think he's writing?' I asked nervously.

'His memoirs.'

I thought Tiberius was being sarcastic, but Marcellus nodded. 'He records everything.'

'Why?' I asked.

'He thinks his heir will read his musings someday and become a better leader.'

Tiberius sniffed dismissively. 'If he only knew.'

'What are you trying to say?' Marcellus demanded.

Tiberius smiled. 'I think you know.'

Marcellus rose from his couch, and I was certain there were going to be blows, when a young boy rushed into the triclinium and everyone turned. With trembling hands, he held up a scroll, and Livia demanded, 'What is it?'

The slave held out the missive. 'Some builders found this while working on the Temple of Apollo, domina. It's addressed to Caesar, and has the stamp—'

Livia grabbed the scroll before the boy could finish. 'Another one!' she shrieked. 'Another actum!' She passed it to Octavian, and as he read, the color heightened in his cheeks. He looked at the slave, who was shaking in his sandals.

'So tell me,' he began with frightening calm, 'were there witnesses to this deed?'

'No,' the boy squeaked. 'When the workers arrived this afternoon, it was already nailed to the temple door.'

Octavian put down his reed pen, and the room fell silent. 'Go,' he said, and the boy ran from the room as fast as his feet could carry him.

Octavian turned to Agrippa. 'This man has access to the Palatine, and is someone who must not have aroused suspicion when he approached the Temple of Apollo.' He stood slowly. 'So what shall we do about this, Agrippa?'

He handed the scroll to his general, who skimmed the contents. 'He wants every slave in Rome to be freed.'

'That's already been established!' Octavian shouted.

'But he must be a senator.' Agrippa read aloud from the scroll:

If you are so worried that Roman culture will change, then stop living off the backs of your slaves, and start doing work for yourselves. Or perhaps you prefer to keep watching wagon trains of a thousand Gauls roll in. Perhaps you would rather condone the slave traders with their pretty Greeks. In which case, you will soon have a Rome in which no one is Roman. You can force them to speak Latin, to wear tunics and sandals, but blood will out.

'Only someone in the Senate would have heard your speech.'

But Juba frowned. 'Senators talk. It could have been anyone.'

'So why don't we do something?' Livia demanded.

'And what should that be?' Juba raised his brows. 'Stand at every temple door in Rome?'

'If that's what needs to be done,' she cried. 'Your job is to—'

'Enough!' Octavian shouted, and immediately Livia fell silent. 'We have heard enough of this!' But a soldier appeared at the door, and the color rose on Octavian's neck. 'What is it?'

The soldier hesitated before crossing the triclinium. 'There – there is news, Caesar. A stockpile of weapons has been discovered in the Forum Boarium. We believe they belong to a group of escaped slaves.'

Agrippa was on his feet at once. 'What kind of weapons?'

'Javelins, swords, daggers, spears, bows, arrows. Plus infantry helmets, armor, and shields. And most of them new.'

Octavian looked from Juba to Agrippa. 'They are planning rebellion.' He stood so quickly that his water spilled across the table. 'I want every slave forbidden from purchasing weaponry anywhere in Rome!'

'But how will the merchants know—'

'Proof of citizenship!' Octavian bellowed.

The soldier nodded quickly. 'But if I may ask a question, Caesar. Where is the gold coming from for these weapons? Most of them were recently forged. If we can find the source—'

'A caravan on the way from Judea to the Temple of Saturn was attacked,' Agrippa said. 'The gold must have been used to buy weaponry.'

Octavian put his hand to his forehead and rubbed his temples with his forefinger and thumb. The triclinium went silent. Even Livia held her tongue. 'You are dismissed.' The soldier didn't need to be told twice; like the boy who had brought in the actum, he swiftly disappeared. Octavian turned to Juba. 'Take us to your villa. I want to see the new statues. This meal is finished,' he announced.

Juba stood up from his couch, and everyone rose, leaving their food whether or not they were finished. We followed him through the triclinium, and once we were outside he led us along the hill to a villa that was perched in a grove of ancient oaks. The shutters of his house were painted green, and the double doors were studded with bronze.

'Juba must be extremely wealthy,' I whispered.

Julia nodded. 'He earned it himself.'

'Through his writing?'

'And antiques,' Marcellus added. 'My mother pays him to find authentic statues from Greece, and he probably has other clients.'

Juba held open the doors for us, and inside, the flooring was *opus signinum,* made from small fragments of tiles and amphorae painstakingly embedded in clay. Wicker partitions divided some of the rooms, and as we walked through the villa I noticed that the couches were carved into fantastical shapes of every kind: gryphons and sea serpents, Gorgons and Sirens. It was the house of a man who had traveled extensively.

'Is that a Grecian Nike?' Tiberius asked as we passed through the atrium.

Juba smiled. 'From the sculptor Phidias himself.'

Octavian paused at several niches to admire the statues that Juba had found. Each time, he ran his hand over the marble, caressing a hand, an arm, the curve of a shoulder. When we reached the library, slaves rushed to light the oil lamps placed in tall candelabra, and the soft glow cast nearly a hundred statues in a warm golden light.

'Magnificent,' Octavia murmured.

'Where does he get them all?' my brother asked Marcellus.

'I travel throughout Rome looking for sellers,' Juba replied, having overheard my brother's question. 'And if I can't find the right statue, I will go to Greece.'

Each of the statues was numbered, and all of them had small bronze plates at the base giving their names and where they were discovered. Octavian busied himself on the other side of the room, showing Livia and Octavia his favorites.

'Look at this one!' Julia exclaimed, pointing to an image of the goddess Aphrodite.

'She looks like you,' Marcellus said. It was true. The sculptor had chosen a model with rich black hair and eyes as dark and soft as twilight. All of the statues were painted, and only a few, whose paint had rubbed off after years of neglect, were flawless white marble.

'Let's find one that looks like you,' Julia said eagerly, taking his arm, and they visited half a dozen statues before Julia decided that Marcellus looked like Apollo.

'We should come here more often,' Julia exclaimed. 'I enjoy Grecian statues.'

'Of course you do,' Tiberius said nastily. 'They speak to your vanity.'

'Well, perhaps we should pick one that looks like you. How about this?' She pointed to a hideous statue of a Gorgon, and Marcellus laughed.

'I think you're being too generous,' he said.

I snickered, and Tiberius shot me a withering look. 'You lower yourself with them.'

Across the library, Octavian regarded a statue of Jupiter. The god's symbol was an eagle, and the proud bird perched on his marble shoulder. Octavian traced its beak with his finger.

'We will find him,' I heard Juba promise sternly.

Octavian looked up into the bird's black eyes. 'I know. And when we do, we will crucify him.'

When we returned to Octavia's villa, Alexander and I pressed our ears against the wall of our chamber, listening to Octavia interrogate Marcellus.

'I want to know where you were while everyone else in this villa was asleep this afternoon!'

'I went for a walk,' Marcellus swore. 'Down the hill,' he added, 'around the Temple of Apollo.'

'Exactly where the Red Eagle's note was found.'

'Mother,' he implored, 'all I did was walk.'

'Without an escort? Without telling anyone?' she challenged. 'The temple priest says he's certain he saw a flaxen-haired man post the actum. How many men on this hill have such light hair?'

'Your brother!' he cried. 'And almost every slave!'

'And do they have access to a temple next to Caesar's villa?'

'Perhaps they snuck in and left him the message. Or perhaps it's one of the workers themselves. Mother,' he protested, 'you don't really believe—'

'Why not? I see you with Gallia. She's beautiful. Perhaps you feel sorry for her.'

'Of course I feel sorry. But to betray my uncle?'

There was silence in the next room, and when I went to speak, Alexander shook his head. Octavia's reply was soft. 'You are idealistic and rash. But I shall hope you are not so rash as that, Marcellus.'

'I promise you, Mother, I'm not the Red Eagle. Look at his writing.'

'Gallia can write. Perhaps you are posting *her* words.'

'And risking everything? Do you know what Octavian would do—'

'I know exactly what he'd do, even if he discovered it was you. And there would be no mercy.'

'I wouldn't need it. I know nothing about this. All I did was go for a walk.'

'Then that was your last walk alone,' she said darkly.

We heard the door open and scrambled away from the wall.

I looked at Alexander. 'Do you really think it could be Marcellus?'

'You heard him. Why would he risk his position as Caesar's heir? He could just as easily wait to become Caesar and change the laws, if that's what he wanted.'

I sat against the back of my couch and drew up my knees. 'Then Gallia?'

'It's possible. She has every reason, and if Octavia already suspects her . . .'

The next morning, I watched Gallia as she carefully laid out a fresh tunic on my couch, and I wondered if those same delicate hands were responsible for crafting the rebellious acta. I noticed my brother watching her, too, moving more slowly than usual with his toga and sandals.

'What is this?' Gallia asked in frustration. 'Do I have to dress the both of you myself? Domina, the architect is waiting for you!'

'It's Selene and Alexander. Not domini.'

When I shoved my diadem back on my brow, she moved to arrange it tenderly among my curls. 'Thank you,' she said quietly.

'You are a princess as much as I am,' I replied.

'Not anymore.' She pressed her lips together.

I would have argued with her, but Octavia appeared in the doorway and waited with her hands on her hips while I fetched my book of sketches. 'I'm coming,' I promised, and followed her into the atrium. 'Do you think Vitruvius will agree to tutor me?'

'I don't know,' she said truthfully. 'He's a very busy man who's never taken a single apprentice. But we can try.' She guided me into the library, where neatly labeled scrolls rose to the ceiling on polished cedar shelves. The architect Vitruvius was already waiting, sitting behind a table with his hands folded in front of him, contemplating the drawing I had given to Octavian. When he heard us approach, his chin jerked up, and his eyes fixed on my book of sketches.

'So you are Selene,' he said, regarding me with his sharp, dark eyes. 'And I hear you like to draw.' His tone was bemused.

'Just look at what she's already done,' Octavia said. 'She has talent. Even my brother thinks so.'

I looked at Vitruvius, with his lean face and angular jaw, and wondered what he was thinking.

'Let me see your sketches,' he said at last.

I gave him my book, and he quietly flipped through it. He studied each page with a critical gaze, pausing the longest over the drawing of my mother's mausoleum. Slowly, he held it up to the light, then lowered it again so that he could question me. 'Is this in Alexandria?'

'Yes. Near the Temple of Isis and Seropis.'

He nodded. 'She can draw,' he said thoughtfully. 'But so can many others. What exactly do you want me to do?'

'Tutor her,' Octavia replied.

'In what?'

'Architecture.'

'A *girl*?' I thought he was going to laugh, but he glanced at my face and asked soberly, 'What does she need with architecture?'

'The same thing my mother needed with eight languages,' I replied boldly. 'She commanded the best diplomats in the world, but she refused to leave anything to someone else that she could do better herself.'

'And what do you hope to do better yourself?' Vitruvius raised his brows.

'Build.'

He leaned back. 'Where?'

I glanced at Octavia, who nodded encouragingly. 'Thebes. It was my mother's dream,' I explained. 'I know what her plans were for it,' I said quickly. 'The entire city was destroyed by Ptolemy IX. But if my brother ever returns to Egypt, I could go with him and build a new Thebes.'

Vitruvius looked at Octavia. 'You know that Caesar will never allow it.'

'He may change his mind.'

But Vitruvius shook his head. 'He will marry her off, and if she's lucky, Livia will not have a say in it.'

'You mean, Livia may decide—'

'She's my brother's wife,' Octavia cut me off. 'Anything's possible. Which is why you must train her, Vitruvius. Show my brother that she has use beyond being some old senator's wife. You can make her your apprentice.'

Vitruvius laughed.

'Why not?' she exclaimed. 'When Octavian showed you her sketch of Alexandria you said it was inspired.'

'It's true. She has a gift. But what does she know about architecture?'

'You can teach me,' I said. 'I already know every type of tool that's used in building, and every architectural style from Egypt to Greece.'

Vitruvius shook his head. 'Building sites are no place for a princess.'

'Then take me with you in the mornings when you leave to do your inspections.'

'Your son has no interest in architecture,' Octavia pointed out.

The color rose in Vitruvius's cheeks. 'Yes,' he said bitterly. 'He wants to be a lover and a poet!'

'Then share your knowledge with me.'

Vitruvius sat forward in his chair, and Octavia said persuasively, 'My brother wants a mausoleum like Queen Kleopatra's. Selene has probably sketched it a dozen times. At least give her the chance to help you with this.'

Vitruvius regarded me in silence. Then finally he said, 'Tomorrow at dawn. Meet me in this library.'

I clapped my hands.

'We will begin with Caesar's mausoleum, and if I'm satisfied with your progress, I may teach you to build.'

'*Thank you!*'

Octavia smiled. 'Go. Or you'll be late to the ludus.'

I met Alexander and Marcellus on the portico and told them what had happened. And when Julia and Tiberius met us on the road, Marcellus said proudly, 'Did you hear? Vitruvius wants to train Selene as an architect.'

'Oh, I'm not sure he *wants* to,' I amended hastily. 'It was Octavia's idea. She pressured him.'

Julia stared at me. 'Why would she do that for you?'

'To give me something to do,' I said awkwardly.

'It's more than that,' Marcellus protested. 'She likes you.' I saw Julia's back straighten. 'You're the half sister to her daughters, after all.'

But it was strange to think of ten-year-old Antonia and seven-year-old Tonia as my siblings.

'They're not much like us, are they?' Alexander asked. We followed Gallia through the crowded streets toward the Forum. It was the last day of Octavian's Triumph.

'No, they're quiet,' Marcellus reflected.

'And charitable,' Tiberius added.

'I'm charitable,' Marcellus protested. 'I give in the Circus all the time.'

My brother laughed. 'And the bet-makers are thankful for it. Will we go again today?'

'Of course.'

'Your mother had Gallia give me several denarii.' Alexander patted a small leather bag at his side.

'You didn't tell me that!' I said.

Alexander looked sheepishly at me. 'Because you were with Vitruvius.'

'And he really wants to teach you?' Julia asked suspiciously.

'Your father wants an Egyptian mausoleum. Octavia convinced him that maybe I can help.'

Julia was quiet for several moments, and I wondered whether she was jealous. 'I've heard that Alexandria is beautiful,' she said at last.

'The most magnificent city in the world.'

'Greater than Rome?'

I hesitated. 'It was three hundred years in the making,' I said carefully. 'All marble buildings perched above the sea.'

'And your mother? Was she as beautiful as they say?'

I blinked rapidly, so that I wouldn't cry as we approached the ludus. 'She wasn't a traditional beauty,' I explained. 'It was her mind.' Julia frowned. She didn't understand that a mind could be beautiful. 'And her voice. It drew men from every corner of the world.'

'Like the Sirens,' Julia whispered. 'I've seen her image in the Temple of Venus and wondered if that's what she was really like.'

Alexander and I stopped walking.

'What image?' my brother asked.

'Her statue in Julius Caesar's Forum.'

'And it's still there?'

Julia regarded him with a puzzled expression. 'Of course. Where else would it be?'

'But why didn't your father tear it down?' I asked.

'The statue of a queen?' Julia was shocked. 'Because she was loved by Julius.'

I glanced at my brother. 'So all of Octavian's rage against her was a lie,' I said in Parthian. 'Just a piece of theater so that Rome would stand against her.'

He turned to Julia. 'Do you think we can see it?'

'I don't see why not. We can go after the exercises on the Campus.'

We studied Homer's *Odyssey* that morning, reciting passages about Odysseus's travels on the wine-dark sea guarded by gray-eyed Athena. When we were finished, Gallia took us back to the Campus Martius, deftly navigating through the excited masses who were waiting for the last victory parade. On the marble portico in front of the stables, Juba and Agrippa were seated next to Octavian, who was showing his sister his plans for a series of buildings. I took a chair next to Antonia, and Livia was silent when I reached for my sketches.

'These are the plans for the aqueduct in Naples,' Octavian was saying, 'and this is the one for the Forum.'

Octavia smiled. 'And did Vitruvius give you the plans for my building?' she asked.

Her brother unfurled a scroll at his side. 'The restoration of the old Portico Metelli,' he said with relish, 'now to be known as the Portico of Octavia, with three hundred new columns and two temples inside.'

'I want there to be a public library within, as well.'

Octavian took notes. 'Good. *Very* good,' he added. 'The plebs will like a library. What else?'

'Perhaps a *schola.*'

Livia's cheeks grew flushed, and she put down her weaving. 'Perhaps I should build a portico as well,' she said. 'What do you think?'

'That would be a grand gesture,' Agrippa remarked, but it was Octavian's approval that Livia wanted.

'Shall I fund my own building?' Livia asked him.

Octavian peered out from under his hat. 'Rome would be grateful for your generosity. But do you have enough time—'

'Of course,' she said swiftly. 'For Rome, there is always time.'

Octavian regarded her with fondness. 'I am lucky in the women who surround me,' he said quietly, and Julia rolled her eyes at me. 'I will make the notes and Vitruvius will hire the men next month.' He stood, and everyone who was riding rushed to follow him into the stables.

When he was gone, Livia smiled. 'A pair of porticos,' she said to Octavia.

'How generous of you.'

She raised her brows. 'The money has to go somewhere. In Gaul, your brother gave me copper mines. And in Judea, entire estates of palm groves. And do you know what he's giving me in Egypt?'

'A temple?'

Livia narrowed her eyes. 'Why would I want that? There's no money to be made from a temple.'

'Of course.' Octavia smiled. 'It's all about money.'

Livia laughed. 'Oh, I see your charity in the Subura. You think you aren't paid for that with smiles, and respect, and women who scrape the floor to kiss your feet?'

'No one has ever kissed my mother's feet!' Antonia exclaimed, and everyone looked at her in shock. Even Vipsania, who was always giggling, covered her mouth.

'It's still payment,' Livia said icily. 'I just like my payment to be worth something.'

'You are a crass woman,' Octavia said.

'A crass woman with papyrus marshes. Dozens of them.' She grinned. 'And there's nothing half as profitable in the east as papyrus. Octavian is giving me my choice of fields. Perhaps Selene will help me choose the most valuable.'

'That's enough!' Octavia stood, and for a moment I wondered if she was going to strike her. 'Gallia, you may take Julia and Selene shopping. Return here before the exercises are over.'

Julia rose swiftly, amazed at her good fortune.

'You may take Selene,' Livia said, 'but Julia is not going.'

'Julia is my niece,' Octavia said. 'She is no blood relative of yours, and if I say she may shop, then she will shop. And if you make her life difficult for this, or I hear that you've punished her for obeying me, then my brother will hear of it.'

Livia's eyes flashed, but she didn't move, and Julia took my arm. Gallia rushed us away from the Campus, and as soon as we were out of earshot, I whispered, 'How do you live with her?'

'She's too busy watching Terentilla to notice me,' Julia answered.

I looked at Gallia. 'Thank you.'

'It was domina's wish,' she said humbly. 'I am only your escort.'

'May we go by the Temple of Venus?' Julia asked. 'Selene would like to see the statue of her mother.'

'It is more than fifteen years old,' Gallia warned.

'I'll still recognize her,' I promised, but when we reached the end of Caesar's Forum and entered the Temple of Venus Genetrix, Gallia saw my confusion and smiled.

'Can you find her?'

Inside the cool marble halls, priestesses stood guard over the temple's works of art. There was a statue of Julius Caesar that was unmistakable, since Caesarion had looked so much like him, and a statue of Venus half-dressed in linen. I skipped the collection of sparkling gems, although this was what caught Julia's eye, and I passed over a stunning metal breastplate adorned with pearls from Britannia. I went from statue to statue, and it was only by the Alexandrian diadem in her hair that I finally recognized her. 'Is this it?' I gasped.

'Kleopatra of Egypt,' Gallia replied.

Julia came to my side and asked eagerly, 'Is that what she looked like?'

I studied the woman's heavy breasts, her long Roman nose, and her pointed chin, then shook my head sadly. 'No.' I could see that Julia was disappointed. 'My mother was much thinner,' I told her. 'With hands that were even smaller than mine.'

'Really? What about her face?'

Although the lips were correct, and the rich amber hue of her eyes, everything else was wrong. 'She was plainer,' I admitted. 'And her nose . . .' I hesitated. 'It was different.'

'So Caesar did love her for more than her beauty.'

I nodded. 'She could speak many languages. Egyptian, Ethiopian, Hebrew, Aramaic, Syrian, Median, Parthian . . .'

'Latin,' Julia put in.

'Of course. And she lived very well.'

'Is it true, what they say about her drinking the pearl?'

I thought of the story my mother had often told to Alexander and me about her second meeting with our father. In an attempt to impress him with her wealth, she had promised him the most expensive feast ever consumed. When he arrived, there was a single goblet of wine on the table. She dropped her largest pearl into the goblet, and when the pearl dissolved she proceeded to drink the wine. I smiled sadly, remembering how my mother could be mischievous. 'Yes. The pearl story was true.'

'I wish my mother were so well known.'

'Is she still alive?'

Julia tensed. 'Somewhere,' she said curtly, and didn't elaborate. 'I heard that your mother showed you how to use eye paints. Do you think if Gallia takes us to the shops, you could show me, too?'

'Domina Livia would not like that,' Gallia warned.

'But we can do it in secret,' Julia promised. 'Please,' she begged. 'We never have any fun.'

Gallia hesitated, and in that moment she was lost.

'Come!' Julia exclaimed. 'We'll go to the street of the Etruscans.'

'Is that where Egyptian goods are?'

'That's where everything is!'

Gallia dutifully led the way, and I wondered what the soldiers guarding us thought when they were forced to linger outside a shop for Egyptian aphrodisiacs and painted beads.

'These were what we used for our hair,' I explained. 'But only on days when there were official ceremonies.'

Julia put her hands in the box of beads, enjoying the feel of the small faience trinkets as they ran though her fingers. 'How many would we need?'

'For your hair? You're not really going to use them?'

'Why not?' She grinned. 'Tomorrow, we're all going to the theater. Before we leave, I can come over, and you can put them in.'

'Livia will never allow it, and neither will Octavia.'

'Who cares what they think?' she asked merrily. 'We'll take them out before anyone can see.' When I hesitated, she gestured to the shopkeeper excitedly. 'The entire box!'

'E-everything, domina?' the old man stammered.

'Yes. Just hurry. You may send the bill to my father.'

He didn't have to ask who her father was.

'Where shall we go next?' she asked eagerly, handing the purchase to Gallia. 'I want to look just like a princess.'

'You *are* a princess.'

'A real one.' There was envy in her eyes. 'With paints and silk tunics and all the things that women should wear if not for Livia. She's just jealous, you know.' I followed her down the streets as she searched for an Egyptian cosmetics shop. 'She wants everyone to be as plain and ugly as she is.'

I noticed that Gallia kept silent, though secretly I was sure she agreed. 'What about this shop?' Gallia asked.

'Are there paints?'

'Of every color.'

We went inside, and Julia wanted a name for everything. Suddenly I knew how Marcellus must have felt when we were riding into Rome and my brother and I had asked him question after question.

Julia held up a jar of ochre.

'For the lips,' I said. 'Sometimes for the cheeks.'

She placed the jar on the counter. 'What about something for the eyes? Like Terentilla.'

'Domina!' Gallia gasped. 'Terentilla is—'

'A whore? I know,' she said brightly.

'But she's married to Maecenas,' I protested. 'How could she be—'

'She was an actress. And we all know there's not much difference between an actress and a *lupa*. But my father arranged their marriage.'

'To one of his closest friends? How can he—'

'Oh, Maecenas isn't interested in women. But he needed a wife, and my father needed an excuse for her to be near him.'

'Then why not marry her himself?' I asked.

'*Terentilla*? Because she doesn't have a clan.'

'None at all?'

'Oh, I'm sure she has *some* clan. But they have no power to speak of. So what would he gain? But she's beautiful, isn't she? What do you think she uses for her eyes?'

I glanced warily at Gallia, whose look was disapproving. 'Malachite,' I said slowly, 'with antimony to line them.'

Julia gathered her purchases on the counter, and when the old man gave a total, Gallia exclaimed, 'Nonsense! You are trying to overcharge.'

'So what?' Julia said. 'My father has plenty of denarii to give him.'

Outside the shop, Julia passed her purchases to Gallia, who shook her head with deep misgivings. 'We should hurry, domina. The exercises will be over soon.'

'But what about Selene?' She turned to me. 'Isn't there anything you want to shop for?'

'I can't. Alexander has our money.'

She waved her hand in the air. 'You can send the bill to my father. He'll never know who bought it.'

I smiled. 'Perhaps in a few weeks I'll get some new reed pens and ink.'

'That's it?' Julia wrinkled her nose, but even when she made such an unbecoming gesture, she was beautiful. A hundred women were walking around us, but men's eyes still lingered hotly in her direction. 'What about the theater?' she demanded. 'What will you wear?'

'Whatever Octavia gives me.'

Julia shook her head. 'Absolutely not. We both need new tunics.'

'Domina!' Gallia protested faintly. 'There is no time for that.'

'Then we'll just purchase the fabric! No fittings,' she promised, and disappeared into the next shop before Gallia could protest further. Inside, bolts of beautiful cloth shimmered in the afternoon light. Silks in peacock blue, celadon green, and pewter gray were laid out among plainer fabrics of every hue. Julia held up a swath of gold silk against my skin. 'This would be beautiful.'

'Domina Livia will never accept it,' Gallia warned.

'Livia doesn't accept anything.' She glanced wickedly at me. 'Let's get it anyway. What can she do once we buy it?'

'She'll take it back! An entire tunic of gold is not for the theater. And if domina Octavia is offended, it will be the end of your shopping trips,' Gallia advised.

Julia hesitated. 'Fine. Then this one.' She chose a bolt of violet silk that would go nicely with her dark skin, and while she arranged with the shopkeeper where to send the bill, I studied the riot of colors on display. *Perhaps I should begin to add color to my drawings,* I thought. Jars of red ochre and dazzling azurite were sitting entirely useless in my chests. I wasn't allowed to wear them on my face, so why not use them as additions to my sketches?

As we left the shop, Gallia said sternly, 'This is it. No more shopping anywhere. Understand?'

'Yes,' Julia said with a hint of mockery. We followed Gallia through the Forum Holitorium, where vegetables were being sold in stalls along the Tiber, and Julia babbled gaily about how I was going to dress her hair, and which colors would go best with her eyes. 'Violet,' she decided, 'to match our new tunics. I'll have our tailor make them tonight, and tomorrow, when I come over we can—'

I stopped.

Julia looked behind her. 'What's the matter?'

In front of a towering column of the Forum, painted with graffiti and splattered with birds' droppings, dozens of infants were lying in baskets. Some of them were wailing pitifully, others were holding up their arms to mothers who would never come. 'What are these children doing here?' I cried.

'They're foundlings.' Julia made to keep walking, but I remained. 'You know,' she said in exasperation, 'children who aren't wanted.'

I looked to Gallia, who nodded sadly.

'You mean, they're just left here, to die?'

Julia shifted uneasily. 'There are wet nurses,' she pointed out. 'That's why they call this the Columna Lactaria.'

'But only some of the children are being fed!'

'Of course. How many wet nurses do you think there are who have nothing better to do with their day?'

I stared at the tired women who were leaning in the shade and doing their best to feed the crying infants. 'But what about the others?' I asked.

'They die. They aren't wanted, Selene.'

Gallia saw my look of horror, and added, 'Not all of them. Some are taken as slaves, and others will go to *lupanaria*.'

'So how is that any better than death?'

Gallia said quietly, 'Even in the most wretched life, there's hope.'

Nothing like the Columna Lactaria existed in Egypt. There were herbs for women who wanted to be rid of pregnancies that happened while their husbands were at sea, and there were childless couples who were willing to adopt from unmarried mothers. Gallia took my arm and steered me away, but that evening, I couldn't stop thinking about the abandoned children.

'What's the matter with you?' Alexander asked testily. 'You're supposed to be helping me with Homer.'

I put away my schoolwork and took out my sketch book. I wasn't in the mood for the *Iliad*.

'Selene, how am I supposed to do this alone?'

'You'll manage. It's not like we haven't read it all before in the Museion,' I said flatly.

My brother stared at me. 'Is this about the foundlings? Julia told me—'

'What?' I snapped. 'That she didn't look twice in their direction?'

Alexander held up his hands in a gesture for peace. 'I didn't know.'

'Well, you should. It was terrible, Alexander.' I blinked back my tears.

'There were children in baskets?' he asked.

'Everywhere. Just left out to die.'

'Surely not all of them—'

'No. Some of them become slaves. And the unlucky ones end up in a *lupanar*.'

'The Romans have strange laws, don't they?' he whispered.

There was a knock on the door, and I said angrily, 'Let's just pretend we're asleep.'

'Don't be ridiculous. There are two oil lamps burning.' He rose from his couch and opened the door, 'Antonia,' he said in surprise.

She looked down at her sandals. Even for a small girl, her feet were tiny. 'May I come in?' she asked. When Alexander scanned the hall behind her, she explained, 'My brother is not allowed to leave his room tonight.'

Alexander stepped aside, and Antonia entered and looked around our chamber.

'Not much like Egypt, is it?'

'Better than prison,' Alexander replied.

She smiled fleetingly, and her eyes came to rest on me. 'I heard you saw the Columna Lactaria today.' When I frowned, Antonia went on. 'Gallia told me. My mother and I go every day to help them. She pays new mothers to suckle the infants.'

'So that's why they do it?' I left my couch and sat on one of the embroidered chairs, indicating that Antonia should do the same.

She seated herself and nodded. 'Yes. Some do it out of pity because they've just lost children of their own. But most of the women have their own babies, and they do it for the denarii.' She looked at me, and I had the strange sensation that she was trying to read my face. 'Was our father charitable?' she asked quietly.

I glanced at Alexander.

'If that means emptying the treasury for his friends,' he said wryly, seating himself across from her on a chair.

Antonia looked at me, and when I offered no reversal, she pressed, 'So he didn't help the poor?'

'Only if they were part of his army. But he built villas,' I said. 'Spectacular villas along the coast.' I could see she wasn't satisfied with this, and I added, 'He was passionate. He loved to gamble, and race horses, and make friends.'

'So the two of you are more like him than I am,' she said, and there was the hint of resignation in her voice.

I cast around for something else to talk about. 'So why don't you study with us in the ludus?'

Antonia regarded me with her light eyes. 'Because I study with my mother by doing charity work.'

'But what do you learn?'

'More than I would by shopping with Julia,' she said softly.

Alexander laughed, but I tensed at the rebuke.

'Oh, I'm not surprised.' Antonia waved her hand. 'Everyone wants to be with her. She's Caesar's daughter. But my mother is as good a teacher as Magister Verrius. And when we aren't reciting poetry together, we're giving out bread in the Subura.'

My brother frowned. 'And you like it?'

'Of course.'

'So why does Marcellus go to the ludus?' I asked.

'Because he will be Caesar's heir. If he doesn't ruin it for himself,' she added.

Alexander leaned forward. 'You mean the Red Eagle?'

Antonia looked over her shoulder.

'We won't say anything,' I promised readily.

Antonia hesitated. 'Yes.'

'But do you really think he could be the rebel?' I exclaimed.

Antonia shook her head, and the ringlets that made her seem so young bounced over her shoulders. 'No. He's too rash. What interests him one day bores him the next. He doesn't have the patience to make so many plans.'

'But you think he could be helping him,' my brother prompted.

Antonia looked down at her small, painted nails. 'My mother says he is idealistic. Anything is possible. But even the mention of rebellion, and our uncle would send him to the island of Pandataria. *If* he was lucky.'

'Is that a punishment?' my brother asked.

She looked at him as though she couldn't believe he'd never

heard of it. 'Yes. Hundreds of men – and women – have been sent to islands to starve, to scrape in the dirt or support themselves by diving for sponges. It's better than being told to open your wrists,' she whispered, 'and that's what my mother says will happen to anyone who isn't useful to my uncle. Men, women, senators, matrons. Look at your parents.'

'Our mother died with the bite of a cobra,' I said sternly.

'It's still suicide. Livia's father, my mother's father, they were all forced to commit suicide. It's how your life ends in Rome,' she said. 'Unless you learn to be helpful in some way.'

'And how will you help?'

'I will marry who I'm told to for the good of Rome and be happy with it.'

'Even if you don't love him?' I exclaimed.

'Of course.' Antonia watched us with her wide eyes, and when neither of us said anything, she added, 'I hope you won't repeat anything I've said.'

'Of course not.' Alexander's voice was firm, and when Antonia stood to go, he asked quietly, 'Is this a warning?'

I could see her cheeks redden even in the low light of our chamber. 'I wasn't sent by anyone.'

'But this is your way of warning us,' he said.

Her silence was as good as a *yes*.

CHAPTER EIGHT

BEFORE THE sun had fully risen above the hills, I dressed myself in a light tunic and sandals.

'I don't know why you're doing this,' Alexander groaned into his pillow. 'It's still dark outside.'

'And this is the only time Vitruvius has for teaching me.'

'But what do you hope to learn? You know everything.'

I laughed, but quietly, so I wouldn't wake Marcellus in the room next to ours. 'Do you think I could build a temple myself?'

'Of course not,' he mumbled. 'That's what workers are for.'

'And how will I know if they're doing it right?'

Alexander opened his eyes to look at me. 'You don't really think you're going to build?'

'Why not?'

He lifted his head. 'Because we're not in Egypt anymore!'

'Someday we will be. And remember what Antonia said,' I warned. 'It might do you some good to get up and come with me.'

But he shook his head, and as he lay back down, I shut the door with more force than I intended. I made my way into the atrium, where clutches of lilies and sea daffodils trembled in the warm morning breeze. I could see candelabra burning in the library, and when I entered, Vitruvius motioned from his desk.

'Come in,' he said wearily, and indicated a chair opposite him. While I seated myself, I saw him watching me, studying the

Greek diadem in my hair, the Alexandrian pearls around my neck, and the Roman *bulla* below them. He heaved the weary sigh of a man whose patience has continually been tested, then folded his hands on the desk in front of him. 'In addition to the Temple of Apollo,' he began, 'which has taken up the better part of two years, I am working on Agrippa's Pantheon and Octavia's portico. Now I shall begin Caesar's mausoleum. That leaves me very little time for anything else.'

'I understand.'

His dark eyes found mine in the dim light. 'Do you?'

'Yes. You are tutoring me as a favor to Octavia. But I'm not here to take up your time. I'm here to help you conserve it.'

His brows shot up. 'And how is that?'

'By helping you design a mausoleum.' When I saw that he wanted to laugh, I added swiftly, 'I know how to draw. I've also learned which kinds of stone are appropriate for building and where to use them.'

'Black lavapesta?' he asked, to test me.

'Flooring. It can be trimmed with white tesserae.'

'Sarnus stone?'

'Flakes can be used on a ceiling to create the impression of an indoor cave.'

'Timber-framed rubble and mortar?'

I grinned. 'Houses too cheap to last the first winter.'

Vitruvius sat back and unfolded his hands. 'Where did you learn this?'

'In Alexandria. We could choose some of the subjects we wanted to study in the Museion, and I chose architecture.'

He watched me with interest. 'And you're determined, aren't you?'

'Yes. I know my drawings are pretty, but they aren't accurate. I want to be able to draw real plans.'

'That takes a knowledge of mathematics. Specifically geometry.'

'Which I've learned.'

'So why didn't your tutors show you how to apply it to building?' he asked.

'They would have, but my education in the Museion was cut short.' I didn't need to say why.

He sighed again, then held out his hand. 'Let's begin with the mausoleum.'

Immediately, I opened my book of sketches to the page with the best drawing of my mother's mausoleum. 'She built it entirely of white marble,' I said, passing my book to him. 'The floors had inlays of mother-of-pearl and the columns were carved into caryatids.'

He studied the image. 'You say it was built entirely of marble?'

I nodded.

'And was there something in front? A tall, pointed pillar?'

'Yes. Two obelisks. Both made of granite.'

Vitruvius took out a stylus and began to write quickly. 'What color were they?'

'Red. Why? Does Caesar want obelisks?'

'He wants exactly what he saw in Alexandria, with very few changes.'

'I can tell you everything,' I promised, and by that afternoon I was so full of my own success with Vitruvius that I didn't even mind when Julia insisted I paint her eyes exactly how my mother painted hers.

'I want to look like an Egyptian queen,' she said, sitting in my bathing room while Gallia painstakingly beaded her hair.

'You understand that before we go to the theater, Domina, all of these beads must be taken out?'

'Yes,' she said impatiently. 'But just this once . . . And then perhaps Selene can draw me.'

'I don't sketch people!'

'But you draw buildings,' she pointed out. 'And how else am I supposed to remember this?'

'I don't know. Look in the mirror.'

'Please,' she begged. 'I can't use a real painter. My father would find out. And after all this trouble Gallia's gone to.' She pouted, and when I looked at Gallia, I saw that I had no choice. Julia would only make Gallia do it over again until I agreed.

I fetched my book of sketches and cursed silently at the idea that one of my pages would have to be spent on Julia. And she would probably want to keep it as well, which would mean tearing a piece from the book.

'Will it be in color?' Julia asked when I returned.

'No. Black and white.'

'But how will I remember the faience beads and paint?'

'By using your imagination.' I twisted the cap off a bottle of ink and carefully dipped my reed pen inside.

Julia studied herself in the mirror while I drew.

'I should have been born in Egypt,' she said longingly. 'Then you would be me, and would have lost your kingdom.'

'But you're happy here, aren't you?' She looked back at me through a fringe of dark lashes, completely unaware of what Alexander and I had suffered.

Gallia clicked her tongue. 'She is a prisoner, domina.'

'But she's living in Octavia's villa,' Julia protested. 'She's going to the ludus and studying architecture.'

'In Rome,' Gallia rejoined. 'Her home is in Egypt.'

Julia sighed. '*My* home should have been in Egypt,' she repeated as Gallia strung the last bead onto her hair. She rose from her chair and studied herself in the polished bronze. 'No wonder you miss Alexandria,' she said thoughtlessly. The swath of violet silk she had purchased had been sewn into a pair of tunics, and while mine hung straight and shapeless as a stick, hers clung to the emerging curves of her body. I had combined red ochre with blue azurite to make a violet paint for her eyelids, and with the faience beads in her hair, she did look like a princess. 'Give me your diadem,' she said suddenly, and when I hesitated, she frowned. 'It's just for the sketch.'

I took off the pearl band that had once symbolized my right to rule over the kingdoms of Cyrenaica and Libya, and although Gallia's eyes narrowed with disapproval, I handed it to Julia.

She nestled it among her black curls. 'Is this how your mother looked?' she whispered.

I knew the answer she wanted. 'Yes.'

'And are you drawing the diadem?'

'If you stay still.'

'Should I sit or stand?'

I hesitated, looking down at my drawing. 'Keep standing. I'll include your sandals as well.'

I was surprised by how still she could be when she wanted something. She stood patiently while I drew the folds in her tunic, then turned quietly when I asked to see her beaded hair in profile. When at last I said, 'Finished,' she clapped her hands together.

'I want to see!' she exclaimed, and when I turned the book toward her, she drew in her breath. She looked first at Gallia, then at me. 'Am I really that beautiful?'

I set my jaw. 'Ink drawings are always flattering.'

'But you'll color it, won't you?'

'With what?'

'I'll have a slave send over paints. Look how beautiful it already is, and think how pretty it will be in color.'

A sharp knock on the door cut off my protest. 'Quick!' I cried. 'What if it's Octavia?'

But Julia didn't move. 'It isn't. It's Marcellus. Gallia,' she said merrily, 'let him in!'

I stared at Julia. 'How do you know?'

She smiled. 'Because I told him to come.'

Marcellus and Alexander entered, and when my brother saw Julia in my crown, he paused. 'Is that your diadem?'

'Just for a moment,' I said quickly.

Marcellus gave a low whistle, and Julia turned for him.

'Well, what do you think?' she asked.

'As beautiful as Selene.'

Julia's eyes flashed angrily in my direction. 'You mean you think we look alike?'

'Of course. I mean no. You're the most beautiful princess of all!' But he winked at me when he said it, and I felt a strange fluttering in my chest.

She grinned. 'And what do you think of my paints?'

'I hope they wash off,' he said seriously. 'Because my mother is coming.'

Julia gave a small shriek of terror, then pushed my diadem at me and fled back into the bathing room. 'Hurry!' she cried. 'The beads!'

Marcellus laughed while Julia scrubbed at her face. 'What did you think would happen?' he asked.

'She's supposed to be doing charity work in the Subura. Don't just stand there. Help!'

The four of us rushed to take off the beads, and Gallia hid them in a small jar next to my couch.

'Not with Selene,' Julia complained. 'I want them!'

'You should keep them here until my mother leaves,' Marcellus suggested. 'Everything makes her suspicious lately.'

Julia's voice was resentful. 'What do you mean?'

Both Alexander and I caught Marcellus's uneasy glance at Gallia. 'Something about the Red Eagle,' he said.

'What? Does she think he's hiding in a jar?'

'No. But trust me, it's better this way.'

Octavia opened the door to our chamber, then stepped back when she saw the five of us together. 'Gallia, what is this?'

'They are preparing for the theater, domina,' she said lightly.

'Do you like my tunic?' Julia asked. She spun around, and there was no evidence on her face that she had been wearing red ochre just a few moments before.

'Is that a new purchase?' Octavia frowned.

'Yesterday. Selene has one as well. There's enough material for Antonia, if you like.'

Octavia smiled thinly. 'Thank you, but I think something more modest suits her better.'

Julia wasn't offended. 'So what play are we going to see?'

'*Amphitruo*,' Octavia replied, her eyes searching the room as if she could sense that something was amiss.

'And do you know who's coming?' Marcellus asked, taking her arm and steering her from our chamber.

'Agrippa, Juba, Maecenas, Terentilla. And, Julia, you'll be happy to know that Horatia will probably be there with Pollio.'

Marcellus glanced back at Julia, and his look was pitying.

'Why? Who's Horatia?' my brother asked.

Julia's gaze narrowed. 'She used to go to the ludus with us. But Livia arranged her marriage last year.'

'So what's wrong with that?'

'Her husband is a disgusting old man – and she was only thirteen.'

I exchanged a look with Alexander as we left the chamber. 'Why would Livia do that?' he asked nervously.

'Because Horatia was my closest friend. She even taught me to swim,' Julia whispered, and her eyes shone with tears.

'And for that she arranged a terrible marriage?'

'She would have arranged a marriage with Cerberus if he had been available. And now Horatia's pregnant with an old merchant's child.'

We reached the portico, where half a dozen curtained litters were waiting, and I shared one with Julia. We had taken an early meal in the triclinium, and the setting sun burnished our curtains red and gold.

'If I were a better person,' Julia said suddenly, 'I would never have let you paint my face.'

'Why?'

'Because if Livia ever discovered it, she would do the same thing to you.'

I sat straighter against the cushions. 'I would never let that happen.'

Julia laughed mirthlessly. 'There'd be nothing you could do. Even Octavia can't change my father's mind once it's made up. And Livia's there all the time,' she added, 'whispering into his ear like Boreas.' I wondered how she knew about the Greek god of the north wind, and before I could ask, Julia said sharply, 'I'm not a complete fool. I listen.' We rode the rest of the way in silence, and when we reached the Campus Martius and the litters stopped, Julia explained, 'We walk from here. My father thinks it looks better to the plebs if we arrive on foot.'

When the six slaves lowered our litter to the ground, I parted the curtains and was helped up by Marcellus. He saw the look on my face and asked, 'A happy ride with Julia, then?'

'You wouldn't understand,' Julia said accusingly.

'Oh, cheer up. Can you remember the last time we went to the theater?'

'Before my father left for Egypt.'

'That's right. And even if Horatia is married to Pot-Bellied Pollio, at least she has the denarii to come.'

'If she had any sense, she'd use it to buy poison for him.'

Marcellus shrugged. 'He'll be dead before she's twenty-five. And then she can remarry.'

'The two of you are disgusting,' Tiberius said.

I hadn't noticed that he was walking behind us with his younger brother. Julia didn't bother to turn around, but Marcellus said swiftly, 'Perhaps your mother can marry you off to some old matron with a sagging *cunnus,* and we can see how you'd like it.'

Seeing my look, Alexander cut his laughter short. 'Octavian is in front of us,' I said in Parthian. 'And everyone else.' Twenty soldiers were escorting us to the theater, and Octavian was flanked by Agrippa and Juba. Their long togas flapped in the late summer's breeze, but beneath them, I could see the shadow of chain mail. Immediately, my brother sobered.

We passed beneath a stunning marble arch into the theater, where terraced stone benches had been built into the hill. Behind them stretched a polished mosaic depicting the masks of comedy and tragedy. On either side of the theater were well-tended gardens and colonnades. Everything looked new, or at least well-preserved. 'When was this built?' I asked Marcellus.

'Twenty-five years ago.'

'By whom?'

'Pompey. He was Julius's great rival. Stone theaters were forbidden in Rome, so he built this outside the walls, and even then the people complained. So he added a temple.' I followed his gaze to the Temple of Venus, perched above the seats of the theater. 'Notice how the seats are arranged?' he asked. 'They're supposed to look like a grand staircase to the temple.' He laughed. 'It's how he convinced them to build. The workers were afraid of angering the gods! Can you imagine such foolishness?' He had spoken too loudly, and his mother turned. Marcellus lowered his voice. 'And that's where Julius Caesar was killed.' He pointed to the rear of the theater.

'I thought he was murdered in the Senate,' Alexander said.

'Sometimes the Senate would meet here in the Curia.'

'That's why my father thinks it's bad luck here,' Julia said suddenly. 'And why he takes so many soldiers.'

I saw no sign of Octavian's nervousness as we approached the padded benches that had been reserved for us in the first row. Instead, he chatted with Terentilla, and I could see from the look on Livia's face that a storm was about to break. As I took my place between Alexander and Octavia, I heard Livia suggest, 'Perhaps we women should set an example for the rest of Rome and take our seats in the upper tiers.' When Octavian looked uncertain, she continued, 'You are Caesar now. Women are not allowed to sit with men in the stadia. Why should it be allowed in the theater?'

'Because we are the ruling family of Rome,' Octavia said, over-ruling her, 'and we know how to conduct ourselves in public.'

'My sister is right. Octavia is an example to all of Rome for charity and virtue. As are you,' Octavian amended.

'And Terentilla?' Livia asked him with a sweetness that was terrifying. 'Is she a part of this family?'

Octavian set his jaw. 'Anyone married to Maecenas is family.'

A young girl was coming toward us, holding her swollen belly, and suddenly Livia's mood brightened considerably. 'Horatia!'

The girl did her best to return Livia's smile. Her seat was next to Julia's, on the farthest end of the bench, but she stopped before Octavian to greet him properly.

'Caesar, it is good to see you in fine health.'

'And you,' he said briefly. 'So where is Pollio, your husband?'

'Speaking with a merchant, I believe.'

Octavian appeared displeased. 'Doing business in the theater?'

'He would do business underwater in the baths if he thought he could make money,' she said with resignation. 'I hope you enjoy the show.'

I inhaled the warm scent of lavender as she passed, and when Pollio appeared, I held my breath.

'Is that him?' Alexander whispered in Parthian.

'It must be,' I replied.

He waddled between the stage and the bench, shaking hands with everyone. His fingers were weighed down with heavy gold rings, and when he came to Juba, he held up his hands. 'The Prince of Numidia,' he announced louder than he needed. 'Do I shake hands, or bow?'

Juba glanced at Octavian. 'I believe we only bow for royalty, Pollio, and as yet, I am not the king of any kingdom.'

Pollio held out his fat hand, and Juba took it without enthusiasm.

'Livia' – Pollio breathed the word like a prayer – 'you put Venus to shame.'

The blatancy of the lie made Octavian frown, but Livia beamed. 'And you could flatter the thunderbolts from Jupiter,' she said.

Pollio moved to Octavian but didn't attempt to shake his hand. 'Caesar.'

'I hear you are conducting business in the theater. Does this look like a market?'

'Of course not. Forgive me.'

'You are a very wealthy man. But that wealth comes from grain contracts granted by Rome. This is not the Forum. If you confuse it again,' Octavian said simply, 'you will find yourself without any business at all.'

As Pollio passed, I whispered to Octavia, 'Is it an offense to conduct business in a place of entertainment?'

'No, but Julius Caesar used to do business when he came to the theater, and it angered the plebs. The people must not come to associate this place with patrician wealth.'

The orchestra began to play, and I glanced down the row at Tiberius, who was telling Vipsania something to make her laugh. On the other side of him, Octavia's daughters were sitting silently, and I wondered if they had ever done anything in their lives that displeased their mother.

A thin actor in a toga came onstage through the curtained doorway. 'We begin tonight as we begin all nights,' he said. 'With a speech!' Several members in the crowd booed, and the actor smiled. 'Perhaps you naysayers would like to give our orator a challenging topic, then?'

Alexander grinned at me. 'Is he joking?'

'No. I think this is really what they do.'

Several members of the audience shouted, 'Athens!' Another shouted, 'Make him talk about the beauty of baldness.' And when one called out, 'The Battle of Actium,' I clenched my jaw. 'How about the value of a cheating wife?' someone suggested, and the actor clapped his hands. 'We have a subject!'

I looked at Octavian, who seemed to be enjoying himself.

A fat orator appeared from the left of the stage. 'The value of being a cuckold,' he began, and the entire audience descended into laughter. 'When the horns of cuckoldry grow on your head, think of all the uses they might have. You can defend yourself without a sword.' He made the motion of charging, and the audience laughed again. 'You could impale your enemies – or scratch an itch.' He rubbed his head on his flabby shoulder. 'There are a thousand uses for a horned man. Not to mention a horny woman.' He went on to extol the virtues of a well-practiced wife, but as he went on to say that men would have fewer duties at the end of a long day, audience members groaned and someone shouted, 'Bring on the bear!'

'I'm not finished,' the orator said angrily, but this only inspired the drunken men to further chants.

'Bring on the bear! Bring on the bear!'

I turned to Octavia. 'Is there really a bear?'

She laughed. 'No. There used to be bears in these theaters. They could do tricks, but they became too dangerous and my brother forbade them.'

'So what do they want?'

'For him to get off the stage and let the play begin.'

The actor who'd introduced the orator came out, and the fat man was led offstage to jeers and hisses.

'I thought he was good,' Alexander said sadly.

Next, the stage was filled with dancing nymphs. Two men appeared in the long-bearded masks of satyrs, and already the audience was laughing. One pranced, the other skipped, and a third masked man entered with a bow and arrow. The first satyr began to recite his lines, and as the third man pointed his arrow toward the audience, I realized what was happening.

'Octavian!' I screamed before I could stop myself, and suddenly Juba was on top of him, pushing him to the ground. The actor's arrow whistled through the air, shattering as it struck the stone bench where Octavian had been sitting.

'In the name of the Red Eagle!' the masked bowman shouted.

Then pandemonium broke out.

Soldiers rushed the stage, but the actor was already gone, and people began fleeing from their seats. Soldiers made a tight ring around us, pushing us toward the exit.

Alexander took my arm. 'How did you know?'

'I saw him nock the arrow.'

MICHELLE MORAN | 189

'But he was just an actor!'

There was the same panic in the air as there had been at the Circus – only this time, someone had tried to assassinate Caesar in the front row of the theater. Outside, there was no time to arrange litters. A cavalcade of heavily armed soldiers escorted us to the Palatine, and I could feel Julia's fear as she pressed my hand. If her father had been killed, everything would have been lost: her villa on the Palatine, her marriage to Marcellus, the succession.

Octavian walked swiftly between Agrippa and Juba, and no one said anything, not even the passersby on the streets. When we reached his villa, he led us into the library. Slaves rushed to light the candelabra, and when they were finished Agrippa locked the heavy metal doors. Juba poured cups of wine, and, for the first time, I heard Octavia weep.

'This Red Eagle,' Octavian said, breaking the silence, 'is now an assassin.'

'I doubt this was the Red Eagle. He spoke with a Gallic accent,' Agrippa said.

'So what stops this rebel from being a slave?' Livia shrieked.

'Look at his acta,' Juba said. 'Are those the writings of a slave?'

'Then what are you saying?' Livia demanded, looking from face to face. 'That this had nothing to do with that rebel?'

Silence fell over the group again, until Agrippa said, 'Yes. This was a slave hoping to share in the Red Eagle's glory.'

Octavian's gray eyes flashed. 'There is no glory in being a traitor,' he warned.

'Of course not. But to the slaves—'

'Tell me, what would happen if I had been killed?'

There was an uneasy shifting in the room.

'Juba,' Octavian said darkly, 'why don't you tell us? You're well versed in history. What would happen to Rome?'

'The thirty tribes would go back to fighting,' Juba predicted. 'They would not accept Marcellus as heir, since he is too young, and the Senate would not accept Agrippa, since he is a descendant of freedmen.'

'There would be chaos,' Octavian promised. 'Instead of going forward, Rome would go backward. It may not have been the Red Eagle tonight, but the man is inspiring rebellion. And there are slaves and freedmen who are covering for him! A man doesn't post a hundred acta without being seen!' He had begun to shout. 'So perhaps we should see what our poor freedmen would rather have. Freedom, or food.'

Octavia gasped.

'We will stop the grain dole for ten days,' he commanded. 'Tell them I must use the denarii to hire personal guards.'

'But hundreds will die!' Octavia cried.

Her brother sat back. 'No one has ever died of a little hunger. Men can go for weeks without food.'

'Not the elderly! Not the sick children!'

'Then perhaps they should have thought of that before they helped a traitor,' Livia snapped. 'This will turn the people against him,' she said eagerly, 'and remind these freedmen why they will always need Caesar.'

Agrippa looked distinctly uncomfortable.

But Octavian was satisfied with his decision. 'When they find the bowman, crucify him.' He stood, and that was our signal to leave. Agrippa unbolted the door and held it open. As we left, Octavian called my name.

I turned, and my heart thundered in my chest.

But Octavian was neither smiling nor angry. 'You surprise me,' was all he said.

CHAPTER NINE

OUTSIDE, SOLDIERS surrounded Octavia's villa, and there was no house on the Palatine that wasn't under guard in case the assassin should reappear. As we entered the villa, Alexander and Marcellus spoke in hurried whispers about the assassination attempt. Then Octavia stopped suddenly.

'Where is Gallia?'

'I saw her with Magister Verrius at the bottom of the hill,' Antonia replied.

'And what was she doing with him?'

'Talking. I don't think she expected us back so soon.'

I looked at Octavia and saw the lines deepen between her brows. Perhaps Gallia wasn't adept at writing Latin, but Magister Verrius certainly was. What if they were writing the acta together? Verrius knew what it was like to be a slave. He was a freedman himself, though he never talked about his childhood with us in the ludus.

Marcellus looked from me to his mother. 'What is it?'

'Nothing,' she said sternly, dismissing us with a wave. 'Go to your chambers.' But as I moved to go, she held me back with her hand. She waited until everyone had left before saying, 'You saved my brother tonight.'

'I didn't do anything. It was Juba.'

'But you saw it first.' Her eyes searched mine in the torch-lit atrium. 'How did you know?'

'I saw him nock the arrow. Then his muscles tensed like he would really set it free.'

Octavia nodded, and her eyes filled with tears. 'Why?'

I knew what she was asking. Why had I called Octavian's name when his assassination could have meant my freedom? What had changed between the Triumph and today? I pressed my lips together and considered my answer before speaking. 'Because he is our future,' I said carefully, and there was nothing I needed to explain. Without him, who knew what would happen to Alexander and me? And if another senator made himself Caesar, what would become of Octavia? Who would feed the poor and bring clothes to the Subura? There would be more bloodshed, more civil war, and the abandoned infants beneath the Columna Lactaria would be food for Rome's dogs.

'I am thankful to the gods for you, Selene.'

I flushed.

'Will you do an errand for me?'

'Of course.'

She took out a key and unlocked the doors to the library. The room was still unbearably warm, heavy with the scents of leather and papyrus. Moonlight silvered the marble busts on the shelves, and Octavia went to one of these statues and took it down. She studied the face by the light of a distant torch. The subject was a handsome man, with a strong jaw and a heavily curled beard. I thought it might be a statue of Zeus, but Octavia said quietly, 'This is Juba's father. I should have given the statue to Juba years ago, but I didn't. Tonight, Juba saved my brother's life. I want you to take this to him.'

My heart sank. I would have happily gone anywhere in Rome. But why did it have to be to Juba's villa? There were a hundred slaves who might have delivered this gift for her, even Gallia, once she returned, and I wondered why Octavia was choosing me. She placed the marble bust in my arms, and because it was smaller than all of the others, it wasn't heavy. She guided me to the door. Although it was dark, the road was lit by hundreds of torches as soldiers patrolled up and down the hill. When I hesitated, she explained, 'My brother's men are everywhere. The Palatine is safe.'

A few of the soldiers nodded in my direction, and I recognized some of them as the guards who followed us to the ludus and back every morning. When I knocked on the door of Juba's villa, the slave who answered glared down at me. He was an older man, with thick hair that had completely silvered, and his face was distinguished.

'Yes?' he demanded.

'I have come with a gift.'

'Dominus does not wish to see anyone right now.'

'But I come from Octavia.' I craned my neck to see inside, and when I tried to step around him, he moved to block my entry.

'No one enters this house tonight.'

'I am coming from Octavia with a bust of Juba's father! What's the matter with you?'

Suddenly, Juba appeared behind him, and the man shook his head in frustration. 'She will not listen, domine.'

'I'm not surprised, Sergius. She rarely listens to anyone,' Juba replied.

Sergius pursed his lips, as if he was personally offended by this, and I purposefully stepped around him. 'I have come with a gift.' I raised my chin.

'So I see. And who am I to thank for this?' Juba asked, taking the bust of his father and passing it carelessly to Sergius.

'Octavia,' I said, 'and she did not give this lightly. Aren't you even going to look at it?'

'I know what it is. A marble of Juba I, King of Numidia.'

'And aren't you grateful to have a portrait of your father?'

Juba smiled. 'Exceptionally grateful. Please relay all of the thanks you so clearly feel on my behalf.' He motioned to the slave to shut the door, but as he stepped away I looked across the atrium, and through the open doors of the library I could see tables upon tables covered in scrolls.

'What are those?' I whispered.

Juba looked behind him, and I was sure I saw his face grow a little pale.

I stepped inside, and this time, neither man made to block my way. 'Perhaps you aren't thankful because you have something to hide.'

'Nonsense!' Sergius said angrily, but Juba raised his brows.

'Wait. Let's hear what she thinks I am hiding.'

The two men looked down at me. One was a prince, the other a slave, but both of them were larger, much more powerful than I. 'Nothing,' I said hastily.

But Juba held out his arm so that I couldn't move, and his black eyes held mine in a piercing glare. 'You looked into my library and announced that I was hiding something. Sergius, why don't you show the princess inside?'

Sergius sighed audibly, then took my arm and guided me across the atrium. In the library, the tables were filled with scrolls, just as I had seen, but on every table was a different colored map. 'Dominus is writing a history of the world,' he said. 'Are you happy now?'

Juba stood behind me, and I could feel his eyes boring into my back. 'There it is. All of my secrets laid out before you. What's the matter, Selene? Were you expecting something else?'

'Not at all,' I lied, and my gaze fell upon a map of Egypt. 'I'm simply wondering why you've added a temple next to the theater of Alexandria when there isn't any,' I said smugly.

But Juba smiled. 'Perhaps there wasn't one before, but there's going to be one now.'

I glanced back at the map. 'Next to the theater?' I cried.

'That is Caesar's wish. Now, if you'll excuse me,' he said, 'I have *secrets* to attend to.'

When I returned to the villa, I didn't see Octavia, but Marcellus and Alexander rose from their chairs as soon as I entered my chamber. I was surprised to see they were both still up.

'Where have you been?' Alexander exclaimed, and the oil lamps flickered in his wake.

'Octavia wanted me to deliver a statue.'

'To Juba?' Marcellus guessed. 'She's been meaning to give him his father's bust for years, but she couldn't part with it. It's a very rare statue, by a sculptor who made very few pieces in his life.'

'And it belonged to Juba?'

Marcellus nodded. 'He was brought to Rome when he was two or three. So up until then, I suppose it was his.'

'But why would Octavia send *you*?' Alexander asked.

'I don't know,' I said defensively, sitting down on my couch and opening my book to an empty page. 'Perhaps it was a punishment.'

Marcellus laughed. 'After tonight? I doubt it. Why? Was he in a foul mood?'

'Isn't he always? He was working on his history of the world.'

'He wants to create a complete history of every kingdom,' Marcellus explained. 'Chart their lands, record their languages, study their people. Perhaps she sent you because she thought it would mean more.'

I drew up my knees and blushed at the thought that I'd been willing to believe that Juba was the Red Eagle. *Everything belongs to Caesar*, he'd told me. Especially him. He would be the last person on the Palatine to betray Rome. Even Agrippa would defy Octavian before Juba would. But I didn't want to think about him anymore. While Marcellus and Alexander whispered over candelight about what had happened in the theater, I took out my ink and stylus and sketched a two-storied building instead. I added frescoed walls and mosaic flooring, and enough rooms to shelter more than three hundred children. When Marcellus stood up to go, he leaned over my shoulder.

'What are you drawing?'

'A building.'

'May I see?'

I held out my sketch. From the outside, it was just like any other building. But the images I had drawn for the chambers inside should have made it clear what it was supposed to be.

'An inn?' he asked uncertainly. 'But why would an inn need so many beds?'

Alexander peered over his shoulder and asked, 'Is this for the foundlings?'

I took my sketch from Marcellus's hands. 'They can't just be left beneath the Columna Lactaria! Think how many must die of exposure. It's a terrible practice.'

'It is.' Marcellus nodded. 'But how would it help to shelter them in a building?'

'Adoptions could be arranged.'

'And the ones who aren't adopted?' he asked.

'Then they can be given to the temples and raised as *akolouthoi*.'

Marcellus frowned.

'Helpers,' my brother said.

'And eventually priests and priestesses,' I added.

Marcellus studied me, and the tenderness in his eyes made my heart beat faster. 'It's a wonderful idea, Selene. And if I ever become Caesar, I will see that it's done.'

'Really?'

'Why not? You're like my mother,' he said. 'You only want what's best for people.' He opened the door to leave, and I was surprised that Octavia hadn't already come in and sent us to bed. Perhaps she was with her brother or Vitruvius.

When Marcellus left, Alexander looked sternly at me. 'Don't think it. He's meant for Julia, Selene.'

'I'm not thinking anything!'

'Yes, you were. And you might as well stop it.'

He blew out the lamp and fell asleep. But I was still awake when a window slowly opened next door. There was a dull thud as something hit the ground outside. I raced to our balcony and threw back the curtains in time to see Marcellus disappear-ing into the darkness. What could he be thinking, with so many of his uncle's guards outside? Perhaps they were in his pay. So far as I knew, word had never reached Octavian about our trip to the Temple of Isis or what Marcellus had told the centurion. But I wondered where he could be going that was worth the risk.

When I entered the library the next morning, Vitruvius studied me with an interested gaze.

'I hear you saved Caesar's life yesterday.'

Heat crept into my cheeks. 'It was Juba who saved him.'

'But you sounded the alarm. You are very quick. And that's why someone as sharp as you will be able to understand this.' He unfurled a long scroll and laid it on the table in front of me.

'Octavian's mausoleum,' I said.

Vitruvius nodded.

Octavian had wanted something as impressive as my mother's tomb in Alexandria, with tall marble columns and a towering dome. But even though the sketch had a similar dome and the mausoleum was surrounded by a round columned portico, the building lacked the grandness of my mother's mausoleum. It was raised above the ground on a circular platform that would probably be made of limestone, with a flight of steps sweeping from the bottom to the top. The stairs were flanked by a pair of red granite obelisks, and although there was simple elegance to it, no one would ever stop in amazement as people had done in Alexandria. I looked up from the sketch to Vitruvius and guessed, 'You have made something simple that won't insult the plebs. Because right now he's afraid of assassination, and of appearing too powerful, like Julius Caesar.'

Vitruvius smiled. 'Indeed. Perhaps last night was the work of a lone man, or perhaps the assassin was really with this traitor the freedmen have taken to calling the Red Eagle. Either way, the people are angry.'

'What will Caesar do?'

'What *can* he do?' Vitruvius rolled up the scroll. 'Enough attempts and the plebs will begin to believe that Caesar is a tyrant. He can build the grandest stadia and baths in Rome, but for himself, it must be something simple.'

'But will he like it?'

'He appeared to like it very much when I showed it to him this morning.'

'He was up?'

'He is always up. Pacing, writing, preparing speeches for the Senate.'

'And will you show me how you executed this?' There were measurements next to every wall shown in the sketch, and near the stairs there were equations I couldn't understand.

'I'm afraid I don't have time for a lesson today.' When he saw my disappointment, he added, 'But in a few days I shall. Until then, these are the chambers inside the mausoleum.' He handed me a scroll on which he'd drawn empty rooms, labeling each one with its dimensions next to it. 'Furnish them,' he said simply. 'Add mosaics, caryatids, fountains. The plebs will only see the outside, so the furnishings can be as lavish as you want. And if I like what you've drawn, I may incorporate it in the final construction.'

I was shocked by the trust Vitruvius was placing in me. 'Thank you,' I said, and Vitruvius smiled. 'These will be my best sketches,' I promised him. I rolled the scroll carefully.

As I was leaving, Vitruvius added, 'Rome is proud of you. Caesar will not forget what you've done.'

I turned. 'Do you think it means that Alexander and I will be sent back to Egypt?'

Vitruvius hesitated. 'Caesar has sent a prefect to rule Egypt in his place.'

'But he could be recalled.'

'He could.' His voice didn't offer much hope. 'But before that would ever happen, Caesar will want to arrange your marriages. You must be very careful these next few years, Selene. You have seen Caesar at his most merciful,' he said quietly. 'But when they find this bowman, he will be crucified. And whoever helped him to get on stage, even if it was Terentilla herself, will die with him.'

I nodded. 'I'll be careful,' I promised.

'And watchful.'

I began by being watchful in the ludus. When Magister Verrius read passages from the *Iliad,* I noticed how he lingered on the passages that described Hector's wife and children, who were sold into slavery. He described Hector's fight as heroic, his death as valiant, and the sacking of his city as the greatest tragedy, since its inhabitants would lose, if not their lives, then their freedom. The longer he spoke about the bitterness of slavery, the more convinced I became that he could be the Red Eagle and that Marcellus was helping him.

Antonia had seen him with Gallia on the Palatine, and while it was possible that Gallia was writing the acta alone, it seemed far more probable that someone with access to supplies of papyrus and ink was behind them; someone whose presence on the Palatine would never be questioned, who had a quick wit and a reason to be angry. And if Verrius and Gallia were lovers, wouldn't that be reason enough to rebel against slavery? Slaves were not allowed to marry unless freed, and on a magister's salary, he could never afford a Gallic princess's freedom.

That afternoon, I studied Gallia as she mended a tunic on the portico at the Campus Martius. She didn't appear worried that someone might approach her with evidence of treachery. Although, when Marcellus announced that it was time for us to go to the Circus Maximus and Juba suddenly appeared at her side, I could see she was surprised. 'Are you coming with us?' she asked Juba.

'Those are Caesar's orders.'

'But we already have guards,' Julia complained. 'Why do we need more?'

'Perhaps you would rather stay at home,' Juba suggested. 'There's nowhere as safe as your own chamber.'

Julia narrowed her eyes, and as we made our way to the Circus she grumbled, 'Now we can't do anything.'

'What do you mean?'

'Juba is here. My father and he are like Romulus and Remus.'

'Didn't Romulus *kill* Remus?' Alexander asked warily.

'You know what I mean!' Julia said irritably. Behind us, Gallia and Juba were walking together, their heads bent in quiet conversation. 'Everything we do will get back to him now. At least Gallia is a slave and knows enough to keep silent.'

I glanced behind me, hoping Gallia hadn't heard what she'd said. 'And what about the guards who always follow us?' I asked. 'Don't they report back to your father?'

'Of course not,' Marcellus answered. 'We pay them.'

'You mean bribery?' my brother exclaimed.

'Just a few denarii. And only when I've gambled too much, or visited a place I shouldn't have.' He winked at my brother, and I wondered if he could mean a *lupanar.*

When we approached the Circus, a large crowd was gathered around the entrance, and Juba said sternly, 'What is this?' He pushed his way to the front and the people fell away from him. 'Another actum?' he shouted. 'Who did this?' Suddenly, no one was interested anymore, and Juba grabbed the closest man by the arm. 'When was this placed on the door?'

The man shook his head. 'I don't know.' He trembled. 'I saw it here this morning after we opened.'

'And no one took it down? Do you understand the penalty for supporting a rebel?'

'It – it isn't support,' he stammered. '*I* certainly don't support it.'

'Then why is it up here?'

'I don't know. I just place bets. I don't patrol the gates.'

Juba ripped down the scroll, and Marcellus stepped forward tentatively.

'May I see it?'

I thought that Juba would refuse, but he shoved the scroll at Marcellus, and we all gathered around. It was written in the same neat handwriting as the previous actum I'd seen, only this time the writer was denouncing the attempted assassination of Octavian, warning that bloodshed would only result in further bloodshed, and that rulers had as much right to a long life as slaves. He reminded his readers that Spartacus had failed, and that no rebellion could ever hope to achieve what votes of conscience by senators could. Then he went on to deride Octavian's punishment of the plebs, promising riots in the Subura once the people began to starve. And there was more – something about helping slaves across the Mare Superum to their homelands. But Juba took back the scroll.

'That's enough. You came here to watch the races. So let's watch them.' He handed the crumpled actum to Gallia, who made it disappear into a beautifully embroidered bag at her side. I was always fascinated to see her clothing, including the embellished bags that no other slave ever carried. But Gallia was Octavia's favorite.

We climbed to the seats reserved for Caesar's family, and when Juba had settled into conversation with Gallia, Marcellus whispered, 'I wonder why this rebel is willing to criticize my uncle, but opposes assassination?'

'Probably because if your uncle died, it wouldn't be the patricians who'd suffer most, but the plebs,' I guessed. 'The rich will always find something to eat. It's the slaves and freedmen who would starve.'

'Do you really think there will be riots?' Julia asked.

'I should think so,' Marcellus replied, keeping his eye on the bet-maker below us. When the man looked in our direction, Marcellus waved him over, taking out a purse full of denarii. 'But they won't be for long. Just as the freedmen are regretting their support of the Red Eagle and feeling hungry, the Ludi Romani will be here to distract them.'

'So you agree with their punishment?' I exclaimed.

'Of course not. But that's what my uncle is thinking.' Marcellus passed the bet maker his purse and said shrewdly, 'The Greens. I hear they have purchased new horses.'

'That's right. Twenty new stallions. All from Arabia.'

Alexander smiled, and I knew at once that he'd been the one to procure this information. 'The Greens,' he said as well, and I gasped at the size of his purse. 'I've been winning,' he explained. 'So what are the Ludi Romani?'

'You haven't heard about the Ludi?' Julia cried. 'They're only the biggest games on earth.'

'We had our own games,' I said tersely.

'Well, the Ludi Romani go on for fifteen days. Chariot races, gladiatorial events, theatrical performances . . .' She glanced uneasily at Juba. 'Perhaps we won't be going to those.'

'And you think your father will want to celebrate after an attempt to assassinate him?' I asked.

'Oh, it's not a celebration,' Marcellus said. 'It's a tradition. Cancelling the Ludi would be like cancelling . . .' He searched for the right word.

'The month of June,' Julia said helpfully.

'Or deciding there will be no more Saturnalia. Besides, it keeps the people happy. All work is stopped on those days, and everyone comes with food and circus padding.'

Alexander wrinkled his nose. 'What is that?'

Marcellus pointed to the bottom of the Circus, where men were carrying thick mats made of rushes. 'Their seats aren't covered like ours.'

Trumpets blared, and as the announcer signaled the start of the race, the gates were raised and chariots thundered onto the tracks. Julia and Alexander yelled themselves hoarse with Marcellus, and I took out my book, opening to the sketches

Vitruvius had given me of Octavian's mausoleum. He wanted designs for inside the building, and, in all likelihood, nothing I produced would be used. But I was determined to surprise him. I would sketch such handsome designs that he would find them irresistible. Perhaps there were other architects he employed who were decades older than me but none of them had lived in Alexandria and seen what the Ptolemies had accomplished. None of them had studied in the Museion, or dedicated years to sketching the most beautiful marble caryatids and mosaics in the world. When I took out my ink and stylus, I noticed that Juba was watching me.

'Sketching a new Rome?' he asked.

'It's a commission.'

'Really? So you are being paid?'

'No. I am doing it to be helpful.'

Juba smiled. 'Such a charitable nature, and not even twelve. Soon you'll be passing out bread with Octavia.'

'I noticed you thanking her this morning,' I retorted. 'So you *did* appreciate the gift.'

He raised his brows. 'Of course. It's the only portrait I have of my father.'

I clenched my jaw, determined not to be goaded by him any longer, and for the rest of afternoon, I made sure he couldn't see what I was drawing.

CHAPTER TEN

ON THE seventh day without the dole, there were riots in the Subura. Although it came as no surprise to anyone but Octavia, the people began breaking into shops, stealing food from vendors in the streets, and setting fire to taverns that refused to defer charges. As we sat in the triclinium eating oysters and thrushes, listening to sweet tones played by a slave girl on the harp, the Subura tore at itself like a rabid wolf. The hungry masses devoured anything that crossed their path – chickens, dogs, even cats. On the eighth night, when a soldier interrupted our meal to announce that a pleb had given up the bowman from the theater, I caught the triumphant look in Octavian's eyes.

'Reinstate the dole tomorrow,' he said. 'Remind the people that I am paying for their grain with my own denarii, and tell them I have sold my statues to buy them food.'

The soldier smiled. 'Certainly, Caesar.'

'And the criminal?' he asked, almost as though it were an afterthought.

'One of your slaves. A kitchen boy, I believe.'

Octavian grew very still. 'Kitchen *boy*, or a man?'

'Sixteen.'

'And you are sure that it's him?'

'He escaped from the Palatine three weeks ago, and the

plebs seem very certain. Even if it wasn't, he's still a runaway.'

Agrippa rose angrily. 'Well is it him, or isn't it?'

'It is,' the soldier said with more confidence. Octavian's decree that slaves could not purchase weapons hadn't mattered. There would always be dealers willing to sell anything for the right price.

'Whip him through the streets,' Octavian said. 'And tomorrow, crucify him next to the Forum.'

Octavia gasped, pressing her silk napkin delicately to her lips, only this time she didn't protest.

'But how do they know the plebs aren't lying, hoping he'll bring back the dole?' I whispered.

Marcellus's usually bright cheeks had grown pale. 'It's possible.'

'And if they tortured him,' Julia pointed out, 'he might confess to anything.'

Octavian didn't appear concerned. He reclined on his couch and continued making notes for his next speech in the Senate. But I couldn't stop thinking of the kitchen boy who'd been condemned to death, and the next day, after our time on the Campus Martius, I persuaded Juba to allow us to go to the Forum.

'To see a dead man?' Julia complained as we made our way there. 'What's the purpose?'

'I want to know if it's really him,' I said.

'And if it isn't?'

'She just wants to know,' Marcellus said. 'I'd like to know as well.'

'There will be no interfering with justice,' Juba warned darkly. He was speaking to all of us, but he looked at me when he said it.

'We understand,' Marcellus replied. 'We just want to go and see.'

Julia sighed heavily, and we walked the remaining distance to the Forum in silence, trailed by Juba and Gallia. When we arrived, there was no mistaking what was about to happen. Hundreds of Roman soldiers stood outside the Senate, shields at the ready and armed with swords. The red plumes of their helmets drooped in the sun, and I imagined how hot the men must be beneath their armor. But none of them moved. Only their eyes roamed the Forum, searching for possible rebels in the crowd.

'All of this, for an execution?' Alexander exclaimed.

'The rebel's supporters might try to save him,' Marcellus explained. 'Or at least give him an easy death.'

'Do you think that will happen?' Julia asked eagerly, glancing around the Forum.

'I wouldn't bet on it,' Juba said curtly.

No one was allowed near the wooden cross, or the boy who would be bound to it. Juba led us to the steps of the Senate, where guards immediately cleared a space for distinguished witnesses. I felt a tightening in my stomach.

'Is it him?' Alexander whispered at my side.

The soldiers had whipped the kitchen boy through the streets, and his bare back was a bloodied mess. But even without shading my eyes from the sun, I could see that the slave had the same height and build as the masked bowman from the theater. 'I don't know. It might be.' I looked at Julia, who had purchased an *ofella* and was munching contentedly. 'How can you bear to watch this and eat?' I demanded.

'It's just an execution. Most are done at the Esquiline Gate. This is the only one I've seen in the Forum.'

'A rare treat,' Juba remarked.

'I wonder why more aren't done near the Senate,' she said.

'Possibly because the Forum is a place of business, not torture,' he snapped.

She popped a last piece of *ofella* into her mouth. 'You're probably right.' She turned to me. 'My gods, just look at these people. All of this for a slave.'

It didn't occur to her that we were part of *these people*, watching as the accused assassin's wrists and ankles were bound to the cross with rope, and listening to his shrieks of pain as he was hoisted into the air. When I buried my face in Alexander's shoulder, Juba remarked, 'What's the matter? I thought you wanted to see this.'

'I wanted to see if he was the bowman!'

'And?'

I nodded, unable to speak. He wouldn't have heard me anyway. The boy's screams were too loud, and as the cross was raised his body sank down on the *sedile*, a crude wooden seat that took the pressure from his wrists.

Finally, even Julia had had enough. 'We should go,' she said. 'I don't want to see this anymore.'

Marcellus agreed. There was no sign of the Red Eagle. No indication that the kitchen boy's death would be swift.

'Imagine if he had tried to assassinate our father,' Alexander reminded me quietly as we left. 'We would want him dead.'

But Octavian wasn't our father, and I couldn't stop wondering what might have happened if I had simply held my tongue.

There was no more talk of the Red Eagle on the Palatine, but Octavian gave a special address to the Senate and requested a force of soldiers whose sole duty it would be to protect him. The Senate agreed, assembling a professional body of men that Octavian called his Praetorian Guard. But after several weeks without any new acta posted in Rome, everyone began to wonder whether the Red Eagle might have gone into hiding.

'Why else would he be silent?' Julia asked on the way to the

Ludi Romani. The streets were swollen with people carrying circus padding to the amphitheater for the start of the Games, and our litter swayed dangerously as the bearers tried to avoid a collision.

'Perhaps he wants to distance himself from the kitchen boy,' I suggested, holding onto the wooden sides.

There was a sudden stop, and Julia jerked forward, steadying herself with her hand. 'Be careful!' she screamed, tearing open the delicate curtains and swearing at the hapless bearers. When she'd twitched the curtains shut, she turned to me. 'For three years now, the Red Eagle has appeared at the Ludi.'

I gasped. 'In person?'

'No. He goes by night and posts acta on the Circus doors. Last year,' she whispered, 'he freed the gladiators who were going to fight in the arena!'

'So you think that there should be an end to slavery?'

Julia looked at me with alarm. 'Of course not! But imagine a man daring enough to free gladiators from their cells.' She sighed. 'Spartacus was courageous. But the Red Eagle,' she whispered eagerly, 'could be anyone. He might not even be a slave.'

I recalled Gallia's meeting with Magister Verrius. Since then, I'd tried several times to speak with her about the Red Eagle, and every time, she'd dismissed me with a wave. 'It would be dangerous to fall in love with a rebel,' I warned.

Julia laughed. 'Plenty of women fall in love with gladiators, and most of the gladiators are criminals.' She opened the curtain and pointed to the merchants on the side of the road. 'You see what they're selling?'

'*Ofellae?*'

'No.' She made a face. 'Look closer.'

'Are those—' I clapped my hand over my mouth.

Julia giggled. The shopkeepers were selling statuettes of gladiators with erect penises. 'Everyone knows that women lust after them.' She let the curtain fall back into place. 'Even Horatia has had one,' she confessed.

I leaned forward. 'Without her husband knowing?'

'Pollio has taken half a dozen of her slave girls. She deserves some happiness.'

'But what if he catches her?'

'It was only once. And he'll never divorce her.'

'How do you know?'

'Because he told my father that he never wants anything but fourteen-year-old girls.'

'And what does he think? She won't ever grow old?'

'Sure. But she will always be small. Like you.' I shuddered at the thought of a man like Pollio taking me to his couch and pressing his naked stomach against mine, just like the man on the Palatine. *I will never let that happen to me again. I will follow my mother to the grave before I'm subjected to that.* I suspected that Julia could read the disgust on my face, because she added, 'Horatia swore that she'd open her wrists before she wed Pollio.'

There was a shrill scream on the other side of the curtain, and Julia rushed to open it again. On the steps of a temple, an old man was thrashing two boys with a whip. They knelt on the steps of the temple and cowered, covering their heads with their arms.

'Why don't they run?' I cried.

'They're slaves.' Julia leaned forward to get a better view. 'In fact, they're Fabius's slaves!'

'You recognize him?'

She threw a look over her shoulder. 'He's one of the richest men in Rome.'

The cries of the two boys were terrible to hear. I covered my ears with my hands. 'But what could they have done?'

'To Fabius? I've heard it doesn't take much more than rebuffing his advances.'

'To *boys*?'

'And girls. And widows. And matrons. Disgusting,' she said, and let the curtain fall into place.

When we arrived, Agrippa made certain that Caesar's box was ready, then returned to help us from our litters.

'This is the new amphitheater,' Julia said eagerly. 'I wonder what our seats will be like.'

Members of Octavian's Praetorian Guard escorted us through the crowd. Armed soldiers cleared away the plebs, but I noticed that Octavian still walked between Juba and Agrippa.

'So what do you think?' a familiar voice asked, and when I turned, Vitruvius was standing with Octavia. He smiled. 'Brand new. Built by Consul Titus Statilius Taurus.'

'It's very handsome,' I said cautiously. The amphitheater towered above the Campus Martius, and even though it was swarming with people, its elegance was undisturbed. The ground floor was occupied by shops tucked neatly between the painted arches, and large columns had been carved like friezes into the sides.

'But?' Vitruvius asked.

'But I would have chosen red granite instead of limestone. The limestone will look dirty in a few years' time.'

Vitruvius smiled. 'I would have to agree with you.'

'Vitruvius tells me you have a strong understanding of geometry,' Octavia said, taking his arm, 'and that he is exceptionally impressed by your designs for my brother's mausoleum.'

When I looked to Vitruvius in surprise, Octavia laughed.

'Oh, he is sparing with his praise. But he's shown me your work.'

'I'd like to see it,' Marcellus said.

'Her sketches are in the library,' Vitruvius replied.

Julia was silent. When we reached Caesar's box with its wine-colored awnings and wide silk couches, she purposefully sat between me and Marcellus, turning her back to me to ask him, 'So who will you bet on?'

'We can place bets on gladiators?' Alexander asked.

'Sure,' Marcellus said. Then he amended, 'Of course, there's no method to it. Not like what you've shown me with the horses. You simply pick a number – fifty, thirty-three – and if that gladiator survives, you win.'

'Are there odds?'

'Alexander!' I said sharply. 'You can't bet on men's lives.'

'I bet on them in the Circus.'

'Those are just chariots.'

Alexander looked abashed. 'Come on, Selene. If I win, I'll give you the winnings for your home.'

'What home?' Julia asked.

'Her foundling home,' Marcellus replied, but not so loudly that Octavian, on the couch next to us, could hear.

Julia stared at me. 'I didn't know about this.'

'It's nothing,' I said quickly.

'Marcellus knows about it.'

'Because he saw the sketch. It's just a place I imagined.'

'For foundlings,' Marcellus explained. 'She's interested in charity, like my mother.'

'How nice,' Julia said, but her tone implied otherwise.

'It probably won't come to anything,' I said.

Julia folded her arms across her chest. 'Why not?'

'Because who would build a home for foundlings? And why would anyone listen to me?'

'I might,' she said pointedly, and most likely for Marcellus's benefit, 'if I were Caesar's wife.'

I was silent.

'You have such a very kind heart, Selene. I wish I were so good.' But I could see that she didn't. She was content to eat *ofellae* during executions and step over wailing infants so long as Marcellus didn't think she was callous. And although Marcellus would never criticize her, she couldn't bear it when he praised me. 'So are you betting?' she asked.

I shook my head. 'If Alexander wishes to bet on death, then he can.'

'Really?' My brother leaned back on the couch so he could see around Marcellus and Julia. 'You won't be upset?'

I refused to answer him.

'Oh, they're going to die anyway,' Julia said.

'And betting on it won't make a difference,' Alexander pointed out.

The bet-maker appeared, and from her couch in front of us, Livia said gleefully, 'Twenty denarii on the first gladiator.'

'To live or die, domina?'

'Die,' she said, and next to her, Octavian passed the man a heavy purse.

'And for you, domina?'

Octavia considered. 'The first five gladiators.'

'Living or dead?'

'Living,' Octavia said pointedly, and her brother smiled.

When the bet-maker came to Alexander, I turned my face away.

'It's not nice, is it?' Antonia asked. She shared a couch with her sister and Vipsania. On the other side of them, Tiberius and his younger brother, Drusus, were rolling dice. 'I try not to watch whenever the men die.'

'Are they all condemned criminals?'

'No. Some are slaves who were purchased for fighting. Aren't there gladiatorial events in Egypt?'

'No. We don't kill men for sport.'

'Oh, there's women, too,' she said sadly. 'And animals.'

'*Here?*'

'Sure. Look.'

The trumpets sounded, and as the gates of the arena were pulled up, a group of sword-carrying men entered from beneath the amphitheater. They wore strange sandals laced up to the knee and short tunics, and I realized with a start that some were mere boys.

'Who *are* they?'

'Telegenii,' Antonia said. 'The consul who built this amphitheater found them south of Carthage and brought them here to fight.'

There was a loud gasp from the crowd in the arena as seven leopards were set loose.

'They're not going to kill the cats?' I exclaimed.

'Certainly. Or they'll be killed themselves.'

I sat forward. 'Is this what you bet on?' I shouted at Alexander.

'No! No one said there would be leopards.'

'What's the matter?' Marcellus asked.

'Those animals' – Alexander pointed wildly – 'are sacred in Egypt. We don't kill them for meat, and certainly not for entertainment!'

'Oh, this is just the opening act,' Julia said. 'There's only seven. Then the real fights will begin.'

Alexander glanced at me, and I could see the fear in his eyes. If our mother had been alive, she would never have forgiven us for watching this.

'Do you think they've brought this to Egypt?' I asked coldly in Parthian.

'Yes,' he said quietly. 'And when we return, we'll forbid it.'

The announcer narrated the fight, and whenever the crowds cheered I closed my eyes and imagined that I was back in Alexandria, where the Museion towered over the gleaming city and philosophers went to the theater for entertainment.

'It's not that bad,' Julia said critically. 'You can open your eyes. They're nearly all dead.'

'The leopards or the Telegenii?'

'The leopards. Only two Telegenii have been killed.'

I opened my eyes, but I refused to watch. Instead I turned and looked at Gallia, who was sitting behind us among the men of the Praetorian Guard. When she caught my gaze, she beckoned to me with her hand. I left my position on the couch next to Julia, and Gallia made space for me on hers.

'Not enjoying the Games?'

'No,' I admitted.

'Oh, but you haven't even seen the best part,' she said dryly. 'When the gladiators are done being savaged, two men will come out and get them. One will be dressed as Hermes, the other as Charon.' The messenger god and the ferryman of the dead.

'What do they do?'

'Collect the bodies. But first, Hermes prods the gladiator with a hot iron, and if he moves, Charon takes a mallet and crushes his skull.'

I covered my mouth with my hand. 'So even if he could survive, he's killed?'

'Yes.' The trumpets blared for a second time, and Hermes made his appearance with Charon, just as she said.

'They have all placed bets on this. Even Octavia. And Julia's enjoying it.'

Gallia nodded. 'I know. But perhaps you judge domina Julia too harshly.'

I glanced up in surprise. 'I don't pass any judgment on Julia at all.'

Gallia smiled as if she didn't believe me. 'She has not had it easy.'

'She's the daughter of Caesar!'

'And what of her mother?'

I didn't know what to say.

'Do you see the woman up there?' Gallia indicated a fine-featured matron several rows above us where the women of Rome were forced to sit apart from the men. The woman possessed a fascinating beauty, and she was watching Julia with attention that never wavered. 'That is Scribonia, domina Julia's mother.'

When Scribonia caught us staring at her, she smiled sadly. I turned to Gallia. 'She's beautiful. Why did Caesar divorce her?'

'She was not obedient. Now she is only allowed to see her daughter from the upper seats of these games.'

'Julia can't visit her?'

'Once a year, during Saturnalia, she may bring her mother a gift.'

I gasped at the cruelty. It was no wonder Julia had been so interested in my mother. And now, all she had was Livia. Bitter, selfish, jealous Livia. 'Do you think she ever visits Scribonia secretly?' I asked.

Gallia gave a little smile. The men of the Praetorian Guard around us were cheering, ignoring us completely. 'Of course,' she whispered. 'But how can secret visits be enough for a mother? Or a daughter?'

I looked around the amphitheater. 'This place is filled with secrets.'

'More than you know.'

I hesitated. 'Are there secrets about my father in here?'

She gave me a long, searching look before answering. 'Yes.'

'Where?'

She indicated a woman seated below Scribonia. Her eyes were painted with heavy shadow, and her long hair was dressed with small gems and pearls. Only actresses and *lupae* wore so much paint in Rome. Gallia said, 'Domina Cytheris.'

'Does she work in the theater?'

'Not anymore. But when she did, she was your father's mistress.' She studied my face to see my reaction, but I wasn't surprised.

'And who is she mistress to now?' I asked. The pearls in her hair and expensive jewels at her throat had not come free, and Charmion used to say that women who couldn't keep their legs closed couldn't keep their purses shut either.

'Dominus Gallus. The prefect that Caesar has sent to govern Egypt.' I gave a small gasp, and Gallia placed her hand on mine. 'I know it is not easy.'

'So why isn't she there with him?' I asked bitterly.

'She has told him she prefers to entertain in Rome.'

I thought of the irony that my father's former *lupa*, an actress who had performed nude on the stage, now had the choice of living in Egypt's palace. My mother had been forced to take her own life, and now a woman like Cytheris could sleep in her bed and paint her eyes with her kohl. But Cytheris had turned down the opportunity. Hadn't she seen paintings of Alexandria? Didn't she want to know what it would feel like to lie in the palace and listen to the waves crash against the rocks while the gulls called to one another on the shore?

I touched the pearl diadem in my hair, and Gallia said tenderly, 'This is why I do not like to tell you these things.'

'It doesn't bother me,' I lied. 'What else?' I ignored the sound of metal on metal and the wild cheering of the crowd. 'Is there anyone else here my father would have known?'

Gallia indicated a young man seated below us, whose light hair and broad shoulders seemed strangely familiar. 'That is your brother dominus Jullus by your father's third wife.'

'He looks just like Antyllus!' Jullus and Antyllus had been brothers, but only Antyllus had made the terrible decision to follow my father to Alexandria. I watched as Jullus tilted his head back with laughter and the golden hair tumbled over his ears – just like Antyllus and Ptolemy. I felt an instant connection to him that I had never felt toward Antonia or her sister. Perhaps it was because I had never had sisters, only brothers. 'I wish I could meet him.'

'Not possible,' Gallia warned sternly. 'You do not want Caesar to think the Antonii are rising again. Better to watch him from afar.'

'Like Scribonia watches Julia?'

Gallia nodded sadly. 'Yes.'

There was a great roar of disapproval from below, and then suddenly everyone was standing. 'What's happening?' I cried.

A Praetorian turned to me. 'One of the gladiators has been wounded.'

'Many have been wounded,' Gallia remarked.

'But this man is a favorite. He has survived combat for three days, and now Charon is coming with his mallet.'

'They will kill a favorite even if he might live?'

'He's been wounded, Princess. His eyes are closed. It doesn't matter to Charon if a physician might save him.'

Although the amphitheater seats rose in tiers, I couldn't see anything above the heads of the people in front of me. I was too small, and there were too many of them standing on their seats. Perhaps it was better. I could hear the crowd's sharp intake of breath as the mallet shattered the gladiator's skull, and Antonia's shriek pierced the sudden silence that had descended over the amphitheater. Octavia rushed to calm her, but she wouldn't be calmed. Her shrieking continued, until Marcellus placed his hand over her mouth. 'Be *quiet!*'

Octavian rose. 'I am done for today.'

'I'm sorry,' Octavia said. 'She's afraid.'

'She *should* be,' he said angrily. 'There will be no more of Hermes and Charon! Agrippa, you will inform them.'

'Then how will the battles end?' Marcellus asked.

'When one gladiator is too tired or too injured to fight.' Octavian turned to Antonia and held up her chin, wiping the tears from her eyes. 'No more death,' he promised, though when the bet-maker returned with various winnings, I noticed that Octavian didn't refuse to accept his.

Inside Octavia's villa, Alexander handed his heavy purse to me. 'For your foundlings,' he said quietly.

I placed the purse inside the metal chest Octavia had recently given to us, and Alexander locked the chest with the key he wore next to his *bulla*. Marcellus and Julia stood at the door, waiting for us to join them.

'Come,' Marcellus urged. 'We can watch the races from my uncle's platform.'

'But won't he be angry?' Alexander asked. 'He said he was done for the day.'

'He was only upset that he will have to pay the *lanistae* three hundred denarii,' Julia said wryly.

'What is a *lanista*?' Alexander asked.

'You know,' Marcellus prompted, 'one of the men who own the gladiators. When a gladiator dies, the sponsor of the event has to pay the *lanistam* for his loss. The Ludi Romani are always sponsored by Caesar, and popular gladiators are worth more.'

'So that means my father will have to pay three hundred denarii just for one man. By banishing Hermes and Charon, he won't have to pay the *lanistae* anything.' Julia smiled. 'You didn't think he did it for poor little Antonia, did you?'

The Ludi went on for fourteen more days, and by September nineteenth, no one wanted to return to Magister Verrius and our studies. Marcellus pleaded with Octavia to let us have one more day, but her answer was firm.

'Your uncle's *dies natalis* is in six days, and there will be two days off for celebration. I believe that is enough.' Octavia walked us onto the portico, where Juba and Gallia were already waiting. 'Do you celebrate birth days in Egypt?' she asked.

'No,' Alexander replied. 'But our father sometimes brought us presents.'

Octavia pressed her lips together, perhaps thinking of the gifts her daughters had never received because their father was with us in Alexandria.

'They were always small presents,' I added swiftly. 'Of little importance.'

'At least he remembered,' Octavia said quietly.

I scowled at Alexander, who understood what he had done. 'He never spent much time with us anyway,' he said. 'Even if it was our *dies natalis.*'

Octavia smiled, but it was bitter. I could feel her watching us as we disappeared down the Palatine. When we reached the Forum, Magister Verrius greeted us at the door of the ludus.

'Enjoy yourselves,' Juba said merrily, and I imagine that Magister Verrius understood what we were feeling, since the next few days were full of games. There was a contest to see who could memorize the longest passage of Euripides, and a game testing our knowledge of the Muses – both of which I won. But Tiberius had memorized the longest passages of both Ennius and Terence, Romans whose works I couldn't be bothered with. By the end of September, our games were over, and Magister Verrius was determined to introduce us to rhetoric, the art of public speaking. Marcellus sighed audibly, and Julia sank lower in her seat.

'Today, I would like you to spend time outside the Senate, listening to the lawyers debate.' When Julia groaned, Magister Verrius ignored her. 'You will follow a trial until its end, and you may *not* choose a trial that ends today.'

'What a waste of time,' Julia said angrily as we walked toward the Campus Martius. Juba and Gallia remained several paces behind. She turned around and glared at them. 'Do you think they might lie for us and pretend that we've gone?'

'What?' Marcellus asked. 'And we'd make up a trial?'

'Well, when are we supposed to watch one?' she demanded.

'We're going to have to forget the Circus,' he said. 'At least for a week.'

'He didn't say how long the trial had to be. We can choose one that ends tomorrow.'

Marcellus gave Julia a long look. 'And be told to do it all over again?'

Julia turned to me. 'I don't know how you stand it. Working with Vitruvius from the break of dawn and studying Magister Verrius's work all day.'

'She likes it,' Tiberius responded on my behalf. 'Some people actually enjoy learning.'

'But *why*? All Vitruvius teaches you is measurements.'

'Measurements to construct a building,' I replied. 'He took me to the Temple of Apollo yesterday. It's almost finished.'

'Really?' Marcellus took a shortcut across the Campus Martius. 'What's inside?'

'A library with gold and ivory paneling. And a statue of the god sculpted by Scopas.'

'Did Juba find it?' Marcellus asked.

I shrugged. 'That's what Vitruvius says.' In the distance, I could see Livia and Octavia on the shaded portico of the stables, both weaving on their wooden looms and sitting as far apart as decorum would allow. When we reached the portico, Octavia stood.

'Juba.' She smiled. 'Gallia. Thank you both for bringing them safely. Are all of my children behaving themselves?'

'Aside from the complaining?' Juba said. 'Yes.'

'You would complain, too, if you had to go to school while everyone else was on vacation,' Marcellus grumbled.

'Ah, the terrible price of being heir,' Juba said.

'He is not heir yet,' Livia snapped.

'Forgive me. *Possible* heir.'

'We all know Octavian wants Marcellus,' Tiberius retorted. 'So why keep pretending?'

Livia looked at her husband, who was swimming with Agrippa while guards kept watch on the bank. 'Octavian has told me he has not decided. There's no reason not to make you heir.'

'No reason in the world,' Marcellus returned sarcastically. 'Come on, Alexander, I want to swim.'

Marcellus and Alexander entered the stables, and Tiberius glowered at his mother. 'Why can't you just leave it alone?' he shouted.

Livia stood swiftly and delivered a slap to his face.

Tiberius turned red, and when he disappeared into the stables, Octavia warned, 'He will come to resent you.'

'How do you know what he will come to do? Are you an augur?'

Julia kept her eyes on the wooden loom in front of her, and

I didn't look up from my sketches, in case Livia turned her wrath on me.

'Get me more loom weights!' Livia shouted at Gallia.

'Don't move,' Octavia said. 'If she wants more weights, she can get them herself. They're inside.'

Gallia hesitated, caught between obeying Octavia and angering Livia further. She met Livia's fearsome gaze without blinking, and when it became clear that she wasn't going to move, Livia stormed from her chair.

Later, when the men returned from their swim, Julia whispered this story to Alexander and Marcellus. We were making our way back to the Forum to observe a trial when she said eagerly, 'And then, Gallia simply refused to move!'

Behind us, Gallia walked between Tiberius and Juba, the incident on the portico forgotten. But Marcellus shook his head. 'My mother is creating trouble for Gallia. She shouldn't have done that.'

'Gallia isn't Livia's slave,' I said heatedly. 'She shouldn't be anyone's slave.'

'Well, she belongs to my mother,' Marcellus replied, 'and my mother is putting her in danger. No one can afford to make an enemy of Livia.'

'I understand why Octavia did it,' Julia said. 'She's tired of Livia thinking she owns all of Rome.'

'She does,' Marcellus pointed out.

'No, my father does! Livia's just a whore with a good marriage.'

Alexander snickered, and I covered my mouth to keep myself from laughing.

Julia smiled naughtily at me. 'Now let's find the shortest trial and get this over with.'

But there was only one trial happening in the Forum. A crowd was growing around the podium where a lawyer was addressing the seated judices, who would eventually return a verdict of guilt or innocence.

'I can't see,' Julia complained. 'What's going on?'

'Two hundred slaves are on trial for the murder of their master, Gaius Fabius,' Juba said.

Julia gasped. 'Fabius?' She turned to me. 'Don't you remember him, Selene? He was the man you saw beating those boys at the temple!'

'And all two hundred slaves helped murder him?' I exclaimed.

'When one slave murders his master, all must be punished,' Juba said levelly.

Suddenly, Julia was interested. 'Do you think we can get a better view?'

Juba raised his brows. 'Certainly.' He took us behind the podium, where rows of slaves were chained together by the neck and we could watch the backs of the lawyers as they addressed both the judices and the crowds.

'Look how young they are,' I whispered to Alexander. Some of the slaves were no more than five or six, and could never have taken part in any killing. I turned to Juba. 'Will they really be put to death?'

'Of course. If they are found guilty.'

'How can you be so callous?' I demanded.

'Because it's not his problem,' Tiberius said. 'What is he supposed to do about it?'

The public lawyer for the slaves stopped talking, and was replaced at the podium by the lawyer for the dead Gaius Fabius. 'You have heard,' he began in a thundering voice, 'pitiful stories of slaves who could not have taken part in the killing. Women, children, old men who are nearly crippled and blind. But what did they see? What did they witness and keep silent about? Make no mistake,' the lawyer said angrily, 'watching and participating are no different! We cannot know which among these dregs stood by while Gaius Fabius was strangled in his chamber, then knifed more than a dozen times.' There was a groan from the crowd, and at the front, seated on wooden benches, the judices shook their heads. 'We must set an example,' he said at once. 'Nearly thirty-five years ago, a similar trial ended in the death of four hundred slaves. That jury understood that a message must be sent. One that discourages any slave from killing his master for fear that *everyone* will be punished. We must stop this now,' he shouted, 'or who will be next? You?' He pointed at an old man on the bench, whose neck was weighed down by heavy gold chains. 'You?' he demanded, looking at a second young man in the toga of a judex. 'Forget what you heard before this. Certainly, a few slave children will die. But are their lives more important than yours? More important than those of your wives and children?'

He stepped down from the podium, and Julia watched with wide-eyed fascination. 'What happens now?' she whispered.

'That's it,' Tiberius said.

'What? No more arguing?' Marcellus asked.

The crowd began to disperse, and Juba started walking. 'No more until tomorrow.'

'But how many days will it go on?' Julia asked.

'As many as it takes.'

She regarded Juba crossly. 'But that could be a month. Even two months.'

'It can't be two months,' Tiberius retorted. 'Courts shut down in November and December.'

'So who decides when it's over?' I asked.

'The judices,' Gallia replied. Until then, she had been silent. Now she added quietly, 'Those poor little children.'

The next day, no one complained about going to the Forum.

Even my brother and Julia were more interested in the fate of the two hundred slaves than in the races at the Circus Maximus. I could hear the people on the streets talking about Gaius Fabius's slaves, and there seemed to be outrage, not at his murder, but at the trial. 'Fifty-three children,' a woman said in the crowd. 'It isn't right.' Though we had arrived at the same time we had before, word had spread throughout Rome and more than a thousand people swelled around the podium and the judices' seats.

'Look how angry the people are! The judices have to set them free!' I exclaimed.

'They don't *have* to do anything,' Juba replied, leading us to the space behind the podium reserved for honored guests. This time, several senators were already there, watching the lawyers arguing. 'The judices will make their decisions based on the principles of justice as they see them, not on the wishes of an angry mob.'

'Then you agree with this?' I exclaimed.

Juba looked at the miserable chain of slaves fettered by heavy iron shackles. Among them was a little brown-haired girl, who smiled when Juba met her gaze. 'I agree with justice.'

The lawyer for Gaius Fabius was at the podium, banging his fist against the wood. 'Would you like to see the murderer?' he demanded, and the crowds cheered. 'Bring him forth!'

The guards stepped forward with a slave who was being held separately, and I whispered to Julia, 'Is that one of the boys Fabius was beating at the temple?'

'Who knows? All Gauls look the same.'

I noticed Gallia shaking her head.

Fabius's lawyer pumped his fist in the air. 'This is the slave responsible for the murder, and he doesn't even deny it!' he cried. 'Which of you thinks that a boy of fourteen could have done it on his own? Strangled his master, stabbed his master, then dumped his master's body into the atrium pool?' There was a general shaking of heads, and the slave looked down at his feet. Like the kitchen boy, he knew he was lost. Then the lawyer inhaled, dramatically. 'Who here believes that slaves are blind?' A few members of the crowd laughed, and I felt a familiar twisting in my stomach. 'Then no one here believes that a murder could take place without anyone hearing. Without anyone suspecting. Without anyone ever seeing this *filius nullius* drag his master's body away from his chamber! There are accomplices,' he promised. 'And we must teach them Roman justice!' He strode away from the podium with the air of a man who knows he has won.

The lawyer for Fabius's slaves looked beaten before he even opened his mouth. His thin shoulders were hunched in his heavy toga, and he looked as if the heat of the day was draining him of color.

'There is no knowing,' he began, 'who saw or heard Gaius Fabius die. There is no one in this crowd who can tell me which of these slaves is an accomplice. Perhaps it was early morning, and while the elder slaves worked, it was the children who witnessed this terrible crime. I do not deny that this slave is responsible.' He flicked his wrist, and the guards took the boy away, holding him near the other slaves. I saw the boy look at an older woman, and felt certain from her tears that this was his mother.

'But who here wishes to punish the innocent?' the lawyer went on. 'The children who have never learned right from wrong?' There was an uneasy shuffling in the crowd, and the men who had laughed wore serious faces now. 'It's true that if you allow these slaves to be put to death, you are sending a message across Rome. But the message is that we are no different from barbarians!' I could see that he had been arguing all afternoon, and the strain was beginning to show. 'Look at these faces,' he implored. 'This one.' He stepped back and held up the chin of the beautiful girl who had smiled at Juba. 'She can't be more than six years old. What has she done to deserve death? She hasn't even lived life!'

I saw Gallia blinking back tears.

'And this child,' the lawyer said. He touched the shoulder of a boy who was not more than ten. 'What might he become if we let him live? He might serve another master well, he might buy his freedom. He might become as wealthy and powerful and useful as Caesar's consul Agrippa!' There was an eager murmur in the crowd, and the lawyer fixed his gaze on the seven rows of judices. 'Have pity,' he demanded. 'Place blame on the shoulders it should rest on. Not upon the innocent!' He left the podium, and for several moments no one said anything.

'Do you think a decision will be made tomorrow?' Marcellus asked.

'It appears that way,' Juba said quietly, and I wondered whether he had been moved by the public lawyer's plea.

As we walked through the Forum, Julia said brightly, 'Who would have thought a trial could be so interesting? Perhaps we should place bets.'

For the first time, I saw Marcellus recoil in disgust.

'What?' she said. 'It's no different from the arena.'

'Perhaps I should not have bet there, either,' he said shortly, and Julia gave me a puzzled look.

CHAPTER ELEVEN

THE CROWD that came to witness the fate of Gaius Fabius's two hundred slaves filled the Forum all the way from the courtyard of the Carcer to the steps of the Temple of Castor and Pollux. We had been allowed to skip our time on the Campus Martius to hear the judges pronounce their verdict, and even Octavian came, with Livia and Agrippa.

'Where are your sisters?' I asked Marcellus. 'And why isn't your mother here?'

He stepped forward to get a better view. Although we were standing behind the raised wooden platform, hundreds of senators jostled around us. 'Trials of this sort upset her,' he said. 'And she'd never allow my sisters to come. They saw a man sentenced to death once and have never stopped talking about it.'

'So you think they'll be found guilty?' I worried.

'Certainly the slave who killed Fabius. The others . . .' He hesitated. 'I don't know. It would be unfair to send them to their deaths.'

'And what could the children possibly have done?' my brother added.

'If the Red Eagle were here,' Marcellus whispered, 'there would be acta on every temple door decrying this.'

'Perhaps he's waiting,' I suggested, 'to see what the judices do.'

Although Octavia had chosen not to come, the rest of Rome appeared to be in attendance. And because Octavian was with us, the lawyers spoke swiftly. Their last arguments were the most moving. Gaius Fabius's lawyer pled for justice, pointing to Fabius's wife in the crowd, who dabbed at her eyes. But the lawyer for the slaves begged for reason, reminding the judices of the children and old women who could not have taken part in a murder. I watched Octavian's face as each judex stood to announce his verdict, and when all of them pronounced the slave boy guilty, he nodded, as if in agreement. There was a deafening cheer from the crowd, and the boy cast a fearful glance at his mother, who buried her face in her chained hands.

'This is it,' Julia said. 'I wonder what they'll do.' She brushed a stray black curl from her forehead and stood on tiptoe to see the faces of the judices.

The first judex stood and announced his verdict for the two hundred slaves. 'Guilty,' he said, and I looked to Octavian, whose face was an expressionless mask. The second judex rose, and when he, too, pronounced a verdict of guilty, the people began to grow restless.

'Perhaps we should leave,' Juba suggested as the third and fourth judex announced their verdicts of guilty.

'Marcellus,' Octavian called sharply. 'Tiberius. We're leaving.'

'But we haven't even heard the verdict,' Julia complained.

'Perhaps you would rather stay here and be killed?' Livia demanded.

The crowd was growing increasingly discontent, and as more judices pronounced their verdict of guilty, some of the freedmen began the chant of 'Red Eagle.'

'Go!' Octavian shouted to us. 'Go!'

The Praetorian cleared a path through the Forum, but as the last judex announced his verdict, the freedmen and slaves became uncontrollable. I could hear the sounds of rioting behind us: statues being shattered, and soldiers clashing with the people. A wave of angry men rushed toward us, and Livia cried shrilly, 'It's Spartacus all over again!' Octavian took her arm, then the guards surrounded us and began to run. The angry slaves didn't need weapons. All they needed was fire and stones.

When we reached the Palatine, Octavia rushed from her portico. 'What happened?' she cried.

'Guilty,' Gallia replied, and Octavia went pale.

'All two hundred will be put to death?' She looked at her brother.

'That was their verdict.'

'But don't you think—'

His look silenced her. We followed him to the platform he had built to watch the races and saw a column of smoke rising from the Forum.

'So the plebs are rioting again,' Tiberius remarked.

Octavian clenched his jaw. 'This will not be tolerated.'

'It's these slaves that are the problem,' Livia exclaimed. 'They have to be controlled! Why not have them all wear one color. Or brand them?'

'A third of Rome's population is in servitude,' Juba reminded her. 'Do you really want three hundred thousand slaves able to identify one another in the streets?'

Octavian pursed his lips. 'That's right. They cannot be branded.'

I stole a glance at Gallia, but her face was impossible to read.

'What about a leniency in the laws?' Octavia asked.

'And that would make these slaves less violent?' her brother shouted.

Octavia stepped back. 'Yes.' I could see that she was holding back tears. 'If they feel that they have a place in court to challenge abusive masters, then perhaps it will.'

Octavian looked to Marcellus. 'And what would you do?' he asked suddenly. It was a test, and Marcellus glanced uneasily at his mother.

'I would bring fewer slaves into Rome,' he said.

Tiberius snorted. 'And who would till the fields? Romans aren't having children. The men don't want to spend the denarii and the women don't want stretch marks.'

Marcellus laughed. 'And how would you know that?'

Tiberius flushed. 'I . . . I listen.'

'It's true,' Octavia said quietly. Behind her, the thick column of smoke was widening. 'Women don't want the risk or the disfiguration.'

Octavian clenched his jaw. 'Then perhaps they need incentives.'

'Such as what?' Tiberius asked under his breath. 'A Festival of Fornication?' At Octavian's look, he immediately fell silent.

'Monetary incentives,' Agrippa said.

'For having children?' Marcellus exclaimed.

'There will be dangerous times,' Octavian warned darkly, 'when there are more slaves than Romans.'

'Then we should banish the Columna Lactaria,' Tiberius suggested. 'Those children all become slaves. Imagine them all rising up—'

'And tomorrow will be the real test,' Agrippa warned. He didn't explain further, but when Gallia and Juba escorted us to the ludus the next morning, I realized what he'd meant.

Julia covered her mouth with her hand, and Gallia made a poor attempt at suppressing a smile.

'I don't believe it,' Tiberius said.

At every temple door, at every crossroads, crowds gathered to read the latest actum. Even on the doors of the Temple of Venus Genetrix, the Red Eagle and his men had nailed their pieces of papyrus. Juba clenched his jaw, and as soon as the plebs saw him approach, one of the acta was immediately torn down. The other one he ripped away himself.

'I don't understand,' my brother said. 'Why aren't the priests taking them down?'

'They're afraid to anger the plebs,' Julia whispered. 'And even if the acta are taken down, people are probably copying them as we speak.'

When Juba returned with the crumpled actum, Marcellus asked eagerly, 'What does it say?'

'Nothing you need to know about.'

'But we're going to read it anyway,' Tiberius argued as we crossed the Forum. 'If not now, then at some other point.'

'We just want to be aware of what's happening in Rome,' Julia pleaded. 'Magister Verrius is always telling us to pay attention.'

Juba smiled. 'I doubt that reading treachery was what he meant.'

'But these are all over,' Marcellus argued. 'There's dozens of them. Do you want us to be the only people in Rome who don't know what the Red Eagle is saying?'

'My father wouldn't care,' Julia promised as we reached the ludus. 'He never keeps these things from us.' It was true. In the triclinium, there was nothing Octavian wouldn't discuss, from banishing *lupanaria* from Rome to prosecuting adulteresses. 'This is how we learn.'

Juba handed the scroll to her. 'I'll be interested in hearing what this teaches you.'

Everyone gathered around Julia. There was no harm in reading, only in speaking, and the five of us read in low voices. It began with a stern warning against murder.

There are a thousand other ways to get revenge. While I cannot advocate stealing from your masters, thievery comes in many different forms. Your lives have been stolen from you. Why, then, should you break your backs attempting to meet the demands of your masters? If it's a farm you work on, be slow with the wheat. If it's a lender you work for, make your records faulty. You cannot be punished for stealing time, or for simple accidents with the reed pen. And if you fear death at the hands of your enslavers, remember, death can come even when you are innocent. Do not forget the two hundred slaves who will die tomorrow with no blood on their hands. Women, children, infants still too young to walk.

The actum went on to list the name of every slave who would be executed at dawn.

'This is terrible,' I whispered.

'How did he find out the name of every slave?' Alexander wondered.

'Are we finished?' Juba demanded. 'Or would we like to go on discussing this in the open Forum?'

Inside the ludus, Magister Verrius was waiting at his desk. He didn't stand to greet us, and he looked as though he'd had very little sleep.

'Did you hear about the Red Eagle?' Julia asked eagerly.

'Yes,' Magister Verrius said curtly. 'And I presume he is the reason we're all late this morning?'

'But we had to read it!' Marcellus protested.

Magister Verrius held up his hand. 'I don't want to know. Just take your seats and begin your work.'

Tiberius hesitated in front of his desk. 'There's not going to be a contest today?'

Magister Verrius shook his head firmly. 'No.'

That evening, Octavian's mood was sour as well.

'What's the matter with everyone?' Julia asked.

Although a harpist's music filled the triclinium, Marcellus lowered his voice. 'What do you think? Tomorrow, two hundred innocent slaves are to be executed.'

She broke open an oyster and dipped it in garum sauce. 'So how does that affect my father?'

Octavian had invited his favorite poets to entertain him. Livy and Maecenas dined next to Horace and Vergil, but even their humor couldn't make him laugh. I saw Terentilla reach for a glass bowl, and when her hand brushed Octavian's, he still didn't smile.

'He thought he had crucified the Red Eagle,' Marcellus guessed, 'and now that the rebel has returned, he's nervous about what might happen tomorrow.'

'I don't see how he can free them,' my brother said practically. 'They're chained inside the Carcer.'

'And they'll be taken by more than a hundred soldiers to the Esquiline Gate for crucifixion,' Julia added. 'There isn't any hope.'

But Marcellus wasn't sure. 'He's managed it before.'

'Without his own soldiers, he'll never manage this,' my brother said.

At the table next to us, Livia rose and addressed the diners. 'Shall we hear the first poem of the night? Horace, give us something triumphant.'

A balding man stood up from his couch and took his place in the center of the chamber. 'Triumphant,' he said musingly. 'But which one of Caesar's many triumphs?'

'The Battle of Actium,' Livia said. 'Or Kleopatra's death.'

Horace smiled. 'An ode, then, to Queen Kleopatra.'

Marcellus looked from me to Alexander.

'We should leave,' I said immediately, but Julia put her hand on my arm.

'Livia wants my father to be upset with you. Don't risk it,' she whispered.

'His mood is already dark,' Marcellus warned quietly. 'Just stay, and try not to listen.'

But it was impossible to ignore the lies that Horace twisted into a poem.

When Horace was finished, my brother looked at me. Although the poem had begun by portraying our mother as a 'drugged' queen, the last three stanzas praised her as a warrior who accepted her death unflinchingly. Horace bowed his head respectfully in our direction, and Octavian stood up from his couch to applaud.

'Magnificent.' He looked at his wife. 'What did you think?'

Livia smiled weakly. 'The beginning had a great deal of promise. Unfortunately, I found the end dispensable.'

Octavian looked down at Terentilla. 'Inspired,' she told him.

I turned to my brother. 'I'm leaving,' I whispered.

'You can't go by yourself!'

'If you don't want to come, Gallia's in the atrium. She'll take me back.'

Alexander hesitated.

'I won't hear another poem about Egypt,' I told him.

'But Octavian will think it's a slight.'

'Then *you* stay.' I stood without finishing my meal, and when I reached the atrium, I searched among the seated slaves for Gallia.

A boy rose from his stool. 'Is there someone you're looking for, domina?'

'Gallia,' I told him.

'She isn't here,' he said quietly.

'Where did she go?'

He hesitated. 'With a man.'

'Magister Verrius?'

He looked down at his sandals.

'I'm a friend,' I promised.

The boy looked deeply uncomfortable. 'Yes. He brings her back here before domina Octavia is ready to go home.'

'Thank you,' I said.

'You won't tell her I told you?'

'Of course not.'

I walked the short distance to Octavia's villa alone. Inside my chamber, I took out my sketch book and studied the drawings. The foundling house was my favorite. It was just a plain villa, with a tiled floor and simple mosaics, but it was more important to me than Octavian's mausoleum or the Temple of Apollo. There weren't enough denarii from Alexander's gambling to purchase the tiles for a single floor, and there would never be enough for the rest of a building, but with my finger I traced the balconies where I imagined the children would look out on the city. Some of the slaves who would be crucified at dawn might once have been foundlings. Perhaps they had even been daughters of wealthy patricians who hadn't wanted to provide any more dowries, or sons of merchants who didn't want to feed any more children. I imagined how different life would be for Alexander and me if we had been brought to Rome as slaves, and when Gallia returned with Octavia and the others, I didn't mention her disappearance with Magister Verrius.

'You missed the best part,' Alexander exclaimed, bursting into our chamber with Marcellus.

'What? Another poem about Egypt?'

Marcellus collapsed on the third couch. 'No. Maecenas mentioned the Red Eagle, and my uncle became enraged.'

'Really?' I put down my book. 'What did he do?'

'He wants to set a trap for the rebel,' my brother said.

'But the Red Eagle's unpredictable,' Marcellus added, 'and never posts in the same place twice. So my uncle is going to have soldiers in plebeian clothes stationed across Rome.'

'And do you think it will work?' I asked.

'If the rebel tries to interfere tomorrow, it may.' Marcellus closed his eyes. 'It's terrible, isn't it?'

'Terrible because you know who the Red Eagle is?' my brother asked.

Marcellus opened his eyes. 'Why would you say such a thing?'

'Because we've heard you leave your room at night,' I said, and Marcellus grew suddenly pale. 'And I saw a shadow move across the garden once. It looked very much like you.'

We both stared at him.

'I'm not the Red Eagle,' Marcellus said firmly. 'How could I ever write such long acta? I can barely finish my work in the ludus.'

'But perhaps you know him.'

'Or her,' I suggested.

Marcellus looked from me to my brother. 'Her? What are the two of you thinking?'

We were silent for a moment, then Alexander said, 'Perhaps it's Gallia, and you're aiding her fight.'

'Against slavery?' Marcellus's voice was incredulous. 'Do you really think I'd be helping a rebel?'

'Where else could you have been going?' Alexander asked quietly, and Marcellus regained some of his color.

'To meet someone.'

'A woman?' I gasped.

He didn't answer my question. 'Sometimes I pay the guards. But surely you don't think they'd cover for me if they suspected I was a traitor?'

Alexander and I were both silent. I crossed my arms over my chest, wondering which woman he could be meeting. A *lupa*? Julia? Some other pretty girl on the Palatine?

Marcellus leaned forward. 'But do you really think it might be Gallia?'

'By herself?' my brother said. 'It's unlikely. But perhaps she knows someone with access to a great deal of ink and papyrus?'

Marcellus's eyes widened, and I knew he was recalling the night his uncle had nearly been assassinated and Antonia had seen Gallia at the bottom of the hill. 'Not Magister Verrius?'

My brother put his finger to his lips. 'Who else has such resources?'

'Or access to the Palatine,' Marcellus realized. He looked at me. 'Do you think it's him?'

'You say you aren't the Red Eagle. You haven't told us where you've been going, but if we're to believe you, who else could it be?'

Marcellus sat back against the couch, but didn't rise to my bait. 'It would make sense. But it could also be a hundred other people.'

'Which is why we can't say anything,' Alexander said swiftly.

'You wouldn't turn him in even if you knew, would you?' I asked.

Marcellus was thoughtful. 'If I knew for certain who it was, and my uncle came to know . . .'

I looked to Alexander. We had been wrong to tell him about Gallia and Verrius.

'I won't say anything,' Marcellus promised. 'But it isn't me.'

When he left, I studied Alexander in the lamplight. 'Do you believe him?'

'I don't know.'

I lay down on my couch and looked at the ceiling. 'So do you think the Red Eagle will save them tomorrow?'

'No. He has every legionary in Rome looking for him. If I were the Red Eagle, I'd disappear for several months.'

I dressed in the darkness, then crept through the atrium to the dimly lit library before dawn broke across the sky. I could see Vitruvius silhouetted against the lamplight, and with his sharp profile he reminded me of a bird. He looked up from his desk.

'Have they been killed?' I asked him.

Vitruvius furrowed his bald brow. 'Who?'

'The slaves being held in the Carcer!'

His face became suddenly tender. 'Executions don't begin until dawn, Selene, but you can be certain that they will die. Those were the orders.'

'From whom? A group of fifty judices, not one of whom has ever known slavery? How is that fair?'

Vitruvius nodded slowly. 'Many things aren't fair.'

'But isn't that what Caesar is for? To make things right?'

'No. Caesar is here to keep the peace. And if two hundred slaves have to die in order to keep the peace in Rome, then he is willing to sacrifice them.'

I stared at him.

'I don't mean to say that's my belief,' he added, 'but that is what Caesar is thinking.'

I took a seat on the opposite side of his desk, but I didn't take out my book of sketches. 'Do you think the Red Eagle will save them?'

'No. And I wouldn't mention his name in this villa. What

began as an annoyance has become a real threat. The boy who was crucified made his attempt in the name of the rebel. You may think this man is brave, Selene, you may even sympathize with those slaves, but do not speak his name around Caesar or his sister.'

I was disappointed that Vitruvius didn't understand, and when I returned to my chamber an hour later so that Gallia could arrange my hair, I told her what he'd said.

'He's right.'

I looked up at her in surprise.

'No one knows whether that boy was working for the Red Eagle.'

You do, I wanted to say, but kept my silence until I could know for certain. Besides, if she had wanted to confide in me, she would have. 'And the two hundred slaves?'

She lowered her head. 'They were crucified this morning.'

I gasped. 'All of them?'

'The smallest children were poisoned.' She saw my look in the mirror and stepped in front of me. 'There is no use in letting this consume you,' she warned. 'You are free, and if you keep away from trouble, perhaps Caesar will return you to Egypt. Then think of the things you could change.'

I closed my eyes and willed myself not to cry. Instead, I vowed that I would be the most talented apprentice Vitruvius could ever want, and that by my twelfth birthday even Octavian would see that I was useful.

CHAPTER TWELVE

December, 29 BC

'HIS WHEELS are smoking!' Alexander exclaimed, rising from our couch. 'Did you see that, Selene?'

A *sparsor* rushed onto the tracks with a bucket of water and doused the chariot's wheels while the driver made frantic motions for the man to hurry. Then the *sparsor* jumped back, and the driver continued racing.

'I don't see how anything can be smoking on a day like this,' I said grimly, tightening my cloak around my shoulders.

Next to me, Marcellus waved his hand. 'Oh, it's not so bad. Wait until tomorrow.'

'What happens tomorrow?'

'From the looks of it, snow.' Julia shivered in her cloak. We had exchanged our silk tunics for cotton months ago, but now that it was nearing the middle of December, nothing seemed to ward off the cold.

'You mean there will be snow on the mountains?' Alexander asked.

'And everywhere else.' Marcellus held out his hand, and the mist left a fine sheen on his palm. 'It would be a shame if it snows during Saturnalia. My mother says once it snowed for three days.'

I exchanged looks with Alexander.

'What's the matter?' Julia asked. 'Haven't you ever seen snow?'

'Only when it was cooling our mother's wine,' I admitted.

Marcellus laughed. 'That's it? But you must have tasted *nix dulcis.*'

I frowned.

'The sweet snow brought down from the mountains,' Julia prompted, 'mixed with honey and fruit.'

Both Alexander and I shook our heads.

'Well, you've haven't lived if you've never tasted *nix dulcis,*' Marcellus said. 'Perhaps there'll be some in the markets before Saturnalia.'

'So what is Saturnalia?' Alexander asked.

Julia grinned. 'On the seventeenth, we'll go to the Temple of Saturn. And for an entire week there's no work and no school. No one has to wear a toga, and even slaves can gamble.'

'Will the Circus be open?' Alexander asked.

I sighed impatiently, but Marcellus laughed. 'It's always open. And I've heard that if it isn't snowing, the Pompeians will be sending up their teams to challenge Rome. We'll have to come down to the stables in advance.'

'There's also a feast every day for a week,' Julia added. 'And people exchange gifts.'

'For what?' I asked.

'Just for fun! They're only small things. Like pretty silks or statues. It's really for the children.'

'And slaves change positions with their masters,' Marcellus added. 'We sit in the atrium where the slaves usually dine, and they use the triclinium—'

'Not this year,' Julia warned. 'My father forbade it. He also said the first feast will be hosted by Pollio.'

Marcellus groaned. 'Why? He never stops talking, unless it's to shove food in his mouth.'

'At least Horatia will be there,' Julia said glumly.

'And how can she move? She's nearly due.'

'Pregnant women can still walk,' Julia retorted. 'She might even have the child by then.'

It snowed on the seventeenth of December. Like a white linen sheath, the snow covered the roads and the rooftops; it froze the fountains and brought every kind of traffic to a halt. A bitter wind blew through the streets of Rome, carrying the scents of charcoal braziers. On the steps to the Temple of Saturn, I tightened Alexander's hood around his face.

'Do I look like a gryphon in this thing?' he asked.

'No. You look like a prince of Egypt.' It was true. The heavy cloak was trimmed in ermine, and the soft white contrasted with his olive skin. Dark tendrils escaped from his hood, and they blew about in the wind, making him look like a statue of young Hermes. 'It's really cold here, isn't it?' I said bleakly.

'It makes you wish we were back in Alexandria.'

'Many things make me wish that.'

As soon as Octavian's ritual in the temple was finished, horse-drawn carriages took us to Pollio's villa. The carriages were normally forbidden in Rome, but the streets were too slick to risk riding in litters. And because the skies were so dark, a dozen torchbearers lit the way. I huddled in my cloak, too cold to speak, and when I stole a glance at Julia, her red cheeks and bright nose announced her misery. I don't remember ever feeling so happy to reach shelter as I did when we entered Pollio's villa. A rush of warm air engulfed us, and the smell of roasted meat filled the vestibulum.

'Thank the gods,' Octavian said. He seemed to be suffering the worst of all. Beneath his woolen cloak, he wore three separate tunics, and there was a brace on his right hand, which Marcellus said stiffened every year with the cold.

Pollio spread his arms. 'Welcome!'

'Take us to the triclinium,' Livia commanded. 'My husband is in pain.'

'Of course!' As Pollio rushed to do her bidding, his heavy fur cloak fanned out around him. 'Of course!'

We passed through the atrium, where elaborate braziers did very little to offset the frigid air. But when we reached the triclinium, Octavian's shoulders relaxed. The room was as warm as any bathhouse. Flowers bloomed from precious gold vases, and garlands twisted around the columns as if it were spring.

'How extravagant,' Livia said critically.

'Where is Horatia?' Julia asked.

There had been no sign of the hostess, and as guests crowded into the room, Pollio hesitated. 'I'm afraid she cannot be with us tonight.'

'Why?' Julia looked around. 'Is she sick?'

'In a fashion.'

'She's not having the baby?' Octavia exclaimed.

Pollio nodded as if he were embarrassed. 'I'm afraid it is bad timing—'

'So why are we here?' Octavia cried.

Pollio frowned. 'Because I promised to host Caesar on the first night of Saturnalia.'

Julia's look was mutinous. 'I want to see her.'

'I'm sorry, but she is in her chamber.'

'And what does that mean? That she should be shut up like some birthing cow while everyone else feasts?' Julia cried.

'Control yourself,' Octavian said firmly, 'and take your couch.'

'But I would rather see Horatia. Please, Father. Please.'

Octavian looked to Pollio. 'Will the child come tonight?'

'If I am lucky. Imagine having to pay for a feast for Saturnalia and a birthing feast as well.'

'Then perhaps my daughter can visit her. It's a comfort to women in labor to have others in their chamber.'

I could see that Pollio wanted to object, but he nodded instead. 'Yes . . . Yes, of course. Up the stairs, to the right,' he directed.

Julia looked at me.

'You're going to go with her?' Alexander exclaimed.

'Why not?'

'Because there'll be blood. And sickness.'

'It's a birth, not the plague.'

'Women don't mind it,' Marcellus assured my brother.

I followed Julia up the stairs, and the pitiful sound of a woman's cries led us to a dimly lit chamber at the very back of the house. When we opened the door, the stench of sweat made my stomach clench, and I wondered if my brother had been right.

Horatia gasped when she saw us. 'Julia!' She was already seated on the birthing chair. She was entirely naked except for a *palla* around her shoulders. Midwives were huddled at the base of the chair where the child would drop through the hole into their arms. Horatia was breathing very heavily, and as Julia rushed forward, I held back. I had never before witnessed a birth.

'Horatia,' Julia said tenderly, and she wiped her friend's brow with her hand.

'It's coming,' Horatia groaned. 'I can feel it.'

'Keep pushing,' a midwife encouraged.

'What have they given you?' Julia asked.

'A little wine.'

'That's it?' Julia cried. 'No verbena?'

'Nothing!' Horatia groaned, gripping the leather arms of the chair. 'Pollio won't allow it.'

'Those are peasants' superstitions!' Julia shouted. She looked at me, and although I felt faint, I helped wipe the sweat from Horatia's brow with a linen square dipped in lavender water.

'I should have used silphium,' Horatia panted. 'I may never even live to see the new year.'

'Nonsense,' Julia said firmly. 'You're healthy, and this is only your first child.'

Horatia gritted her teeth, and when she screamed, I was sure her cries could be heard above the harpists in the triclinium. For several hours we remained like this, encouraging and fanning the air into Horatia's face. Then finally one of the midwives cried, 'It's coming, domina! Keep pushing!'

Horatia looked up into Julia's face. 'Thank you.' She began to weep. 'Thank you for coming.'

'Don't thank me! Concentrate!'

Horatia gripped the arms of the chair, and her face was a mask of terrible pain. Again and again she strained, screaming, crying, then finally pushing a child into the world in a rush of blood and water. I held my breath, and Julia cried out, 'A girl! It's a girl!'

'No,' Horatia whispered. The midwives swaddled the crying infant in wool, and Horatia sat up on the birthing chair. 'It can't be!'

'It's a girl, domina. A healthy child.'

'But he wanted a son.'

'So next time—'

'You don't understand!' She looked from the midwife to Julia in desperation. 'He will never accept it!'

'Of course he will!' Julia took the baby girl into her arms while the midwives packed Horatia's womb with wool. 'Look.' Julia stroked the little nose with her fingertip, then placed the infant gently in her friend's arms. I had never seen her so tender with anyone.

Tears welled in Horatia's eyes. She took the crying baby to her breast, but the infant refused to suck. 'She's not hungry.'

The eldest midwife smiled. 'Leave it to the *nutrice*. That is her job.'

'What will you name her?' Julia asked.

Horatia was silent, stroking her daughter's brow with two fingers. Then she said, 'Gaia. Like the Greeks' Mother Goddess.' She held Gaia for a little while, as the music and feasting went on below us.

'You must wash, domina. It isn't healthy to stay here with all this blood.'

Horatia passed her daughter to Julia, and then the midwives helped her into the bathing room.

'She's beautiful, isn't she?' Julia said.

Gaia had the thick hair of her mother, and her dark eyes were already open.

'Do you think that Pollio will be terribly angry?' I asked.

'Probably,' Julia admitted. 'But she'll have a son next time. Do you want children?'

In fourteen days I would be old enough to marry, and when my monthly blood came, to have children of my own. 'Yes, but not for many years.'

'I would like them now,' she confided.

'At twelve?'

'Horatia is only thirteen. And now she has a little girl of her own who will always love her. Who will never abandon her.'

I was reminded of what Gallia had said about judging Julia too harshly, and suddenly I felt sorry for her. She had a father who valued her only for what marriage she could make, and a mother she could visit only in secret. Although my parents were gone, I had always known I was loved. And my parents had only ever left me in death.

When Horatia emerged from the bathing room, she walked gingerly. The midwives were careful in their movements, slowly helping her into an embroidered tunic and heavy new *palla* trimmed with fur. Only married women wore the *palla*, and I could see the admiration in Julia's eyes as the midwife draped her friend in the beautiful mantle. Horatia held out her arms for her new daughter, and I thought that Julia handed the infant back with regret.

'May Juno bless her first day,' the gray-haired midwife intoned, 'and may Cunina watch over the cradle.'

'Will you go to him now?' Julia asked.

'Absolutely not!' The midwife clicked her tongue. 'Dominus must come to her in their chamber. He must accept his daughter first.'

We followed Horatia down the hall to the chamber where she and Pollio slept. A slave was sent to fetch Pollio from the festivities, and we waited outside while Horatia sat on a chair with her infant daughter in her arms.

'Is he coming to name the child?' I asked.

'No. That happens in eight days with the *lustratio*. This is the *tollere liberos.*'

There was no time to ask Julia what that meant. I could hear Pollio's heavy footsteps on the stairs, and when he reached the landing, he looked expectantly at Julia. 'Is it a son?'

The midwife inclined her head. 'Your wife is in there, domine.'

Pollio entered his chamber, and before the door swung shut behind him I could hear him demanding, 'Is it a son?'

Julia's dark eyes flashed at me. 'He doesn't even care if she's well.'

'What a terrible marriage.'

'They're all terrible,' she said bitterly.

'But yours won't be.'

She gave me a long, calculated look. 'If my father doesn't change his mind.'

There was a shriek on the other side of the wall, then the door was flung open, and Pollio emerged. 'Take it away!' he ordered the midwives. I looked inside the chamber, where Horatia's daughter lay alone on the floor.

'Pollio, please!' Horatia ran after him.

'I said a son.' He turned on her. 'Not a daughter. A *son*!'

'But I will give you a son. Pollio, *please*, she's ours!'

'She belongs to the gods.' He made his way down the stairs, and Julia rushed to Horatia so that she wouldn't faint. 'Take her to the dump,' Pollio called over his shoulder.

Horatia fell on her knees. 'Please!' she begged. 'Take her to the Columna Lactaria. Give her a chance!' But Pollio was gone. She looked up into the face of the midwife. 'Don't take her away,' she pleaded, but the midwife had already gathered the child in her arms. 'You can't take her away from me!' Horatia shrieked.

Hot tears burned my cheeks, and I realized that my hands were trembling. 'Don't do this,' I said.

The midwife's look was firm. 'It's dominus who pays me. They are dominus Pollio's orders that I follow.'

'But don't take her to the dump. She's a child. She hasn't done anything wrong.'

The woman's smile was full of vengeance. 'Neither did those two hundred slaves.'

'So what?' Julia cried. 'Because slaves die, patrician children must die as well?'

The woman didn't respond.

'Let me give you denarii,' Horatia said desperately. 'Please. Just don't take her to the dump.'

The midwife hesitated, then turned to the other slaves and

snapped, 'Go!' The women swiftly disappeared, some down the stairs, others to separate chambers. When the hall was empty, the midwife said, 'Two hundred denarii.'

Horatia went pale. 'That's my entire dowry.'

'And this is your daughter's chance at life. Maybe someone will take her, maybe they won't, but at the dump the wolves will eat her.'

'Wait.' Horatia was trembling. 'I will give you the money.'

Julia stared at the midwife, who looked back at us without any remorse.

'You are no better than a beast,' Julia said.

'And isn't that what slaves are supposed to be? Beasts of burden?'

Horatia returned with several heavy purses, and the midwife stuffed them beneath her cloak. 'How will you carry her?' Horatia asked worriedly.

'Just fine.'

But even if Gaia survived, she would likely end up in a *lupanar*, abused from the time she was old enough to speak. My mother had told me there were men who liked girls too young to understand what was happening to them. Tears rolled down Horatia's cheeks, and Julia whispered, 'Isn't there someone who can adopt her?'

'How could I arrange it without Pollio knowing?'

The midwife pulled her cloak over the child, and I turned away from the terrible scene. While Horatia and Julia wept, I made my way slowly down the stairs. In the triclinium, the harpist was still playing, and Pollio was raising a cup of wine in toast.

'What happened?' Alexander asked.

'It's a girl,' I told him.

Marcellus frowned. 'Was she deformed?'

'No. Pollio wanted a son, so he ordered that she be put out.'

'As a foundling?' he cried.

I nodded.

Octavia rose from her couch and came over to me. 'Where is Horatia?' she asked quietly.

I told her the story, even the part about the two hundred denarii and the Columna Lactaria. When I was finished, her face was hard.

'What do you think will happen to her?' I asked.

'The infant or Horatia?'

'Both,' I said.

Octavia drew a heavy breath. 'If they survive, they will live the rest of their lives in terrible sadness.' She walked back to the table where Octavian was reclining between his wife and Terentilla, then whispered something into his ear. He glanced briefly at me, then rose from the couch.

'What is this?' Pollio exclaimed. 'The dessert has not even come.'

Octavian's voice was clipped. 'I hear that your wife has given birth,' he said. 'It would be rude of me to stay, when you belong with her.'

Pollio's fat mouth opened and closed like a fish's.

'Marcellus,' Octavian said sharply, 'go and find Julia.'

Pollio looked around him. 'But we cannot let Saturnalia be interrupted by women's matters.'

'The children of Rome matter to everyone,' Octavian said coldly. 'Even foolish men like you.'

Several dozen guests remained in the triclinium, but everyone who had come with Octavian prepared to leave.

'Congratulations,' Agrippa said, not knowing what had happened in the upstairs rooms.

Pollio's face took on the color of unbaked dough. He led us

through the atrium to the carriages outside. 'Are you certain?' he protested. 'It's cold. Perhaps you would like to stay the night!'

Octavia turned and said quietly, 'I'm sure your daughter would have liked to stay the night as well. When you shiver, remember how cold it is in the dump.'

On the ride back to the Palatine, I thought of Horatia's daughter freezing beneath the Columna Lactaria while the rest of Rome drank wine beside crackling fires and ate roasted meats. And once all of his guests left, Pollio would probably climb under the covers next to his wife, demanding her attention even as her breasts leaked milk through her bindings. The thought made me wince, and while Julia wept softly, Alexander and Marcellus exchanged doleful looks.

When we reached Octavia's villa, Juba excused himself, but Agrippa and Octavian remained, settling with the rest of us in the warmth of the library, where Vitruvius's plans were spread across the tables. No one said anything, until Julia broke the silence.

'What about a home for foundlings?' she asked.

Marcellus looked up from his place near the brazier, and Alexander caught my eye.

'A place where mothers can leave their infants and they can be adopted by freedwomen and citizens,' she said. 'Selene has drawn sketches of what such a house might look like.'

'And how would that help Rome?' Octavian demanded.

'We would be saving lives. Roman lives,' Julia protested.

'And increasing the number of mouths on the dole,' Livia retorted.

'Not if citizens were to adopt the infants!'

'And who would want to do that?' Livia asked. 'When a woman

is barren, she takes a child from a slave. Why would she need a dirty foundling?'

Octavia recoiled. 'I doubt that there was anything dirty about Horatia's child.'

'How do you know? Did you see it? The child was probably deformed.'

'It was perfectly healthy!' Julia exclaimed. 'I was there and so was Selene.' She turned to her father. 'If there was a foundling house—'

'It would be too costly,' Octavian overruled her. 'There is a Columna Lactaria for a reason, and the plebs are satisfied. We do enough by paying *nutrices* to suckle infants.'

'But most of them die!' Julia cried.

'Then that is the will of the gods.'

She looked at me, but I knew better than to speak.

'You do enough for these people,' Livia assured Octavian. 'Free grain, free baths, even men who fight fires and patrol the Subura watching for crime. How much are you supposed to give?'

'As much as possible,' Octavia said.

'Then why don't *you* fund this foundling house?' she demanded.

'If my brother thought it was a good idea, I would.'

Everyone in the library looked to Octavian, who was shaking despite the warmth in the room. 'My wife is right. We do enough.'

Julia's eyes shone with tears, and I saw Marcellus pat her knee tenderly.

'And Horatia's child?' Julia whispered.

'It was a girl,' Octavian said simply. 'The incident was an unlucky beginning to Saturnalia. But I plan to end this night with good news.'

I couldn't imagine what kind of news could dispel the

unhappiness that had settled over the library, but when Octavian looked to Agrippa, his general announced, 'I am getting married.'

Julia gasped, and I wondered if she feared that she might be the bride. 'To whom?' she ventured.

'My daughter Claudia,' Octavia said.

'My sister?' Marcellus exclaimed. He looked at his mother. 'How come I didn't know about this?'

Octavia smiled primly. 'Well, now you do.'

For the rest of Saturnalia, Julia kept a vigil for Horatia's daughter, going every day to the Columna Lactaria to search for her. For seven days we battled the wind and rain, holding each other on the slick cobblestones while Juba and the Praetorian guards shone the light of their bronze lanterns on the empty streets. But on the eighth day, Gallia demanded to know what Julia would do if she found the infant.

'I would bring her home!'

'What? To your father's villa?' Marcellus asked. 'Be sensible, Julia. Someone has taken her.'

'But who?' she shouted, and her voice echoed across the icy courtyard. The marketplace was closed for the last day of Saturnalia, and anyone with good judgment was at home, hunched in front of a brazier, cooking lamb in the kitchens and drinking hot wine.

'It might have been a well-meaning citizen,' Alexander said.

'But what if it was the owner of a *lupanar*?'

'Well, there's no way of knowing which it is,' Juba said. 'No one's going to return her now.'

Julia stared at the column where thousands of women had left their infants over the years. The courtyard was silent.

'The rain is about to come,' Juba remarked.

We followed him back to the waiting carriage, and inside,

Julia fretted over the night we had visited Pollio. 'I should have taken Gaia from the midwife.'

'And what would you have done with her, domina?'

'Found her a home!'

'With whom?' Marcellus asked. 'Where?'

Julia looked at Juba. 'What do you think has happened to her?' I knew why she was asking him. Of everyone in the carriage, he would give the answer that would come closest to the truth.

'A freedman found her and took her home.'

'But how do you know?'

'Because no patricians live near the markets or would ever want to be caught there at night.'

'But what if it was a freedman with a *lupanar*?'

'Don't you think it's more likely that men of that sort were indoors, celebrating the first night of Saturnalia?' he asked. 'Not standing in an abandoned marketplace waiting for foundlings, when those can be had any other day of the week.'

This settled Julia's mind a little. But even when Alexander and I turned twelve on the first day of the New Year, she was quiet during Octavia's celebration of our *dies natalis*.

'Tomorrow,' Octavia offered her kindly, 'why don't you come and help me prepare for Claudia's wedding?'

Julia looked up from the crackling brazier, where cinnamon sticks burned among the charcoal to scent the triclinium. 'What about your slaves?'

'Oh, they can do the tedious work. The cleaning, the cooking. But who will help me with the tunic and veil? There are only two weeks before my daughters come home from Pompeii and Claudia marries.'

So through the miserable month of January, while ice still covered the fountains and Octavian wrapped himself in furs,

Julia helped Octavia prepare. On the way to and from the ludus, she told us about the jewels Claudia would be wearing, what her sandals would look like, and how her carriage would be decorated for her trip to Rome. But when I asked her why Octavia's eldest daughters were living so far away, she looked from me to Alexander and hesitated.

'You can tell them,' Tiberius said on our way back from the ludus. 'It's not as though it's their fault.'

Julia nodded uncertainly. 'Octavia had to give them away in order to marry Antony. Then, when Antony left her, Claudia and Marcella chose to remain with their aunt in Pompeii.'

I was quiet for a moment. After all of the unhappiness my mother and father had brought into her life, it was surprising that Octavia treated us with any kindness at all.

My brother shook his head. 'I have no idea why your mother treats us so well.'

'She loves children,' Marcellus said simply. 'Wait until you meet my older sisters. We're all very similar.'

'You mean they gamble?' Tiberius asked.

'He means they're both blond with blue eyes,' Julia said, ignoring Tiberius's quip. 'They're his only full sisters.' She turned to me and added brightly, 'You should help us with the planning.'

'Oh yes,' Marcellus said. 'It's so much fun. Much better than watching the races, which is what we *could* be doing.'

Julia swatted him. 'Alexander enjoys it.'

'Because he likes you girls. I can't stand all the talk of hairnets and paint.'

'Come help us,' she begged me. 'Vitruvius doesn't need you every day.'

'He probably doesn't need me at all.'

'Nonsense,' my brother said as we walked. Across the

courtyard, Gallia and Juba were waiting for us, bundled into their warmest winter cloaks. 'Just yesterday,' Alexander boasted, 'he told her that when the weather turns, he'll be taking her with him on his inspections.'

'A *girl*?' Tiberius cried.

'What does that matter?' Julia retorted.

'What business does a girl have with construction? Look at her! She can't even lift a brick.'

'I can take measurements,' I said sharply. 'And I can sketch a design for the flooring or the rooftop better than any of Vitruvius's old men.'

Tiberius laughed. 'So what is Vitruvius going to do? Introduce you as his apprentice?'

'I'll be going in the mornings before the builders get to work.'

He smiled. 'So he *is* ashamed.'

'Leave her alone,' Marcellus warned.

'Does that mean you won't help us?' Julia pouted.

'Yes,' I said firmly.

By the time we arrived home on the Palatine, half a dozen litters crowded the portico of Octavia's villa.

'The priestesses are here,' Gallia warned. 'Be silent when you enter.'

Juba and Tiberius followed us into the atrium, where the priestesses of Juno had arranged themselves around a brazier. Octavia held an unfurled scroll above the flames, while Agrippa fanned the fire with his hand.

'What are they doing?' I whispered.

Julia leaned over so that her lips were at my ear. 'The scroll Octavia is holding is a calendar. When the priestesses decide there has been enough smoke, they will interpret the burn marks and determine which days are *dies nefasti*.'

I drew away from her. 'Bad-luck days?'

'March, May, and all of June are unsuitable for weddings. So are the Kalends, the Nones, and the Ides of any month, and any day following those. And no one can be married on the day of any religious festival.'

'Is it really bad luck?'

She rolled her eyes. We listened as the priestesses chanted to Juno, the goddess of motherhood and marriage. Octavian, holding a wax tablet and a stylus, stood next to his sister. He was wearing a heavy fur cloak that was too big around his shoulders. I could see that he was bitterly cold, keeping away from the open roof, where rain was falling into the icy pool. His face had turned as white as his cloak, and the only color to be seen in it was the gray of his eyes.

'That is enough,' one of the priestesses said.

Octavia immediately withdrew the calendar, and the priestess who had spoken held it up to the dim light from above. The other women stopped chanting, and the only sound was the patter of rain.

'Not February second,' she said.

Octavian scribbled something with his stylus, and I noticed that the polished ivory brace on his right hand now extended all the way up his arm.

'Is your father well?' Alexander whispered to Julia.

She nodded. 'He is like this every winter.'

Even on the worst days in Alexandria, I had never seen my father look so weak.

'Not February tenth,' the priestess said.

Octavian made another mark on his tablet.

'The best day in February will be the twelfth.'

Octavian looked up from his tablet. 'The day before Lupercalia?' he challenged.

The priestess would have responded, but suddenly lightning

cracked through the sky and thunder shook the walls of the atrium.

'The augurs!' Octavian shouted. 'Go to the *collegium* and bring the augurs!'

Alexander turned to Marcellus. 'What's happening?'

'Thunder,' he replied fearfully. 'It's a terrible omen.'

Lightning flashed again, and the thunder clapped, bringing with it a fresh torrent of rain. Octavia said curtly, 'Get to the library!'

We crowded into the library, where Juba helped Octavia light the oil lamps until the paneled room glowed a burnished orange. The priestesses huddled together near the brazier, but it was the woman who had spoken who looked the most fearful. If the augurs came and declared that the gods were upset with her pronouncement, it might mean any number of terrible things for her.

'What does this portend?' Octavian asked. He was looking at Juba, who had taken a seat next to the brazier. Outside, rain poured into the fountains and pool.

'We should wait for the augurs,' Juba said.

I was close enough to hear Tiberius whisper to Juba, 'You don't really believe it means anything? It's the precursor of rain. That's it!'

'The augurs are coming,' Juba said firmly.

'But you don't believe them! Tell the truth. Even Cicero mocked the augurs.'

'And Cicero ended his days with his head on the rostrum,' Juba said forcefully.

Some of the priestesses whimpered, and an uneasy silence fell over the library. I imagined the augurs tucked in comfortably on their couches, buried beneath heavy piles of blankets until a slave summoned them into the rain and wind. What sort of mood would they be in when they arrived? Angry enough to condemn a priestess of Juno?

When a slave appeared at the door, everyone sat up. 'They're here, domine.'

Octavian rose. 'Bring them in!' He looked at Agrippa. 'Nothing must go wrong with this marriage. It must be blessed by all of the gods.'

The first augur who entered looked eager to please. He shepherded the others inside the crowded library, and addressed his first question to Octavian. 'We are humbled to be of service, Caesar. Is it the thunder that brings us here today?'

The priestess of Juno explained what had happened, and Octavian added, 'As soon as she made the pronouncement, it came. There had been no thunder the entire morning. For days, there hasn't been any lightning.'

'And where did the lightning come from?' the augur asked.

'The east,' Juba said.

Octavian frowned. 'I didn't see that.'

'Because you were writing. I was watching the skies.'

The first augur lifted his arms. 'Then it is a sign of blessing!'

Octavia placed her hand on her heart, and her brother persisted, 'Even though the chosen day is the day before Lupercalia?'

A second augur nodded. 'The gods have spoken.'

Tiberius gave Juba a triumphant glance, but Juba was too polite to respond with anything but a curt nod. *He's lying*, I thought. *He doesn't believe in this and just wants it to be done. No one can know whether it came from the east or the west.* But no one said anything, and Agrippa's wedding date was set for the twelfth day of February.

CHAPTER THIRTEEN

February 12, 28 BC

CLAUDIA STOOD in the middle of her mother's chamber while a dozen slaves rushed around, plaiting her hair into six even braids and fastening her crimson veil with flowers. She was giddy and shy, always blushing and surprisingly naïve for a nineteen-year-old woman. Perhaps because her skin was so light, every passing emotion colored her face a curious shade of pink. It would begin in her cheeks, then spread to her nose, her ears, and finally her neck. I noticed that Marcella had the same coloring, as if her face were an open scroll waiting to be read.

'The Romans certainly do things differently than the Egyptians,' Alexander remarked.

'Why? What do Egyptians do for marriage?' Claudia asked.

'The bride and groom take a special bath.'

'Together?' she cried.

Julia smiled. 'How lovely.'

'How vulgar,' Livia retorted, but no one was listening. She had complained that my brother was allowed in the chamber while Claudia's veil was being fitted, but Octavia had rightly pointed out that it was no different than watching someone put on a cloak. And there was no more skin showing on Claudia than if she had been mummified in linen like Osiris. Her long tunic was fastened at the waist by a girdle, and like a vestal virgin, she wore her veil so that it covered the rest of her body, including the top half of her face.

'Don't be nervous,' Octavia murmured. 'Agrippa is one of the finest men in Rome.' She turned to Marcella, who was seventeen. 'And you will be next.'

Marcella nodded sadly.

'You aren't going to be lonely without me?' Claudia worried. 'You can come and live with me if you get tired of Pompeii.'

'And get in the way of your baths?' Marcella teased. 'No, our aunt needs me.'

'Then you will kiss her for me, won't you? And tell her I love her, even as a matron?' I could hear that Claudia was about to cry, and her sister wrapped her arms around Claudia's waist.

'Of course I'll tell her.'

I noticed that Octavia's eyes looked sad. After so many years of separation, she had ceased to be like a mother to them. She had lost that special bond as surely as Horatia had lost Gaia.

Claudia lifted the hem of her tunic so that she could walk without tripping, and a pair of crimson sandals peeked out. She held out her arms so that we could see.

'Beautiful,' Alexander said.

'As beautiful as an Egyptian bride?'

'Even prettier,' he lied.

We could hear the music and laughing from the atrium, where the pool was illuminated by floating lamps and the dusk was held at bay by hundreds of candelabra. There was no special procession as there was in Egypt. We simply walked with the bride to the granite altar that Octavia's slaves had carried in. A ewe had been slaughtered earlier, so that the augurs could again declare this a favorable day.

'Look at all the people,' Claudia said anxiously.

Patricians from all across Rome had come for the evening's

celebration, and Octavia said, 'This is an important marriage. If something were to happen to my brother, who do you think would take his place? Marcellus is still too young.' She squeezed her daughter's hand, and Agrippa approached the altar with Octavian and Juba at his side. His eight-year-old daughter, Vipsania, stood on his right, looking curiously at the woman who was to become her stepmother.

'She's lucky,' Julia whispered, noting the direction of my gaze. 'Claudia will be good to her.'

The laughter in the atrium grew muted, and senators in their best togas stepped closer to the altar to hear what was being said.

'*Ubi tu es Agrippa, ego Claudia.*'

'*Ubi tu es Claudia, ego Agrippa.*' Agrippa raised Claudia's veil, and the entire atrium shouted '*Feliciter!*'

'That's it?' Alexander asked incredulously. 'All of that preparation for this?'

Julia raised her arms and clapped. 'It's done!'

Flute players led the way to the triclinium, where the couches were draped in saffron-dyed fleece to match the bride's attire. A tall spelt-cake had been decorated with flowers, and as I bent to inhale the fragrance, Livia said merrily, 'Soon it will be you.' When I straightened, she called to the old man next to me, 'Catullus, have you met Princess Selene?' The deep black of his eyes was masked by a rheumy film, and his hands shook with some ailment of age.

The old senator lowered his cup of wine to smile. 'A pleasure.'

'Such a pretty girl, isn't she? Her mother had four children, and probably could have had more.'

Catullus raised his brows.

'So tell me,' Livia said, 'is it true that you are looking for a wife?'

I felt the color drain from my face, and I was too terrified to turn or leave the conversation.

'Yes.' The old man nodded slowly.

'Well, perhaps you would like to spend some time with Selene.'

My heart was beating rapidly in my chest.

Catullus frowned. 'Doing what?' he asked cautiously.

'Oh, for now, just discussing a few things,' Livia answered.

'And exactly what would he have to discuss with a child?'

I had never been so thankful to see Juba.

'My gratitude for your concern,' Catullus said swiftly to Livia, 'but I believe I am wanted over there.'

Livia watched Catullus leave, then fixed her gaze on me. 'You will *never* return to Egypt.'

'And how do you know she wants to return?' Juba asked.

Livia laughed sharply. 'Because I know this one. She would have tried to run away if she didn't think my husband might return her to Alexandria.'

Octavia appeared as silently as Juba had. 'Livia,' she said sweetly, 'I hope you're not taking out your anger on Selene. It's not her fault my brother has disappeared with Terentilla.'

Livia raised her chin. 'He'll never leave me. Terentilla's nothing more than a theater-whore.'

'He left Scribonia,' Octavia reminded her.

'Because I had something to give him.'

'What?' Octavia asked. 'A patrician name? Do you think he needs that now?'

'I remember a letter once,' Livia said pensively. 'I believe it was from Marc Antony, calling your grandfather a freedman and a rope-maker from the town of Thurii. Do you really think that without my family the senators will sit quietly – just sit – while the descendant of a rope-maker makes laws for them?'

I recalled my father calling Octavian 'Thurinus' once, and now I understood.

But Octavia only smiled. 'Yes. And when that time comes,' she suggested, 'let's hope your friends outnumber your enemies.'

There was a loud cheer in the triclinium as the bride and groom took their first sips of wine from the same cup. I noticed that Juba had disappeared. Octavia held out her arm to me. 'Shall we?' She led me to a table where Marcellus and Alexander were teasing Julia about how lavish her own wedding was going to be. But when Julia turned and smiled at me, I didn't have it in my heart to be merry.

The celebration carried on almost until morning, when Octavian returned and announced that it was time for the groom to lead his bride to her new home. Senators began singing crude songs to the blushing bride, and flutists and torchbearers led the way while the guests followed. When we reached the portico of Agrippa's villa, my brother stumbled over the first step and fell.

'*Alexander!*' I exclaimed.

'What?' He giggled. Marcellus and Julia giggled, too.

'The three of you are drunk!' I accused.

'It's the Falernian wine,' Julia protested. She looked at Alexander, still sitting on the first step of the portico, and they all collapsed into laughter.

'Julia, Marcellus, Alexander,' Octavia snapped. 'Get yourselves home.' Next to her, Gallia shook her head disapprovingly.

'But the bride hasn't even—'

'I don't care.' She cut off Marcellus's protest, then looked down at me. 'You may stay.' It wasn't an offer. It was a command.

Alexander threw a pleading look over his shoulder at me, while Marcellus helped him up and the three of them stumbled away.

'You are the only one with any sense,' Octavia muttered.

On the steps outside Agrippa's villa, Claudia was crowning the doorposts with wool, then anointing them with wolf's fat to bless her new home. When Agrippa carried her over the threshold, he was followed by dozens of drunken senators eager to watch him lay Claudia on her bridal couch and take off her girdle. I would have gone as well, but Livia's voice cut through the merriment.

'What's the matter, Senator?' A thin man in a toga had just emptied his stomach into an urn. He rose shakily to his feet, and Livia told him, 'You should get yourself home.'

'And miss the untying of the girdle?' He gave a leering laugh and made to go inside, but Livia stopped him with her hand.

'I will send a slave with you. Gallia,' she instructed. 'Take Senator Gaius back to his villa.'

I saw that the senator was about to protest, until he caught sight of Gallia. Then his smile grew wider.

Gallia hesitated. 'Are you sure you wouldn't rather have an escort of men, domine?'

'Not tonight,' he said eagerly. 'And the bottom of the hill isn't far,' he promised.

Gallia searched for Octavia, but she had followed Claudia into Agrippa's home. Without her, Gallia could never disobey Livia. 'Of course, domine.'

Livia followed the pair of them with her eyes, and when the cheerful throng of senators and well-wishers reemerged, she took Octavian's arm. 'A successful night,' she said happily to him. 'Shall we retire?'

A cock crowed in the distance, and Octavian stifled a yawn. 'It's time.'

Guests were summoning their litters, and tired slaves, who had taken too much wine, staggered beneath the weight of their masters. I heard exclamations of horror as one litter bearer or another fell down.

Octavia turned to Juba. 'Is it too late to ask you about a statue?'

'I doubt I will be getting much sleep,' he replied. The disappearing celebrants were making enough noise to reach the ears of Persephone as they called to one another in the gloom and shouted for the slaves to be more careful.

'It's a gift I purchased for my daughter,' Octavia said. 'But I'd like to know that it's authentic before she takes it.'

We walked together to Octavia's villa, and I wondered if I should mention what had happened with Livia. But before I could say anything, Octavia turned. 'Where is Gallia?'

'Gone,' I told her.

She frowned. 'With Magister Verrius?'

'No. Livia sent her with a senator to take him home.'

Juba asked swiftly, 'Who? Which one?'

'A man named Gaius.'

He exchanged looks with Octavia, who put her hand on her stomach. 'Dear gods,' she whispered. 'When did he take her?'

'When everyone went inside to see Claudia's bridal couch.'

'I know where he lives,' Juba said at once. 'Below the south shoulder of the hill. I'll go.'

'Wait! I know a shortcut,' I told him.

'Where?'

'Behind the Magna Mater.'

Octavia gasped. 'Through the woods?'

'We used to use it on our way to the ludus. Before Juba started coming with us.'

Octavia looked at him. 'Do you know it?'

'No one uses the woods,' he replied.

'We did! Marcellus convinced Gallia to take us that way. I can show you,' I promised. 'Gallia would never use it in the dark, but you'll get down faster.'

Octavia motioned swiftly. 'Go. Both of you!'

Juba didn't protest. He grabbed a torch from a soldier and led me through the press of drunken men and litters to the Temple of Magna Mater. 'So where is it?' he demanded. 'I don't see a path.' He handed me the torch, and I picked out the trail we had used every morning.

I had never been in the woods at night, and I was thankful to have Juba behind me, despite his antagonism. 'Over here,' I said, lighting the way. I remembered the night that Juba had saved me. 'What if he attacks her on the road?'

'With so many soldiers watching the Palatine?'

When we reached the bottom, he took the torch from me and we raced together through a cluster of houses. His scarlet cloak billowed behind him, and the way the moonlight crowned his long hair made him seem more handsome than he was before. We stopped at a house being watched by a group of guards, and Juba approached the first man.

'Has a slave girl entered here?'

'That is none of your business.'

Before the guard could blink, there was a dagger at his throat and the other men withdrew. The torch extinguished itself in a puddle. 'Let me repeat my question,' Juba said. 'I come from Caesar's sister Octavia, who would like to know if the Princess of Gaul, her favorite slave, was taken inside.'

The other guards slowly lowered their swords, and the man with the blade to his neck swallowed convulsively. 'Yes, she's inside,' he whispered.

Juba swept past him, and I kept several paces behind as he threw open the doors to Gaius's house and shouted, 'Gaius Tacitus!' There was the sound of shuffling in a chamber off the atrium, and slaves hid behind columns as Juba approached. 'Gaius Tacitus!' he shouted again, and this time, Gaius appeared at the end of the atrium. His toga had been discarded, and he was dressed in his thinnest tunic.

'Juba.' He smiled. 'And the little princess of Egypt, already budding into a woman.'

'Where is she?'

'Who?'

Juba crossed the room, and immediately, Gaius backed away. 'You mean the Gallic whore?'

There was a moan from inside a chamber off the atrium, and Juba shoved Gaius's head against the wall. 'Gallia!' Juba shouted.

I rushed inside, where Gallia was curled up on the couch. Her pale skin was bared to the moonlight coming through the open shutters, and only her long hair covered her nakedness. 'Gallia!' I cried, and she looked up at me with blackened eyes.

'Selene.' She had fought him and lost.

'She's hurt!' I screamed, and rushed to give Gallia my cloak. There was no sign of the tunic she had worn to the wedding, or the handsome leather shoes that Octavia had given her. 'Come,' I told her.

But Juba warned abruptly, 'Stay inside!'

We listened to the sound of men scuffling, and when I tried to help Gallia to her feet, I saw that her ankle was swollen.

'I'm sorry,' I told her. 'I'm so sorry.'

'It isn't your fault.'

'But I was there. I saw when Livia sent you.'

'And how were you to know what this man would do?'

'Octavia knew! She sent Juba, and if I had told her sooner . . .'

There was silence outside, and then Juba appeared. 'Gallia,' he said, taking her into his arms in a single sweep. She didn't cry out, despite her bruises.

'Please take me to Magister Verrius,' she whispered.

I followed them out of the chamber and saw Gaius bent double, clutching his stomach. Blood trickled from his mouth and his wounds. I wondered how many women he'd forced himself on, and then how Juba would explain the murder of a senator.

Outside the house, the guards shifted uneasily. 'What . . . what happened?' one of them asked.

'Go inside and find out,' Juba told them darkly. He carried Gallia to a house in a small copse of trees, where smoke coiled from the opening above the atrium. When he reached the door, he didn't have to knock. Magister Verrius opened it and saw at once what had happened.

'Gallia!'

Her lip began to tremble, and Magister Verrius led the way through his atrium to a woman's chamber where the scent of lavender hung in the air. Juba placed her gently on a couch, then followed me outside the room while Magister Verrius took Gallia into his arms. I heard her beginning to tell him the story. Then Juba closed the door and we were alone.

'She should have said no to Livia!' I cried.

'She's a slave. She doesn't have that privilege.'

'But what if this happens to her again?'

'It probably will.'

I couldn't understand Juba's callousness. There was weeping on the other side of the door, along with exclamations of rage from Magister Verrius, who had never raised his voice to us in the ludus. 'So how will you explain the senator's death?'

'I will say he challenged me. Only you were there to see it.'

His dismissiveness riled me. 'Don't you care about what happened tonight?'

'Of course I do, or I would never have risked my life to kill Gaius. But aside from freeing every slave in Rome and joining ranks with a traitor, what would you like me to do?'

I thought of the denarii Alexander had won at the races, but rejected the sum as being too small. Then I touched my mother's necklace of pink sea pearls. The golden pendant alone could buy Gallia's freedom; the rest could support her for many years. I unclasped my mother's last gift to me, then handed it to Juba.

'What am I supposed to do with this?'

'You deal in old statues and jewels,' I told him. 'I want you to trade it for me and buy Gallia's freedom.' If Gallia was freed, she would never have to obey the commands of a citizen again.

He raised a single brow. 'And what makes you think that Octavia will accept it?'

'The denarii from this necklace could feed half the mouths in the Subura.'

'I doubt she needs denarii.'

'Are you refusing?'

He took the necklace and held it up to an olive oil lamp.

'It's real,' I told him.

'I would expect no less from a princess of Egypt. Was it the queen's?'

I blinked away my tears. 'Yes. But if Octavia accepts the payment, I don't want you to tell Gallia who it came from.'

'How charitable.'

'It isn't charity!' I was the reason for what had happened to Gallia. She had defended me once when I had refused to wear Livia's beaded dress, and made an enemy of a woman who wished to see everyone else suffer. 'I owe this to her,' I whispered.

If it hadn't been the start of Lupercalia and the beginning of a week's holiday from the ludus, I would never have woken in time to meet with Vitruvius the next morning. When I opened my eyes, Alexander had already left the chamber, and the windows, which usually looked over a dark and richly wooded garden, were brightened by the winter's milky sun. I listened for a moment for sounds outside my chamber, wondering what time it was and where everyone had gone. Did they know about Gallia? Would Juba be punished for killing a senator?

I dressed as quickly as I could and simply pushed back my

hair with my diadem. When I looked in the mirror, only the golden *bulla* stared back at me. I had traded my mother's last gift for Gallia's freedom. In everything he did, Juba was swift. Surely by now some woman was placing my mother's pearls around her neck, admiring them in a large bronze mirror without ever knowing what they had meant. I closed my eyes to keep the tears from falling, and wondered whether Octavia had accepted the denarii.

I opened my door and listened for Marcellus, but the halls that were normally filled with his laughter were silent. When I peered into the library, I saw Octavia and Vitruvius sitting together. As soon as Vitruvius saw me, he rose. 'Octavia would like to speak with you,' he said quietly. I searched his eyes for some indication, but his face was a mask. When he shut the door behind us, I looked at Octavia.

She motioned for me to sit, then she folded her hands and heaved a heavy sigh. 'A terrible thing happened last night.'

'Yes. Very terrible,' I said quietly.

'But you may have helped save Gallia from death.'

'I did nothing. It was Juba,' I said, just as it had been Juba who had saved Octavian from assassination.

She studied me with her soft eyes. 'And it was Juba who came this morning with enough denarii to manumit Gallia.'

I lowered my gaze to my lap.

'So I freed her.'

I looked up swiftly.

'I am ashamed to say that for all my charity, I was not as generous as you were to Gallia.'

'It was my fault she went with Gaius. I should have stopped her!'

'And defy Livia's command?' Octavia laughed mirthlessly. 'There's nothing you could have done.'

'We could have found her sooner!'

'You found her before Gaius strangled her, Selene. And if he had succeeded, there would be no one in Rome to tell the tale. Do you think his guards would have given him away? His slaves?'

'Where is she?' I whispered.

'She will live with Magister Verrius now.'

'And you aren't angry?'

Octavia didn't say anything. She clasped her hands, then unclasped them. 'I am sad that I had to tell Gallia she was free when it wasn't my generosity that freed her. And I am sad that I will be losing my closest friend. I have been selfish in wanting to keep her a slave. Perhaps I have been selfish in many things.'

'No. You are the spirit of Empanda,' I said earnestly, thinking of the goddess of charity. 'And even Empanda must have coveted something.'

'At the expense of a life?' She stood, and I wasn't sure whose life she meant. That of Gaius, who had died by Juba's sword, or Gallia, whose life had been given to slavery. 'It is possible that Gallia will return,' she said. 'But not before she has recovered.' I rose from Vitruvius's chair and followed her across the room. At the door, she paused. 'However, if there are other slaves you wish to free, Selene, I would save your denarii. Gallia may be a friend to me,' she warned, 'but I am no Red Eagle.'

I missed the Festival of Lupercalia. While Alexander and Marcellus sacrificed a goat in Romulus's cave and watched while young men were putting on the skins of the sacrifice, running down the Palatine, and whipping anyone in their path with strips of goatskin, I sat alone in my chamber and sketched. From my room, I could hear the shrieks of the women. They were the ones who stood in the path of the whip to ensure fertility over the coming year, and when there was no more screaming, I heard Marcellus's voice and assumed that everyone had returned.

Alexander was the first to enter the chamber, and when I saw his face, I jumped from my couch.

'What happened?' I cried.

He laughed. 'It's not mine. It's goat's blood.'

'What for?'

'The Lupercalia! And if you hadn't been sleeping, you could have come. But I felt too sorry to wake you.'

'Sorry for me, or sorry for Gallia?' I demanded, and immediately he sobered. 'You think you're going to be King of Egypt someday, acting like this? After you saw what endless feasting and drinking did to our father?'

'It isn't endless,' he said quietly. 'It's just one morning.'

'Which happens to come after a night of bloodshed!'

'I heard what you did,' Marcellus whispered. 'My mother said you bought Gallia's freedom.' Behind him, Julia and Alexander both exclaimed, 'You freed a slave?'

'And Octavia let her go?' my brother pressed.

'It appears that way.'

'Do you think Gallia will return?' Marcellus asked.

'Your mother said it was possible. If I were Gallia, I would leave Rome altogether.'

'Livia was happy this morning. But when she hears what you've done, she'll be beside herself,' Julia said fearfully.

'Then no one will tell her,' Marcellus replied firmly. 'Gallia doesn't know who it was, and Livia won't either.'

But my brother scowled at me. 'You never cared about the slaves in Alexandria.'

'And in Alexandria, we had a kingdom. Here, what's the difference between us and Gallia?'

'Citizenship,' Julia said.

'No,' my brother said. 'A roll of the dice. We could just as easily have been made slaves.'

'The children of a queen?' Julia exclaimed.

'Wasn't Gallia the child of a queen?' my brother asked.

She made a face. 'The Gauls are barbarians.'

'And what if tomorrow your father decides that Egyptians are barbarians?' I asked.

Marcellus and Julia were silent.

'Please promise you won't say anything,' I begged, but even though Julia nodded, I wondered whether she could keep such a secret.

That evening, as we walked to Octavian's villa, Marcellus waited until my brother was ahead of us to whisper, 'You have a very kind heart, Selene.'

I was glad there was only a sliver of moon. That way he couldn't see the rush of blood to my cheeks.

'I had always hoped to set Gallia free when I became Caesar. I wasn't sure how my mother would take it. You've done what I was afraid to do.'

'It was nothing.'

'I don't think so,' he said tenderly.

Our eyes met, and I wondered for a moment if he was going to kiss me. Then Julia, in one of her new silver tunics, appeared on the portico, waving to us. Marcellus turned, and we said no more.

CHAPTER FOURTEEN

June, 28 BC

GALLIA RETURNED before our summer progress to Octavian's palace in Capri. With the entire villa in a state of upheaval, she appeared one morning at Octavia's *salutatio* and asked whether she still had need of an *ornatrix*. Her blue silk tunic was sewn with seed pearls, and her long hair was swept back with a tortoiseshell band that gleamed in the bright light of the atrium. The bruises Gaius had left her with were long gone, and in their place shone healthy, pampered skin. As soon as Octavia saw her, she began to weep – tears of joy, and probably relief. She celebrated Gallia's return that evening with roasted peacock from Samos and rare oysters from Tarentum.

'Does that mean you will be coming with us to Capri?' Marcellus asked. We were sitting together in the triclinium, where Gallia had never been allowed to eat with us before.

Gallia fanned herself with her hand. 'You think I want to stay behind in this terrible heat?' she teased. Freedom suited Gallia: from the gilded ornaments in her hair to the expensive silk stola embroidered with gold. No one mentioned what had happened with Gaius, and Juba had not been punished for the killing.

But when Gallia and I were alone together on the morning of our departure, I asked her quietly, 'Have you been well?'

She seated herself on my traveling chest, considering my question. 'I have healed,' she said. 'And, of course, it is good to be free. There is no one who can give me orders now,' she said firmly. 'Only Caesar.'

'And does Octavia pay you?'

She smiled. 'More than Magister Verrius makes at the ludus. And I no longer have to sneak away at night to see him. We are married.'

I was shocked. 'Since when?'

'Since the week Octavia gave me my freedom.' But she put a finger to her lips. 'It would not go well for his teaching if Livia discovered this. Caesar respects him, but Livia . . .' Her blue eyes narrowed into slits. 'She does not approve of freedwomen marrying born citizens. I will try to keep it from her as long as possible.'

'And will Magister Verrius come to Capri?'

'Of course. Who would spend the summer here if he could escape it?'

We left the crushing heat of Rome on the first of July, and it occurred to me that only a year ago Ptolemy had been alive. I thought of his dimpled smile, and the way his cheeks used to look like little apples when he laughed. But thinking about him only brought me pain, and I tried not to remember. Instead, I focused on the journey. It would be a long ride to the shore of Naples. We were setting out at night so that a formal send-off wouldn't be necessary. This way, Octavian could leave without drawing attention to the fact that while the plebeians were suffering in the searing heat, the wealthy were escaping to their cool villas by the sea. Agrippa and Juba rode on horses ahead of the Praetorian Guard, and the sleeping carriages that followed behind them bumped along the cobblestones. We were the only people using the actual road. Few horses were shod, and to save the unshod horses' hooves, most carriages traveled on the grassy shoulder of the Appian Way.

Alexander and I shared a carriage with Marcellus and Julia. I watched with rising envy whenever Marcellus's leg brushed against hers or he arranged a pillow behind her back. They played games with their eyes when they thought that no one was looking, and Julia smiled more than she ever did in Rome.

'Wait until you see Capri,' Marcellus said as we left the stagnant air of the city.

'Is it like the Palatine?' Alexander asked carefully. The last time Marcellus had been excited about a journey, we had arrived in Rome, where smoke belched from the cooking hearths and the temples were covered in graffiti. Now, I no longer noticed the crude drawings scrawled across the steps of the Senate.

'There's no comparison,' Julia said. 'On the Palatine, my father pretends to be the humble servant of Rome. In Capri, we actually live like the ruling family.'

'It's my uncle's Sea Palace,' Marcellus explained. 'There'll be a beach and horses, and we'll take you to the Blue Grotto.'

'Are the buildings beautiful?' I asked eagerly.

'You'll be sketching all day,' Marcellus promised. 'Why do you think Vitruvius is coming?'

'Possibly for your mother.'

Marcellus laughed. 'And for the beauty, too.'

It was three days by carriage, but at twelve years old, we thought the journey endless. We made up games to pass the time, but mostly we looked out the windows and watched the sleepy towns and roadside shrines go by. Several inns advertised bread, wine, and a girl for the night, all for one denarius, but we never stopped in any of those places. I tried to read some of the scrolls that I had packed. I chose *The History of Naples* and

The Guidebook to Troy, but reading made me sick, and even the fresh sea air couldn't quell my nausea.

When we finally arrived on the shore of Naples and stepped onto the ships that would take us to Capri, it was my turn to feel strong while the others held their stomachs and moaned. Alexander and I raised our faces to the crisp morning wind and closed our eyes.

'It feels like home, doesn't it?' he said.

I sighed. 'Yes.' The high calcareous cliffs with their lush vegetation plummeted into the sea, creating grottoes and bays where children were swimming or fishing along the rocks.

'Someday, when we return to Egypt,' my brother promised, 'we'll commission a new *thalamegos* and sail like this up and down the coast of Alexandria. I'll never get enough of the water.'

Vitruvius came up behind us. 'There it is,' he said, and I heard the love in his voice.

Perched on a promontory so high above the sea that even the spray couldn't reach its gardens, the Sea Palace looked like an eagle carved from stone. Marcellus was right. It had nothing in common with Octavian's squat villa on the Palatine.

'I don't understand. Why doesn't he rule Rome from here?'

'Because alienating the Senate didn't work very well for Julius Caesar,' Vitruvius replied. 'I don't think he wishes to repeat that history.'

It was a shame. Slaves with bronze and ebony litters carried us to the palace, where terraced gardens looked out over the water, and the portico commanded a stunning view of sunlit vineyards and golden fields. I was the first from my litter, then Vitruvius.

'It renews your faith in architecture, doesn't it?' he remarked. He ran his hand lovingly over a caryatid, pausing to rest it on the figure's marble cheek.

'You built this, didn't you?' I realized.

He grinned. 'My first commission. And I know that school is done for the summer, but if you wish, I will continue to tutor you here. There'll be no measurements to take or mosaic flooring to plan, but the inspiration—'

'Yes,' I said at once.

He laughed. 'We can begin with a tour.'

Octavian stepped from his litter, announcing that dinner would be at sunset in the summer triclinium, and in the remaining time we could explore. Marcellus and Alexander wanted to go to the stables, and immediately Julia moved to go with them. Marcellus looked over his shoulder at me. 'Aren't you coming?'

I glanced at Vitruvius. 'To the stables?' I hesitated, watching Julia take Marcellus's arm. 'No, I . . . I'm going with Vitruvius.'

'Then we'll see you later,' Marcellus said easily. The pretty trio turned away, my handsome brother, Julia, and Marcellus.

Vitruvius saw my face and promised, 'There's an entire summer to spend with them.'

'And who wants to listen to Julia's chattering anyway?' Tiberius demanded. I hadn't seen him emerge from his litter, and I wondered whether he'd been hiding until his mother had gone inside. He looked to Vitruvius. 'May I come on your tour?'

'I didn't know you were interested in architecture.'

Tiberius shrugged sheepishly. 'If Selene's interested, I might be, too.'

We followed Vitruvius into the palace, where the entrance tesserae of colored limestone spelled out the Latin greeting AVE at our feet. The halls were frescoed with scenes from the *Odyssey*, mainly images of sailors and ships. Once we reached the atrium, Vitruvius stopped, letting me stand long enough to take it all in. Long white curtains fluttered in the breeze, brushing against blue mosaic floors. Everything had been painted in shades of the sea: cerulean blue, deep midnight, turquoise.

'It's nothing like Rome,' I said wonderingly. The walls were ornamented with painted apses and niches. 'And look at the marble edges on the pillars!'

'And the painted ceilings,' Vitruvius added.

'How were all of these made?' Tiberius asked.

'The frescoes? Selene can tell you.'

'By applying three coats of mortar and three coats of lime mixed with powdered marble. Then the artist painted on the wall while the mixture was still damp.'

'You've learned a lot about this,' Tiberius remarked.

'She's a good student.'

He nodded thoughtfully. 'I'm not surprised. She's my only real competition at school.' Although he was unbearably arrogant, I couldn't help being flattered. 'You should show her the library,' he said to Vitruvius.

'That's where we're going.'

It was magnificent. Heavy wooden shelves from ceiling to floor were crammed with scrolls. Seabirds had been carved into the wood of the ceiling, and beautiful urns filled the niches. Vitruvius explained how the shelves had been built, then took us through the triclinium and the guest chambers, pointing out small features like fluted columns and barrel-vaulted spaces painted in sea green and gold. Every room we entered was richly furnished. There were marble-topped tables and couches faced with bronze. Even the chairs were inlaid with precious ivory. When we reached my chamber at the top of the stairs, I saw that I would still be sharing with Alexander, but the room was so large that it was impossible to see all of its corners from the doorway. Straw hats and feathered fans had been laid on our tables, and thick leather sandals for walking along the rocks had been left out for us as well. I stepped onto our balcony overlooking the sea.

'Is it as beautiful as Alexandria?' Tiberius asked earnestly from behind.

I didn't lie. 'Yes.' I turned to Vitruvius. 'How long did all of this take?'

'My entire youth.'

'And the most difficult part?'

He indicated the immaculate gardens with their shady bowers and small marble temples.

'Can we see them?' I asked eagerly.

He led us down the stairs and through a pair of doors that opened onto a portico. There were gardens in every direction, some colonnaded, others terraced to the sea. Vines trailed from painted bowers, and as we walked beneath them, he explained the difficulty.

'A garden is like an onion,' he said. 'It takes layer after layer to make it whole. First the earth has to be cultivated, then the landscape rearranged.' He pointed to thickets of myrtle and boxwood, then showed me the orchards where peach trees grew among lemons and figs. 'But it's the small details that make it complete.'

Sea daffodils and lilies spilled from heavy urns. And where fountains bubbled merrily, Carystian marble gods raised their arms to the sun. As we reached the bottom of the garden, Vitruvius pointed to the heated bathing pool from which swimmers could look out over the sea. Even in Alexandria we had never had such pools. And there were many more things he showed me that afternoon that rivaled Egypt for beauty.

When we returned to the triclinium in time for the evening's meal, I saw that Alexander had put on a new tunic, while I was still in my traveling clothes.

'So what did you do all day?' he asked.

'Looked at architecture with Vitruvius and Tiberius.'

Julia popped open an oyster. 'That's it?'

'There's a great deal more to the palace than you know,' Tiberius retorted.

Marcellus raised his brows. 'Such as?'

'The slaves' chambers,' I said. 'And have you seen the baths that they use?'

Julia laughed. 'Who would want to do that?'

'You might,' I said sternly. 'They are some of the most beautifully frescoed pools I've ever seen. And their rosewater is better than what you use in Rome.'

Julia wrinkled her nose. 'Really? Why are the slaves living so well?'

'Because we only come here once a year,' Marcellus guessed. 'The rest of the time they're doing as they please. Your father doesn't call this the Land of Do-Nothings without a reason.' He smiled at me. 'I'd like to see their baths.'

'I'm sure Vitruvius will take you.'

'Or you can.'

Everyone at the table paused. My brother darted a look of warning at me. Then Julia said lightly, 'You can take all of us. Tomorrow afternoon.'

Marcellus shook his head. 'I heard your father say we'll be visiting Pollio.'

Julia lowered the oyster in her hand. '*What?*'

'Pollio is always lending money to the treasury,' he explained. 'And you know he comes to the sea every year—'

'So my father's planning on spending the day with a murderer for a handful of denarii?' Julia cried.

Marcellus put his finger to his lips, but Octavian was busy

talking about antiquities with Juba. 'At least you'll get to see Horatia,' he offered.

'And then what?' she hissed. 'Ask if she's enjoying the sea?' She pushed away her plate of food and stood. 'I'm not in the mood for this anymore.'

She left the triclinium, and Marcellus was caught between going after her and remaining with us.

'Oh, just let her be,' Alexander suggested. 'My sister can talk to her.'

'Why me?' I exclaimed.

'Because you're a girl and understand these moods.' Since I had experienced my moon blood several months before, Alexander had suffered a few of my irrational tantrums.

'Yes,' Marcellus pleaded. 'Better you than us.'

'And you wouldn't rather go?' I asked temptingly.

Marcellus shook his head. 'She's vile when she's angry.'

I suppressed a smile and stood. So long as we weren't sitting at Octavian's table, no one cared when we left the triclinium. I found Julia on the balcony of her chamber, illuminated by torchlight and watching the waves. 'Marcellus?' she asked eagerly, and her shoulders sagged a little when she saw that it was me. 'Selene.' Her pale tunic fluttered in the breeze, and I realized that her cheeks were wet.

'I'm sure your father isn't doing this to hurt you,' I said.

'No.' She spun around. 'Livia is. You think my father can't borrow gold from a thousand other men? Why Pollio?' she demanded. 'Why tomorrow, just as we're free from the ludus and beginning to enjoy ourselves?' She stalked from the balcony, and I followed her into her chamber. Her eyes were brimming with tears. 'I won't go.'

'Don't give Livia the satisfaction,' I told her. 'She wants to see you alone and upset while all the rest of us are out together. And if you don't go tomorrow, she'll know she's found a way of excluding you. She'll only do it again.'

Julia sat on her couch. 'You saw what she did to Gallia,' she said. 'Without lifting a finger. If I go, she'll only find another way to hurt me.'

'Then tell your father!' I seated myself on one of her chairs.

'Do you think he would listen?' She laughed scornfully. 'I'm like one of his Setinum wines being aged to perfection. And when the time is right, he'll sell me off to Marcellus.'

'But I thought you *wanted* to marry him?'

'Of course I do. But my father doesn't care about that. I could loathe Marcellus, and we would still be married.' Her voice grew very still and frail. 'You were lucky to have a mother,' she said. 'Even if Gaia survived her first night at the Columna, she'll never know her real mother. Just like me.'

'But your mother is alive—'

Her eyes flashed. 'And banished from the Palatine! No one invites her to dinner for fear of displeasing my father. She has no friends, no husband. She doesn't even have me. Do you know where she is right now?'

I shook my head.

'In Rome, suffering with the plebs. She doesn't have the denarii to purchase a summer villa, and do you think my father cares? If I could, I would leave this island behind and sweat through the heat of Rome to be with her. Instead, I get to suffer here.'

When she bent her head and I realized she was crying, I moved from my chair and put my arm around her shoulders. There was nothing to say, no way of changing Rome or her father. I simply listened to her cry, and was thankful I had come instead of Marcellus.

*

Before we left for Pollio's villa, an augur was summoned to determine whether the day would be auspicious for dining with a friend. We stood in the colonnaded garden beneath the increasing heat of the sun, waiting for a flock of birds to pass overhead so that the augur could divine from their pattern of flight whether this would be a *dies fastus* or a *dies nefastus*.

Tiberius sighed heavily, and Marcellus looked immensely bored with the whole procedure.

'Where are the damn birds?' Octavian swore.

The augur shifted nervously on his feet. 'I am afraid the gods do not work on mortal schedules, Caesar.'

Livia pointed wildly to the north. 'Blackbirds!' she exclaimed, and everyone turned to face the augur.

Julia closed her eyes, and I could almost hear her thoughts. *Please proclaim it a* dies nefastus.

The augur spread his arms. 'There will be good fortune today!' he announced. 'This is a *fastus*.'

Tiberius stood swiftly. 'Good. Let's go.'

I saw Juba smile wryly at him while Octavian gave his thanks to the augur. A dozen curtained litters were waiting for us outside the villa, and I shared mine with Julia.

'I was hoping he'd declare it a *dies nefastus*,' I admitted as the litter began to move.

'I knew he wouldn't. All the augurs look at my father's face before making a proclamation. If he doesn't look as if he wants to go, then it's a *dies nefastus*.'

'So your father doesn't really believe in it?'

Julia's eyes went wide. 'Of course he does.'

'But how—'

'He believes what he wants to. Just like you with your Isis.'

'And what does that mean?'

'Well, have you ever seen her?' Julia challenged. 'Has she ever come to you in a moment of need?'

'Isis works her miracles unseen.'

Julia cocked her head and gave me a disbelieving look. 'You believe what you want to.'

I refused to dignify her insult with a response. Instead, I pushed open the curtains and looked out at the blue expanse in front of us. Villas were strung along the rim of the sea like pearls, bright white and gleaming in the sun.

'You see that villa over there?' Julia asked. 'That's Pollio's.'

I had intended to be angry with her, but instead I inhaled. 'The one as large as a city?'

'Yes. And wait until we go inside,' she said resentfully. 'It's bigger than anything you've ever seen. Even the palace at Alexandria,' she promised.

Julia wasn't lying. Although his villa in Rome had been sprawling, Pollio's villa on Capri had been built to house more than three thousand people, most of them slaves. The walk was more than a mile from his handsomely frescoed portico to the gilded triclinium, where the stars in the ceiling were made from silver and the sun on the wall from beaten gold. And as Pollio escorted us through chamber after chamber, he pointed out his newest purchases.

'That is an authentic Myron,' he said, naming one of the most famous Greek sculptors in the world. 'And that is my eel pool.'

'Eels?' Octavia made a noise in her throat. 'What for?'

'Entertainment! Would you like to see them?' He didn't wait for her answer before leading us to the far corner of the atrium to a vast pool large enough to fit a small boat. But no one would have attempted to sail on that lake. Beneath the murky waters, sharp-toothed fish writhed between the rocks. What sort of man kept eels for entertainment?

I didn't step to the ledge, and I noticed that even Marcellus kept his distance. 'Where do they come from?' he asked.

Pollio made a grand gesture with his arm. 'All across Capri. I have my slaves find them for me.'

'That must be very dangerous,' Juba remarked.

Pollio smiled. 'It is. Shall we see them feed?'

When no one objected, he ordered a slave-boy to bring him a handful of rotten meat from the kitchens. When the boy returned, he was careful not to step too close to the pool.

'Your meat, domine.'

'Go ahead,' he ordered the child, 'throw it.'

The boy trembled. '*Me*, domine?'

'Yes! This is Caesar who's waiting!'

The slave-boy moved timidly toward the ledge, then quickly tossed his handful of meat into the pool. Pollio watched proudly as the eels swarmed around the offering, snapping their jaws and attacking one another in order to get to the food. Their teeth gleamed like small razors in the lamplight, and Octavia suggested faintly, 'Shall we continue?'

Pollio looked up. 'Oh, yes. But did you see how they attack?' he asked Octavian eagerly. 'They're absolutely vicious creatures!'

We walked past elaborate partitions made from ivory and a wooden chair whose back was carved in the shape of an eagle. 'Every piece in this villa has a story,' Pollio boasted. 'That chair once belonged to a Gallic chieftain.'

'Vercingetorix?' I asked.

Pollio looked surprised, as if a bird had opened its beak to speak to him. 'That's right. And over there is my newest addition,' he said. 'A second library for my collection.'

'What about a second triclinium?' Livia said shortly. 'One that doesn't require a litter to get there.'

Pollio laughed loudly at what was obviously meant to be a criticism. 'I already have two triclinia. Can you imagine the first villa to have three? Of course, if Caesar were to suggest it, I would be more than happy—'

'My wife was joking,' Octavian snapped.

'Of course.' Pollio laughed nervously. 'Who could afford three rooms for dining?'

We came to the summer triclinium, where Horatia was waiting patiently for her guests in an exquisite tunic of apricot and gold. Immediately, her eyes met Julia's, and I could see that she wanted to speak privately with her, but she did her duty and politely escorted the guests to their couches. The tables overlooked the water, and the warm wind smelled of sea salt and wine.

'Just like Alexandria.' My brother sighed, patting down his hair.

'Did you spend your entire lives near the sea?' Marcellus asked. Julia and Tiberius seated themselves on opposite sides of him, while across the room, Pollio and Horatia would be eating with Octavian.

'Every day. Playing in the water, collecting seashells by the rocks . . .'

'I'd like to go to Egypt,' Julia said wistfully, and I wondered how many times a day she wished she were somewhere else.

'Someday,' Marcellus whispered, 'if I become Caesar, we'll return Alexander and Selene to their thrones, and in return they'll show us Alexandria.'

Julia looked at her father. Now that winter was over, the color had returned to his cheeks, and he appeared strong. 'That could be many years,' she said fearfully.

'Already wishing death on Caesar? That's how treachery begins,' Tiberius warned.

'No one said anything about death,' Marcellus said.

But Tiberius grinned. 'I know what she meant.'

'You don't know anything,' Julia retorted angrily. 'You smile and listen like a sickly cat hoping for a scrap of meat to run to my father with. You think I don't know that you tell him everything we say?'

He snorted. 'As if I cared enough to do that. Try Juba. He's the spy.'

But Julia sat forward. 'You hope that if you tell my father everything, he'll trust you enough to send you to war alongside Agrippa. Maybe even make you a general, and you'll never have to come back here.' She snorted. 'But that's never going to happen. My father will keep you here, dancing like his puppet until he's gone. The heir.' She looked from Marcellus to Tiberius. 'And the spare.'

There was a crash of crystal on the mosaic floor, and everyone turned.

'You stupid son of an ass!' Pollio shouted. He leapt from his chair, thundering toward the old man who cowered on the floor.

'Please, domine, I didn't mean—'

Pollio lashed out with his foot, kicking the slave squarely in the jaw. The old man fell back against the shattered glass, and Horatia rushed from her couch.

'Please, Pollio—'

'This is the finest crystal we own!' he shouted.

Julia and Tiberius exchanged glances; their own bickering was silenced.

'This *asinus* has broken one of my largest vessels. Octavia wanted to know why I have eels?' He turned to the guards at the door of the triclinium. 'Take him to the pool!'

The old man clasped his hands before his bloodied face. 'Please, domine.' His voice became hysterical. 'Please! Kill me here, but not the eels.'

I looked from Agrippa to Juba, desperate for one of them to do something. Then Octavian stood. He held his crystal goblet in front of him, dropping it on the floor and watching it shatter into a thousand pieces. No one spoke. No one even dared to breathe. Octavian proceeded to smash every piece of crystal on his table. The pieces scattered across the floor, and some of the children covered their ears at the terrible sound. At last, when there was nothing more to destroy, Octavian asked, 'Will you be feeding me to the eels as well?'

'Of course not, Caesar,' Pollio said.

The old man had tears in his eyes.

'How many men have you killed this way?'

'Seven,' the old man whispered from the floor.

'And all of them deserved it!' Pollio challenged, his chins wagging with indignation.

'And this slave. Does he deserve it?' Octavian asked.

Pollio considered his answer before speaking. 'Not with an example such as Caesar before him,' he said wisely. He was not as great a fool as he looked.

'You are generous, domine,' the old man said. He trembled, and the sight was pitiful. Octavia turned away.

'Yes, dominus Pollio is very generous,' Octavian said. 'So generous, he will be freeing you tonight.'

Horatia gasped. But for the first time, Pollio had the sense to bow his head humbly and accept Octavian's pronouncement.

The next morning, on every temple door in Capri, the Red Eagle posted his first actum in praise of Caesar.

It became the subject of every conversation for the next two weeks. Clearly the Red Eagle had come out of hiding now that enough time had passed since the kitchen boy's crucifixion. But where was he residing on Capri, and how had he known what had happened in Pollio's villa?

'Perhaps it's one of Pollio's clan,' Marcellus speculated, dangling his feet in the swimming pool. The four of us were drying off in the sun. Since we were no longer in Rome, Julia and I were allowed to swim, but only inside the villa where no one could see us in our breastbands and loincloths.

'Or it could be anyone who heard the news from Pollio's villa,' my brother said. In the days after Pollio's slave had been freed, people as far away as Pompeii came to know of what had happened. We watched as Vipsania splashed at the other end of the pool, completely naked. Both Julia and I, though, now had something to cover. I noticed Marcellus was watching us with new interest – Julia in particular, whose wet band of cloth pressed against her breasts. I had the unkind urge to get up and block his view.

'But if it's someone who has visited Pollio,' Julia reasoned, 'the person must be wealthy. Pollio doesn't admit any other kind.'

'What about a slave in his house?' I asked. 'Or one from this house who's been there?'

But my brother frowned. 'It wouldn't be like a slave to compliment Octavian.'

The speculation continued throughout the summer, and everyone was suspect, even Juba and Agrippa. But there were no more acta on Capri, and the Praetorian guard stationed at every temple door idled their nights away rolling dice and watching owls hunt for prey. By the end of August, Octavian announced a reward of five thousand denarii to anyone with useful information on the Red Eagle.

'Who do *you* think it might be?' I asked Vitruvius. We sat in the library with the final plans for the Temple of Apollo. A grand staircase swept from Octavian's home to the temple, where a vast library already housed his favorite literature. In a few days, when we returned to the oppressive heat of Rome, the last touches would be added, and the temple would be dedicated.

'If I knew,' Vitruvius said, 'I would be five thousand denarii richer. Now find me the measurements for the landing.'

'Is there going to be a mosaic?' I asked eagerly.

Vitruvius smiled. 'We will include the one you sketched.'

I gave a little cry of joy. After nearly a year of working with Vitruvius, this was the first design of mine he was going to use. I had sketched mosaics for Octavian's mausoleum, and column designs for Agrippa's Pantheon, but none of them had been included.

'Don't grow too excited,' Vitruvius warned. 'We have to finish by October. And you're going to oversee the laying of the tiles.'

I didn't care how much work it meant, or how many hours before the ludus I would have to rise to oversee the mosaicists' work. When I told my brother, he stopped packing his trunk to look up at me. 'And you *want* to do this?'

'Of course. Why wouldn't I?'

'Because we're about to return to the sweltering heat. How will you be able to work?'

'It will be morning. And I don't suffer the way you do.'

'I'll never understand it,' he said enviously, closing his trunk. 'Only you and Octavian can endure it. Our mother would never have survived.'

Alexander seated himself next to me. Two years ago, our mother and father had been alive. Ptolemy had been running through the palace halls with Charmion chasing after him, threatening to pinch his ear. There had still been hope of saving Egypt then. But now it was lost, and there was no telling whether we would ever return. 'What do you think will happen if Octavian determines not to send us back?'

'Exactly what we've thought all along. He'll find us marriages and we'll remain in Rome.'

'And doesn't that frighten you?'

'Of course it does! But what can we do?'

I was quiet for a moment. 'If Caesar died,' I whispered, 'Marcellus would return us to Egypt.'

My brother's gaze immediately went to the door. 'Be careful, Selene. There's no telling who's listening in this villa. Marcellus thinks the Red Eagle is working with someone inside.'

'Like Gallia?'

'It's possible.' He stood and opened the door. When he was sure there was no one outside, he closed it again and came back to my couch. 'In five months Marcellus is going to have his *toga virilis* ceremony. Has he told you about this?'

I shook my head.

'At fifteen, every boy puts aside his *bulla* and becomes a man. Octavian will probably announce Marcellus's official engagement to Julia, and if he does, it will be clear to everyone who his heir is intended to be. Octavian will want to catch the Red Eagle before this happens. He can't afford to be embarrassed at such an important time. Be very careful what you say and to whom you say it.'

'Why? You don't think he suspects *us*?'

'I don't know. But even Agrippa's and Juba's chambers have been searched.'

I made a face.

'I know,' he said. 'They're desperate.'

'Has Gallia's name ever been mentioned?'

'I don't think so. But it's impossible to know whom the Praetorian Guard are watching. Including Marcellus.'

I was quiet for a moment. 'And what does Marcellus say about marriage?'

My brother gave me a long look. 'Nothing you want to know about.'

'So he's in love with Julia?' I exclaimed.

'I don't know.'

'But what does he say?'

My brother hesitated. 'That she is beautiful, and they have the same passion for the Circus.'

'But she doesn't even care about the Circus! She only goes for him.'

'What do you want me to tell you, Selene? He's mentioned that he thinks you're pretty.'

'He has?'

'Many men think so,' he said dryly.

'But what else has he said?'

'That's it. I'm sorry. You know whom he's been promised to; you're wasting your time thinking about him.'

That afternoon, ebony litters were arranged to carry us to the ship. No one was particularly happy about leaving, least of all Marcellus, who couldn't bear the thought of returning to the steam bath that was Rome.

'If we had vacations like every other family,' he complained on the portico, 'we'd be here until October.'

'I don't believe we're like every other family,' his mother reminded him.

'Yes,' Tiberius said mockingly. 'There is the small matter of governing Rome.'

'That's what the Senate is for.'

'So when you're Caesar, is that what you plan to do?' Tiberius asked Marcellus. 'Give the reins of government to the senators and sit back while they steer?'

Octavian appeared, and everyone fell into an uneasy silence. 'Wave good-bye to the Do-Nothings,' he said as he crossed the threshold of his palace. 'This is the happiest day of their year.'

Livia laughed, and Octavia smiled fleetingly at her brother's strange sense of humor. But Marcellus crossed his arms over his chest.

'I'm tired of the ludus,' he grumbled, and he turned to find a sympathetic ear in Julia. 'I don't want to wait until I'm seventeen to leave school. I don't think I can stand it for another two years. Especially not when we could be here.'

She patted his arm. 'It's better than hard labor,' she said teasingly. 'Selene' – she turned to me – 'why don't you ride with your brother?' Julia climbed into a litter after Marcellus, and I watched their shadows on the curtain for a moment before my brother pulled me into a second litter.

'Don't obsess about it,' he said sensibly. 'Just be glad he doesn't want you.'

I stared at him in amazement.

'Well, how would that turn out?' he demanded. 'What do you think Julia would do?'

'Turn against me.'

He nodded. 'She's not all pretty tunics and jewels.'

'I notice you stare at her enough.'

My brother laughed. 'I have no interest in Julia. Trust me.'

'Why? I thought you said she's beautiful.'

'She is. She also belongs to Marcellus. And no matter how much we may wish otherwise,' he said darkly, 'that's not going to change.'

I thought of Julia and Marcellus laughing together in the litter next to ours, their shadows growing closer and closer, and tears of frustration blurred my vision. My brother put his arm around my shoulders, and I let my tears roll down my cheeks. Then I noticed I wasn't the only one. My brother's handsome cheeks were wet. But I was too absorbed in my own misery to ask why.

CHAPTER FIFTEEN

February, 27 BC

A FEW months after our return from Capri, Octavian dedicated
the Temple of Apollo, and the feast that followed lasted until
the early hours of the morning. But it was nothing compared
to the reception being planned for Tiberius and Marcellus,
who had both turned fifteen recently and would now celebrate
their coming-of-age during March's festival of Liberalia. Julia
insisted on new tunics for the ceremony, and wasn't satisfied
with the bolts of cloth we had purchased over the winter
holiday.

'This has to be something special,' she'd said as February
drew to a close. She'd begged her father to let Gallia take us to
the Forum Boarium, where barges from Ostia unloaded their
goods. This way, we could barter for cloth before any other
woman in Rome had a chance to see it. He finally agreed a week
before Liberalia, and with seven of the Praetorian guard we
followed Gallia into the cattle market.

'How can anyone stand this?' Julia complained, holding up
a ball of amber to her nose.

'This was your idea,' Gallia reminded.

'But look at these people. They're so poor.'

Gallia gave me a weary look. 'Welcome to Rome.'

Unsatisfied with Gallia's response, Julia turned to me. 'Have you ever seen so much dirt? I'll bet these people don't even bathe.'

'It's their work,' I said. 'They can't help it, dealing with cattle all day.'

'Even so.' She passed her hand in front of her nose. 'If my father wasn't so obsessed about his reputation among the plebs, he could have ordered the bargemen to just bring their cloth to the Palatine.'

The odor of cattle excrement really was overwhelming. On either side of the road, concrete apartment buildings teetered three and four stories high, and I wondered how the inhabitants could live with such stench and noise around them. We passed the bronze bull that occupied the center of the marketplace, and Gallia warned us to watch for cutpurses.

'You never know what sort lurks around here. And sometimes—'

A woman screamed on the other side of the Forum Boarium, and suddenly people were running. Julia grabbed my arm. 'What is it?' she cried.

For a moment, we couldn't see anything; and then a space cleared in the middle of the Forum, and Gallia shouted, 'Bulls!' The guards fanned out around us, but as the two animals charged, the soldiers scattered.

Julia and I pressed ourselves against the side of an apartment building. As the bulls drew closer, Gallia shouted, 'Move!'

But there was nowhere for us to run. I closed my eyes as the first bull charged past us through the open door of the apartment building, missing us by a hairsbreadth. But the second bull lowered its head. It had no intention of following its brother, and as it ran toward us, Gallia's screams rang out like a whistle. Then, suddenly, the massive bull staggered, and from the corner of my eye I caught a glimpse of a blond man with a bow and arrow on the balcony of an adjacent building. A second arrow pierced the air, then a third and a fourth. The bull bellowed with rage, turning to see where the attack was coming from. In those precious moments, a soldier leapt forward and speared the beast with his metal *pilum*.

The bull collapsed at Julia's feet, and when I looked up again to see the blond bowman, he was gone. But men were still shouting in front of us, and two of Octavian's guards leapt over the bull and dragged us away from the building. Above our heads, the first bull was roaming the balconies.

A crowd of shouting merchants were warning anyone inside the building to flee. The bull didn't understand its confinement, and in its anger it was pushing its horns into the rails and ramming the walls again and again. Then there was a terrible crack, and the bull looked up as if it sensed what was about to happen. The balcony gave way, and in a shower of concrete, the bull fell to its death where Julia and I had been standing. There was a moment of shocked silence from the crowd, then a sound like thunder rumbled above us as the upper stories began to crumble.

'Go!' one of the guards shouted, and the men ran with us before we could be engulfed in dust and debris. When we stopped to look behind us, the upper floor of the apartment building was gone.

Julia began to shake. Our tunics were covered in dust, and merchants from across the Forum Boarium were running to see what had happened. 'The man on the balcony . . .' She trembled. 'He saved our lives.'

We looked to the apartment balcony where the bowman had been standing, and one of the guards approached the building. As he reached the door, he stepped back quickly. 'Gaius, Livius, take a look at this!'

We followed the men to the door.

Fastened with the same type of arrow that was used to fell the bull, an actum had been posted about the mistreatment of slaves on the Aventine. At the bottom of the sheet of papyrus, written in hasty lettering, the rebel had added:

So long as freedmen and slaves are forced to live in buildings made of thin brick walls and concrete mixed with more water than lime, there will be deaths, and those deaths stain Caesar's hands.

There was a frenzy of excitement as people around us realized who the archer must have been. The guards Octavian had sent with us burst into the building and raced up the stairs.

Julia gripped my hand. 'Do you think he's still up there?'

'No,' Gallia said. 'He's probably long gone.'

'But what could he be doing here?' I asked.

'Many men keep several apartments,' Gallia said. 'This could be his third or fourth home.'

When the guards returned, they were carrying bottles of ink and a copy of the same actum that was posted on the door. The eldest of the guards introduced himself as Livius. His short gray hair exposed the hard, chiseled planes of his face. He looked first at Julia, then at me. 'What did you see when those arrows killed the bull?'

Julia hesitated. 'A . . . a man on the balcony.'

'And what did this man look like?'

'I couldn't tell.'

Livius's eyes bored into mine.

'I couldn't tell either,' I added swiftly. 'A bull was headed right for us!'

'Why?' Gallia asked. 'What has the landlord said?'

'He tells us he's never seen the tenant in that room.'

'But someone must have rented it!' I exclaimed.

Livius smiled slowly. 'He says that money simply appears whenever the rent is due, and that men don't ask questions in the Forum Boarium.'

'That's true,' Gallia offered.

'It may be true,' Livius returned hotly, 'but no man is invisible. Someone has seen him. Someone in that building. And when Caesar hears of this,' he warned, crumpling the Red Eagle's actum in his hand, 'the men he sends won't be interested in excuses.'

We began the walk back to the Palatine, and Julia whispered, 'Marcellus and Alexander will never believe this. I told them they should have come with us instead of going to the Circus!' Her fear had turned to excitement with the appearance of the actum, and even though our shopping trip was aborted, she remained in high spirits. 'We'll return tomorrow,' she promised gaily. 'And we can show them where we were almost killed!'

'There may have been people who died inside that building,' I chided.

'And there would have been two more if the Red Eagle hadn't saved us!'

When we returned to Octavia's villa, Julia wanted everyone to know how we had almost lost our lives, and that evening in the triclinium, she repeated the story. 'That's when the Red Eagle saved us,' she said breathlessly.

Her father lowered the scroll in his hands. 'What?'

Julia looked uneasily at me before turning to Octavian. 'It was him. He shot the bull just as it was coming toward us. Didn't the guards tell you?'

I could see that Livia was growing enraged, but Octavian

remained perfectly calm. 'And how do you know it was the rebel?' he asked evenly.

'Because the same kind of arrow was used to hold the actum to the door.'

Marcellus whispered severely, 'Stop talking.'

But Octavian was already on his feet. Obviously the guards hadn't told him. When they'd reported finding the Red Eagle's apartment, they had failed to mention the fact that the rebel had saved Julia and me. Octavian seated himself on Julia's couch and put his arm tenderly around her shoulders. 'So he saved you.'

'From death,' she said. 'Right, Selene?'

I nodded.

'And did you get a chance to look at him?'

I could see Alexander and Marcellus holding their breaths.

'I . . . I don't know.'

'This is very important,' Octavian said gently. 'See if you can remember.'

Julia frowned. 'Yes. Yes, I did. He had flaxen hair and strong arms.'

Octavian stood. 'Thank you,' he said. 'Tomorrow, buy whatever silks you would like.'

Julia grinned, clearly proud of herself.

That evening, in the privacy of my chamber, I railed against Julia's foolishness. 'What's the matter with her?'

My brother sat on his couch and shook his head.

'A man's life is at stake!' I cried.

'And it may be someone she loves.' He leaned forward, and his voice dropped low. 'Marcellus wasn't at the Circus this afternoon.'

'What do you mean?'

'We went together, then he asked whether I wanted to have a little fun. I thought maybe he meant he was going to visit

the *fornices*, so I told him no, but he was gone for so long even
Juba and the Praetorians couldn't find him.'

'None of them?'

'Only seven were with us.'

'So what did they do when he returned?'

Alexander gave me a long look. 'They warned him that if he
ever did that again, our trips to the Circus would be finished.'

'They must have been furious. But where did he say he went?'

My brother turned up his palms, and I noticed how large his
hands had grown. He was taller than me now. Women had begun
to stare at him in the streets, and Julia liked to run her fingers
through his hair and ask for his opinion on her tunics. I wondered
what kind of husband he'd make, but couldn't bear the thought
of being apart from him. What if Octavian decided to send him
back to Egypt and keep me in Rome? Or, worse, send us to
opposite ends of Rome's vast territories. He was watching me
with the light amber eyes the two of us shared, and their
expression was anxious. 'He didn't. Marcellus just elbowed me
in the side and said, "You know." Is it possible he was the
bowman, Selene?'

I thought back to the afternoon when the bull had been
charging us and I had caught only the briefest glimpse of a man
on a balcony. 'His hair was golden. But I was too far away to
see his face.'

'Well, what if his performance in the ludus is just an act?
What if he's smarter than any of us give him credit for?'

I thought of Marcellus – laughing, silly, always quick with a
jibe – and shook my head. 'He's brash enough for it. But you've
seen his writing in the ludus, Alexander. It can't be him.'

'Handwriting can be disguised.'

'But you're forgetting that there's Magister Verrius as well.
They both have the same light hair and eyes.'

'Except Magister Verrius wasn't the one who went missing.'

'How do you know? He could have left the ludus as soon as we did.' We stared at each other in the lamplight. 'Magister Verrius or Marcellus,' I said, 'Julia has all but given him away.'

'What do you think Octavian would do if it was Marcellus?'

Fear, as cold as ice, traveled down my spine. 'He would kill him,' I said with certainty.

My brother closed his eyes. 'You need to speak with her.' He looked at me, and his gaze became intense. 'She needs to understand what she's done.'

As a reward for the information Julia had given him, Octavian allowed silks of every color to be brought to the Palatine, fresh from the barges of Ostia. Julia directed the merchants to Octavia's atrium, where Livia couldn't spoil the fun. But before she could begin choosing, I pulled her aside and whispered harshly, 'I hope you understand what these silks cost.'

Her black eyes widened innocently. 'I only told him the truth. You saw him, too. He was probably a slave. He had hair like every other German or Gaul.'

'With access to the Palatine, and Capri, and rich enough to keep apartments across Rome? What slave do you know who has that kind of wealth?'

'I don't understand.'

'You're not that foolish,' I said cruelly. 'Of course you do. There are only two men on the Palatine who fit that description. Magister Verrius and Marcellus.'

She blinked slowly, as if considering it for the first time. Then her eyes filled with tears. 'No... can't be.'

'Why not? Yesterday, while we were in the Forum Boarium, Marcellus disappeared from the Circus, and the gods only know where Magister Verrius was.'

Her hand flew to her mouth. 'My father would never suspect them—'

'Of course he would. And even if he didn't, then Juba would. He was there when Marcellus left and even he couldn't find him. And Juba reports everything to your father.'

'No.' She backed away from me. 'It can't be Marcellus. Why wouldn't he tell me?'

I raised my brows, given what she'd already done.

She panicked. 'But what does he care about slaves? He likes to gamble on horses and have fun.'

'What about the Temple of Isis?' I challenged. 'He cared about those slaves.'

'Because they happened to cross paths! He's rash and foolish.'

'And idealistic,' I reminded her.

'Why, Selene?' The distress on her face was real, and I almost felt sorry for her. 'Why did I have to tell my father?'

'Whatever you do, keep your silence from now on.'

'But what if it's too late?'

We both looked across the atrium, to where Octavia and Claudia were marveling over the different silks. Neither of them appeared worried. 'We would know if Marcellus were being accused.'

But when the festival of Liberalia came, I wondered whether I was wrong. Octavian was an actor. If he wanted to hide his suspicions from his sister, how hard would it be? He appeared in time for Marcellus's dedication and seemed to be enjoying himself. He even led the way to the lararium, where Marcellus took off his *bulla* and offered it with wine and incense to the Lares, asking that the spirits guide his transition to manhood. But I noticed that Caesar's arm was around Tiberius's shoulders, and that Livia's mien was less dour than usual. 'Shall we proceed to the Capitol?' Octavian asked jubilantly.

Julia was dressed in a silk tunic of the deepest red, and her hair was arranged in a golden net sewn with seed pearls. But even though Marcellus couldn't keep his eyes off her, she was pale with worry. 'What's the matter with my father?' she whispered. 'Why is he so interested in Tiberius suddenly?'

I didn't know, and I didn't want to guess.

'You don't think—'

I put a finger to my lips. 'Not here.' I held up my green tunic to keep the hem from getting dirty as we walked, and I shivered in the cool March wind.

'Would you like my cloak?' Marcellus offered.

'Alexander is carrying one for me.'

'Well, perhaps you should put it on. There are bumps up and down your arms.'

I felt embarrassed that he had noticed such an intimate thing. My brother handed me my cloak. We had purchased enough cloth from the merchants of Ostia to outfit a garrison, and Marcellus smiled when he saw me in my new silk. 'Very handsome.'

'Julia's cloak is new as well,' my brother pointed out.

I glared at him.

'The Princesses of the Palatine,' Marcellus flattered. 'And what more fitting tribute to a pair of princesses than Liberalia?'

He was joking, of course. As we reached the bottom of the Palatine, a procession of boys passed by pulling a cart with a towering statue of a phallus.

'What is that?' I cried.

'Haven't you ever seen one?' Tiberius asked snidely.

'The boys are the Salii,' Julia said, ignoring him. 'Liberalia is a fertility festival.'

'Like Bacchanalia back home,' my brother prompted.

'But what are they singing?'

'No one knows,' Marcellus said delightedly. 'The song is so old that the meaning has been forgotten.'

The young Salii were wearing the sort of bronze breastplates and shields that even Juba, who dealt in antiques, would have considered extremely old. No one had fought in such outfits for centuries, and I wondered how the boys could even walk. As the stone phallus rolled by on its cart, women tossed rose petals in the air, clapping and cheering as if the statue were the fertility god himself. Octavian had forbidden us from the festivities of Liberalia the previous March, telling us that we had only a few years to study in the ludus and the rest of our lives to celebrate Liber Pater and his splendid endowment. Now I saw what he meant. When we reached the Capitol, a second giant phallus had been decorated with flowers and mounted on the Tarpeian Rock. Julia giggled, and Marcellus asked my brother what he thought it would be like to have a pair of *colei* that big.

'Painful,' he replied.

'Not as painful as what's about to happen.' Marcellus heaved a sigh. 'Welcome to the Tabularium.'

The Tabularium was a solemn place, with a façade of peperino and travertine blocks masking a stark interior of concrete vaults. It was the Hall of Records where Marcellus and Tiberius would proudly register themselves as citizens, but none of the men who passed us smiled. Liberalia meant nothing to them down here, where Rome's scrolls were guarded like gold and the sun never penetrated its labyrinth of vaults. An old man in a toga took us into a chamber where the names of the most important clans in Rome were etched into the walls. He fetched the scrolls of the clans Julii and Claudii, and we waited in the dimly lit space while Marcellus and Tiberius read the names of the men who had come before them. A reed pen and ink were produced, and the old record keeper instructed each of them to sign at the bottom of his clan's list. By the time we emerged into the sunshine, even Octavian had had enough of the gloom.

'I should build a more cheerful office for them,' he mused. 'Would you like to make that your first contribution to Rome, Tiberius? I will gift you the denarii to rebuild the Tabularium.'

Tiberius was genuinely grateful. 'I would like that very much.'

Julia returned my panicked look. Then Octavian approached Marcellus and clapped him heartily on the back. 'And what about you? What will be your first contribution to Rome?'

'How about a new Circus?' Marcellus asked eagerly.

Tiberius laughed. 'Don't you think you gamble enough?'

Octavian was displeased. 'Perhaps there is something else you would prefer.'

Marcellus looked desperately from his mother to his uncle, considering their passions. 'What about a theater?'

Octavian smiled. 'Better.'

Tiberius clenched his jaw, and I saw Marcellus exhale.

'The Theater of Marcellus. That shall be my gift to you.'

'And Selene can design it!'

Everyone turned. I held my breath while Octavian regarded me with his inscrutable gray eyes. 'How old are you now?' he asked suddenly.

'My brother and I are thirteen.'

'A very mature thirteen,' Octavia put in. 'She designed the mosaic floor in the Temple of Apollo, and Vitruvius has her working on the Pantheon.'

Octavian shaded his eyes with his hand. 'So why didn't Vitruvius tell this to me?'

'Because she's a *girl*,' Livia said, 'and her place is at the loom.'

'It's a beautiful mosaic,' Octavia retorted. 'Girl or no, her skills are useful to him.'

Octavian considered this. 'Where is he today?'

'Working on the Pantheon,' she told him. 'After that it will be the Basilica of Neptune, the Saepta Julia, your mausoleum, and my portico.'

Octavian turned his attention back to me. 'When do you come up with these designs?' he asked curiously.

'In the morning, before ludus. Vitruvius takes me with him sometimes.'

Octavian seemed to find this funny. 'And what do you do?'

'Measurements,' I said firmly, refusing to let him dismiss my work. 'I've also laid tiles.'

'What?' Livia sneered. 'Like a mosaicist?'

'Yes. If the mosaicist needs help or direction. I also want to learn for myself.'

Octavian regarded me for a moment. 'A princess who doesn't mind work.' He looked meaningfully at both Marcellus and Julia. 'Something my own family can learn from.' There was an uncomfortable silence before he added, 'It sounds like Vitruvius is busy enough with his projects. If he wishes you to help with my nephew's theater, I see no problem with that.'

Livia's mouth worked into a tense line, but Marcellus smiled triumphantly at me. On our walk to the Forum, where he and Tiberius would exchange their boyhood togas for the white *toga virilis*, he whispered, 'That was very well done.'

'What?' I asked guilelessly.

'Your talk of laying tiles. My uncle tends to keep people around him who are useful.'

'So you've said. And what about you?'

Around us, flutists played, and children sang songs to Liber Pater and his consort Libera, whose blessings would make them fertile once they were married. In Alexandria, we knew Liber Pater as Bacchus, though I had never seen so many garlanded phalluses even in Bacchus's temple. Marcellus smiled conspiratorially at me, a flash of white teeth in a handsomely tanned face. 'I'm his sister's son. The heir and the spare' – he glanced at Tiberius – 'remember?'

Tiberius leaned over my shoulder and said softly, 'Be careful. Your secrets are making Julia jealous.'

I saw Marcellus tense, and when I looked behind me, Julia's eyes were hard as stone. That evening in the triclinium, she wanted to know what we'd been whispering about.

'Who your father will make his heir,' I replied.

A harpist began to play, for wealthy patricians and their young wives had come to celebrate the heir and the spare's coming-of-age. Julia moved closer to me on our dining couch. 'And do you think my father suspects Marcellus?'

'He's giving him the denarii to build a theater. How suspicious could he be?'

She nodded slowly. 'So you weren't talking about the Red Eagle?'

I sat back. 'Why wouldn't I tell you?'

'Maybe you think I'm not trustworthy anymore.'

'If Marcellus ever said anything to me, you'd be the first to know.'

She watched me suspiciously. 'My father is a very good actor,' she said. 'I've seen him lie to Livia as if his words were pure as gold.'

'I'm not lying,' I swore. 'I would tell you if I heard anything. Haven't you asked Marcellus yourself?'

'Of course. He always denies it.'

'Well, Marcellus never confides in me,' I said glumly. 'He talks to Alexander.'

This settled her a little. 'Just because my father was being generous today doesn't mean he isn't suspicious,' she admitted, toying with her food. I had seen Julia lose her appetite only once before. 'Do you know what they call understudies on the stage?' She didn't wait for me to answer. 'Shadows. And if my father has even the slightest suspicion that Marcellus isn't shadowing him, that will be the end. I will marry Tiberius, whether he's my stepbrother or not, and Marcellus will disappear.' I realized she wasn't angry with me so much as she was angry with herself, and her eyes gleamed with tears.

'Perhaps he isn't the Red Eagle,' I said hopefully.

But Julia simply looked toward her father and didn't reply.

In the hour before dawn, shouting echoed in the atrium, then the sound of hobnailed boots filled the halls. For a moment, I was in Egypt again, huddled with my brothers on my mother's bed on the day of her death.

'Alexander!' I pushed away my covers.

He jumped up. As we rushed to put on our cloaks, I could hear Marcellus's raised voice in the hall. Alexander flung open the door. Octavia, Vitruvius, Marcellus, and his sisters were standing in a circle outside Marcellus's chamber, watching the soldiers move in and out of the room. When Marcellus saw us, his face lost its color.

Agrippa was there. 'We found him at the Circus,' he said. 'In the *fornices.*'

Octavia covered her mouth with her hand.

'It's not what you think!' Marcellus protested.

'So then what were you doing?' Octavian emerged from Marcellus's chamber, and his look was violent. 'Not writing acta, I hope.'

Marcellus stepped back. 'Is that what this is about? You think I'm the Red Eagle?' I could see he wanted to laugh, and might have if the accusation hadn't been so serious. 'Because I leave at night to visit a few *lupae*, you think I'm a traitor?'

Octavia shrieked, 'You were visiting dirty *lupae*?'

Vitruvius put a calming hand on her arm. 'Every boy has been there.'

'Not the heir of Rome!' Octavian shouted.

Juba appeared from Marcellus's chamber, wiping his hands on his tunic.

'What did you find?' Octavian demanded.

'Just a few lewd paintings.'

'I told you!' Marcellus cried. 'You've seen my work in the ludus. Do you think I could really be responsible for the acta? I don't have the patience!'

Octavian considered this. 'Perhaps you are too secure in the belief that you will be my heir. Remember, Marcellus, I loved Fidelius as well,' he said, reminding him of the young soldier he had killed outside the walls of Rome. Then he turned to his sister. 'Keep a better watch on your child.'

The halls emptied of soldiers, and when Octavian's men were gone, Marcellus moved toward his mother.

'I don't want to see you!' she cried, pushing him away.

'But it's not what you think. Mother, just listen!' He leaned over and whispered something in her ear that made her step back and look at him anew. 'Please don't tell Octavian,' he begged.

'Everyone back to your rooms,' Octavia ordered. 'Go to sleep.'

But the vestibulum was suddenly filled with a woman's cries for help, and everyone froze.

'It's Gallia,' Marcellus said, recognizing her voice. 'I'll bet they've taken Magister Verrius!' He glared at his mother. 'I guess any blond on the Palatine will do.'

Gallia burst into the hall, looking as if she had run all the way from her house at the bottom of the Palatine. In a weeping tirade, she confirmed Marcellus's fears. 'What has he done? Was it something he taught?'

'No,' Marcellus said angrily. 'There's information that the Red Eagle looks like a Gaul, but they haven't found him yet. So now anyone with light hair is suspect.'

Gallia looked to Octavia.

'It's true,' she said quietly. 'My brother was here searching Marcellus's chamber.'

She gasped. 'His *own nephew*?'

Octavia raised her chin. 'No one is above suspicion.'

Gallia put her head in her hands. Even that night at Gaius's villa she hadn't wept. But the sobs that racked her body made everyone turn away. Her own pain hadn't been enough to break her, but now that it was Magister Verrius ...

Octavia put her arm around Gallia's shoulders and told Vitruvius to fetch some blankets. We followed her through the hall into the library. There would be no ludus in the morning, and there was no use telling us to go to sleep. A slave arrived to light the brazier, and we sat together around the fire, drinking warm wine and huddling in our cloaks. Marcellus looked the worse for his night.

'He's probably been taken to the Carcer,' Octavia guessed. 'They'll search his rooms, and when they don't find anything to suggest he's a traitor, they'll set him free.' But she hesitated. 'He isn't a traitor, is he?'

Gallia put down her cup more loudly than she probably intended. 'I have lived with him for nearly a year. I think I would know if he was the Red Eagle!'

Octavia nodded. 'Then once they're finished going through his scrolls—'

'So let them read! I hope they enjoy Simonides and Homer!'

The fire crackled in the brazier, and an uneasy silence settled over the library. Vitruvius returned with blankets and warm *ofellae*, but no one felt much like eating.

As dawn broke over the sky, doing its best to lighten the leaden clouds, little Tonia put her head in her mother's lap. 'It's time for ludus,' she said. 'Why aren't they going?'

'Because there's not going to be any ludus today. Antonia, take your sister back to your chamber.'

Although I would certainly have argued with my own mother, Antonia rose quietly and did as she was told. The ensuing stillness in the room felt crushing.

'Did you hear about the theater?' Octavia asked to fill the silence.

Vitruvius nodded. 'Caesar has approved of Selene's help,' he said quietly. 'I look forward to seeing her ideas.'

The conversation lapsed into silence, and just as my eyes were becoming too heavy to keep open, a shadow darkened the doorway.

'Verrius!' Gallia cried. She rushed from her seat and threw her arms around his neck, searching his face for signs of torture.

'He wasn't there long,' Juba assured her. 'The soldiers searched his rooms and didn't find anything.'

'Of course they didn't!' Gallia said harshly. 'What did they do to you?' she asked tenderly.

'Nothing. Juba arrived to get me out before they could even put me in chains.'

Tears dampened Gallia's cheeks. 'Thank you, Juba—'

'So nothing was found tonight,' Octavia cut in angrily. 'Not here, not in the ludus, and not in Magister Verrius's home.'

Juba's gaze did not waver. 'Those were my orders.'

'And what have you been *ordered* to do next?' she demanded.

'Inform you that Octavian is resigning from office.'

CHAPTER SIXTEEN

27–26 BC

BY THE next day, there was no one in Rome who hadn't heard the news. Thousands of people flocked to the Senate, where Octavian had promised to relinquish his powers and resign his office in its entirety. Soldiers kept peace in the courtyard outside, where the men looked solemn and a few hysterical women were beating their chests. We stood around the open doors of the Senate, where a space had been cleared for us, and I heard Octavia say, 'Make way!'

Vitruvius appeared with a young man at his side, and for a terrible moment I wondered if he had taken a new apprentice.

'Alexander, Selene. My son Lucius,' he said.

Lucius gave me a dazzling smile. He was shorter than my brother, but, like Octavian, he had small heels on his bright golden sandals. When I extended my hand, his kiss lingered. 'So you are the one who is bearing my burden,' he said gratefully. 'Without you, I would be chained to ink drawings and cement.'

I laughed. 'It's a pleasant burden,' I told him.

'Well, with someone as pretty as you watching over them, the builders must be begging for more work.'

Marcellus laughed at this empty flattery, but Lucius just turned his attention to my brother. 'Alexander—'

'There he is,' Marcellus interrupted, pointing through the open doors into the Senate. 'He's taken the podium!'

Octavian was dressed in a plain white toga, and nothing on his person gave any indication that he was Caesar. He was flanked by Juba and Agrippa, and behind them stood the Praetorian Guard. Although Alexander and Lucius were whispering, everyone else in the courtyard was silent.

I had asked Julia whether her father was doing this because of the Red Eagle, but she'd only laughed. 'There's nothing he does without planning it first. He's probably considered this for months. Years.'

'Then you don't think he plans on giving up his power?'

Julia had given me a wearied look. 'No,' she'd said with practiced cynicism. 'He would only be doing this if he thought it would increase it.'

I didn't see how resigning his office would make Octavian more powerful than he already was. But as he rose to speak, the senators began to revolt. They shouted for him to remain, citing the civil wars that had ripped Rome apart before he had taken power and swearing that this would happen again if he refused. Men pumped their fists in the air, cursing like sailors from Ostia. But Octavian raised his arms and the room fell silent.

'It is time,' he shouted, 'for me to give up the reins of power and return the Republic to the citizens of Rome.'

'He can't mean that!' Marcellus exclaimed.

Octavia twisted her belt strings nervously in her hands. But Livia was smiling, and I thought, *Julia's right. He doesn't mean that.*

'I believe we all remember my adoptive father, Gaius Julius Caesar, who stood before you only seventeen years ago in the purple robes of *imperium*, with a laurel wreath on his head. Notice that I come before you with none of the trappings of

Caesar. I am a humble servant, one who remembers his history well.'

'Then you remember the civil wars!' a senator shouted.

'Yes,' Octavian conceded. 'But I also remember my father,' he said harshly, 'stabbed to death for attempting to build an empire!'

There was pandemonium in the Senate. A young boy in the doorway repeated Octavian's words for those standing in the courtyard, and the frenzy outside soon matched the turmoil within.

Octavian raised his arms, and again the senators fell silent. 'Having done what I can for Rome,' he went on, 'I now lay down my office in its entirety. To you, the esteemed senators of Rome, I return authority over the army, the laws, and the provinces. You are free to govern not just those territories which you entrusted to me, but also those which I fought and won for you.'

Seneca leapt violently from his seat. 'This is not acceptable!' he cried. 'You fought against Antony, you crushed the kingdom of Egypt, you rebuilt our city and sent forces to police our dangerous hills. You took a republic in chaos and made it into an empire, and we will never allow you to resign!'

Vitruvius turned to Octavia. 'Is he paying Seneca?'

She shook her head. 'I don't know.'

'He doesn't have to pay him,' Livia snapped. 'The senators don't want a return to civil war. Without Octavian's leadership, the clans will go back to fighting and tearing each other apart like wolves.'

'Let us take a vote!' one of the senators shouted.

There were hums of approval, and Octavian raised his hands. 'Then I submit my departure to you,' he acquiesced.

Seneca addressed the chamber. 'We are voting on the future of Rome,' he said. 'There is not a man here who doesn't know what Octavian has done for this city, for this empire, for *all* of you! Do you want to return to the days of anarchy? The days of civil war?' he threatened. 'Octavian is not another Julius Caesar. He is something different. *This* is something different. We can share power, and for the first time in the history of Rome, create a joint way of ruling. So let us give him a name in honor of his difference, of his victories, and his sacrifices to build a better Rome. Let us call Gaius Octavius . . . Augustus.'

There was a roar of approval from the senators, and only a few men remained seated on the benches. From the platform, Octavian bent his head humbly.

Livia looked toward the sky. 'He's done it,' she murmured. The gods seemed to have been watching over her. 'He's made himself emperor.'

The senators resumed their seats, and only Seneca remained standing. 'As for leaving office,' he continued, and a chorus of protests met the words, 'we shall have a vote as to whether Augustus shall be allowed to resign.'

It was a grand piece of theater, and when all of it was done, we watched as Octavian reluctantly accepted control over the provinces of Syria, Iberia, and Gaul for ten years. Egypt would still belong to him, and the command of more than twenty legions was his as well. But the rest of the provinces and their comparatively small legions would be governed by the Senate, and they would be allowed to choose which praetors would oversee them. The celebration in the streets that followed was as loud and wild as any military Triumph. It was as if Augustus were coming home again victorious from battle.

In Octavia's villa that afternoon, we prepared for a celebratory feast. Gallia arranged my curls into a loose bun and slipped pearl-tipped pins into my hair. I imagined how beautiful the pins would have looked with my mother's necklace, then commanded myself not to think about it. Gallia's freedom and happiness were worth any number of necklaces, and no necklace could bring my mother back. Gallia swept the slightest hint of malachite across my lids, then allowed me to wear a pair of pearl earrings Julia had given to me for Saturnalia. When Alexander saw me, he hummed with appreciation.

'Be careful,' he teased. 'All of those senators will be here tonight, and they're probably tired of looking at Octavian.'

'Did you even hear what was happening?' I asked critically. 'Or did you spend the entire time talking with Lucius?'

'Of course I heard! He's kept his power for ten more years, and we're all to call him Augustus.'

I looked up at Gallia. 'Is it true? Will even Octavia call him that?'

'Yes. Romans are always changing their names.'

I thought of the mausoleum that Vitruvius had already started to build, and all of the inscriptions that would have to be changed.

'So do you think he planned this?' Alexander asked, seating himself next to me at the mirror while Gallia perfumed my neck.

'Julia says he did.'

'So does Lucius.'

'And what does Lucius know?' I demanded. 'He lives with his aunt.'

My brother raised his brows. 'Not anymore. He's been talking to his father. Octavia has said he can come and live here.'

'He's quite the charmer.'

We sat together in silence for a moment. Then I glanced in the mirror. 'Do you really think I look pretty?'

'Enough to turn every head in the triclinium,' he promised. 'And me?'

I laughed. 'You're always handsome. And what does it matter? There's no one you have your eye on.'

He smiled uneasily.

'Is there?'

'No,' he confirmed. 'It would be foolish to begin anything. We don't know what Octavian – Augustus – has in mind for us. He could give you to a senator as old as Zeus and me to a witch like Livia.'

'Don't say that,' I whispered.

'It's true. That's why Lucius won't stay with his aunt. She thinks she's found a wife for him. Some horrible hag with a villa in Capri. And he's only a year older than we are.'

'When will he come here?' I asked.

'This evening.'

'So quickly?'

'The more time he spends with her,' my brother said, 'the more time she has to bring women home to meet him.'

'But Vitruvius has to approve any marriage.'

'Lucius says Vitruvius trusts his sister's judgment.'

'So does he think he'll escape marriage by coming here?'

'Perhaps. Not every man marries, you know. Maecenas didn't have a wife for years. And Vergil's in his forties and has never married.'

'They are *poets*, Alexander. And probably Ganymedes.'

But my brother didn't seem bothered by the reference to the handsome Trojan boy who was abducted to Olympus to become the lover of Zeus. He simply shrugged. 'Maybe.'

For the rest of the night, I studied Alexander. Even when Marcellus poured my wine and complimented me on my earrings, I watched the way my brother talked, how Julia laughed at everything he said, and how Alexander's eyes never left Lucius. The only time their gazes were parted was when Augustus stood from his couch in the triclinium and declared that tomorrow, another startling announcement would be made.

Julia shook her head. 'If my father weren't consul, he'd be an actor.'

'Is there a difference?' Marcellus asked, and I detected a note of bitterness in his voice. He said he had forgiven his uncle for accusing him of treachery, but I wondered whether he could forgive him for sending guards to pull him out of the *fornices.*

'What do you think he'll announce?' I whispered. I looked to Julia and Marcellus, but it was Lucius who spoke.

'War.' When everyone turned to him, he added, 'My father says that Augustus wants a new triumphal arch. When he was asked what it was for, he said his continued battle against Gaul, and war in Asturias and Cantabria.'

'Vitruvius never told this to me,' I said, hurt.

'Augustus only asked for the arch this morning.'

'There is rebellion in Gaul,' Marcellus conceded. 'And the Asturians have gold, while the Cantabri have iron. They'd be valuable territories. Not to mention that Cantabria is the last independent nation in Iberia that isn't Roman.'

We all looked at Octavian, bundled in his warmest winter toga and fur-trimmed cloak despite the mildness of March's weather.

'If he goes to war,' Julia confided, 'I only hope he takes Livia along with him.'

On the Ides of April, Julia got her wish. Not only was Livia going to travel with Augustus on the campaign to put down the Gallic rebellion, so were Juba, Tiberius, and Marcellus.

'You can't go!' Julia said desperately, watching Marcellus pack for what might be two, even three years abroad.

He laughed. 'It's only Gaul. Do you know how many legions have been there before?'

'But anything could happen. Why risk yourself like this?'

'Because someday, if this is ever my empire, I will have to go to war alone. Without your father, or his generals, or Juba.'

'And Agrippa?' Lucius asked. He sat next to my brother on Marcellus's couch, where a heavy chest was being filled with sandals and clothes. Since he had moved into the villa and started attending the ludus with us, he and my brother had become inseparable, working on their poetry together, gambling at dice, even betting on the same horses in the Circus. I didn't understand my brother's fascination with him, yet Julia found the pair of them irresistible, laughing like a hyena whenever the three of them were together.

'He'll stay behind to govern Rome,' Marcellus said.

My brother started. 'But isn't he—'

'The architect of my father's wars? Yes,' Marcellus replied. 'But someone needs to watch over the Senate.'

'Agrippa went to Egypt,' I pointed out.

'And every man who wanted Rome for himself was on the battlefield. Now they're dressed in *togae praetextae* and call themselves senators.'

I was impressed by Marcellus's eagerness. Tomorrow he would be riding out with five legions to a war from which he might never return, yet there was only excitement in his voice. I thought of the dangers he would face and the painted Gallic fighters hiding in the thickly wooded passes. I was sure that Isis would never be so cruel as to abandon someone so young and filled with promise. But then why had she abandoned Ptolemy and Caesarion? Where had she been when Antyllus was murdered at the base of Caesar's statue and my parents lost their kingdom to a thin, weak sapling of a man?

There were tears from nearly everyone the next morning. Julia clung to Marcellus and wept. Then he whispered something in her ear and tenderly wiped away her tears with his finger. When he came to me, he didn't whisper anything. I was ashamed to admit how afraid I was that he would never come back. But I refused to weep like a child.

'What, no tears?' Juba asked. 'He's about to fight the fearsome Gauls and Cantabri.'

'Isis will watch over him,' I said firmly.

'Perhaps she can use her wings to fly us to Gaul.' Tiberius laughed. 'Then we won't have to worry about barbarians hiding in the trees along the road.'

'Enough,' Livia said, and for once I was thankful to her. I could feel the sting of tears in my eyes, and Juba watched me curiously while Marcellus straddled his favorite horse. The Campus Martius was filled with onlookers, waiting for the soldiers to begin their march so they could scatter laurel branches in their path.

I was standing close enough to the horses to overhear Livia whisper to Tiberius, 'I'll be in the carriage. If anything happens, you know what to do.'

'Of course,' he said curtly.

'And you won't be fool enough to stand in the way of any arrow meant for Marcellus. If the gods wish him to die, you must not challenge their will.'

Tiberius looked at me and saw that I was eavesdropping. I looked away.

Livia walked to Octavia and kissed her sister-in-law good-bye.

'A safe journey,' Octavia said without conviction.

Livia smiled. 'Don't worry for Marcellus. He's a capable man. And, of course, I'll watch over him like a son.'

I almost protested, but Octavia had wept all morning, and now the tears came afresh. From atop his horse, Marcellus passed her a small square of linen, which she pressed to her nose.

'It's nothing, Mother. A short fight and then it's over.'

Octavia nodded, pretending to believe him, and as the legions moved out, Alexander put his arm around my waist.

'He'll be back,' he promised.

'How do you know?'

'Because Juba and Agrippa have trained him.'

I watched Juba mount his horse. He had saved both Gallia and me from death, and I felt certain he would do the same for Marcellus. Women whistled in his direction, raising their tunics above the knee, and I suspected that some of them were *lupae*. 'Why are they interested in him?' I demanded.

'Because he's handsome,' Alexander said.

I gave him a look.

'It's true,' he admitted. 'You may not like him, but the women of Rome obviously do.'

I supposed that Juba was somewhat attractive. His hair was thick and long, a rich color as dark as his eyes. His muscled thighs were exposed on the horse, and I imagined that his chest was just as handsomely sculpted. But he would never have the same easy laugh as Marcellus. There was no one like Marcellus, and as I blinked back my tears, my brother patted my shoulder.

'Augustus doesn't want anything to happen to him. Marcellus won't see any of the dangerous fighting. But it'll be lonely in the ludus,' he said understandingly.

'And the Circus. And the triclinium.'

'At least you have Julia.'

She was my only consolation as the long months passed and Saturnalia approached without any hint that the soldiers would be returning home. We wandered the holiday markets together with Gallia and seven of the Praetorian Guards, but it was strange without Marcellus's constant chatter and with no one to look pretty for.

'When Marcellus returns home,' Julia said, pausing above a wide selection of wigs, 'perhaps I'll be blond.'

I laughed. 'What? Like a *lupa*?'

'No, like Gallia! Look how beautiful she is.'

'Because I am light,' she told Julia. 'With blue eyes and pale skin. You are a Roman. Dark is your color.'

Julia pouted. 'Then how will I surprise him?'

I glanced in the mirror above the shopkeeper's head, wondering whether I would look good with golden hair. But the thought of wearing a slave girl's shorn-off tresses turned my stomach. *Marcellus is not for me*, I thought firmly. *If he comes home safe, it will be to Julia.* But I couldn't help feeling just a little triumphant that I would have something more than a new wig to show him when he returned. The construction of the theater had already begun near Octavia's portico, and when given a choice of designs, I had asked Vitruvius to build something like the Circus, with three stories of arches veneered in white travertine and topped by Corinthian columns. He was allowing me to sketch every mosaic and all of the important friezes inside. I picked up one of the shopkeeper's statuettes and smiled to myself.

'What? Are you thinking of worshipping Roman gods now?'

I looked down and realized that I was holding a statuette of Mars. 'Of course not!' I put down the statue at once.

Julia laughed. 'He looks like Agrippa, doesn't he?'

The round marble face and short, cropped hair did look a little like him. 'He must be a very loyal man,' I remarked. 'All of this time your father has been gone, and he's never once betrayed him in the Senate.'

'Agrippa would lay down his life for my father. His eldest brother chose the wrong side in the war against Julius Caesar. He fought alongside Cato, if you can imagine, and when Cato was defeated, Julius Caesar took Agrippa's brother as a prisoner. It was my father who intervened and saved his life, so Agrippa feels as though he owes him,' Julia said. 'Sometimes, he comes to our villa just to check on Drusus and me. Of course, there's the Praetorian Guard to watch over us, but he comes anyway.' She lowered her voice. 'And he never betrayed me that night in the Circus.'

I paused. 'What night?'

'When my father went searching through Marcellus's room thinking he was the Red Eagle! Agrippa found us renting a room near the *fornices* and never told my father that I was there as well.'

There was a sudden pressure on my chest so hard that it hurt to breathe. '*You're* the one Marcellus was sneaking out to meet?'

Julia giggled. 'Didn't your brother tell you?'

'No!'

'Well, you should talk to him more often.'

When we returned to the Palatine, I stormed into my chamber, startling Lucius and Alexander at their work.

'What's the matter?' my brother asked. 'Shopping didn't go well?'

'You lied to me!'

He scrambled to a seated position on the couch, scattering his scrolls from the ludus. 'About what?'

'You never told me Marcellus was meeting with Julia in the *fornices*!'

'I just found out! Julia only told me a few weeks ago.'

'Weeks?' I cried. 'And were you ever going to tell me?'

'He was waiting for the right time.'

I glared at Lucius. 'So you know about this as well? My brother tells *you* everything, but keeps his own twin in the dark?'

'It wasn't meant to be that way,' Alexander argued.

'Then how was it meant to be?'

Alexander moved across the room and shut the door. 'He was meeting with her. I knew it would hurt you and I didn't want to see you upset.'

'So better to see me embarrassed,' I said heatedly. 'Better that I learn about it while shopping in the Forum!' Then another thought occurred to me. 'So Marcellus isn't the Red Eagle.'

'It's still possible,' my brother said. 'Haven't you noticed that since he's been gone, not a single actum has been put up?'

'It could also mean the rebel is smart enough to make it look like him.' I crossed my arms over my chest.

'I'm sorry, Selene,' my brother said quietly.

'I wonder how long they've been—'

'Only a few months before he left,' he assured me. 'Before then, he was seeing a *lupa*.'

I gasped.

'Everyone's done it.'

'Have you?' I challenged.

'Of course not me!' He glanced at Lucius. 'I mean everyone else.'

I seated myself and closed my eyes, wishing that if I kept them shut, I would never have to see Alexander, or Lucius, or Marcellus's bright face when he returned and whispered into Julia's ear.

Lucius perched himself on the arm of my chair, and I opened my eyes. 'Come with us to the odeum today,' he said.

'Yes,' Alexander replied. 'You never come. And you're the one who professes to like poetry.' Since Lucius had moved into Octavia's villa, my brother had begun going with him to the local odea. The little covered theaters hosted musical competitions and poetry readings. And since Marcellus had left, my brother was visiting the odea even more frequently than the Circus. 'Come on,' Alexander pleaded. 'The one on the Campus is the prettiest little theater you've ever seen.'

'It might even give you some ideas,' Lucius prompted.

'Ovid is going to be there,' my brother said temptingly.

'And who is Ovid?'

Alexander and Lucius looked at one another. 'Just the greatest young poet in Rome!' Lucius cried. 'Come with us!' He took my arm, and I allowed myself to be led to the Campus Martius, where a small stone building welcomed visitors with a handsome mosaic and an ivy-covered arch. Because it was nearly Saturnalia, a green and saffron canopy fluttered over the crossbeams, invoking the colors of fertility and protecting the patrons from the December drizzle. Two men of the Praetorian Guard took seats behind us, and Alexander explained what was about to happen.

'Today is for poetry,' he said. 'You see the young man with the red cheeks waiting to go on stage? That's Ovid.'

'How old is he?' I exclaimed.

'Sixteen.'

'And his family lets him perform?'

'Not everyone's father refuses to acknowledge the value of literature,' Lucius said.

'What about Horace and Vergil?' I asked.

Alexander wrinkled his nose. 'Augustus owns them. All they write is politics now. Ovid writes about what's real.'

When I frowned, Lucius said, 'Love,' then added quickly, 'and love's pain.'

I crossed my arms. 'And you think I want to hear about love's pain?'

'Shh,' Alexander said. 'Just listen.'

Ovid took the stage, and immediately the patrons of the Odeum hushed. This was not like Octavian's theater performances, where men stood from their seats and threw dates at the actors and chanted, 'Bring on the bear.' The audience was composed mostly of young men. A few women sat with their friends, giggling and pointing, but everyone grew silent when Ovid declared, 'I call this "Disappointment." '

Several men chuckled.

'Why is that funny?' I whispered.

'Because he's always talking about his triumphs,' my brother said.

Then Ovid began:

> But oh, I suppose she was ugly; she wasn't elegant;
> I hadn't yearned for her often in my prayers.
> Yet holding her I was limp, and nothing happened at all:
> I just lay there, a disgraceful load for her bed.
> I wanted it, she did too; and yet no pleasure came
> from the part of my sluggish loins that should bring joy.
> The girl entwined her ivory arms around my neck
> (her arms were whiter than the Sithonian snows),
> and gave me greedy kisses, thrusting her fluttering tongue,
> and laid her eager thigh against my thigh,
> and whispering fond words, called me the lord of her heart
> and everything else that lovers murmur in joy.
> And yet, as if chill hemlock were smeared upon my body,
> my numb limbs would not act out my desire.
> I lay there like a log, a fraud, a worthless weight;
> my body might as well have been a shadow.
> What will my age be like, if old age ever comes,
> when even my youth cannot fulfill its role?

The audience laughed uproariously, and Ovid continued:

Ah, I'm ashamed of my years. I'm young and a man: so what?
I was neither young nor a man in my girlfriend's eyes.
She rose like the sacred priestess who tends the undying flame,
or a sister who's chastely lain at a dear brother's side.
But not long ago blonde Chlide twice, fair Pitho three times,
and Libas three times I enjoyed without a pause.
Corinna, as I recall, required my services
nine times in one short night – and I obliged!
Has some Thessalian potion made my body limp,
injuring me with noxious spells and herbs?
Did some witch hex my name scratched on crimson wax
and stab right through the liver with slender pins?

He went on to describe the shame of not performing, and I stared at my brother in disbelief. When Ovid was finished, the entire audience was on its feet.

Alexander turned to me. 'Well, what do you think?'

'It's disgusting and crass. Is this all that he does?'

'You didn't like it?' Lucius exclaimed, wiping the tears of laughter from his eyes. 'He has other material, too,' he promised. 'Entire odes to his mistress Corinna.'

'The one he took nine times?' I asked dryly.

'It's meant to be satire,' my brother said. 'I thought you'd find it funny.'

'Perhaps I'm not in the mood.'

'But the theater is handsome, isn't it?' he asked.

Grudgingly, I admitted that it was. For a little stone building crushed between two shops in the Campus Martius, it had a certain charm. It wasn't anything our mother would have frequented in Alexandria, and she would never have condoned our enjoying coarse Latin poetry in a Roman theater with golden *bullae* around our necks. But then, our mother was gone, and Egypt had been swept up in Augustus's new empire. Marcellus had been all that made my exile bearable. When I listened to him laughing in the halls of the villa or shouting at the teams in the Circus Maximus, I could forget for a while that Charmion and Ptolemy were dead, that I would never return to the Egypt of my childhood, and that my father's memory had been expunged from Rome.

Alexander and Lucius tried their best to cheer me, and for a while there was news from Egypt that seemed hopeful. Cornelius Gallus, the poet and politician whom Augustus had set up as prefect over my mother's kingdom, had fallen from favor and committed suicide. What better time to turn to me and Alexander than now, when Egypt was without a leader? But news arrived just as swiftly from Gaul that a new prefect had been found. So even as Saturnalia came and went, I found little to be happy about.

When my brother and I had our fourteenth birthday on the first of January, Julia presented me with a beautiful pair of gold-and-emerald earrings, but her generosity did nothing but irk me.

'We should go to the Forum,' she said eagerly, 'and pick out a silk tunic to match them.'

'And who would I wear it for?' I demanded, ruining the light mood in the triclinium, where Octavia had hung Saturn's sacred holly branches from the ceiling, and their waxy leaves reflected the lamplight.

Julia frowned. 'What do you mean? For yourself. For Lucius.'

'All Lucius does is stare at my brother.'

Julia looked at the pair of them rolling dice in the corner of the triclinium. 'So do you think they're more than friends?' she asked.

I looked at her aghast. 'Of course not!'

'They spend all their time together,' she pointed out.

'So do we,' I whispered. 'And I'm not your lover. Marcellus is.'

She glanced swiftly at Octavia. 'Please don't tell her, Selene. She would never forgive me if she knew. Please.'

I wanted to reply with something cutting, to tell her that Octavia knew already, but the need in her eyes was too urgent. And why was it her fault that she was the one destined for Marcellus, and not I?

'So you don't like the earrings?' she asked hesitantly.

'Of course I do.' I attempted a smile. 'They're beautiful.'

'Then we'll shop for something to match them tomorrow!'

I tried to be in a better mood when we went to the Forum. Even though the weather was grim and a cold mist hung over the streets, I followed Gallia down the Via Sacra in my warmest cloak.

'At least it's not snowing,' Julia said. 'Imagine what it must be like in the mountains of Gaul.'

'How cold does it get there?' I asked Gallia.

'Very bitter,' she replied. 'When the snow falls, even the animals go into hiding. Every year there are children who starve for lack of food, and the old women without families are prey for the wolves.'

Julia shivered. 'No wonder my father's letters are so pitiful. He's sick all the time. And weak.'

'The Gallic winters can do that. If he is wise,' Gallia said, 'he will leave his most hearty men there and take the rest south toward Cantabria.'

Julia looked at me, and I knew she was thinking of Marcellus. Somewhere in the cold mountain ranges of Gaul, he was suffering with Juba, Augustus, and Tiberius. Their men were probably wishing for the comforts of home, where holly hung in bright sprigs on their doorposts and the rich scent of cooked goose filled their halls. Some of them would never live to see another Saturnalia, and I wondered how Livia was managing in such a bitter place. *Probably just fine*, I thought acerbically. *She has Augustus all to herself, and Terentilla is eight hundred miles away.*

When we reached the Forum, Julia wrapped her cloak tighter across her chest. 'Perhaps we should have left this for another time. Let's take the shortcut,' she suggested.

Gallia led the way through the Senate courtyard, where despite the bitter weather, lawyers were arguing a trial. The heavily dressed men stood at two separate podiums, shielded from the light rain by a thin canopy. A crowd of onlookers had gathered, and I pulled at Julia's cloak. 'Do you think we should see what's happening?'

'In this weather?' she exclaimed.

'But look at all the people. It might be another trial like the one for the slaves of Gaius Fabius.'

Julia hesitated, torn between the warmth of the shops and curiosity. 'Only for a moment. And only if it's good.'

We stood behind the platform in the space reserved for senators and members of what was now the imperial family. A young defendant had been placed between two soldiers, but it was obvious from her clothes that she was no pleb. The fur of her cloak brushed her soft cheeks, and the sandals on her feet were new and made of leather. Her long braid had been threaded carefully with gold, and no man would have passed her on the street without thinking that she was pretty. It was her lawyer's turn to speak at the podium, and she listened with downcast eyes.

'You have heard Aquila's lawyer tell you that this girl was once his slave,' he said angrily. 'You have heard him lie like a dog from his mouth and say that she was stolen from him as an infant. So how can Aquila tell that this girl is the same child he purchased fifteen years ago? Does she have the same plump cheeks?' he demanded. 'The same fat legs and ear-piercing cry?' The crowd in front of him laughed a little. 'And why has Aquila suddenly come forward now claiming that she is his former slave? Could it be that she is pretty?' The crowd shook their heads in disapproval, and a heavy man in a fur cloak narrowed his eyes at them. 'Could it be that he has lusted after Tullia for months, and knowing that she is the daughter of an honorable centurion, he has decided that this is the only way to have her?'

'Liar!' the lawyer for Aquila shouted.

'I can prove to you that I'm not lying! This girl you see before you has never been a slave, and I will bring a dozen people who witnessed her birth and who will vouch for her identity.'

'And who are these people?' Aquila's lawyer challenged. 'Slaves who can be easily bought off?'

'Not as easily as judices,' Tullia's lawyer retorted, and there was a stiffening of backs among the seated men. 'It's true. The midwives of Rome are slaves, but I will bring to you her mother, her father, even her aunts, and you will see the resemblance—'

'They can see a resemblance between you and me!' Aquila's lawyer scoffed. 'See? We both have short hair and dark skin. Does that make me your child?'

Several of the judices laughed, and an uneasy feeling settled in my stomach.

'Tomorrow, I bring witnesses,' Tullia's lawyer promised. 'And when this case must be decided, I ask that you use reason. What man would wait fifteen years before bringing charges of kidnapping? Why Tullia? Why now? And remember,' he warned ominously, 'that the next time a man wants to abuse a pretty citizen, she could be your sister, your daughter, even your wife!'

The judices rose, and the crowd began to disperse.

'It's over?' Julia exclaimed. 'Why not bring the witnesses today?'

'Because it is raining heavily now,' Gallia pointed out.

Neither Julia nor I had noticed. We watched the soldiers escort the girl from the platform, and the eyes of the man in fur watched her hotly. She avoided his gaze, looking instead at the weeping woman still standing in the rain. *Her mother*, I thought sadly. Next to the woman a broad-shouldered centurion placed his hand on his heart in a silent promise. The girl seemed to tremble, then her legs gave way beneath her.

'Tullia!' the man shouted, and I was sure he was her father.

The soldiers lifted her swiftly back onto her feet, and the centurion spun around to the fat man in his furs. 'I will kill you!' Her father lunged, but several soldiers moved quickly to stop him.

'Let the judices decide!' Tullia's lawyer pleaded.

'He's paid them off!' the father accused. 'Even her lawyer knows that their pockets are filled with this maggot's gold!'

Aquila straightened his cloak. 'Be careful,' he warned. 'Masters can discard slaves who are no longer useful to them.'

The two men stared at each other for a moment, then the centurion hissed, 'If I were you, I'd watch myself. Even maggots have to sleep.'

More soldiers rushed to separate them, splashing through the mud before violence could be done.

'We must come back tomorrow,' Julia said suddenly.

'You will not like it,' Gallia warned. 'The judices have been bought.'

'How do you know?'

'You saw their faces. Who were those men laughing for?'

'Aquila's lawyer,' Julia realized. 'But that isn't fair!'

Gallia turned up her palm. 'It is foolish to think that rot can be confined to a single fruit. Once slavery is planted, everything decays.'

We didn't do much shopping. The rain was falling in heavy gray sheets, and when we reached the shop of a wealthy silk merchant, we huddled around his sandalwood brazier until the rain subsided and we could go out again. Julia purchased a few bolts of cloth in acknowledgment of his hospitality, and instructed him to send the bill to Augustus.

That evening, in Octavia's triclinium, Julia described what we'd seen in the Forum. As she came to the part about the judices being bought, Octavia sucked in her breath.

'The judices of Rome are men from honorable patrician families.'

'I'm only repeating what the lawyer said.'

'And isn't it suspicious that a man would wait fifteen years before claiming one of the prettiest girls in Rome as his slave?' Vitruvius asked. 'Can it really be said that *all* patricians are honorable?'

'Perhaps we should go tomorrow,' Agrippa suggested. He looked at his wife.

'I wouldn't mind the rain,' Claudia replied. 'We could dress warmly. And our presence might inspire the judices to act on their consciences.'

I was surprised by the simplicity of her thinking. Assuming the judices had really been bought, no one's presence would speak louder than gold. Agrippa might appear for one day of the trial, but how long would it hold his attention? And what would he do if the judices ruled that Tullia was Aquila's slave? As Octavia had said, they were men from honorable families. Charging them with corruption would be a heavy thing.

*

Before Alexander blew out the oil lamps in our room that night, I turned on my side to face him. 'It's a dirty system, isn't it?'

'No more than in Egypt. And where's the better way?'

'Perhaps if they forbade slavery—'

But my brother laughed sadly. 'And do you think the patricians would allow that? All of their fields, which make them rich, would have to be tended by workers they actually paid.'

'So what? They're all wealthy enough.'

'It would never pass the Senate. Even if Augustus paid the senators to vote in favor of banishing slavery, they'd be risking their lives. The plebs would revolt. The patricians aren't the only ones with slaves. And in the end, what would it accomplish? Men would simply forbid their slaves from leaving on punishment of death, and the courts could run every day from now until next Saturnalia before they found judges willing to punish slave killers.'

I was quiet for a moment, angry that he was right. 'Are you going to come tomorrow?'

My brother hesitated. 'Vergil has a reading—'

'And you would rather be at the odeum instead of watching a trial for a girl's life?' I sat up on my couch. 'Whenever Vergil is invited to the triclinium, you and Lucius hang on his every word,' I said accusingly. 'What is it about him? He's just an old Ganymede.'

'You shouldn't say that,' my brother replied.

'Why? Isn't it true?'

'Yes. But he writes about male love in a way that makes it beautiful. If you read some of his works, Selene, you might change your mind.'

I stared at him. 'You aren't in love with Lucius, are you?'

My brother blushed.

'With a *man*?' I exclaimed.

'We haven't done anything,' he said defensively. 'Just kissed.'

I regarded my brother. His namesake, Alexander the Great, had taken men to his bed and counted the soldier Hephaestion as one of his greatest loves. But he had also taken a wife and given Macedon an heir. 'So what do you think you will do when Augustus returns and wants to arrange a marriage for you?' I whispered, 'Refuse?'

'No one refuses Augustus. So why spend my last free years – maybe only months – at a trial whose outcome I can't change, when I can be with Lucius?'

We stared at each other from our couches, and I tried to determine what I felt about this.

'I'm sorry, Selene. It's nothing I can help.'

'Have you even tried—'

'Of course,' he said swiftly.

'Why didn't you tell me this before?' My voice broke.

'I thought you'd be disappointed.'

He waited for me to tell him I wasn't; that his desire for Lucius was as normal as Marcellus's desire for Julia. But I kept my silence, forcing him to explain.

'There are many men who aren't attracted to women. Look at Maecenas. You don't think it's a coincidence that Terentilla's never had a child? Maecenas isn't interested, while Augustus has her drink the juice of the silphium plant to keep her from getting pregnant by him.'

'How do you know that?' I demanded crossly.

'I heard it from Maecenas.'

'So men who love other men pass on their secrets to one another?'

My brother raised his brows. 'Don't women?'

'And what does Vitruvius think of you two?'

'He doesn't know. Or maybe he doesn't want to.'

'So this is why Lucius didn't want to marry,' I said.

My brother nodded. 'Yes. But unless he can support himself or find a generous patron, he will have to someday. And then we'll both be miserable, instead of just one of us. That's why I have to encourage his readings in the odeum. There's nothing I can do about slavery, Selene. But I can help change Lucius's life.' He held out his hand to me, and slowly I took it.

'This isn't how I imagined our lives would be when I was Queen of Libya and you King of Armenia.'

Alexander laughed sadly. 'Our father had great plans, didn't he? The kingdom of Parthia hadn't even been conquered and he crowned me its king.' We both smiled, remembering our father's irrepressible belief in himself. 'Do you think it's fate that we'll lead unfulfilled lives?'

I drew back. 'Of course not. Augustus may still make you king.'

'After he's married me off to some widow.'

'But you're a man! You can do as you please – send her off to the country or keep her in Rome while you return to Egypt. Maecenas is content enough.'

'But what about you?' His voice was so gentle and full of concern that tears sprang to my eyes.

'I don't know.'

'If you can forget Marcellus, perhaps you'll find someone else.'

'For what purpose? To have my heart broken again? This isn't Egypt, Alexander. When Augustus returns, he'll find me a husband that's convenient for him, not me. It could be someone like Catullus or even Aquila. And there would be nothing I could do if he forbade me from visiting you in Alexandria.'

'I would never return without you,' he swore.

'Yes,' I said firmly, 'you would. It's your destiny.' I looked outside. The gardens, which shone blue and green every summer, were still dreary and soaked with rain. 'I don't think unhappiness is fated. Look at Gallia. She was forced into slavery and still found happiness.'

'Because you freed her! But even as citizens we aren't free. Everything we do, from the food we eat to the clothes we wear, is determined by Augustus!'

'And you've always been the one telling me to be practical. But now look. You've lost your heart to Lucius, and it's making you crazy.'

My brother turned away. 'It would all be different if Augustus died in Gaul, wouldn't it? Marcellus is old enough now to be Caesar and he would let us marry whomever we wanted. Then we could return to Alexandria.'

'Augustus's letters to Octavia are always short,' I said eagerly. 'And Julia says she heard that he spends most of his days sleeping. He isn't strong.'

My brother raised his eyes. 'From your mouth to Isis's ears,' he whispered.

CHAPTER SEVENTEEN

BEFORE ISIS could make a decision about my brother's prayer, she acted on one of my silent pleas. I was leaving the library, where Vitruvius was making the plans for the Pantheon's final steps, when Octavia rushed in, too anxious to even realize I was there.

'He's back!' she exclaimed. 'And they're all over Rome. We finally have *proof* it wasn't Marcellus!'

Vitruvius rose from his desk. 'Another actum?'

'On the temples of Apollo, Jupiter, Vesta, Castor and Pollux, even Venus Genetrix. It's short, just a few lines calling people to the trial of Tullia. But Marcellus isn't here, and there's not a chance in Hades he could have done it!'

I rushed back to my chamber to tell Alexander the news, and my brother remarked, 'So he wasn't lying.'

When Lucius met us on the portico, he grinned widely at me, as if he already knew what my brother had revealed about him last night, and that I had come to accept it. 'I heard from my father about the actum. Now all of Rome will be at the trial.'

'I should think the weather will keep some people away. The old won't want to come. And certainly not mothers with their children,' I said.

But my prediction was wrong. Despite the dampness in the

air, there wasn't any rain, and even matrons with babies on their hips came to see what had drawn the Red Eagle out of hiding. For months he had not posted a single actum. Whenever we went to the ludus, I glanced at the doors of the temples we passed and felt a keen disappointment. The Red Eagle's absence had only made me more certain that he was Marcellus, but the latest message removed all possibility.

Thousands of people had gathered in the Forum. Even Octavia had been watching the trial since morning. She explained to us what was happening, and when she saw that Magister Verrius had come with us, her eyebrows rose.

'This case has implications beyond one little girl,' he replied to her unspoken question.

Since the night of Magister Verrius's arrest, Augustus's spies had been following him constantly. If they hadn't found anything yet, there was nothing to find. And now, with Marcellus in Gaul, the two men who had seemed most likely to be the Red Eagle were suddenly innocent. Alexander and Lucius stepped back, letting me stand in front of them so I could see what was happening. If a foreigner to the city had looked out over the handsomely dressed crowd of senators and their fur-cloaked wives, he would have thought he'd happened upon a theatrical performance. But the danger to Tullia's life was real, and I wondered whether somewhere in the crowd, the Red Eagle was listening to her lawyer as he tried to persuade the judices of her freeborn birth.

'I have brought before you the maiden's mother, her father, two aunts, and an uncle who all swear before Juno that she is the daughter of centurion Calpurnius Commiodus,' Tullia's lawyer was saying. 'Only purchased women have sworn that she is Aquila's slave. Whom will you believe?' he demanded. 'Citizens of Rome, or slaves?'

'Correct me if I am wrong,' Aquila's lawyer retorted, 'but I believe you produced slaves as witnesses as well.'

'With citizens! Where are your citizens?' Tullia's lawyer challenged. 'Not a single pleb has come forward to vouch for Aquila's lies. Why is that?' The crowd began to hiss. 'Perhaps Aquila spent all his denarii,' he speculated, 'paying off other people.' He looked piercingly at the judices – a warning to them that if Aquila's gold was in their pockets, they had better beware.

The crowd raised fists of anger, shouting threats to the seated men in togas. I saw Aquila flinch as someone hurled a lettuce from the crowd and one of the judices was hit on the head. The judex rose in a fury, turning to the spectators. 'Since you cannot behave yourselves, we are done for the day. Trial will resume tomorrow!'

There was near mutiny.

'Can he do that?' Alexander exclaimed.

'Any of the judices can stop the trial,' Magister Verrius said. 'I suspect they will deliver a verdict in the morning.'

'And will we come to see it?' Julia asked.

Magister Verrius looked at Octavia. She surveyed the madness, and two small lines appeared between her brows. 'Only with an escort of the Praetorian Guard. This courtyard will not be safe if the judices determine that Tullia was a slave.'

As we returned to the Palatine, I asked Magister Verrius who he believed the Red Eagle might be. For once, Julia stopped complaining about her hunger and listened. Even Alexander and Lucius were attentive.

'Someone wealthy, with a personal interest in slavery and the education to write eloquently about it.'

'And someone who is willing to risk death by crucifixion if he's caught,' Octavia added.

'*When* he's caught,' Agrippa said sternly. 'And it will be only a matter of time. A priest will see him posting one of his acta and think of the five-thousand-denarii reward. Or perhaps it will be a passing slave, or a young matron with seven children to feed. There are many people in Rome whose lives could be changed by five thousand denarii.'

'And what would he be crucified for?' I asked.

'Inciting rebellion,' Agrippa answered swiftly. 'Disturbing the lives of good citizens of Rome and provoking assassination.'

'I thought the kitchen boy had nothing to do with the Red Eagle,' my brother said.

'There are men who will take secrets with them to their graves, no matter the cost,' Agrippa replied. 'He could have known the Red Eagle personally.'

But I didn't believe it. Faced with the most terrible kinds of torture, what man wouldn't speak to save his skin?

For the rest of the afternoon, the Red Eagle was all anyone wanted to talk about. And that evening, in Octavia's triclinium, Julia whispered, 'Perhaps he'll slit Aquila's throat in the night and the trial will end.'

'But has he ever killed before?' Alexander asked.

'Of course. Dozens of times,' Julia told him.

'How do you know?'

'Well, how else has he posted so many acta without a single person fingering him? He must kill his witnesses.'

'Perhaps he uses disguises,' I suggested. 'Or goes in the night when everyone is sleeping.'

Julia tilted her head at me. 'Have you seen these streets at night? Julius Caesar forbade traffic from entering Rome during the day. As soon as the sun sets, there are thousands of merchants on the streets. Not to mention cutthroats and *lupae*.'

'But what would they be doing at the temples?' I argued. 'They'd be in the Forum, where the shops are.'

'The Temple of Venus Genetrix is in the Forum,' Lucius pointed out. 'And he's posted there.'

'Then perhaps he goes in the guise of a merchant,' my brother said.

We argued about it until Octavia determined it was time for us to retire to our chambers. Then Lucius followed us into our room and reclined on the same couch where Marcellus used to lie, the couch meant for Ptolemy. 'It's better that we went to the trial today,' he said. 'I don't think there's anyone in Rome who believes that Tullia was a slave.'

'If the judges decide otherwise, there will be riots,' I predicted.

'Julia should like that,' Lucius remarked.

'She likes anything so long as there's action,' my brother said. 'It has to be lonely in her father's house with only Drusus to talk to.'

'And now, only the slaves,' Lucius remarked. 'When do you think they'll be coming home?'

'Months yet,' Alexander replied. 'Maybe even years.'

'But Marcellus might return before Augustus,' I said hopefully. 'He's not a seasoned soldier. There's no reason for Augustus to keep him there so long.'

From my lips to Isis's ears. In two days, my second plea was answered. First, the Red Eagle had returned to Rome. Then, before the sun even peeked through the slats of my shutters, there was a clamor in the atrium; laughter and shouts of tremendous joy.

My brother sat up on his couch and looked at me.

'They've returned!' I shouted. I threw off my covers and dressed as quickly as possible. I didn't bother with my hair and my tunic was a mess, but when I flung open the door and saw Marcellus, I regretted not taking more time with my appearance. The eleven months he'd been away had turned him into a man. He was taller than I remembered, with broader shoulders and a leaner jaw. He looked well fed and rested, and he was dressed in a soldier's scarlet cloak and nail-studded boots. Antonia and Tonia were both laughing, touching the hunting horn that hung from a strap across his chest and pointing to the double-edged sword at his side. Octavia beamed with pride, and Vitruvius could not have looked happier if Marcellus had been his own son.

Marcellus grinned when he saw me. He crossed the atrium with open arms. 'Selene.' I let him take me to his chest and inhaled the scent of rain and leather from his muscled cuirass. 'Look at you,' he said, pulling away. 'A woman now.'

I'm sure I blushed, and I was thankful that the room was lit only by oil lamps. 'Eleven months is a long time to be gone,' I replied. 'You've changed as well.'

'Really?'

'Of course! Don't you see it?' Antonia asked. 'Your hair is longer.'

'And your feet are bigger!' Tonia exclaimed.

Marcellus laughed. 'Well, if you think I've grown, you should see Tiberius.'

'He's come home with you?' I frowned.

'Along with Juba. Augustus and Livia plan to remain until the rebellion in Gaul and the war in Cantabria are finished.'

'But that could be years,' Octavia worried.

'Or just a few months. Most of the Gallic rebellions have been crushed. It's just a matter of Iberia now.' Marcellus saw my brother and smiled. 'Alexander.' The two embraced, and Marcellus complimented my brother on his height. 'How is it that you can be two years younger than me and still as tall? It must be the Roman sun. It's not as strong in Gaul.' There was a squeal of delight from behind him, and when Marcellus turned,

Julia came into view. She was dressed in a tunic of diaphanous blue silk, with turquoise at her ears and around her neck. I looked like an underfed peasant compared to her, with her perfectly plump waist and ample chest. Only my brother and I were close enough to hear Marcellus catch his breath. 'Julia.'

She ran to him, and he held her in his arms and kissed her cheek. Behind her came Juba and Tiberius, both wearing short scarlet cloaks.

'Already the happy reunion,' Juba said, watching me.

'Juba!' Octavia's smile was wide. 'And Tiberius,' she said delightedly. 'But why didn't anyone warn us of your coming?'

'We thought it should be a surprise,' Marcellus said, letting go of Julia. 'So was it?'

Octavia's eyes shone with tears. 'Yes.'

'We won't have to go to the ludus today, will we?' Julia pleaded.

Octavia laughed. 'No. Today will be a day of celebration! Faustina,' she called to one of her slaves, 'let Magister Verrius know there will be no ludus today. And invite him to a feast tonight.'

'But what about the trial?' I said with concern.

Marcellus looked from one face to another. 'What trial?'

Octavia explained what had been happening in the Forum, and how this morning a verdict would be given on Tullia's fate.

'I don't know.' Marcellus looked at Julia. 'I was rather hoping to spend some time at home—'

'And we can send a slave to hear the verdict,' Julia added.

'But you were the one who suggested going!' I exclaimed. 'Aren't you interested in what happens to her?'

'Sure, but Marcellus just returned, Selene. He's tired.'

He didn't look tired to me.

'And probably hungry.'

'Starving.' He groaned.

I looked from Julia to Marcellus and wondered how I could

ever have believed that Marcellus had the compassion to be the Red Eagle.

'I'll go with you,' my brother said swiftly.

'I'm happy to go as well,' Lucius said.

'Not by yourselves,' Vitruvius warned.

'I can take them.'

Octavia turned to Juba. 'But you've only just returned,' she protested. 'Aren't you tired?'

'Perhaps if we hadn't stopped at every inn along the way,' he said, looking meaningfully at Marcellus, 'I would be more road-weary. As it is, I feel quite rested. Besides, the princess seems to have a soft spot for slaves, and I'm interested to see which victim has inflamed her sympathy this time.'

I crossed my arms over my chest, and my brother's look warned me not to say anything that might cause Juba to withdraw his offer.

'Then you must be careful,' Octavia cautioned. 'The plebs are extremely angry about this.'

'You aren't coming?' I asked.

Octavia looked uncomfortable. 'I believe I will spend this day with Marcellus.'

In the end, only four of us went, and Lucius conversed cheerfully with Juba along the way.

'So are the Gauls as barbaric as they say?' he asked eagerly.

'Look around. Half of Rome is filled with them.'

'But in their native lands, do they really feast on men's flesh and walk naked through the woods?'

'Not that I've seen,' Juba replied.

'But their horses are finer than anything in Rome,' my brother said. 'That's true, isn't it?'

'Yes,' Juba said. 'They train them better, and the steeds seem to be of better quality. You know, their goddess Epona is a horse.'

'I notice you don't make fun of that,' I remarked.

Juba smiled. 'That's because everyone knows the Gauls are barbarians. The Egyptians, on the other hand, are reputed to be fine thinkers.'

'And was the weather as terrible as Augustus wrote?' Lucius asked. 'Octavia read us letters that talked of snow falling for weeks.'

'The Gallic mountains are forbidding,' Juba admitted. 'Hundreds of soldiers died, and many more would have followed if the rebellion had lasted. Wounds that may be survivable in the summer drain the body differently in winter.'

'So how did Augustus survive it?' I asked.

'He left after a month of rain.'

'He left?' Alexander repeated incredulously. 'Where?'

'The northeast of Iberia at a place called Tarraco. And I suspect that's where he'll remain until his generals finish the Cantabrian war.'

My brother stopped walking. 'Then he isn't fighting?'

'No,' Juba said simply. 'Augustus was not built for warfare.'

Alexander looked at me, then continued moving, and I could hear his thoughts as clearly as if he were speaking them aloud. Our father, who had never been sick a day in his life, had died so that a weakling could rule an empire he couldn't even defend personally. Our mother would have clothed herself in deerskins and eaten strips of human flesh before leaving her soldiers hungry and cold in the mountains of Gaul. She would have donned armor herself and fought like a man before turning and fleeing for warmer climes.

'So this is it,' Juba said as we arrived in the Forum. 'The latest trial to stir up the passion of the plebs and Princess Selene.'

I ignored his taunt and he led us to our regular place behind the platform. Because we were early, the judices had only just begun seating themselves, but a swarm of spectators already filled the courtyard. The lawyers for Aquila and Tullia mounted the rostrum, and the girl at the center of the trial was brought out, with two soldiers for guards. Her face was stained with tears, and she was trembling. I searched for her mother and father in the crowd, and saw them closest to the platform, smiling and encouraging her to be strong.

I turned to Juba. 'Do you think it's funny now?'

'You mistake me,' he said coldly. 'This has never been funny. Just a sad, short spectacle of human injustice like most other trials this courtyard has witnessed.'

I stepped back. 'Then you hope she will go free?'

'If what Octavia has told me about the trial is true, then yes. I am sorry if this disappoints you. I know how you cherish the thought that I'm indifferent to human suffering.'

I looked back at the lawyers, who were wearing long cloaks in case of rain. The two men waited patiently to begin, and when the last of the judices were seated, the lawyer for Tullia addressed them. He made a plea for reason and sanity, asking that the seated men remember their own daughters, sisters, and wives. Then Aquila's lawyer spoke on behalf of his client, reminding the judices of Aquila's reputation as the Aventine's most reputable banker. There were jeers from the crowd as he said this, but no one attempted to rush the platform or throw food. Hundreds of soldiers stood in formation around the Forum, and when the judices rose, there was total silence.

'Aquila,' the first judex announced. 'Aquila,' said the second, and the third said the same.

'What does it mean?' I whispered.

'They are voting in favor of the banker,' Juba said, 'and we are about to witness what plebian rage looks like.'

The soldiers around us began to tense as one by one the judices stood and announced for Aquila.

'Perhaps we should leave,' I said uneasily.

'*Some* of them have to find in favor in Tullia!' Alexander exclaimed. 'They can't *all* be bought.'

But judex after judex rose and said, 'Aquila.' The crowd was becoming volatile, shouting insults and threatening revenge. But as the last judex rose, the courtyard fell silent.

'Aquila,' the old man said, and suddenly Tullia rushed past the rostrum into her father's arms. But instead of laying her head upon his chest, she fell to her knees and exposed her neck. It happened so swiftly that even the guards were taken by surprise. Then shrill screams echoed across the Forum as the plebs realized what had happened. The centurion had killed his own daughter in order to save her from slavery and rape.

Lucius covered his mouth with his hand, and even Juba looked pale. We didn't wait to see what would happen. I had seen plebian anger at the Circus Maximus and the trial of Gaius Fabius's slaves, but this was outrage on a different scale. Juba took my arm, and Alexander and Lucius followed swiftly behind us. 'Move!' Juba shouted at the people around us. 'Move!' By the time we reached the Palatine, a fleet-footed slave had already told Octavia what had happened, and dozens of people were gathered on Augustus's platform, watching the conflict in the Forum. Something was burning in the courtyard of the Senate, and I presumed it was the rostrum where Tullia's father had killed her rather than let her be violated. The small flecks of scarlet darting in and out of the Forum had to be soldiers attempting to put out the fire, but small fires had already started up in other places.

'They're burning their own livelihoods,' Tiberius said scornfully.

'They don't care,' I told him. 'They're sending a message to the Senate.'

'And what is that?' he demanded. 'That the plebs can't be

trusted to watch an open trial? That from now on, trials should be held in secret?'

'She was alive,' Julia said plaintively. 'Just yesterday, she was alive.'

Agrippa looked murderous, and I wondered if he was thinking of his daughter, Vipsania. 'I should have gone today.'

'It wouldn't have changed anything,' Vitruvius assured him. 'The judices were bought.'

Octavia remained silent, watching the small fires burn across the Forum. One by one they were being put out, but the sound of the raging mobs was carried on the wind.

'Do you think her father will be charged with murder?' I asked no one in particular.

'She was the property of Aquila,' Juba replied. 'His slave. If he wishes to ask for money in reparation, he may.'

'Someone should kill him in his sleep,' Julia hissed. 'He should be slaughtered the way Tullia's father slaughtered her.'

The young slave girl Faustina approached Octavia with hesitant steps. 'Domina, the cook says the feast is ready.'

'It's too soon,' Octavia snapped, and the girl flinched. I had never heard Octavia raise her voice to a slave.

'We can watch the fires burn or go inside,' Vitruvius said. 'Either way, the girl is gone.'

It wasn't a merry homecoming. What was supposed to be a festive celebration in honor of Marcellus's return with Tiberius and Juba became a subdued meal. Magister Verrius and Gallia joined us in the triclinium, and there was a purposeful silence about what was happening below the Palatine. But after a little music and several courses of wine, Marcellus described for us his feats in battle, and Tiberius even honored us with a poem composed after a bloody clash. I heard my brother whisper to Lucius that *he* could have done much better, and when Marcellus saw the intimacy between them, he looked at me. I smiled helplessly, and when he nodded, I wondered how long he had known about Alexander.

'So tell me about Rome,' Marcellus said to me.

There was not much to tell. Only that the Pantheon was nearly done, and that building had begun on his theater months ago.

'Shall we see it tomorrow?' Marcellus asked eagerly.

'You mean, after the ludus?' Octavia reminded.

If Magister Verrius hadn't been there, I'm sure that Marcellus would have rolled his eyes. Instead he smiled politely. 'Of course. So tell me,' he added excitedly to Vitruvius, 'what does it look like?'

Vitruvius smiled. 'Don't ask me. Ask Selene. She is your architect.'

'*Really?*'

'Didn't you say the design should be left up to her?' Vitruvius asked.

Marcellus grinned. 'So?'

'It looks like the Circus Maximus,' I said. He slapped his knee, and I'm sure I felt my heart expanding. 'There's three stories of arches, and columns in the Corinthian style.'

'Is it big enough to hold races?'

'Marcellus!' Octavia reprimanded.

But everyone laughed, and when the evening was finished, Juba caught me watching Marcellus and Julia. He was telling her good-bye, promising that he would see her in the morning and that there wouldn't be any more wars for a very long time.

'Their marriage was arranged years ago,' Juba said. 'There's no use staring.'

'I wasn't staring,' I said angrily.

'Then what were you doing?'

'Observing.' Before I could think of something far more clever to say, he was gone.

His comment rankled me the entire night. I thought about it when I should have been asleep, and even turned it over in my mind the next morning while I should have been concentrating on what Vitruvius was teaching me. But when a commotion erupted in the atrium, I forgot about Juba entirely. I looked up at Vitruvius, and he rose from his chair.

'Is someone shouting?' I asked him.

'I don't know.'

We both went to see.

'On every basilica,' Faustina was saying, 'an actum as long as your stola. And news that Aquila has been murdered!'

'In his sleep?' I cried, thinking of Julia's request.

'No.' She turned to me. 'On the Aventine. Left for dead like a pig and not a single person willing to come forward as a witness.'

'Is it any wonder?' Octavia whispered.

My brother and Lucius hurried into the atrium. 'What is it?' Lucius looked to his father.

'Plebian justice,' Vitruvius replied.

There were seven more acta between the time of Tullia's trial and our progress to Capri in July. Agrippa's soldiers stood guard at every temple and basilica in Rome, so the rebel began posting on the windows of merchants' shops, making those shops instantly popular with the plebs. And when the merchants were threatened with imprisonment, he posted his next actum on the heavy cedar doors of Augustus's villa. The sheet was taken down before any of us could read it, but enough slaves had seen it on Augustus's door to send the story spreading like fire throughout the city.

CHAPTER EIGHTEEN

I COULD see the relief on Octavia's face when summer finally came, and she could escape the plebian hostility for Capri. She'd said nothing to me about her charity in the Subura, but Vitruvius admitted that at some homes, people had begun to turn away her help, preferring to beg or steal for their food than receive it from a patrician.

As our ship sailed from Naples to the little island where Augustus's Sea Palace rose from the rocks, Alexander turned to me. 'I wonder if the Red Eagle is following us.'

I looked from the rails to Octavia and Vitruvius, who were sitting on the deck, shaded from the sun by a thin linen canopy. 'Every home on Capri will be searched if he dares to post anything there again,' I told him.

'I wouldn't be surprised if they have soldiers in disguise across the island, waiting for him to make a mistake.'

'It didn't work in Rome.'

'Rome isn't an island,' my brother said.

But after a week of sun-bleached days spent lounging in the Sea Palace, there was no sign of the rebel, and the men of the Praetorian Guard began to relax at their posts. They tossed dice, ate fish, and were willing to place bets on nearly anything, from the fastest-moving boats passing on the sea to the height of a palm tree.

Without Augustus or Livia to watch us, there was almost nothing we couldn't do. Even Tiberius and Drusus enjoyed themselves a little, joining us on Marcellus's daily boat trips into the Blue Grotto, where Roman patricians had turned the sea cave into their own bathing pool. The walls were painted with images of Neptune rising from the waves, and small statues of the bearded sea god rested in niches carved into the rock. Toward the end of the summer, when Claudia became adventurous enough to come along, both Agrippa and Juba paddled with us to the cave.

'What do you think makes the water so blue?' Claudia asked. It was as if something was lighting the sea from underneath, turning the water the brilliant shade of cornflowers.

'It's the opening down there,' Juba said from the boat, pointing to a gap in the rock that was completely submerged. 'That's where the sunlight enters and lights the water from below.'

'First in!' Marcellus shouted, tearing off his tunic and diving into the water in his loincloth. Claudia immediately averted her gaze, but Tiberius and Drusus stripped off their tunics and dove overboard, too.

'Are you coming?' Drusus called to Vipsania.

She stood at the edge of the boat. 'It looks a little cold.'

'Nonsense!' Lucius exclaimed. 'Let's go!' He pushed Julia and Vipsania from the boat before they had time to take off their clothes, and Alexander followed.

'Are you going in?' I asked Claudia, stowing my sandals in the prow of the little boat where they wouldn't get wet.

'In my breastband and loincloth?'

'Why not?' I took off my tunic. 'We come here every day.'

She looked uneasily at Agrippa and Juba, who were already swimming.

'Go,' I persisted. 'Your husband doesn't mind. Look at Vipsania.

Do you think he would let his daughter do something dishonorable?'

Claudia hesitated, then took off her tunic and slowly, timidly dipped her foot into the water.

'What are you waiting for?' Marcellus cried, pulling her in.

'Marcellus!' she shrieked, but once she was completely wet, she giggled. 'It's warm in here. Like bathwater.'

'You see?' I told her. 'It's not so bad.' I slipped over the side of the boat and swam up to Marcellus. Immediately, Julia was at my side.

'Can you imagine being here at high tide?' Claudia asked worriedly. 'The water would rise and we'd all be trapped.'

'It's not high tide for another few hours,' Marcellus said.

'Besides,' Julia added, 'there's a secret path over there to the mountain.' She indicated the end of the cave, where a limestone platform led to a series of steps.

'Have you ever used it?'

Julia shook her head.

'Then how can you be sure it works?'

'Because we saw a goat come through it once!'

Claudia looked to her brother to confirm the story.

'It's true,' Marcellus said. 'Ask Agrippa if you don't believe me.'

She swam away to her husband, and Julia said critically, 'She's so nervous.'

'Like all my sisters,' Marcellus said. 'Why do you think Antonia and Tonia aren't here?'

'Because your mother forbids it?' Julia guessed.

Marcellus shook his head. 'So long as I'm with them, they're welcome to come. But they're afraid. They'd rather be playing their lyres or planting boxwood in the garden.'

Julia wrinkled her nose. 'How boring.'

'They're like my mother,' Marcellus observed. 'They enjoy the simple, quiet pleasures.'

And there was something very endearing about their simplicity that evening while everyone played dice in the summer triclinium. Neither Antonia nor Tonia gambled, and Vipsania and Drusus were deemed too young to play. So the four of them sat together on a couch, quietly watching the roll of the dice. Only Alexander, Lucius, and Julia remained in the game. Marcellus whispered eager tips to Julia, and once in a while Juba or Agrippa would look up from their reading to see who was winning.

Julia rolled, and Lucius exclaimed, 'Four Vultures!'

She groaned. 'I'm finished.'

'But no one's thrown a Venus,' Lucius protested. 'The next roll could be yours.'

'It's always the next roll with you two. You can keep my denarii in the pot.'

'Your loss,' my brother said temptingly, but she didn't care. He and Lucius battled it out, and by the time Lucius won, I realized that Marcellus and Julia had disappeared.

I looked around the triclinium. 'Where did Marcellus go?'

'With Julia,' Tonia said. 'Out to the gardens. I think they're sitting in the gazebo.'

'Which one?'

'Near the statue of Fortuna. Would you like me to show it to you?'

'Leave them alone,' Juba said, looking up from his reading. 'They've gone there for a reason.'

'And how do you know?'

'I have eyes.'

I rose swiftly from my chair, and Tonia asked eagerly, 'Would you like me to show you?'

'Yes,' I said stubbornly.

'You're wasting your time.' Juba's voice grew irritable. 'If you think you're in love with him, you're no different from any of the girls at the roadside inns. Besides, it's Julia he's meant for.'

'So everyone says.'

'So Augustus says.' When Juba saw me pause, he added, 'The letter came today. Octavia will probably announce it tomorrow.'

Tonia was still looking up at me; her small hand reached out toward mine. 'Shall we go?'

For a moment, I didn't answer. Then, when the mist finally cleared from my mind, I told her, 'Just take me to the baths.'

Tonia chatted about silly things along the way – what color the flowers should be on her balcony and which food I liked better, thrush or quail. She wanted to know if I had ever seen the animal called a giraffe, and told me that I should visit her uncle's zoo in Rome as soon as we returned. Nothing she talked about was of any importance. She spoke only about simple, insignificant things, and for that I couldn't have been more thankful.

But when Octavia gathered us all in the triclinium the next morning and announced that she had wonderful news from Iberia, my heart sank in my chest, and I wished I could have as simple a life as Tonia. Instead, I had spent the night hoping that Juba had been wrong, that he had only told me such things to try and torment me. But now, Marcellus's long-awaited marriage to Julia was going to be made a reality, and Augustus wanted Agrippa to take his place in the ceremony on the auspicious day of December twenty-fourth.

As soon as Octavia spoke the words, my brother looked at me, and Lucius patted my arm in an understanding gesture. For the next four months I would have to be cheerful and happy for Julia, and there would be a dozen things she would want me to help her with: tunics and cloaks, new sandals and bridal jewels. There was more news as well, but I hardly heard it. Marcellus was to be honored by being made an aedile, in charge of Rome's public entertainments for an entire year, which would mean access to nearly unlimited funds in order to impress the plebs. When Tiberius heard this, he sat back in his seat and groaned. 'I hope Augustus knows what he's doing.'

But the final news made time stop entirely. In honor of his service to Rome, Juba, Prince of Numidia and unswerving friend of Augustus, was being made King of Mauretania. It would be a client kingship in which he served the purposes of Rome, but even so – Mauretania adjoined his ancestral land of Numidia, where his father and grandfather had ruled before him. I met my brother's gaze across the table, and while everyone celebrated the happy news, Alexander seated himself next to me.

'You see,' I whispered in Parthian. 'If it can happen for Juba, it can happen for us.'

'Yes, but he's twenty-two and he's spent his life being useful to Augustus, serving him, protecting him, fighting alongside him. What have I done?'

'Nothing. But you haven't been given the chance!'

'At least you have your work with Vitruvius.'

I was quiet for a moment. 'Perhaps that will be enough for us both.'

We looked across the triclinium at Juba, who was being congratulated by Agrippa and Claudia. 'As soon as you're comfortable in your new palace,' Agrippa was promising him, 'we plan on making the journey south for a visit.'

But Juba laughed. 'I don't expect I'll be leaving anytime soon. There's the matter of a war in Cantabria to finish. I'm not sure how Augustus would feel about returning home to discover that I'd left him.'

Julia and Marcellus were by themselves on the farthest couch in the triclinium, and I could see that she was weeping. He kissed the tears of happiness from her cheeks in a way that made my heart ache, and I reminded myself sternly, *It's about continuing to study with Vitruvius so that Augustus will let me return to Egypt; it's not about falling in love with a Roman – however winsome he is.*

But it was difficult to remember what I had left to hope for as Julia dragged me to every shop in the Forum in search of the perfect bridal clothes. There had been a message from Iberia that whatever Julia wished for her wedding should be ordered, and that every senator in Rome would be invited to the celebration.

'Look at all this cloth,' Julia complained in November, with only a month left before her marriage. 'Wool, linen, heavy winter silks. How can any of these be used for a veil?' We had gone to shop after shop looking for something suitable, but she'd found nothing. She sat down on the shopkeeper's chair while the old man scurried around us, presenting us with options.

'There has to be something,' Lucius protested. 'What about that red stuff over there?'

'It's too thick.'

My brother held up a swath of red silk.

'Too shiny,' she ruled.

'There are no more shops,' Gallia reminded her. 'What about inviting the merchants from Ostia to the Palatine?'

'She's already done that,' I said dryly.

'Then how about choosing something from the one hundred shops we've already been to?' Marcellus suggested.

Julia's eyes filled with tears. 'You don't care what I wear.' She stood angrily. 'I could show up in a peasant's *palla* and it wouldn't matter at all!'

Marcellus exchanged a wearied look with me. 'You're right.

It wouldn't.' He went to her. 'Because what matters to me isn't the veil.' He lifted her chin tenderly. 'It's you.'

Alexander whispered in Parthian, 'You have to feel a little sorry for him. This is what the rest of his life is going to be like.'

Julia calmed a little, but the crisis of the veil wasn't resolved until eight days before the wedding, as we were bidding Magister Verrius farewell. Our days in the ludus were finished. Beginning with the new year, Alexander and Lucius were going to join Marcellus and Tiberius in a separate school for rhetoric, where they would learn how to speak in public and argue law cases. Julia would be in charge of her own house, a magnificent villa near Agrippa's on the Palatine, and instead of studying Homer or Vergil, she would be holding her own *salutatio*, doing charity work, and commissioning buildings in her own name. Because school was finished for me as well, Vitruvius paid me the honor of asking whether I wished to study with him in the daytime and oversee some of the work on the theater, Agrippa's Pantheon, and the new basilica being built in honor of Julia's marriage. Only this time, when he asked, it was not because Octavia pressured him to.

The six of us waved goodbye to Magister Verrius, and though Julia was the one who had enjoyed the ludus least, she blinked back tears as we crossed the courtyard toward Juba and Gallia for the very last time. Though Juba was king of a foreign land now and could have left our security to the Praetorian Guard, it was a mark of his loyalty to Augustus that he remained as Marcellus's personal protector. Julia sniffed loudly, and when Marcellus gave her his linen square, she used it to dab at her eyes. 'You know what this means, don't you?' she wailed.

'Our childhood has passed,' Alexander said quietly.

'Who cares about our childhood?' she said heatedly. 'There are only eight days to find cloth for a veil!'

Marcellus gave Julia a desperate look. 'Why don't you go shopping with Selene,' he suggested. 'Juba can take us back—'

'We've been to every store,' I interrupted. 'There's nowhere in Rome we haven't gone.'

Julia's look was miserable. Everything was ready. Her handsomely embroidered cloak of red and gold. A tunic woven from the finest silk. Her pearl-encrusted sandals, her bangles, her underclothes. Only the veil remained. Marcellus looked as if he were about to weep himself. And then I remembered.

'I think I have something. In the chest I brought from Alexandria – some swaths of red silk.'

Julia gasped. 'Can we see them?'

I glanced at Marcellus, who smiled at me with the deepest gratitude, and was forced to admit to myself that my revelation was not entirely altruistic. 'Of course.'

Marcellus exhaled audibly. 'I'll bet Selene has something that would be absolutely perfect.'

Julia shot him a look, but when we returned to the Palatine and I opened the chest that had been locked for more than four years, she reached forward for the first swath of silk and exclaimed, 'This is it!' It was the material left over from a chiton I had worn to my mother's last feast. It had been the Feast of the Inseparable in Death, when my parents had invited everyone who had been close to them to dine one last time. I hesitated, wondering whether or not I should tell her.

'You probably don't want that one,' I said finally.

But she had already draped it over her head. 'Why not?'

'Because it was the cloth I wore to my mother's last dinner.'

'The feast of a queen,' Julia whispered, regarding herself in the mirror. The red contrasted beautifully with her mass of black hair, and she didn't care what the material had been for.

'It might bring you bad luck.'

'Nonsense,' she said. 'That's only superstition.'

'Your father wouldn't think so.'

'And do I look like him?'

No. She looked like the most beautiful bride who would ever be carried across the threshold of a villa. Pearls imported from the Indian Sea gleamed on her dark neck, and in eight days, when her hair was dressed in similar ornaments, Marcellus would be the envy of every man in Rome. I let her take the silk, but as she was folding it into a neat square for her seamstress, she sat down on my bathing room chair, and tears began to well in her eyes.

'What's the matter?' I exclaimed. 'You have your veil. Everything is ready.'

She nodded, as if she knew it was foolish to cry. 'I know.'

'Then what's wrong?'

She looked up at me, and her dark eyes suddenly appeared enormous, as if they belonged to a child. '*She* won't be there,' she whispered, and immediately I was ashamed of my resentment. No one in the world knew Julia better than Marcellus. Her father, her stepmother, even her stepbrother only cared what happened to her so long as it advanced their will. In a world of pretty silks and pearls where everything was theater, Marcellus was her only real happiness, and her mother wouldn't even be able to meet him on the wedding day. I took a seat next to her and offered her my hand. There was nothing I could say, so instead we sat together in silence and I thought of how selfish a friend I had been.

The excitement of Julia's wedding didn't stop me from wallowing in my own misery in private. Though I put a smile on my face and helped Julia with everything a bride might need – packing her chests, choosing her perfume, finding the right silk tunic for her wedding night – I still felt an empty ache in my heart when Marcellus looked at me or I heard him laugh in his mother's villa and knew it would be one of the last times I would ever have that sound wake me in the morning. Yet Marcellus was bursting with happiness. He was marrying a woman he loved, and who loved him back. There would be spectacles and entertainments to plan for an entire year, and before long Augustus would make him consul and officially name him the future emperor of Rome.

Two nights before the wedding, Marcellus crept into my chamber, where Alexander, Lucius, and I were whispering about the war in Cantabria and how it might be many years before we'd have to see Livia's sour face again. Since the announcement of his wedding, he had stopped coming to us, and I presumed from the nightly creaking of his window that he was visiting Julia instead. But he took up his old position on the third couch, and my brother asked eagerly, 'Well, what's it like to be getting married?'

Marcellus smiled. 'Wonderful. Frightening.'

'How can be it be frightening?' I teased.

'Well, think of the responsibility,' he said. 'Now, there will be a house to maintain, and slaves to buy, and—'

'You're not really going to buy slaves?' I exclaimed.

'Of course he is,' Lucius said. 'How else is his house going to run?'

I stared at Marcellus.

'I will treat them properly,' he promised swiftly. 'I would never send them away for getting pregnant.'

'Or push them into an eel pool,' I added, 'or whip them for broken dishes.'

'Certainly not!'

I crossed my arms over my chest. 'Will you pay them?'

He hesitated. 'I . . . well . . . sure. Why not? Every Saturnalia, they can all receive presents. Julia can take care of that.'

'Why can't you?'

'Because I'll be too busy planning the Games.' He grinned widely. 'There's the Ludi Plebei, the Ludi Apollinares, the Ludi Megalenses, and the Ludi Ceriales.' He looked at my brother. 'And you'll help me, won't you?'

My brother couldn't have been more pleased with any request. They spoke at length about horses, and floats for parades, and which animals from Augustus's zoo would be the most likely to awe the plebs if they were used as part of the opening processions. Marcellus didn't speak again about marriage, but before he left, he paused at the door one last time and looked back. 'Lucius and the twins,' he said, his voice filled with regret, 'I'll miss our nights together.'

When he shut the door and Lucius left, I turned on my side and faced the wall. Alexander knew enough to simply blow out the oil lamp. Then he kissed my hair and whispered that it would be better in the morning.

But it wasn't. It was the last day of Saturnalia, with all of the shops in the Forum closed, and a hundred different things still to be arranged. There was the matter of the food, and reminders had to be sent across Rome to the homes of butchers and bakers to ensure that the proper amounts would be delivered the next morning. Wine, honey, vinegar, and garum had to be available in considerable quantities, and despite the fact that it was a holiday, merchants arrived throughout the day with heavy chests and barrels. Nothing more important than this wedding would ever happen beneath Octavia's roof, so the slaves rushed from room to room with wash-buckets and brooms, using feather dusters on the most delicate statues and ladders to reach the highest mosaics. Marcellus went to spend the day with Julia, and when Alexander asked whether I'd like to join him and Lucius at the odeum, I shook my head.

'What will you do, then? Sit out here on the portico and feel sorry for yourself? It's cold,' he protested. 'Come to the odeum. There'll be warm beer and *ofellae*.'

'I'm fine. Besides, there's work to be done in the theater.'

'Over Saturnalia? Even Vitruvius isn't working.'

'There's just a few things I'd like to see to,' I lied. 'It's important.'

But my brother knew me better. 'Selene, you care more about that theater than Marcellus does. He'll probably step inside it once.'

'That doesn't matter!' I said angrily. 'It's my project. Vitruvius gave it to me, and I'll see that it's done right. Work doesn't stop just because it's a silly Roman festival.'

I convinced Octavia to let me go, and two Praetorians were sent with me to Marcellus's theater. I took my book of sketches, although truthfully there was nothing I planned to sketch. I simply wanted a place away from the madness of preparations; a place where I could sit one last time to remember how simple life had been before engagements and weddings and bitter envy.

We crossed through the Forum Holitorium, where the vegetable stalls were shut for Saturnalia, and though the guards wanted to take the shortcut, I refused, thereby avoiding the Columna Lactaria, where Horatia's daughter had been abandoned. This winter hadn't brought any snow, but gray clouds curtained the sun, casting a pall over the city and darkening the streets. When we arrived, I could see that the guards were worried about rain. There was only one *umbraculum* between us, so they gave it to me and waited beneath the arches while I inspected the empty theater.

A great deal of work had been completed since the building's conception: the *cavea*, where more than ten thousand spectators could sit; the stage, which would soon be covered in mosaic; and the three tiers of arches supported by columns in each of the Greek architectural styles, first Doric, then Ionic, and finally Corinthian. Every day for nearly a year I had come here, with either Vitruvius or the guards, and watched the men build. I had been allowed to choose the artwork and mosaics, and the workers knew better than to slight me, since Vitruvius had made it clear that I was as important to this theater as Marcellus himself.

I walked to the stage and ran my hand along its edge. The wood had been smoothed to perfection, and when I was sure that there were no splinters, I seated myself so that I looked out on the *cavea*. Years of hard labor would be required to complete the rest of the theater. Builders would grow from boys to men here, as I had grown from a girl to a woman in the time since it had started. I thought of my excitement when Marcellus first asked Augustus whether I could help in its creation. I'd believed it was Marcellus's way of showing special favor to me, and it had been, only not the kind I'd imagined. He didn't really care about this theater, and tomorrow he would take Julia as his bride. She would press her soft cheek against his chest as he carried her into their villa, and once he untied her girdle their new life would begin. I could feel the sting of tears beginning in my eyes. Then a figure appeared at the back of the theater, and I stood swiftly.

'What are you doing here?' I exclaimed.

Juba smiled as he advanced. 'I saw the guards and thought there might be trouble inside. I didn't realize you had come here to cry out your sorrows. But I suppose that every tragedy deserves a stage.'

'I'm not crying,' I said sternly.

Juba raised his brows. 'My mistake.'

'I came here to make some final plans. This area,' I said unconvincingly, 'still needs a mosaic.' I stepped down and strode purposefully past him. And then it occurred to me. 'I know why you're here,' I gasped. 'Augustus wants you to spy on me!'

Juba laughed at my foolishness. 'Do you really imagine that I have so little to do with my time?'

'Then why aren't you packing? Leaving for Mauretania on the next ship?'

Immediately, I regretted my words. He stepped back and said quietly, 'Perhaps I still have business in Rome, like making sure my slaves have a place to go when I'm gone.' He moved to join the guards, and the three of them talked about the war in Cantabria, completely ignoring me. When I finally asked to be taken back to the Palatine, the four of us walked the short distance in silence.

It was a wedding that even the wealthiest merchants would be talking about for many years. Thousands of people filled the villa from the triclinium to the gardens, where charcoal braziers kept away the winter's chill and lanterns lit the rose-trimmed paths. Between every column, swaths of the richest blue and gold silks fluttered in the breeze, and handsomely dressed slaves rushed between the senators offering them cups of the best Chian wine. When Marcellus slid a gold and emerald ring onto Julia's finger, the thundering shouts of 'Thalassa!' on the hilltop were probably heard all the way down by the Circus Maximus, and the feast that followed lasted into the third watch.

'It will be us next,' my brother said ominously as we rested in the triclinium. His hair had taken on a burnished sheen in the soft light of the oil lamps, and I saw Lucius staring at him from across the room.

'Perhaps Augustus will never return,' I said.

But my brother wasn't so hopeful. 'Then Livia will take care to arrange it from Iberia. She sends Octavia letters every week. And you know what happens in seven days.'

We would be turning fifteen. Alexander would prepare for his coming-of-age ceremony at the festival of Liberalia, and more men would be inquiring about my availability for marriage, since this was the age by which even the most restrictive fathers realized they would have to let their daughters go. I twisted my napkin nervously in my hands.

We both looked at Julia and Marcellus, laughing and happy in their newly wedded bliss. He had taken her up in his arms, and a long procession was forming to escort them into their new villa. As they passed our table, Julia's gaze met mine and her smile faltered. I knew she was thinking about her mother. I stood up and pressed her hand. 'Someday, when you are empress . . .' I whispered. Her face brightened, and as Marcellus carried her away, I made a silent prayer to both Isis and Serapis that Julia would always be this happy. Time and again she had been kind to me, and I had repaid that kindness with jealousy. She had been denied the love and affection of her mother; now, at least, she would have it from a husband.

'Do you want to go with them?' I asked Alexander.

'No. It will only be depressing,' he said.

Secretly, I was thankful. Although I was curious to see what her villa was like, I had no desire to watch Marcellus untie Julia's girdle, then lay her down on his bridal couch while men sang lewd songs and made grunting noises. 'I'm going to go to sleep, then,' I told him.

'Don't wait up for me.'

'But it's almost morning!'

My brother smiled. 'And there's still a few amphorae of the Chian left.'

When I awoke that afternoon and looked across the chamber, I saw that Alexander's couch hadn't been slept on.

It was three days before we saw Marcellus and Julia again. They remained in their villa enjoying each other and their sudden freedom, and Marcellus didn't even attend school with the *rhetor*, which sent his mother into a rare fit of rage. She burst into the library while Vitruvius was showing me the formulas he had used to build the dome on the Pantheon.

'Three days!' she cried. 'He hasn't studied with the *rhetor* in three days!' We both looked up, and Octavia rubbed her temple. 'If this is a sign of things to come—'

'He's a newlywed,' Vitruvius pointed out calmly. 'I'm sure it's not a sign of anything but love.'

Octavia saw my face and mistook my pain for disapproval.

'You see?' she exclaimed. 'Selene understands. That's why she comes here with you every day when she could be shopping with Julia or studying Plato. I will warn him this evening.'

'At his first feast?' Vitruvius asked. 'He'll be playing the host.'

'He can play at whatever he'd like so long as he studies! Even from Iberia,' Octavia warned, 'Livia keeps her eye on Rome. You think I don't know what her slaves are writing? And if Augustus should discover what Marcellus has been doing – lying in bed, watching the races from his balcony – don't think there aren't plenty of other choices for heir.'

Vitruvius gave a hollow laugh. 'Like who? Tiberius would rather be castrated.'

'And would Livia care? She would put him through the trials of Hercules if she thought it would bring him closer to power. When I'm finished speaking with Marcellus,' she demanded, 'you must speak to him as well.' Only after Vitruvius nodded gravely did she look down at the scroll we were working on. 'Is that the Pantheon?' she asked.

'Yes. Selene and I are about to oversee the installation of the gods, and by the time your brother returns, it will be finished.'

'Then there's been news?' I asked swiftly. I looked at Vitruvius and Octavia, but neither of them seemed inclined to answer.

'Only half of Cantabria has been subdued,' Octavia said. 'The war may take another six months, even though he promised to be here for the unveiling.'

'I can ask Agrippa whether he wishes to postpone it,' Vitruvius said uncertainly.

But Octavia shook her head. 'No. It wouldn't be right for such a great building to stand empty.'

'Come with us,' Vitruvius said imploringly. 'You haven't seen the construction in more than a year, and you can write to your brother about what's been completed.'

'He'll be jealous.' She smiled sadly. 'Agrippa tells me it's unlike anything that's ever been built.'

Vitruvius offered her his arm. 'You'll have to judge that for yourself.'

Octavia invited Gallia to come with us, and when we arrived, their eyes were drawn upward to the pediment, where sculptors had inscribed: MARCUS AGRIPPA, SON OF LUCIUS, CONSUL FOR THE THIRD TIME, MADE THIS BUILDING. There was nothing unusual about the outside of the building. It was a colonnaded porch of simple concrete and brick. But as we passed through the great bronze doors into the Pantheon, I heard Gallia whisper something in her mother tongue.

Nothing in the world had ever equaled it in beauty or grandeur, not even in Alexandria. From the rich marble flooring to the internal colonnades, light and color worked together to create something that had never been done before. The dome was decorated with octagonal and hexagonal shapes, making it appear like a honeycomb to anyone who was standing beneath it. In the center was a large, perfectly round opening, an oculus, which let in the only light.

Gallia's gaze traveled from niche to niche, where workers were using oiled polishing cloths to prepare them for the reception of the marble statues. When she repeated her amazed sentiments in Gaulish, Juba stepped from the shadows and replied, 'It's impressive, isn't it?'

I looked at Vitruvius in surprise. He explained, 'He has come to inspect the statues for flaws and authenticity. They only arrived this morning.'

Juba and Gallia spoke for a moment in her language, then he turned and greeted Octavia and Vitruvius. But when it came to me, his voice was not so merry. 'I don't believe there are any mosaics that need finishing.'

'I am here to make measurements for the statues,' I retorted.

He turned to Vitruvius. 'What?' he asked with mock indignation. 'You didn't think I would consider that before buying them?'

Vitruvius looked genuinely apologetic, but Juba slapped his back good-naturedly.

'Of course,' Juba laughed. 'There is no point in hauling a marble statue across the chamber if it's only going to be returned.' He took Gallia and Octavia on a short tour of the building, and while they were busy I helped Vitruvius take the measurements. I hoped desperately that one of the statues would be too tall or too wide for its niche, but, frustratingly, Juba was right. They all fit.

'Well?' Juba stood over me when we were finished.

'They're fine,' I said shortly, rising and dusting my hands on my tunic.

'A perfect job,' Vitruvius complimented. 'And very handsome sculptures, Juba. Are they all Roman?'

'Only the Venus is Greek. For some reason, I was drawn to her face.'

I looked across the Pantheon to the statue of Venus. Perhaps it was my own vanity that made me think I recognized her. But the nose and possibly the light, painted eyes were similar to mine. Then Gallia dropped her voice and whispered, 'She reminds me of Caesar's mistress.'

'Terentilla.' Juba nodded. 'Yes. Perhaps you're right.'

That evening, I dressed more carefully than usual for Marcellus's first feast. I put on my favorite tunic of blue silk and a belt of silver cloth to match my sandals. Then Gallia arranged my hair in a handsome bun on the top of my head, using long silver pins to hold it in place. The result in the mirror was extremely pleasing, and even Gallia was impressed. She sprayed me with a blend of violet and jasmine.

'You have turned into a real beauty,' she said. 'Hera would be jealous if she had to compete with you.'

I laughed. 'How do you know that story? It's a Greek tale.'

'I read. And sometimes, Magister Verrius tells those tales to me.'

'Does he miss us?' I asked as we walked to the portico.

'What do you think? He has Drusus and Vipsania now for students. They do not study much.'

Poor Magister Verrius, I thought. *He probably imagined that Julia and Marcellus were the laziest students he'd ever have to teach.*

My brother and Lucius were already on the portico, gambling with dice. 'Don't you ever stop?' I teased.

My brother looked up, and a smile touched his lips. 'Nice.' He rose to his feet. 'Exceptionally nice,' though he gave me a warning look.

As we walked cross the Palatine, I clenched and unclenched my hands. 'So what do you think their villa will be like?' I asked.

Alexander smirked. 'Without any slaves? A mess.'

'Octavia will have lent them some,' I said. 'And I'm sure Julia took cooks from her father's house.'

'We'll see,' he said eagerly as we came to their doorstep. A young slave I had seen in Octavia's villa answered.

'*Salvete*,' the girl said in greeting. The glow of the setting sun burnished the gold trim on her tunic, and I was certain it was a touch that Julia had added. She wanted even her servants to wear gold. 'Please.' She stepped aside. 'Come in.'

Our small party entered the vestibulum, and Claudia made noises of appreciation. The floor was made from white Carrara marble, and the elegant murals and stucco decorations had been polished to a shine. Although many people had been here on the night of the wedding, few had taken the time to study the architecture, and as the young girl led us through the atrium, I could see Vitruvius appraising every niche and alcove. The judgment he passed must have been favorable, since he looked at Octavia and smiled.

When we reached the triclinium, Marcellus and Julia rose from their couch, and Alexander whispered, 'Look at the tables.' They were made from cedar wood and inlaid with both jasper and ivory.

'Welcome, Mother,' Marcellus said jubilantly. 'So?' he asked eagerly. 'How do you like it?'

'Beautiful,' she admitted. 'All the marble and light. Especially in the atrium.'

'Julia's going to buy the rest of her furniture tomorrow. We still need a lararium and couches for the guest rooms. Please, sit wherever you'd like.'

I had been worried about what the seating arrangements would be, but they were the same as for every other evening on the Palatine. Octavia sat with her daughter and son-in-law, and Vitruvius and Juba joined them. Drusus and Vipsania ate with Antonia and Tonia at their own small table, while the rest of us sat with Julia and Marcellus.

'Your own villa,' I said enviously. 'So what is it like?'

'Wonderful,' Julia gushed. 'No one to tell you what to do, or when to wake up, or where to go.'

'And the pool overlooks the Circus,' Marcellus added. 'It's too cold for it now, even though it's heated, but in the spring, you're all welcome to come.'

'It must be quiet in Augustus's villa without me,' Julia said.

Tiberius raised his brows. 'Yes. There's no one to pick on now but the slaves.'

She laughed, and I thought, *Already, marriage has changed her. She would never have let him have the last word before.*

'And have you seen the upstairs?' Julia asked me.

'No, not yet.'

'There's an entire room just for bathing, and a chamber that looks out over the Forum. Come!' She stood. 'Let me show you around.'

'But what about your guests?'

She waved her hand dismissively. 'They won't miss me during the *gustatio*. Let them have a few drinks and some oysters.'

She took me up the stairs and pointed out the small details that she knew I would like: the onyx floor with its sleek fur rugs, the insets of blue and yellow marble on the ceilings. The tapestries, draperies, and awnings all looked new, and I asked her, 'Who owned this villa before?'

'Some old man who died without children. My father bought it for me six months ago and had all of the tasteless furniture removed. You should have seen what was here. Only now, there are no tables and almost nothing to sleep on.'

I saw what she meant. In the bridal chamber, although the windows were beautiful and the floor had been polished, there was only a single couch.

Julia saw my look and crossed her arms over her chest. 'It's worse than my father's villa, isn't it? Even the Vestals live better than this!'

I was forced to agree with her.

'Come with me tomorrow,' she begged. 'We'll go shopping in the Forum.'

'I have to work with Vitruvius.'

'What? Every day? No one has a better eye for design than you.' I hesitated.

'Please. He'll understand. Just tell him your next project is going to be my villa!'

The next morning, we set out for the Forum. Alexander came with us, shadowed by two Praetorians, and Julia remarked, 'I'm surprised you're not with Lucius. I can't remember the last time I saw the two of you apart.'

My brother wrapped himself tighter in his cloak. Although no rain had fallen yet, the wind was bitter. 'He's with his father. He wants to show him some things he's written and ask for his opinion on finding a patron.' He looked at me. 'Do you think there's any hope?'

'I don't see why not. It's not as though Vitruvius doesn't have a patron himself.'

'Yes, but it's Octavia and he's sleeping with her. We were hoping for a patron who's content simply with art.'

'Has he tried Vergil?' Julia asked. 'Or Horace?'

'They both have more than a dozen writers whom they help fund. And Maecenas is interested only in Ovid.'

'Then why can't *we* be his patron?' Julia asked suddenly. 'Marcellus and I are married, and now both of us have our own funds.'

My brother stopped walking. 'Really?'

'Why not? Octavia has her writers, and it's probably time that I have mine!'

My brother laughed. 'Lucius will be absolutely beside himself.'

'There's only one condition,' Julia stipulated. 'In all of his work, I want to be young and pretty, even when I'm old and fat.'

'Eternally beautiful,' my brother said. 'Duly noted.'

When we reached the shops along the Via Sacra, Julia wanted to go into them all. By the afternoon, we had chosen nearly everything she would ever need: chairs and chests made of citron wood, tripods with heavy bronze basins for incense and whose legs were decorated with gryphons' heads and claws, tables made of rosewood, ivory-handled mirrors, hip baths in the shapes of sea-dragons and swans.

'Your villa's going to be like the Royal Palace of Alexandria,' my brother promised.

'Really?' she asked eagerly.

'Prettier,' I said, though it disturbed me that I was beginning to forget what the rooms in the palace had looked like. Sometimes, when I took out my book of sketches and flipped through the pages, I was reminded of a chamber I'd forgotten entirely, or an alcove where Alexander and I had played as children. Sometimes I wondered how much Alexander remembered, but I was afraid of asking and upsetting him.

'All right,' Julia announced. 'Just one more thing. A tapestry for the atrium.'

We followed her into a shop near the Senate, and Alexander nodded appreciatively. 'Impressive.' On the walls hung tapestries and marble plaques depicting every sort of mythological scene. On one tapestry, Odysseus navigated his ship past the cliffs of Scylla. On another, Romulus and Remus fought about the walls of Rome. My brother stood immediately in front of a plaque depicting the Greek twins, the Gemini. 'Like our mother used to call us,' he said quietly. 'We should buy this for our room.'

'Absolutely not! It's too expensive.'

'Then let me buy it for you,' Julia said. When I started to object, she shook her head sternly. 'In three days, it'll be your birthday, and this can be my gift.'

'Julia, this is too generous,' I protested.

'After all you did for me before my wedding? Nonsense,' she said, and snapped her fingers. The man behind the counter came over at once, and when Julia pointed to the marble plaque, his eyes went wide. 'Have this sent to Octavia's villa,' she instructed. 'You know the place?'

'Of course, domina.'

'And you see that tapestry of Venus and Vulcan? That should go to the house of Julia Augusti.'

'This is a very kind present,' my brother said. 'Between this and Lucius's patronage, I don't see how we can ever leave Rome.'

She grinned. 'Good. When Livia returns, I'll need trustworthy friends on the Palatine.'

CHAPTER NINETEEN

25 BC

ON THE morning of our fifteenth birthday, Alexander woke me with a kiss. 'Felicem diem natalem, Selene.'

I bolted upright. 'What's the matter? What?'

Alexander laughed. 'Nothing! I'm wishing you a happy birthday. Julia and Marcellus are here. They want to take us to the Circus, and then to the theater.'

'Already? What time is it?'

'Almost noon. Good thing you weren't meeting Vitruvius today. You must have had too much wine last night.' My brother grinned. We had stayed up long past midnight, laughing and talking, but most importantly, helping Marcellus plan for the Ludi Megalenses.

I rushed into a heavy tunic and cloak, sweeping up my hair into a loose bun, and while I dressed, Alexander regarded the handsome marble plaque of the Gemini.

'Do you really think the war will be over in six months?' he asked worriedly.

'I hope not. The longer Augustus stays in Iberia, the better for everyone.'

There was a knock at the door, and Alexander called brightly, 'Come in.'

I'd expected Julia or Marcellus, but it was Octavia who

appeared, carrying honeyed cakes and a letter. I glanced at Alexander, and he touched the *bulla* around his neck. While I would wear mine until the day of my marriage, he would offer his to the Lares today. As long as we wore our *bullae*, we were no threat to anyone. But what would Augustus do with us now?

'*Felicem diem natalem!*' Octavia exclaimed. 'Fifteen years old and a new year before you.' She set the cakes down and smiled. 'I hear that my son is taking you to the Circus. That doesn't seem like much of a treat for Selene.'

I smiled briefly. 'We're going to the theater afterward. Marcellus says it will be a comedy.' I looked at the letter in her hand.

'From my brother,' she said meaningfully. 'Seven came yesterday. One was for Agrippa, and a few were for generals in his army. But this one,' she said, taking a spot on the third couch where Marcellus used to sit, 'might interest you. Perhaps you'd like to hear it?'

Alexander looked at me, and both of us nodded. Octavia unfurled the scroll and read:

On this, the fifteenth year of their birth, I hope you will wish the Gemini well. There is nothing nearly as momentous as the passing from childhood to adulthood, and it is an occasion that merits serious consideration. When I return, it will be my foremost duty to see that a good marriage is made. Be sure to warn the princess Selene, so that when the time comes she has made herself ready.

Octavia looked up at me with a triumphant smile.

'That's it?' I panicked. 'What about Alexander? What about our return to Egypt?'

Her smile faltered. 'I'm sure that will all come in time. My brother's still at war. When he returns—'

'But why does he have to wait? When Gallus committed suicide,' I challenged, 'Augustus named a new prefect while he was still in Gaul.'

'That was a different situation,' she said uneasily. 'For now, we should celebrate this news. Another wedding!'

Alexander reached for my hand. 'And what if we don't want to be married?' he asked.

Octavia frowned. 'Every girl wishes to marry at least once. And what man doesn't want to take a wife?'

'We don't,' I said. 'Alexander and I enjoy each other's company, and I don't see any reason why we should part.'

Octavia lowered the letter to her lap. 'But this is good news, Selene. You'll have a house of your own, like Julia and Marcellus.'

'Who love each other!' I protested. 'You know better than anyone what comes of an unwanted marriage.'

She flinched, and though I regretted hurting her, it was the truth.

'And what will Alexander do,' I asked, 'given to a girl he doesn't even know?'

'Most husbands don't know their wives. It's an arrangement—'

'That we don't want!'

She sat back, shocked by my reaction. But clearly Augustus had known, otherwise he wouldn't have warned her to prepare me. 'We shall discuss this in a few months,' she said. 'But I see no reason why the two of you should have to be parted simply because you'll be married.'

'What if one of us goes to Egypt and the other to Greece? Or what if Alexander isn't sent to Egypt at all, and we're sent to live at opposite ends of the empire? Livia might marry us off to anyone.'

'This is not a decision to be made by Livia. It is one my brother shall make.' She rose, looking deeply regretful. 'I should not have read this to you. This day should be free from worry. They will be good matches,' she promised, 'and happy marriages.' But I didn't see how she could ensure that.

Julia and Marcellus were waiting for us in the atrium, and when they saw our faces, they wanted to know what had happened.

'A letter from Augustus,' my brother replied.

'Apparently, we're to be married,' I said.

'To whom?' Marcellus exclaimed.

'Not Tiberius?' Julia asked in alarm.

I recoiled. 'No. Livia would never allow that.'

'Well, so long as it's not him,' she said brightly, 'how bad can it be?'

'Think of Horatia,' I retorted, 'or any number of terrible marriages. In Egypt, women are allowed to choose their husbands.'

Marcellus put his arm around my shoulders. 'Just remember who is heir,' he whispered, and I smiled despite myself.

Aside from the contents of Augustus's letter, it was a wonderful day, the best birthday I could remember having. As usual, Alexander won his bets at the races. It had rained the night before, but he knew which horses preferred wet tracks to dry, and after taking out the small scroll on which he recorded past performances, he bet on the Whites.

'Fifty denarii to the Prince of Egypt,' the bet-maker said, handing him a heavy red purse. 'And another fifty for you.' He passed a second purse to Marcellus.

We took the winnings with us to the Forum, where we all bought *nivem dulcem* even though we were freezing, then washed it down with warm honeyed wine.

At the theater, Lucius critiqued the dreadful speech making

and the five of us shouted, 'Bring on the Bear!' It was an awful play, but none of us cared. We laughed at the senator who fell asleep in his seat, and at the woman whose snores were disturbing the actors. By the time Alexander and I returned to our chamber, the sun had long since set, and the guards looked ready to collapse.

'*Felicem diem natalem*,' he repeated, then embraced me tightly. 'Sleep well.'

'Where are you going?'

He smiled.

'And you don't think Octavia will know?'

'It's just for one night.'

'It's been many nights,' I said sternly. 'The slaves talk.'

'Then let them. In six months,' he added darkly, 'we'll both be married. We might as well enjoy our freedom while we can.'

I watched as he disappeared down the hall, then shut my door and blew out the oil lamps. As I was closing my eyes, I imagined that I heard footsteps in the atrium, and I wondered if my brother had changed his mind. But the door didn't open, and I fell into a deep sleep filled with strange dreams.

Then, suddenly, I awoke with a start. There was the sound of sandals slapping against marble, then a wail like the scream of a wounded animal tore through the villa, shattering the stillness. Doors were being opened and shut, and slaves were shouting to one another for lamplight. I rushed from my couch and put on my cloak, but I couldn't find my sandals. By the time I found them, I could hear women crying and Vitruvius's voice shouting orders over the madness. I fumbled with the door, unable to find the handle in the darkness, then flung it open and stepped into the hall.

Outside, Antonia and Tonia were already up, shivering in their heavy linen sheaths.

'What's happening?' I cried. But neither would answer me. 'Who's screaming?' I followed their gaze to Lucius's room, then cried out, 'Alexander!'

Antonia reached out to stop me. 'Don't go in there,' she pleaded.

'Why?' Slaves were running with hot water, then Vitruvius appeared with bottles and bandages. I approached the chamber slowly, as if still in a dream, and when I saw what had happened, my legs nearly gave way beneath me.

'Take her away from here!' Vitruvius shouted.

A dozen different men were attending to Lucius, who had been wounded in the chest and was lying on the floor. But on the couch, still dressed in his white tunic and cloak, Alexander wasn't moving. Several slaves stepped forward to take me away, but I shrieked at them wildly, 'Leave me alone!' I rushed to Alexander and took him by the shoulders. Blood seeped through his shirt onto the linens. A deep gash ran along his neck, and when I felt his cheeks they were already cold. 'No,' I whispered again and again. 'No!' I screamed so that Isis could hear me.

Hands lifted me up, and men began saying things I didn't understand. There was light, and I saw books and sketches. Someone had laid me down on a couch in the library. Gallia and Magister Verrius appeared, followed by Juba and Agrippa. There were times when I wasn't sure if I was sleeping or awake. As dawn came, Gallia pressed a cup into my hands.

'Drink.'

'I can't.'

'You've been crying all night. You need fluid,' she instructed.

I drank, but didn't taste anything. I could hear Juba questioning the slaves in the atrium, and when he came to me, I turned my face away.

'Selene,' he said gently.

I closed my eyes.

'I know you don't wish to speak, but if we're to find who did this—'

'Just tell me,' I whispered. 'Is my brother . . . is my brother gone?'

Both Agrippa and Juba were standing above me, but neither of them spoke.

I opened my eyes. 'Is he dead?' I cried.

Gallia rushed to my side. 'Selene, he was attacked. He had no chance.'

Tears blurred my vision, then suddenly my mind was as clear as ever. I remembered Augustus's letter to Octavia. 'You want to know who did this?' I demanded.

'Yes,' Juba said.

'Then find Octavia! Tell her to bring you Augustus's letter!' Juba frowned at me.

'Do you think I'm lying? Find Augustus's letter!' I shrieked.

I heard a slave go running, and when he returned, Octavia was with him.

She handed the scroll to me with trembling hands. 'What do you want?' she asked nervously. 'What's in the letter?'

I read the first line to myself, just to be sure I wasn't mistaken, but it was there. *On this, the fifteenth year of their birth, I hope you will wish the Gemini well.* The Gemini. Meaning Castor and Pollux. The twin sons of Leda, and the brothers to Helen of Troy. Except Castor was killed, leaving Pollux all alone.

I continued reading, only this time, louder:

When I return, it will be my foremost duty to see that a good marriage is made. Be sure to warn the Princess Selene, so that when the time comes she has made herself ready.

Tears burned my cheeks, and I looked from one face to the other. 'A good marriage,' I repeated. '*One!* And why just one?' I shouted angrily. 'Because he knew my brother would never be married!' When Octavia gasped, I sat up and read: '"There is nothing nearly as momentous as the passing from childhood to adulthood, and it is an occasion that merits serious consideration." If these words aren't a death sentence, then what is? He wanted Alexander dead! The last of the Ptolemies. Antony's son. And at fifteen, a man!'

'No!' Octavia wouldn't believe it. '*No*,' she whispered.

Agrippa said firmly, 'We will find these men, and they will be tried.'

But it was a lie. All of it was a lie. Augustus had paraded us through the streets of Rome and made a show of raising us before the people. But always, in the back of his mind, he knew that my brother would never live to wear the *toga virilis*. First Caesarion, then Antyllus, now Alexander . . .

Thunder clapped overhead, and I heard Juba say, 'Leave the princess alone. She needs her rest.' When Octavia hesitated, he told her firmly, 'Go and tend to Lucius.'

My other half. My twin. 'How will I live without him?' I whispered.

Gallia placed a warm cloth on my head. 'By getting some sleep.'

'But I don't want to sleep!' I sat up and searched the room desperately. 'I want to see him.'

'He's being dressed for burial.'

'Where?' I cried. 'In an unmarked grave? Beneath a plain tombstone on the Appian Way?' I looked up at Juba. 'You must have known about this,' I accused.

'Don't be ridiculous.'

'Only one man on the Palatine kills for Augustus.'

His jaw worked angrily. 'And that man isn't me.'

'I want you to leave.' When he didn't move, I screamed violently, 'I want you away from here!'

Hurt flickered across his face, then he turned and walked toward the door.

'Juba!' Gallia called after him.

'What are you doing?' I demanded 'He knew about this. He probably planned it!'

'Don't be a fool,' Gallia said strictly. 'He would never do such a thing!'

'How do you know? Who else knows Augustus's closest secrets?'

'His wife,' she said when Juba was gone. 'Livia knows everything.'

'And Livia isn't here!'

'But her slaves are.' She pushed me firmly to the couch. 'They will find them,' she promised, 'but you must rest. There is nothing you can do for him now.' Her voice broke, and though she turned, I could see that she was crying.

But she was wrong. There was still one thing I could do.

CHAPTER TWENTY

I WOULDN'T let him be buried without a mausoleum, and because Octavia feared that the last of the Ptolemies would end her life by suicide, she wrote to Augustus, and he approved. My brother's body was kept in the Temple of Apollo while workers from the Pantheon, the basilica, and the baths worked day and night for three months to finish. And in the time it took to build his tomb, I saw no one unless they came to me.

When Marcellus first heard the news of my brother's death, he'd sworn vengeance on Livia and even Augustus, but I'd warned him that if he spoke a word against his uncle, he would suffer next. It was better to wait, I told him. To bide his time until he became emperor. But as winter melted into spring, he was still angry, and even when the Red Eagle posted acta across Rome denouncing the imperial family as murderers who treated their guests like slaves, killing them off with impunity, he wasn't satisfied. No perpetrator had been found for the crime, and though Lucius survived and could describe his assailants, nothing was done. No one spoke of how Alexander had been found in Lucius's room. It was as if their love had never existed.

I ate alone. I worked alone. And when I asked Octavia to move me from the chamber I had shared with Alexander, she placed me next to Antonia, who came to me at night and brought me food.

'Do you think you will return to the triclinium?' she asked.

It was April, and I shook my head. 'Not until the mausoleum is done.'

'But it's finished,' she protested. 'His funeral is tomorrow.'

I blinked away my tears. The priests of Isis and Serapis had embalmed my brother's body, and I had gone to visit him every day in the temple. What would it be like not to have him near me? 'I'm not sure the tomb is done,' I said.

'But what will you do?' Antonia cried. 'Work on it forever?'

I turned and looked at her. She had her mother's gray-eyed innocence. 'Yes, I will.' And I would make the mausoleum my second home. When Augustus returned and married me off to some decrepit senator, I would leave my husband as often as possible. And when he'd go searching for me, he'd find me sleeping by Alexander, the two of us together in a marble eternity.

Antonia's eyes filled with tears. 'But it isn't natural.'

'No. And neither was my brother's death.'

The funeral began on the Palatine, and as the procession wound its way through the streets, thousands of people came to see the murdered Prince of Egypt. He was borne on a bier, carried by slaves, and preceded by the imperial family. I walked at his side, while Lucius and Vitruvius walked behind me. I could hear Lucius weeping, the deep, heart-wrenching cries of a man completely gutted by grief, and if I hadn't been so embittered I might have gone to offer him some comfort. But I had no reserve of sympathy left in me. It had been cut away with Alexander's life.

As we reached his mausoleum on the Appian Way, I wondered which of the people among us had been responsible for my brother's death. But everyone's mourning appeared genuine, and whenever Octavia looked on Alexander, sobs racked her body. An Egyptian embalmer had disguised the wound across my brother's neck, and if not for the thin layer of gauze across his face, Alexander might have been sleeping. The beautiful curls he had taken such care of were still dark and lustrous, topped by his pearl diadem. He was the last of the male Ptolemies and my only hope for returning to Egypt. He was my twin and my closest friend. And now, his short life was over.

We entered the cool recesses of the tomb, and Julia stifled a sob with her fist. The marble plaque she had purchased to celebrate our birthday hung above the sarcophagus. When Castor, who was mortal, had died, his immortal twin chose to join him in the sky. They were the Gemini, and now Alexander had gone to Elysium to wait for me.

The priests of Isis and Serapis lifted my brother's body from the bier into the coffin, singing Egyptian hymns that no Roman would recognize. And when I placed my book of sketches in Alexander's sarcophagus, I saw Vitruvius cover his eyes with his hand. As the lid was lowered my knees grew weak, but Marcellus steadied me, and I saw Juba flinch as if something about this disturbed him deeply. He regarded us from across the chamber with eyes as hard as onyx, and I thought, *If justice truly exists in this world, my brother will be avenged.*

Then Roman hymns were sung, and Maecenas read a long poem in honor of the Ptolemies. Even Tiberius was shaken. His eyes were red as if he'd been weeping, and when he placed a heavy wreath at the front of the tomb, I noticed that his hands were unsteady. But when the ceremony was finished, I could still smell the oil of cedar and myrrh used to perfume my brother's body, and as long as it lingered, I wanted to remain in the mausoleum.

'Selene,' Lucius said when all the others had left and were standing outside. 'I'm so sorry.'

I didn't say anything to him.

'I'm sorry it wasn't me. Because I know that's what you wanted.'

Tears welled in my eyes, and my guilt became unbearable. I took my brother's lover into my arms, and the pair of us wept together. 'It was the will of Isis,' I told him, which only made him weep harder.

'But why?'

'I don't know. Only she knows.' When our tears were spent, I looked at Lucius, and I was sure he had aged ten years in those three months. 'There's a reason you weren't killed,' I said. 'The gods are saving you for something great. You have a patron.'

'But what does it mean without Alexander?'

What did anything mean? I let him walk me out into the sunshine, and I felt angry with the world, with the sun for still daring to shine when my life was so dark.

Although everyone expected I would rejoin Octavia's meals in the triclinium, I remained shut away in the library, sketching additions to Alexander's mausoleum and the shrine I wished to purchase for him in the Forum.

One afternoon Julia came to the library with a letter. She could see that I was working on something for Alexander, but she interrupted me anyway and said, 'You should see this.'

She offered me the scroll and I read, 'We can easily forgive a child who is afraid of the dark; the real tragedy of life is when men are afraid of the light.' They were Plato's words. I looked up at her.

'For you,' she said quietly.

'From whom?'

'Me.' When I was silent she continued, 'We will find whoever did this, Selene.' But her words died away at my look.

'It's been four months,' I reminded her harshly.

'I know. But my father won't be emperor forever. And when I become empress, I swear to you, there won't be a plebian in Rome who doesn't remember Alexander. But you can't go on living this way,' she pleaded, 'afraid of being happy, afraid of the light.'

'It makes me happy to be in the dark,' I told her.

But Julia gave me a disbelieving look. 'You go to his mausoleum every day. What do you do?'

'I plan. I work!'

'And how much more work can there be?'

'Plenty. I want to build a shrine.'

'That's fine,' she said. 'And then what?'

'Maybe a statue,' I said, giving back her scroll. 'Possibly a bust.'

'And where does it end? What will you do? Spend until your treasury is gone?' She was shaking her head. 'It's too much, Selene. You have to live. When my father returns—'

'Then I'll be *forced* to live. Only I won't have to worry about being separated from Alexander, because he's already gone!'

Her lower lip trembled, and she pushed Plato's words toward me. 'I'm sorry,' she said, though for what I wasn't sure.

I watched her leave, then summoned two of the guards to take me to the Appian Way. As we walked down the Palatine, Juba saw me and stepped forward.

'What?' I demanded. 'Are you here to kill me as well?'

'I hope you're joking.' He glanced uneasily at my guards.

'Augustus saved my brother like a bull for the slaughter, so why shouldn't I be next? And who better to do the job than you?'

I turned to leave, and he whispered something to the light-haired guard. The man nodded gravely, and, as we left, I didn't bother asking him what had been said. But when we reached the mausoleum and I saw what had been done, I spun around.

'Who did this?' I gasped.

The light-haired guard replied, 'Juba.'

Next to the sarcophagus, in the only light of the chamber, stood the most magnificent statue of Alexander that any sculptor could have crafted. He was sculpted in marble, with eyes painted brown and hair that clustered in perfect ringlets around his diadem. I went to the statue and touched his face, his nose, his lips, his chin. It was as though he were alive, and nothing I could ever have commissioned would have equaled what this artist had done.

I approached the light-haired guard and asked him, 'Are you sure?'

He nodded. 'We helped him bring it here.'

Deep humility and regret silenced me, and the dark-haired guard whispered kindly, 'There are many men who will miss your brother. You are not alone.'

'Then you don't think Juba killed him?' I whispered.

The men exchanged looks. 'Princess, why would he kill a man he was helping to support?'

When I didn't understand, the dark one explained. 'Who do you think has been putting all that gold in your treasury since you've been here?'

'Octavia.'

Both guards made a face, and the light-haired one said, 'Maybe she gave you a couch and food, but it was Juba's denarii in the Temple of Saturn. We should know. We counted the coins.'

I looked from one guard to the other. 'But . . . but why?'

'Maybe he felt sorry,' the dark one speculated. 'His mother

was a Greek. Captured and sold into slavery when she was young. It was his father who freed her. Then both of them met their end the same as your parents. He knows what it's like to lose a kingdom and have to work even for the tunic on his back.'

I thought of all the gold my brother had squandered at the races, and the times when I had purchased furs and silks without ever questioning how the money had appeared. Then suddenly an image came to mind of the Greek statue that Juba had found for the Pantheon, and a deep flush crept across my cheeks. Gallia had thought the Venus looked like Terentilla, but that wasn't why Juba had wanted it. There had been a tender expression in his eyes when I'd caught him looking at me that afternoon. Perhaps his help had been charity at first, but now . . .

As I hurried back to the Palatine, I tried not to think of Juba's full, solemn lips turning downward when I'd accused him of Alexander's murder. How many times had he watched me pining for Marcellus? And how could Marcellus have understood our suffering?

That evening, I decided to appear in the triclinium. For more than four months, I'd worn only black, but Gallia picked out a tunic of deep violet and gold, something my brother had once praised when I wore it, and commanded me not to weep while she brushed soft azurite above my eyes and a little ochre on my lips.

There was a surprised murmur in the room as I entered, and I noticed with a pang that the table where Alexander and I used to sit was no longer there. Instead, it had been moved next to Octavia and Vitruvius, and this was where Marcellus and Julia were reclining. Immediately a space was made for me next to Juba, whose strong profile was silhouetted against the candle-light. As I took my seat, there was an uneasy silence.

'Welcome back,' Claudia said, and each person offered a quiet welcome. Then, slowly, conversation resumed, and it was as if I had never been gone. They were careful not to laugh too much, and even Tiberius held his tongue. But it was Juba who concerned me most, and finally I turned to him.

'I was wrong,' I said.

'About what?' he asked shortly.

'You. I underestimated your . . . your generosity. And the statue of my brother was very kind.'

'It wasn't for you. It was for Alexander.'

I flushed. 'Either way. It was very thoughtful and—'

'Make no mention of it.' He stood. 'It is time for me to say *valete*,' he announced. 'There is a great deal to prepare if Augustus is approaching.'

'He's coming back?' I exclaimed.

Juba regarded me gravely. 'With fifty thousand members of the Alpine Salassi.'

'As prisoners of war?'

'Slaves,' Tiberius said. 'Although only Juno knows where they're going to fit in a city already swimming with Gauls.'

Everyone looked at me, and I realized why I hadn't been told. They didn't want me to panic. They were afraid I might take my own life the way my mother took hers when everything was lost and Augustus was on the horizon. From the first time he had seen us in Alexandria, Augustus had known when my brother would die. A grown son of Marc Antony and Kleopatra would be a rallying point across the empire; a threat not only in Egypt but in Rome. There had never been hope of returning to Egypt no matter how hard we worked to become useful to him.

'Why don't you come with us?' Julia asked quickly. 'Marcellus and I are going to the theater.'

I shook my head.

'You should go,' Octavia prompted. 'It's a Greek play tonight.'

'Sophocles,' Marcellus said.

'No. I think I will go to my chamber.'

Vitruvius gave a meaningful look to his son, so I wasn't surprised when someone knocked on my door that evening and it was Lucius.

'Did your father send you?' I asked.

For a moment, Lucius considered lying. Then he admitted, 'Yes. But I would have come anyway.'

I let him inside, and his eyes grew big. It was a little Egypt, with rich swaths of red silk hanging from the walls, and bronze incense burners in the shape of sphinxes. An ankh hung over my couch next to an image of Isis. I no longer cared if I upset Augustus or if the slaves wrote to Livia about my chamber. What more could be done to me? What else could I lose?

'So is this what Alexandria is like?' Lucius asked.

I laughed sadly. 'A pale imitation.'

He seated himself on my leather chair, casting about for something to say. 'I guess you've heard that the Senate has voted to give Augustus tribunician power for life. That's even bigger than the consulship.'

'Yes. He owns the world now.'

'But not you.'

I looked up.

'No one can keep you from drawing, Selene. No matter what happens, you'll still have the support of Octavia and Vitruvius. And do you know what Julia and Marcellus are doing? They're making plans to build a house for foundlings, and they say it's in honor of you.'

'Did they ask you to tell me this?'

'No.' This time, his answer was firm. 'But I lost a great friend, too, and some days, even when I don't want to carry on, I do.'

He blinked rapidly. 'You know that Augustus arrives tomorrow.'

Immediately, thoughts of Augustus's death returned, and I wondered whether someone might assassinate him.

'There are reports that he's sick,' Lucius went on. 'We all know that he's never been strong. Even the mild weather in Iberia hasn't been enough to keep him in good health. When he comes, please don't do anything rash.'

'What makes you think I would?'

He gave me a long look. 'You aren't known for your prudence.'

'Perhaps someone else will do it for me, then.'

'You are the last of the Ptolemies, Selene. There is no one else after you whose veins carry the blood of Alexander the Great and Kleopatra. Be careful, or everything your grandfathers fought for will be snuffed out.'

'It already is.'

'No. Not unless the last Ptolemy dies.'

When word was sent ahead from the walls of Rome that Augustus was about to enter the city, we gathered in the Forum, and I thought of Ptolemies who had come before me and wondered what they would do. I knew what my mother had chosen, an honorable suicide over ignominy. But what would she have done if she were standing on the steps of Saturn's temple, wearing a Roman *bulla* and waiting to greet the man who had murdered her family?

I searched the temple steps for Juba, who had come here every month to deposit denarii in a treasury chest for Alexander and me without ever telling us. When I couldn't find him, I asked Agrippa.

'He's been sent ahead to inspect the spoils. The Cantabri left behind thousands of statues.'

'Why? Where did they go?'

'They chose death over slavery,' Agrippa said solemnly.

Next to me, Gallia's blue eyes narrowed, and I imagined how difficult it must be for her to witness a second subjugation of her people.

The war trumpets blared, and from the sound of the crowds lining the Vicus Jugarius it was evident that the army had arrived. I felt someone squeeze my hand.

'He's coming,' Julia said, but there was a nervousness in her voice that made me wonder how happy she was.

Drums beat out a rhythm to the approaching horses' hooves, and Octavia shouted, 'There he is!' White horses with red plumage came into view, and then Augustus, the triumphant conqueror of foreign lands, appeared at the head of his army in a golden chariot. I could see at once that he had lost weight, but a muscled cuirass disguised his weakness, and the paleness of his face was covered with vermillion. Livia rode behind him in a chariot of her own, followed by all the generals who had really won the war. The crowd worked itself into a frenzy as thousands of Gauls rolled by in filthy cages and soldiers held up urns of gold, amphorae, and silver *rhyta*.

Augustus stopped before the Temple of Saturn. Because no one wanted to hear the misery of the weeping Gauls, soldiers rolled the cages into the courtyard of the Basilica Julia, where they'd be kept until the prisoners could be sold. Augustus descended from his chariot, and the cheers that rose as his victorious generals gathered around him must have deafened the gods. Agrippa held out a golden laurel wreath, and I turned my head, disgusted by the spectacle. Instead I watched the soldiers outside the basilica as they attempted to organize more than five hundred cages. It was madness, and from my vantage point on the steps, I could see more soldiers hurrying from the basilica to help in the fray.

But as I watched, I realized that the supposed reinforcements *weren't* soldiers. The men were dressed as legionaries, in the right sandals, crested helmets, and scarlet cloaks, but black masks covered the top half of their faces. I gasped. The Red Eagle had come to free the Gauls! The men were working swiftly, opening cage after cage and instructing the prisoners to remain where they were until the signal was given. Somehow, the Red Eagle had come by keys, and as lock after lock opened, I could see the prisoners rushing to the sides of their cages.

Then one of the soldiers on the temple steps followed my gaze and saw what was happening. 'They're escaping!' he shouted, interrupting Augustus's Triumph. 'The prisoners are escaping!' he cried.

From across the courtyard, one of the masked men looked up and realized they'd been seen. 'Go!' he shouted, and though he'd spoken in Gaulish, I was familiar with the word from Gallia's reprimands. The doors were flung open and thousands of prisoners began to flee. Panic ensued in the basilica's courtyard, and the *liberatores* discarded their masks. Soldiers, uncertain who was on their side and who wasn't, fired arrows indiscriminately into the crowd. One arrow struck the rebels' leader, and I saw him clutch his shoulder in agony.

'He's been hit!' I shrieked.

Gallia rushed forward. 'Come back here, Selene!'

'But he's been wounded!'

It didn't matter that I ran. Everyone was moving, and it was impossible to remain on the steps of the temple. Smoke rose from the rooftop of the Basilica Julia, and a woman screamed, 'The basilica's on fire!' While thousands of people ran from the flames, I rushed toward them. A woman with two children in her arms warned me to turn back, shouting that the fire would take the entire building. But I followed a trail of blood into an abandoned shop, and I heard a man behind the counter breathing heavily. I rushed to him, but as soon as he saw me, he turned his face away. 'Go!' he growled.

'I'm here to help you!'

'How? By getting yourself killed?'

'No! There's a tunnel. It leads to the House of the Vestals, and from there you can escape.'

'Then tell me where it is, and get yourself out of here.'

'I can't describe it. You'll have to trust me.'

He hesitated, and when he turned, I covered my mouth in shock.

'*Juba!*'

'Who did you think you would find?' he asked grimly. 'Marcellus?'

I ignored the sting in his words and bent over him. He was losing a great deal of blood, and I ripped my tunic to make a bandage. My hands trembled when I touched the heat of his skin. 'But the man who saved us in the Forum Boarium was blond. Even Julia saw him.'

'And there are such thing as wigs,' he said sharply.

'Then what about the actum while you were in Gaul?' I tried not to think about the sudden wetness on my tunic, though I knew it was his blood.

'There are others who seek an end to slavery as well.'

I was aware of my hair brushing his chest as I tied his binding. It took several knots before it stayed in place.

'That's enough,' he said gruffly.

'Where is the point?'

He drew my eyes to a bloodied shaft on the floor, and though my stomach clenched, I could see that its point was still intact. Nothing remained in his body, but if he wasn't stitched soon, it might not matter. I offered him my arm, and he took it without complaining.

'Can you run?'

'Yes.'

We rushed through the Basilica Julia. Smoke was beginning to fill the halls, and Juba leaned more heavily on me than he probably intended. I could feel he was weakening, and quickly I tried to recall one of Vitruvius's sketches. The basilica housed law courts, offices, and shops, and the Vestals had wanted a tunnel from their temple so they could reach the shops without being seen. But to which shop had it led?

'Are you sure you know where you're going?' he demanded.

'I've seen the sketch more than a dozen times.' I led him inside a silk merchant's *taberna* and looked around. The shop had been abandoned, and customers had fled without taking their purchases. I grabbed a woman's tunic and flung it over my shoulder. I would change before we reached the Palatine.

'Where is the tunnel?'

'I don't know! But it's here.'

Juba stepped behind the counter, where a heavy curtain covered the wall. With a flick of his wrist, he swept it aside, revealing an open door. He stepped inside first, and when he was sure that it was safe, he leaned on my arm and allowed me to guide him. There was nothing inside to relieve the darkness, and as we hurried, I felt my way along the wall.

'You should change,' he said.

I stopped walking, and though I knew he couldn't see me as I undressed, my cheeks grew warm at the thought of him there. I remembered the last time I had stood in my breastband and loincloth in front of him. We had been in the Blue Grotto, and I had tried to keep myself from staring at his half-naked body in the water. 'What should I do with the bloodied—?'

'Give it to me. Now hurry.' As we continued down the tunnel, his breathing grew more labored.

'Where will you go when we reach the temple?' I asked.

'To the Palatine.'

'And how will you explain your wound?'

'The soldiers were shooting at everyone,' he said shortly. 'They'll simply think I was in their way.'

'But will Augustus believe it?'

He didn't reply, though when we reached the end of the tunnel, I thought for a moment he might say something more. Instead, he reached down and offered me his dagger.

'What's this for?'

'You don't remember your first trip down the Palatine alone?'

'But that was at night!'

'And do you think that criminals disappear in the day? I'll be behind you,' he promised. 'But you must leave first. When the path is clear, I want you to whistle. Then start walking. All the way to the Palatine.'

My hand trembled violently as I took the dagger. I slipped it safely beneath my belt, then opened the door and stepped out onto the marble portico outside the Temple of Vesta. I was shocked to see that the entrance was empty. *Everyone has gone to see the fire*, I thought. I whistled immediately, and when I heard the door open, I began to walk. Gallia knew where I had gone, and it was possible that Tiberius had heard as well. If I returned to the Palatine with Juba, only a fool would fail to realize what had happened.

Throughout the city, men were rushing to the Forum. Even merchants were abandoning their stalls to see the fire that was consuming the basilica. It took all my resolve not to turn to see if Juba was still behind me. When I reached Octavia's villa, there was no one on the portico, and I knew at once where everyone must have gone. But before I could reach the platform in front of Augustus's villa, Gallia came running.

'Where is he?' she cried.

I thought of Juba bleeding inside his villa with no one to help him, and did my best to look unconcerned. 'Who?'

Gallia gave me a long look before whispering, *'Juba!'*

I leaned closer. 'How do you—'

'I have been in his confidence since the Red Eagle first appeared,' she said quickly. 'Who do you think posted his acta while he was gone? Is he safe?'

I told her what had happened, and her face went pale. 'Stay here, and say absolutely nothing.'

I panicked. 'But where are you going?'

'To find Verrius.'

I mounted the platform and tried to avoid Augustus's interested gaze. Immediately, Marcellus and Julia cried out.

'Where have you been?' Julia exclaimed.

'I was caught up in the rush,' I lied, hoping I was as good an actor as Augustus. 'I didn't know where you went. And when I looked back, everyone was gone.'

Augustus studied me. It had been a year since he had last seen me. 'They thought perhaps you'd been crushed,' he said.

'Of course not! I escaped.'

'But hundreds of people were trampled,' Julia said. 'Did you see?'

I shook my head.

'Then you must have seen the Gauls escaping from their cages! It was the barbarian invasion all over again,' she said breathlessly.

Augustus watched for my reaction, but I refused to give one. Then he turned abruptly to Livia and said, 'I'll be in my chamber.'

Octavia rushed to his side, and I noticed that both Agrippa and Tiberius were absent.

When Augustus was gone, I looked to Julia. 'Is he sick?'

'My father has been ill since Iberia. He says this afternoon will be the death of him, and he's told Agrippa to find the Red Eagle whatever the cost.'

'I heard the Red Eagle was wounded,' Marcellus added, 'and Tiberius thought you ran after him.'

'He's a *traitor*. Why would I do such a thing?'

'That's what I said. But he thought you would try and escape from Rome.'

Although all I wished to do was run to Juba's villa, I remained on the hill and watched the fire burn. When at last even Julia was tired of the show, she asked Claudia whether there was to be a feast.

'No. Your father needs his rest. Perhaps in a few days, when the Red Eagle is dead, there will be a celebration.'

Julia looked at me. 'Will you dine with us?'

'Not tonight. I'm not feeling well,' I lied again.

I hurried back to my chamber, hoping that Gallia would be waiting for me, but the room was empty. Then I spotted something dark peeking from beneath my pillow. It was small black box. I picked it up and read the note that was attached. 'In case tomorrow never comes,' it said. I opened the hidden box and took out a necklace of pink sea pearls – my mother's last gift to me. The one I had given to Juba to purchase Gallia's freedom. Tears blurred my vision as I put on the necklace. He must have left it in the morning, not knowing whether he would survive the day. And now, his fate was up to the gods.

I paced my room, desperate for any news, and when Octavia returned, I asked if she'd seen Gallia.

'She's gone home,' she said, and I noticed the half-moons beneath her eyes. She looked drained, as if she'd stayed up for nights on end without sleep. 'A fever is spreading through Rome,' she added, 'and Gallia tells me that both Magister Verrius and Juba are ill. The physicians say my brother may be suffering from the same sickness. But you are safe.' She reached out and caressed my cheek. A tear wet her finger, and I noticed that she was crying as well. 'Shall we pray?'

I followed her into the lararium, where she lit a cone of incense and we knelt before the gods. She whispered her prayers to Fortuna, and I made my silent ones to Isis. I promised all sorts of things to the goddess, swearing to marry whomever Augustus chose, even if he was vile, so long as she would spare Juba's life. And I vowed to endure my suffering in silence. I would not complain. I would not be embittered. If she would grant Juba's health, I would never weep in self-pity again.

But the night passed without word, and the next morning, Gallia was nowhere to be found. I paced the library until Vitruvius put down his stylus and insisted I go outside for fresh air. 'If you are worried on behalf of Magister Verrius, you needn't be. I saw him this morning and he looked well.'

'You did?' I cried. 'Where?'

Vitruvius looked at me strangely. 'On the Palatine. Coming from Juba's villa.'

'And what did he say?'

'That Juba is ill.'

'And was Gallia with him?'

Vitruvius shook his head. 'No. Not that I saw.'

I hurried onto the portico, hoping to catch a glimpse of Magister Verrius, but the only person hurrying toward Octavia's villa was Agrippa. When he saw me, he smiled.

'Excellent news,' he said triumphantly.

'Has the Red Eagle been caught?'

'Even better. He's dead.'

I felt my heart stop in my chest, but Agrippa went on.

'Two men caught him last night attempting to post an *actum* on the Temple of Apollo. He was already hurt, but they ran him through with a *gladius* as he fled.'

Suddenly the world was spinning. It was Alexander's death all over again. 'And is . . . is there a body?'

'No. But judging from the amount of blood he left behind, there's no chance that he survived.'

He went inside to share his triumph with Octavia, and I held on to a column to keep myself from falling. I had to find Gallia. Gallia or Magister Verrius would know what had happened. I raced to the bottom of the Palatine without bothering to demand a guard. I banged on Magister Verrius's door at the end of the street. When no one answered, I peered through the windows, and a child who was passing by stopped to stare at me.

'There's no one there,' he said.

'How do you know?'

'I live next door. They haven't been back all night.'

'What about this morning?'

The boy shook his head.

'Not even Magister Verrius?'

'No.'

I took the shortcut back up the hill. I didn't dare to approach Juba's villa, but I went to the Temple of Apollo to see for myself. A group of Praetorians were gathered at the entrance, and I recognized two of the guards as the same men who'd accompanied me to Alexander's mausoleum. They were talking quietly between themselves, admiring the stain across the marble steps. It was just as Agrippa had described it. No one could lose so much blood and survive. I could feel my throat beginning to close, and the world was growing dark around me when the light-haired guard from the mausoleum shook my arm.

'It's only blood. Nothing to be worried about.'

'Who stabbed him?' I whispered.

'We did.' He pointed from himself to the familiar dark-haired guard beside him. 'I expect we'll both be amply rewarded.'

I felt sick to my stomach. Suddenly, nothing made sense anymore. When I returned to Octavia's villa, I shut myself in my room. Charmion, Ptolemy, Caesarion, Antyllus, Alexander, both of my parents. And now Juba; the man who had cared for me all along, protecting me, writing about the injustices I cared passionately about as well, all in the guise of the Red Eagle. It no longer mattered to me whether I lived or died. I lay down and closed my eyes, hoping that someone would steal out of the shadows as they had four months before, only this time, that it would be my life that ended.

But when I awoke, the sun was still high. No one had come to murder me in my sleep. There was noise in the atrium, and when I opened the door, Octavia and Vitruvius were whispering. They stopped when I appeared, and both of them looked at me.

Octavia approached. Her face was full of concern. 'Augustus would like to see you,' she said.

'Really?' I asked indifferently. 'Is he angry?'

'I don't know. He is very ill, Selene. And preparations are being made . . .'

I could see she was on the verge of tears, and I softened my voice. 'He has always recovered.'

'But this time it's fever. He's asked us to bring you.'

When I nodded, she released her breath. She had expected a fight, but I no longer cared what happened to me. I followed her into Augustus's villa, where dignitaries crowded together in the atrium, and even Julia and Marcellus were there.

'He's asked to see you,' Julia said nervously. 'Do you know why?'

I shook my head.

'I think you're going to be married.' When I didn't react, she went on fretfully, 'No one knows who it is. I don't think even Livia knows. But he's making all his plans. He's even given Agrippa his signet ring.'

'The one belonging to Alexander the Great?'

She nodded.

'So Agrippa's his heir?'

'Until Marcellus is twenty.' I could see the fear in her eyes. 'Oh, Selene.' She took my hands, but I didn't move. 'Whatever happens, I am here. It will be all right.'

Octavia guided me to the stairs and pointed upward. 'The first door on the right.'

I mounted the steps, and as I approached the door, I was aware of a rushing sound in my ears. But why was I afraid? It didn't matter what future Augustus decided for me now.

I opened the door and realized that I wasn't entering a chamber, but Augustus's office, Little Syracuse. The walls were adorned with maps and scrolls, and where there weren't books, there were statues. A pale-looking Augustus was seated behind his table, hunched over like an old man trying to fend off the cold. With his hand, he offered me a seat.

'Kleopatra Selene,' he said.

'Emperor Augustus.'

He smiled at the title, but didn't disagree. 'Do you know why I've called you here?'

I didn't lie. 'Julia says it has something to do with my marriage.'

'Yes.' He studied me. 'You've grown very beautiful in my absence.'

'Many things have happened in your absence,' I said shortly.

He raised his brows, but instead of growing angry with me, his voice became strangely regretful. 'Yes, they have. And once we die, what we leave behind is not what is engraved in stone monuments, but what is woven into the lives of others.'

'Pericles.'

He nodded. 'And I have not woven much happiness into your life, have I?'

I dug my nails into my palms to keep myself from weeping.

'Before I die, I wish to change that, Selene.'

'Are you going to bring Alexander back from the dead?'

He hesitated. 'You understand, I hope, that a grown son of Marc Antony and Kleopatra would always be a risk to the stability of Rome so long as he was alive.'

'The stability of Rome, or the stability of your rule?'

'Is there a difference?'

'He never wanted to be Caesar!'

'Many men have no intention of being Caesar. But when offered the opportunity by discontented senators, how many would turn it down?'

I bit my lower lip.

'I did not bring you here to discuss death,' he said quietly. 'I brought you here to give you a new life. You had a very fine education in Egypt, and in Rome you have proven yourself capable of rule. If you will accept a dowry of five thousand denarii,' he began, 'I wish to make you Queen of Mauretania.'

The study began to spin so quickly that I gripped the sides of my chair. 'I don't understand,' I whispered. 'I thought that Juba—'

'Is ill? Yes, but he's young and very strong. Men like him recover quickly, and he's waiting for you in the other room.'

I stood so quickly that my seat nearly toppled over.

Augustus smiled. 'At the end of the hall.'

I don't remember whether I ran. I must have, because when I opened the door and Juba took me in his arms, I was breathless.

Immediately, I inspected him for signs that he'd been wounded again. 'I don't understand,' was all I could say. 'I don't—'

He put his finger to my lips. 'The men at the temple were mine. There was no attack.'

'But the mess—' I whispered.

'It was bull's blood. I think I'm going to survive.'

'And your shoulder?'

He pushed his tunic away so I could see where Magister Verrius had neatly stitched him closed, and in the bright light of the chamber, I knew there'd never been a more beautiful man. From the time I'd been taken from Alexandria, he must have known that Augustus had intended me for him. Then I thought of the times he'd seen me weeping for Marcellus, and the many times I'd goaded him for being nasty when all of it had simply been an act to keep away suspicion, and my eyes began to burn.

'I hope you're crying with happiness,' he said, 'and not with disappointment.'

'How could I be disappointed?' I cried.

'Perhaps you wanted someone else.'

I ran my fingers through his hair. 'No.' I searched his eyes, which were filled with kindness, and I drew my fingers over the handsome contours of his face. 'I want you.'

'Me, or the Red Eagle?' he asked cautiously.

'Perhaps both.'

'But you know that the Red Eagle is gone,' he said. 'I've done what I can in Rome. Someone else must continue the fight.'

'Like Gallia?'

'And Verrius, and many other good people. But Augustus would have suspected it was me eventually. So I'm afraid your Red Eagle is dead,' he said with regret.

'Dead?' I asked him. 'Or just flown away to Mauretania?' When he didn't say anything, I added, 'I suspect it's the latter.'

'There will be no more rebellion. No more daring acts of kindness,' he warned.

'You mean we won't get to run through burning buildings?' I could see he wanted to laugh, but instead he watched me intently. 'What? Why are you staring at me?'

'I'm not staring. I'm observing.'

I smiled through my tears. 'And what do you observe?'

He brushed his lips against my ear. 'A brave young woman who has always fought for what was right, even when it was unpopular. A woman who can't return to the land of her birth, but is welcome to cross the seas and rebuild Alexandria in mine. And a woman who has suffered enough in Rome and deserves happiness for a change. Will you come to Mauretania and be my queen?'

He drew back to look at me, but I held him closer. 'Yes.'

'Just yes?'

I nodded and pressed my lips against his.

AFTERWORD

Selene

Selene and Juba were married in 25 BC, and, true to his word, Augustus gave Selene a magnificent dowry. The union of Kleopatra Selene and Juba II became one of the greatest love stories ever to come out of imperial Rome, and for twenty years they reigned side by side in an extraordinary partnership that began on the voyage to Mauretania. When they reached their new kingdom, they settled in Iol, renaming it Caesarea in deference to the man who had made them king and queen. Once this public declaration of loyalty was made, however, Selene began rebuilding their capital in the image of the greatest city on earth: Alexandria. Before long, their court became known as a center for learning, and the images that archaeologists have discovered at Caesarea (such as a basalt statue of the Egyptian priest Petubastes IV, a bronze bust of Dionysus, and a statue of Tuthmosis I), speak loudest about Selene's true loyalties.

While Selene erected monuments in honor of her Ptolemaic heritage, Juba charted the lands around his new kingdom. In the process he was credited as being the first person to 'discover' the Canary Islands, naming them Insularia Canaria, or Islands of the Dogs, after the fierce canines that inhabited them. He also penned the treatise *Libyka* and discovered an important type of medicinal spurge, which even today is called *Euphorbia regis-jubae*. Pliny wrote that Juba was 'more remembered for the quality of his scholarship even than for his reign,' while Plutarch considered him one of the 'most gifted rulers of his time.' Two or possibly three, children were born to Juba and Selene during their marriage. Their son Ptolemy inherited the throne.

Augustus

Despite his grave sickness, Augustus recovered and ruled for another thirty-nine years. Nearly everyone he loved passed on before him, including Terentilla, Agrippa, Maecenas, Octavia, and even Marcellus. At seventy-five, when it was clear that the end was approaching, he asked Livia to take his life by surprise. He wished to orchestrate his death just as he had orchestrated everything else. When Livia poisoned his food, Augustus died in 14 AD. He left behind explicit instructions on how to govern Rome, even going so far as to describe the tax system in minute detail. His heir was Livia's son, Tiberius.

Julia

Julia and Marcellus enjoyed their wedded bliss for only another two years. In 23 BC, Marcellus died suddenly, ending a brief life that would likely have seen him as emperor had he survived. He was buried in Augustus's mausoleum, which can still be seen today in Rome. With no clear heir, Augustus ordered Agrippa's immediate divorce from Octavia's daughter Claudia, and the eighteen-year-old Julia was given to her father's forty-two-year-old general and closest friend. Five children resulted from their marriage, but when Agrippa died in 12 BC, Julia became a widow again. This time, with fewer heirs to choose from, Augustus married Julia to her stepbrother Tiberius. But

Julia rebelled, taking as her lover Selene's half brother Antonius, the son of Marc Antony and Fulvia. When Augustus discovered this, he arrested his own daughter for adultery and treason. Antonius, like his father, was forced to commit suicide, and Julia was banished to the island of Pandataria. Only her mother accompanied her into exile, where they were forbidden from having visitors other than those specifically sent by her father. After five years, Julia was allowed to return to the mainland, though she was forbidden from entering Rome. Upon Augustus's death, one of Tiberius's first acts was to confine Julia to a single room in her house. She died of starvation.

Tiberius

Before becoming heir to the Roman Empire, Tiberius was ordered to marry Agrippa's daughter Vipsania. Their marriage proved to be an actual love match, and for seven years they remained loyal partners, producing a son whom Tiberius named Drusus, after his own younger brother. But when Agrippa died in 12 BC, Augustus ordered Tiberius to divorce his pregnant wife and marry Julia. The shock caused the loss of Vipsania's second child, but the divorce proceeded, and Tiberius never forgave Augustus. In the years to come, Tiberius haunted Vipsania's doorstep, threatening her new husband, Gallus, with death. After several more encounters, Augustus forbade Tiberius from ever seeing Vipsania again. Upon becoming emperor, Tiberius declared Vipsania's husband a public enemy, imprisoning him and killing him by starvation. After Julia's death, he never remarried. Jesus of Nazareth is believed to have been crucified during the reign of Tiberius, which lasted twenty-three years.

Octavia

After the sudden and devastating death of Marcellus, Octavia retired from public life, spending her time quietly doing charity work and raising her grandchildren. Her daughter Antonia married the renowned charioteer Lucius Domitius. Although the marriage was a deeply unhappy one, it produced three children, one of whom, Antonia, would become the grandmother of Emperor Nero. Octavia's youngest daughter, Tonia, married Livia's son Drusus, and the two of them enjoyed a happy marriage for nearly seven years until Drusus died in a riding accident. Their children were the famous general Germanicus, the beautiful Livilla, and the future emperor Claudius.

HISTORICAL NOTE

LIKE OTHER historical novelists before me, I am deeply indebted to those who have spent countless years interpreting, researching, and writing on the world of ancient Rome. Those scholars have allowed me to depict, to the best of my abilities, what life was like more than two thousand years ago when the children of Marc Antony and Kleopatra were taken from Egypt and raised for several years on the Palatine. If Selene and Alexander seem incredibly precocious for their ages, that is because they were the extremely well-educated children of a queen considered to be one of the most learned women of her time. Like today's child actors, they would have been raised in an adult world with adult expectations, and clearly Selene's education was sufficient to see her made Queen of Mauretania.

Nearly all of the characters in the book represent real people whom Alexander and Selene actually met, and I based their personalities on what was written about them and preserved in the historical record. From Augustus's love of the theater to Agrippa's building of the Pantheon – where you can still see his name etched into the pediment today – I tried to ensure that the characters remained true to their historical selves. The major exception to this would be my invention of the Red Eagle. While the Red Eagle did not exist, there is evidence to suggest that Juba was deeply disgusted by the culture of slavery in

Rome. After his arrival in Mauretania, slavery there slowly disappeared, and it's not surprising that he would identify with those who had been enslaved, given the fate he might have suffered had it not been for his illustrious ancestry. Both of the slave trials in the novel were based on events which supposedly took place in ancient Rome, and I believe they help to illustrate just a few of the moral issues that arose from human bondage. Such trials also serve as a reminder of how frequently fact is stranger than fiction. Take, for example, Pollio's attempt to feed a slave to his eels, the escaped bull in the Forum Boarium that plummeted to its death from a second-story balcony, and Augustus's obsessive note-taking: all are based on the historical record. Even Magister Verrius's use of games in the *ludus*; the tribe of Telegenii who fought leopards in the arena, and Octavian's carelessness in Alexander the Great's mausoleum, which resulted in the corpse's broken nose: all come from contemporary accounts. And even though we might think of some of the amenities in the novel as exclusively modern, the heated pools, elegantly shuttered windows, tourist guide books, and much else were present in Imperial Rome.

It is astounding to think of what the Romans accomplished more than two millennia ago when the average life expectancy was less than thirty years. Some of the most enduring buildings can be traced back to both Agrippa and Augustus: the famous Pantheon, the Basilica of Neptune, the Saepta Julia, the Forum Augusti, and many of the baths. Augustus and Agrippa furnished these places with their favorite statues, and just like many other Romans, they were avid collectors of antiquities, particularly anything that came from Greece. Contrary to what we see today in museums, nearly all of their marble statues were painted, many of them in garish colors such as bright red, turquoise, yellow, and orange. Though it's strange to imagine people who lived two millennia ago collecting antiques, in many ways Roman society was startlingly similar to our own. The Romans were fond of the theater; they used handshakes for introductions; and many of the leading thinkers, such as Cicero, mocked prevalent superstitions and even belief in the gods. Children played with dice and puppets, while adults went to the races to place bets and meet friends. Everyday humor was notoriously crass. All across the city of Pompeii, graffiti preserve ancient Roman sarcasm. And when the emperor Vespasian knew he was dying, he told his sons wryly, 'I think I'm becoming divine.'

There is a reason so many of us are drawn to ancient Rome, and I believe it's because we recognize ourselves in these people who lived more than two thousand years ago. Consider the following quotes, some of which you might think were excerpts from modern-day writings:

A human body was washing ashore, tossing lightly up and down on the waves. I stood sadly waiting, gazing with wet eyes on the work of the faithless element, and soliloquized, 'Somewhere or another, perhaps, a wife is looking forward to this poor fellow's return, or a son, perhaps, or a father, all unsuspecting of storm and wreck; be sure, he has left someone behind, whom he kissed fondly at parting. This then is the end of human projects, this the accomplishment of men's mighty schemes. Look how he now rides the waves!'

Petronius, *Satyricon* 115

I was happy to learn from people who had just visited you that you live on friendly terms with your slaves . . . Some people say, 'They're just slaves.' But they are our fellow human beings! 'They're just slaves.' But they live with us! 'They're just slaves.' In fact, they are our fellow slaves, if you stop to consider that fate has as much control over us as it has over them . . . I don't want to engage in a lengthy discussion of the treatment of slaves, toward whom we are very arrogant, very cruel, and very abusive. However, this is my advice: 'Treat those of lower social rank as you would wish to be treated by those of higher social rank.'

Seneca the Younger, in a letter to a friend

She who first began the practice of tearing out her tender progeny deserved to die in her own warfare. Can it be that, to be free of the flaw of stretchmarks, you have to scatter the tragic sands of carnage? . . . Why will you subject your womb to the weapons of abortion and give poisons to the unborn? . . . The tigress lurking in Armenia does no such thing, nor does the lioness dare to destroy her young. Yet tender girls do so – but not with impunity; often she who kills what is in her womb dies herself.

Ovid *Amores*

What's come over you? Is it because I go to bed with the queen [Kleopatra]? Yes, she isn't my wife, but it isn't as if it's something new, is it? Haven't I been doing it for nine years now? And what about you? Is Livia really the only woman you go to bed with? I congratulate you, if at the time you read this letter you haven't had Tertulla or Terentilla or Rufilla or Salvia Titisenia or the whole lot of them. Does it really matter where you insert your prick – or who the woman is?

Marc Antony, in a letter to Octavian that was preserved by the biographer Suetonius

In the Petronius quote, we recognize the very human fear of death and the sense of loss it creates for those who are left behind. In Seneca's letter, we see that even though slavery had long been an institution, there were those who clearly felt uncomfortable with it. Ovid takes up the long-running abortion debate, while Marc Antony's letter mocks Octavian for being a hypocrite where extramarital affairs were concerned. These sentiments now seem surprisingly modern, for we still live with the relics of their ancient world. The first newspaper is widely considered to have been Julius Caesar's daily acta diurna, and the phrase *Senatus Populusque Romanus,* meaning 'the Senate and the People of Rome,' is still used today. In fact, its initials, *SPQR,* can be seen throughout the city, on everything from billboards to manhole covers.

Yet even with such abundance before me, I did allow myself some deviations from the historical record. Because both of Octavia's eldest daughters were named Claudia and both her youngest daughters were named Antonia, I changed two of their names for the sake of simplicity (to Marcella and Tonia). And while it was *haruspices* who examined the entrails of animals in order to determine favorable signs from the gods and *fulguratores* who interpreted lightning and thunder, I chose to call them both 'augurs' so that I wouldn't overwhelm the reader with too many foreign terms. Similarly, I have chosen to limit the use of Latin noun declensions for the sake of English reader simplicity.

Other changes I made included the invention of both Gallia and Lucius, who did not, so far as we know, exist, and a few of the dates within the novel, which were altered slightly. (Also, the month of August was known as Sextilis during the dates this novel takes place, and was only later renamed Augustus in Octavian's honor.) I did not include the Roman habit of kicking instead of knocking on doors, and for the sake of storytelling, I had Queen Kleopatra act shocked upon hearing the news that Octavian had taken his uncle's name, when in reality she must have known much earlier. And while I tried my best to remain anachronism-free, I admit to failure where some words, like *books* (which were really *codices* at that time), are concerned. Yet for the most part I attempted to remain as close as possible to proven history. After all, that's why we read historical fiction – to be transported to another time, and to be astonished at ancient people's lives and traditions, just as they would probably be astonished at ours.

GLOSSARY

akolouthos: Greek term for an acolyte or helper. The plural is *akolouthoi*.

Amphitruo: A popular sexual comedy written by Plautus.

atrium: An open area in the center of many Roman homes.

bulla: An amulet worn around the neck by Roman children for protection against evil. A boy would wear his *bulla* until he became a Roman citizen during his *toga virilis* ceremony, while a girl would wear hers until the eve of her marriage.

calamistrum: A curling iron.

caryatid: A pillar or other architectural support sculpted into the shape of a female figure.

cavea: The semicircular seating area of a theater, arranged in tiers.

Cerberus: a three-headed mythological dog that guards the gates leaving Hades.

chiton: A long garment worn by both Greek men and women and held together at the shoulders by pins.

colei: Testicles.

Columna Lactaria: A column in Rome at which unwanted infants were abandoned, and where wet nurses or adopting parents might feed those who survived.

cunnus: The female genitalia.

diadem: A royal crown and symbol of authority.

dies natalis: Birthday.

dies nefastus: An unlucky day in the calendar, during which no official business could be conducted. The plural is *dies nefasti.*

domina: Mistress. Used when the female subject of sentence is spoken of as a superior; also used to address a female superior.

domine: Master. Used to address a male superior. The plural is *domini.*

dominus: Master. Used when the male subject of sentence is spoken of as superior.

equites: Knights, who were members of the lower aristocratic order.

Fasti: A Roman almanac of the year, listing festival days and *dies nefasti,* among others.

filius nullius: 'No one's son' (a bastard).

fornices: Archways or vaults. Roman prostitutes' habit of soliciting in archways leaves its trace in the word 'fornicate.' The singular is *fornix.*

Forum Boarium: The cattle market.

Ganymede: A young homosexual, after the beautiful lover taken by Zeus in mythology.

Gaul/Gallic: Terms that refer to continental western Europe between the Rhine and the Pyrenees, inhabited by Celtic tribes. This area included what are now the Low Countries, Switzerland, and Northern Italy (Cisalpine Gaul).

gustatio: The appetizer or starter course of a meal. Often consisted of a light salad, lentils, or pickled vegetables.

himation: A Greek garment that was worn over a chiton and often used as a cloak.

ignobilis: Of low birth.

judices: The jurors in a public trial, usually comprising of citizens, and drawn from the higher social orders. The singular is **judex.**

kyphi: Incense, used for medical purposes and in Egyptian religious rites.

lantisa: A manager/trainer for gladiators.

lararium: A small shrine room for honoring the household's gods.

Lares: The household gods or protective spirits that were honored in the lararium.

Liberalia: the festival of Liber Pater and his consort Libera, celebrated on March 17. This was also the day when boys who had come of age would put aside their *bullae.*

liberatores: Liberators.

ludus: School. Also used to refer to the public games that were intended to serve as a festival of thanks to the gods. The plural is **ludi.**

lupa: She-wolf. a derogatory term for a prostitute. The plural is *lupae.*

lupanar: A brothel.

Lupercalia: A pastoral festival held February 13–15.

lustratio: A purification ceremony, often involving animal sacrifice, to purify people (especially newborns) as well as places, crops, armies, and buildings.

Mare Superum: The Adriatic Sea.

nemes headdress: The blue-and-gold-striped head cloth worn by Pharaohs of ancient Egypt (prior to action in story).

nobilitas: Nobility.

nutrice: a wet nurses. The plural is **nutrix.**

odeum: A building used for musical and theatrical events. The plural is *odea.*

ofella: The ancient Roman version of pizza made of baked dough but without the tomatoes, as tomatoes were unknown to the Romans at that time. The plural is *ofellae.*

ornatrix: A woman skilled in hair arrangement and makeup.

palla: a shawl worn over the arms and shoulders

pilum: A long spear or a javelin.

pleb: Plebian; member of the lower classes.

portico: The roofed entrance porch at the front of a building.

rostrum: Speaking platform in the Senate, made from the prows of ships that the Romans captured in various sea battles.

Salii: a group of young male priests of Mars, the Roman god of war.

salve: Greetings. *Salvete* is the form used in addressing more than one person.

silphium: An extinct plant commonly referred to as a 'giant fennel.' The Roman author Pliny the Elder wrote about its use as an herbal contraceptive.

SPQR: *Senatus Populusque Romanus,* or 'the Senate and People of Rome' This ubiquitous 'signature' of the Roman state appeared on legionary standards, documents, coins, and a great deal more.

sparsor: The person whose job it was at the races to douse the smoking wheels of a chariot with water.

spelt-cake: A cake made from a precursor to modern strains of wheat.

spina: The barrier in the center of the Circus Maximus; it separated the outbound and inbound laps of the race.

stadia: Plural form for a Roman measure of distance; one *stadium* was 200–210 yards in length.

stola: A long, pleated dress worn over the tunic; the traditional garment of Roman women.

stylus: A metal writing implement, used to inscribe on wax tablets. The reverse, flat end of the stylus could be used to scratch and flatten, or 'erase,' mistakes.

tablet: A wax writing pad that could be reused by warming the tablet and melting the wax.

taberna: A shop or alehouse. The plural is **tabernae**.

thalamegos: A type of ancient Greek ship. The name means '-cabin-carrier.'

tiet: The sacred knot of the Egyptian goddess Isis.

toga praetexta: A long woolen robe, worn by Roman citizens as a tunic. The *praetexta* had a single crimson stripe, and was often worn by magistrates, by priests, and by boys too young for the *toga virilis.*

tollere liberos: The lifting of a newborn into the air by its father, signifying his acceptance of it into the family.

triclinium: The dining room in a Roman household, so named for the three couches on which diners reclined and ate.

tunic: A garment worn by both men and women in ancient Rome, either under the toga or by itself.

univira: A woman who has had only one husband.

Ubi tu es Agrippa, ego Claudia: 'Where you are Agrippa, I am Claudia.'

umbraculum: an umbrella or parasol, typically carried by slaves for their wealthy Roman mistresses.

valet: Farewell. *Valete* is the form used in addressing more than one person.

vestibulum: The narrow hallway that connected the atrium of a Roman house with the street outside. These hallways often contained welcoming messages or decorations in the form of mosaics or murals.

ACKNOWLEDGEMENTS

As always, I owe the greatest thanks possible to my infintely patient and incredibly supportive husband, Matthew. After more than a decade together, you still inspire me to choose the great love stories of history to write about. To my mother and brother, who have always been supportive of my writing career, I am deeply indebted to you both. And to my father, who instilled in me his love of ancient Roman history – I only wish you could have been here to read this. I think you would have enjoyed a break from your heavy ancient tomes to do some lighter reading, and I feel sure that you would have loved the Red Eagle, given your interest in the doomed Spartacus and his slave revolt. An homage to the dashing heroes who populate the works of Baroness Emmuska Orczy, Alexandre Dumas, and Barbara Michaels, the antics of the Red Eagle – who was based on historical rebels who came before and after him – would have pleased you no end. Thank you for always taking the time to teach me and for being such a wonderful father.

I must also mention my debt of gratitude to the brilliant Classics scholar, Dr James (Jim) T. McDonough Jr., and his wife Zaida, who were there to answer my many questions about ancient Rome. Jim, your careful notes and historical advice were absolutely invaluable to me, and this novel is immensely richer for your detailed input. Any mistakes are entirely mine.

For those who would like to read more about Selene's life, I highly recommend Duane W. Roller's excellent book *The World of Juba II and Kleopatra Selene*. Thank you so much, Duane, for taking the time to answer my questions about Selene's world. And to Jon Corelis, whose translation of Ovid's poem 'Disappointment' appears in the book, I am incredibly thankful. Your website is a gold mine, and your translations inspired me during many a marathon writing session.

To my former students Brynn Grawe, George Mejia, Ashley Turner, and Ashley Williamson, who helped me sort through my towering piles of research on such subjects as fermented fish sauce and peacock brains, I am deeply appreciative. If I can persuade you to be my research assistants for my next book, I promise to give you notes on things that are much less revolting! And to Shaun Venish, whose intricate map of Augustus's Rome appears at the front of the book, I am in awe of your talents.

Of course, no acknowledgments page would ever be complete if it did not recognize the editors who molded the clay into something worth reading. Heather Proulx and Suzanne O'Neill have been absolutely magnificent, and I am a lucky author indeed to have had their discerning eyes on my manuscript. It's not all the time that an author can say she's found a great friend in her editor, so, Heather, I know how lucky I am to be working with you! And I am very much looking forward to exploring the world of Madame Tussaud in our next book together.

I also owe an enormous thank-you to my wonderful copy editor Janet Fletcher, who worked tremendously hard to make this novel gleam. And, of course, a huge thank-you goes to Crown's amazing team: Patty Berg, Tina Constable, Dyana

Messina, Jennifer O'Connor, and the many people who have worked behind the scenes. I am deeply grateful to Allison McCabe, who originally purchased *Cleopatra's Daughter* for Random House. And I'd like to thank my agent, Anna Ghosh, as well as my foreign rights agent, Danny Baror, who has seen to it that my novels can be read in more than twenty languages.

With every published book, an author is indebted to more people than he or she can ever name. So to everyone who helped to bring *Cleopatra's Daughter* to readers around the world, thank you so much.